THINKWELL BOOKS

THE LEAF BLOWER

Jeff Weston was born in 1970, in Bolton, Lancashire. He graduated in 1999 from Manchester Metropolitan University with a degree in English literature and commenced a career in stockbroking the following year. He is the middle son of an electrical engineer and barmaid / housewife and author of three novels (*The Leaf Blower*, *Mutler*, *Wagènknecht*), three plays (*The Relationship*, *Directions*, *The Broken Heart Ward*) and a collection of short stories (*Homage to Hernandez and other stories*). His writing has crossed over into sports journalism (*Pitchside, Ringside and Down in the Table Tennis Dens*) and book reviews / feature articles for psychotherapy magazines.

G000071037

'A modern *Lord of the Rings*. A study of childhood interactions and the damage that never quite leaves us.'

Bill Wood

'*The Leaf Blower* pits a naïve son and a world-weary father together and admirably shows us that truth is grey - often many, many things - once we get old.'

Ade Kolade, former researcher, University of Manchester

'Crucial Italian history is woven into this book around the time of Woodrow Wilson and America's anti-immigrant sentiment. The case of Sacco & Vanzetti is given its due against the backdrop of corrupt officials and willing flunkeys.'

Andrew Routledge

'Reading about George Minty I, Green Suit and Warwick alone makes one smile in the face of 'regular' society.'

Helen Taylor

'A dark, Orwellian trip which reveals how the world is controlled and castigated.'

Amy Maddox, protester

'Religion, imagination and spirituality versus science and technology. Which wins? Which seduces our minds?'

Robert Perrin, teacher

'Jeff Weston has written a book that deserves to be read *and* discussed: a rumbustious bravura of a novel which provokes the intellect and furrows the brow. The central protagonist is Arnold Debrito, a naive guide to the intersections between personal histories and the Grand Narratives that shape our time. If truth is to be found, it is to be located in disruption, on a path cleared by the almost messianic figure of *The Leaf Blower*: blowing away the pretensions of the rich (wedded to the false truths of the city), shoving aside the certainties of science and taking issue with God and religions which have created "an army of indifferent beings". Debrito reminds me of Woody Allen's Leonard Zelig, an unreliable character at the centre of great events, but at the same time on the periphery, tumbling through life in search of understanding. This book is both provocative and entertaining and, like Anthony Burgess and Ian McEwan, unafraid to ask questions and address the fundamental thought in our head: What does it mean to be civilized?'

David Stephens, author of *The Disappeared*

'Tender. Courageous. Fascinating. A trip through those post-school years when finding things to love becomes survival itself.'

Sue Thornborrow-Jones, Age UK volunteer

'Weston takes us on an odyssey of angst, through history, politics, the minefield that is family, the secrets and lies, the betrayals, until the loner, the outsider – the 'us' – is pitched against the unknowable 'them'; a frightening new brand of cold-hearted capitalism.'

Chris Robinson, author of *Can't Pay, Won't Pay*

'Language that mesmerizes. Words which sink into us and make us more than we are. *The Leaf Blower*'s richness is its harmony, its page-turning brilliance, its dedication to historical injustices. This is not Weston's best. That remains *Wagenknecht* – the last of the 'trilogy'. But it is beautiful and different – snobby in a *good* way. Can anarchists be fine examples to mankind? it asks. Yes, if conditions give them no other option. Yes, if the absence of that which cows them introduces more peace.'

Pinklon Wilson, refuge collector

Jeff Weston

THE

LEAF

BLOWER

THINKWELL BOOKS

Written by Jeff Weston 2000-04.
Cover design by Alejandro Baigorri.

Interior formatting by Rachel Bostwick.

Published by Thinkwell Books, U.K.

First printing edition 2024.

For Aeeee & Maooo

...shallowness and moral vacuity went out together
one night in the pitch black of unreason and dancing cheek
to cheek very quickly spawned grotesque idiot children,
children whose incapacity for self-doubt enabled them to
push the concerns of honest people off the front page of the
times and gradually back through the world, beyond the
weather, finally make sport of them before using them to
wrap up something dead.

Elliot Perlmann
Three Dollars

Apathy is laughter
And laughter is rife

Jeff Weston

CONTENTS

FOREWORD

For a few mad moments, when thinking of potential titles for my first novel, I considered *Thatcher's Abortions*. Growing up in the early-eighties North, thrown out of school (and, in my case, home) at 16 with three O-levels (much like Weston's Debrito), our only options were the dole or Youth Training Scheme (YTS). Expelled, not yet fully-formed, we were unable - in vital ways - to *live*.

In the end I decided the title implied actually undergoing abortions, was too negative and so settled on the more poetic, Chinese Horoscope-inspired *Fire Horses*. One thing I didn't remove from the book though was the fury and impotent rage we felt on being denied the dignity of work - seeing our planet ravaged by revolutionary capitalism. We were young, looking for answers, and the politics of the Hard Left seemed to provide answers, as they often had to young people who sought change, excitement and certainty.

If it hadn't been for gurus, I wouldn't be here. My mum and dad, working-class children of Communists and socialists, met at a Socialist Labour League event; Gerry Healey – in some ways an older, more corrupt Leaf Blower – told my 17-year-old mum he would sleep with her on the eve of the revolution. She picked my dad instead, and the revolution never came and was never televised.

The journey embarked on by Arnold Debrito, the subject of Jeff Weston's enthralling novel, is thus a familiar one. The quest for answers. The impatience with systems. What makes Debrito's pilgrimage more interesting is the profession he falls into: the markets, a world of which I know nothing and Weston apparently knows a great deal (if only enough to know, in the words of screenwriter William Goldman, that "Nobody knows anything").

This duality – between Debrito's beliefs and his occupation – provides the narrative with tension and nuance, but it also does much more. By describing and part-explaining those infamous dates, Black Monday and Black Wednesday, the book illustrates the boom and bust insanity of the markets, the impossible lust for perennial growth and the reliance on colonial exploitation in the form of the outrageous execution of Ken Saro-Wiwa.

This is an unapologetically ambitious book, taking in radicalism, capitalism, the history of Italian anarchists in America, educating the reader about Sacco & Vanzetti as Philip Roth did with the Weathermen in *American Pastoral*. There is something Ballardian in Weston's prose; not just the way he describes buildings, the passing of cars, the dark underpass and neglected city zone, but the people. What could be a more Ballardian name than Pendlebury? English, unthreatening, close in fact to King Charles' mythical hamlet of Poundbury, that artificial tribute to an artificial past where serfs were not serfs and overlords were paternal benefactors.

In *Fire Horses,* I wrote: "There's a photograph by Andreas Gursky in the Tate I never tire of looking at, Chicago stock exchange, thousands of traders in tribal colours. Capitalism equals loneliness; the meek shall inherit the mortgage." Weston's book encapsulates that madness, that yearning for change, that nagging feeling something is wrong. We might not have all the answers; we might not have any. But at least we are looking, still asking. Still fucking angry.

Mark Piggott, 10 December 2023

CHAPTER 1

Pendlebury. His name was Pendlebury. He wore his black, greying hair slicked to the side, yet could not prevent its tumbling forward when he least desired it. This, to me, spoke of madness; a physiognomical chink which allowed us to judge him before even hearing his words...words which were few from the start and even fewer as the months progressed.

It was 1986 when I first met him. We were both sixteen and among a supposedly 'select' group of individuals; individuals that had either failed to get into a real college or, quite simply, were not aware of our eligibility for further education. We – all of us – were set to become one of three things: a secretary, an engineer, or a computer hack. I chose the latter and so did Pendlebury. Where this mighty vocational step was to lead us, I had no idea.

From the outset, we worked inside an old church; a granite-constructed offering stripped of its pews and laden with unfashionable desks, coarse surfaces and plastic, paganistic chairs. The external architecture seemed to register its disgust of this fact, as if its forefather had been gutted in the manner of a simple river fish. For my part, I enjoyed getting off the bus and walking to a destination – any destination - other than school for the first time in over a decade. I was a young man whose consciousness was half-tuned to the stifling adult set, yet at the same time, half-ready to be led.

As apprentices, each of us received around thirty-five pounds per week (a phenomenal amount to an ex-paperboy). Some of the 'workers', as a result, took to tasting the local brew on a regular basis. Others bought computer games and clothes, whilst avoiding the issue of keep, or rent, with their parents. I, personally, saved for a car...a quite glorious bright yellow Mk.II Escort (Cost: £550). And Pendlebury? It was difficult to tell exactly where his funds went. The clothes remained the same: starched jeans that didn't appear to be available in any high-street shop; a long, black, gothic coat that Edgar Allan Poe would have been proud of; a brown sweater that was ironed maybe once a fortnight. There were no vices, no habits, nothing. He appeared to walk everywhere, living in the locality, and had never been seen with a pint in his hand (if only he had been stood in the public house to begin with). For this, I admired him, if only out of wonderment.

In the few weeks we had all been working at this government-funded establishment, bonds had been made, common-room chairs had been unofficially assigned....and Pendlebury – constantly on the outside of things – had been threatened; not because of any unrulyness, but because he did not 'fit in'.

'You fucking gothic bastard, Pendlebury,' came the lambasting, with an almost Oxford intonation given that the initial expletive was unabbreviated. 'Shift the stinking coat from my chair.'

Titters surrounded the not-so-gentle reprobation. Others added to the gothic theme by salting their comments with bats, castles and all manner of early nineteenth century generalisations. I watched from the other side of the room – comfortable amongst two half-decent peers. It was a situation not too dissimilar to the others. Pendlebury, clumsy and seemingly inarticulate, took a hold of his black jacket and backed away. He didn't wish to lengthen his pain, nor spar with this foppish crowd, and so stood amongst the shadows of the feeble library that acted as perimeter to the room. Gazing at the spines and fingering them self-consciously, he appeared desperate for obscurity, anonymity – something which would steal him away from this hell; something which would paint his face like that of a regular kid: impertinent, unassailable, cavalier.

On this occasion I caught his eye. Through the scrum of the packed room, he registered his vulnerability with me and me alone. I turned away almost immediately. I was a sixteen-year-old not given to accepting pariah-status lightly. It shamed me because I suspected I knew the weight of his troubles, along with their tiresome encumbrance. There were mainstream ideas I still had to dally with, however, and so Pendlebury was to be left abandoned like an indigenous tribe villaged in the flood-line of a dam development. Altruistic I was not, unlike my mother. She was the baker of cakes for the family, thinking herself fortunate to eat just one, whereas I......I was gluttonous for a reasonable level of acceptability; something which was in danger of being steered off course should I have associated with Pendlebury.

I turned to my peers and indulged in routine banter. There was nothing much doing in terms of philosophical insight or unruffled intuitiveness, yet the staid manner in which we conducted ourselves suited the wider scheme of things. It was inconspicuous. It was sensible. It was deplorable.

After this Pendlebury no longer sought me out, either visually or, one felt, psychically. He seemed to strengthen his resolve, both professionally and socially; the latter reflected by the fact that I would walk behind him for a distance of five hundred yards each evening on the way to the bus stop – his march in front of me never letting up despite my obvious presence. I would, upon waiting for my ride, watch his taut yet sinewy frame bowl its way along the streets, until either a row of Victorian terraces intervened in my field of vision, or I myself was commandeered by a large, orange, community bus (a pre-MkII Escort necessity).

Watching Pendlebury this way for weeks on end – the same routine each evening - became a hobby of sorts.....a fascination even. He was dismissed as a buffoon by the others and ignored increasingly, however, a map, a pattern, a Pendlebury paradigm was beginning to build in my own mind through the constant 'surveillance'. I felt like a personality sneak thief, a traitor to Pendlebury's brave doggedness, yet my own sanity had become snagged and somehow dependent upon the nature of this young gentleman's endeavours.

Mondays he would always turn off into Dickinson Lane; a rather derelict and forsaken area which housed some of society's fringe members. The following three days were usually the same. Fridays, however, he would walk past like a soldier on weekend leave; a soldier perhaps tired of his barracks and the uninspiring faces that regularly surrounded him; a solider, moreover, that saw these precious forty-eight hours as a mellifluent release or a time to plot alternative pastures.

Pendlebury, I always noted, seemed not jolly but certainly less forlorn come Friday afternoons, as if grasping a comely knowledge that none of us could even begin to conceive. Because of this my own Fridays began to take on a rather cerebral edge. It wasn't necessarily the instinctive need to know which now mattered, but the intellectual chase with regard to Pendlebury's manoeuvring and pigmented mindset.

On the first occasion that I trailed him (beyond the bus stop) – some three months after college had begun – it was thus key data which interested me: the type of faces which may have been waiting for him (were they beautiful and consoling constructions primed for the sadness which Pendlebury ultimately carried?); the area or location (was it somehow befitting of Pendlebury's real self?). Upon finally stopping after a trek of some three or four miles (a distance perfectly manageable to Pendlebury without breaking speed) I found myself gazing into a reasonably well-heeled street; a semi-detached haven quite inverse to the hapless aura of Dickinson Lane.

Here, lawns were impeccably mowed, litter was a byword for hardened soul and the birds undoubtedly sang sprightly tunes in the spring and summer months. There was an urban calm about the area rather than a rural prodigiousness, yet that was enough. Pendlebury, whilst waiting at the door of one of the houses, seemed conscious of the transition. He gazed around with a fresh inquisitiveness. His lips purported what could easily have been a smile. Every detail of the surrounding area, in fact, appeared absorbable without a rebuke from one's finer sensibilities.

As the door to the house eventually opened I think I knew who or what to expect in a strange, anticipatory way. The gent, in his mid-forties, looked magnanimous – profuse in his understanding of life's darker side. There was no joyous greeting or meticulously executed razzmatazz....just a hand on the Pendlebury shoulder and with it a firm commitment of sorts. It was the first time I had seen Pendlebury interact with another human being. It was the first time I had seen him alive and less inhibited. After a brief glance up at the sky from both of them, they went inside – the door shutting definitively.

I stood there – on the corner of the street – for a few more minutes, unable to partake in their world any longer, yet engrossed in the nothingness they had left behind. I imagined their chatter, so vast when set against the rough subterfuge espoused by everyone else. I attached an immenseness to their existence, even though I knew little of their motives. I........I wished for Monday – for the unctuous mannerisms of my fellow college goers, knowing that in amongst them would be Pendlebury.

CHAPTER 2

I had signed up for this apprenticeship college with three O-levels to my name (Maths 'A', Computer Studies 'B' and Business Studies 'B'). On the morning that my results came out, my mother had been travelling on a bus coming back from town and had happened across a few of my street buddies (friends who attended a different school to mine). Aware of my meagre total, she simply stressed my mathematical 'genius' quietly and assuredly, avoiding talk where possible of my failure in Physics, Control Technology, Art and Woodwork, not to mention English (Language and Literature). I didn't hear from these friends again – I only heard that they were in the big league (the land of A-levels) whilst I was scrapping for a YTS certificate. My mother's dignity, I suppose, revealed a truth which I still have trouble assimilating: that friendship is at the mercy of performance. The irony two or three months later was that I had become the cream in academic terms given my new setting; an O-level being something bestowed upon enlightened ones.

The news of this and particularly my statistical 'prowess' came about as a result of an early feel-good exercise once within the walls of the old church. We were each given thirty seconds in front of a rather archaic camera wherein we had to describe an achievement we were proud of. The practical abilities of my new colleagues became apparent from this point on. Some would enthuse about re-wiring a domestic appliance, whereas others would talk of computer programming. I, having nothing much else in my locker at the age of sixteen, subtly flaunted my 'A' grade in mathematics. It registered immediately. They were unaware of the geared fluency behind such a result (my teacher resembling a bearded, East European basketball player, whilst possessing the ability to pluck my latent talent like a guitar string), yet they commended it as if hoping to hire me for a bank job.

Pendlebury, pushed to the back of the queue unceremoniously, had *his* thirty seconds not long after: 'I….I think some of you…are fools. Big fools. Knowing this is a great achievement.' Had it been said with a whiff of irony then perhaps the watching faces would have forgiven such an outburst. As it was the invidiousness was lost on no one. Two teachers immediately sprang to their feet and barricaded Pendlebury in. The camera was switched off – not before editing out Pendebury's 'ill-judged' choice of words. It was later to remind me of a paragraph in an Orwell novel; Pendlebury a kind of social experiment in his own right merely speaking a harsher truth than people were used to and suffering in the process. I looked at his face as it incurred the wrath of almost everyone in the room. Diplomacy was not etched on it. What was, seemed anachronistic: indifferent to the Thatcher years. Pendlebury was striving for something which these people would never permit and because of that I began to see part of myself in him.

This abiding memory together with the face of the magnanimous gent stayed with me for much of the weekend. How the two images collided fantastically disturbed me. I recalled the teachers' stares at Pendlebury as if he had committed a catastrophic offence. And then I recalled the image of only hours ago: peaceful, complete and, if puritanical, then something unseen in spurious contemporary circles. Some teachers protected their corn it seemed, their tiny reputations, ahead of a sharper judgement, and as a consequence I found myself possessing less and less resistance to marginal or bohemian ideas. Pendlebury's disenfranchisement upset me. It bore the hallmarks of an adulthood whose existence I had suspected yet never fully acknowledged, perhaps in the hope that the sun really would smile at the moon one day.

Saturday, I grew up I suppose. I walked around the house not only like a man about to turn seventeen, but like someone sitting up in a hospital bed; someone with a genuine take on life following a period of hardship. I chatted to my parents (my mother mainly) about the choices I had made, about the incident on the bus. I was concerned and I needed good, solid answers that would cement my feet for a while. Why hadn't anyone taken me aside to extol the merits of higher education? Why did I feel restless after only seven months as an apprentice?

My father shifted uncomfortably in his chair. He was a gruff, yet somehow polite individual. 'You're seventeen, Arnold. When you reach thirty, *then* you worry. *Then* we eject you from the family home.' It was succinct, neat and orderly, and following its delivery my father left the room. I looked across at my mother. She smiled as she always did, aware of a fuller meaning; aware of the reassurance that emanated from the bones of my tradesman father. And then, as we considered our next lines, a final volley, ensemble, swept its way in from the hall: 'Sacco and Vanzetti...'

It had the same impact it always did, although referring to an incident some sixty years ago. Sacco and Vanzetti, two hard-working - if semi-anarchic - Italian migrants (living in America) had been electrocuted quite wrongly following a prejudiced murder trial. My father, with his scant knowledge of American history and quarter Italian blood, had somehow decided that these two individuals were to be our - the Debrito family's – beacons of hope; our liberators in the face of oppression of any kind. It was now ten years since he had first pulled me aside and whispered their names, and yet the resonance still held strong.

Now, left with my mother's benevolent and attentive presence, I became both cohesive and incohesive, discursive and exact. I indulged in the ramblings of someone seven *years* out of school, rather than seven months: 'There was an instance a couple of years ago – I was reading Melville's *Moby Dick* as part of my English assessment. It was a book I saw as simply relating to a crew's troubles at sea. As such, I read it in quite an artless manner. After a few paragraphs I was interrupted. "Do you not understand the allegorical and philosophical might of this work, Arnold?" the teacher infused. "Are you unable to grasp the undertones which hint of evil?" I was fourteen. It was probably only the third novel I'd ever read. Why did she have to be so damn ungracious? What kind of teacher exposes a kid – average class position 21 out of 28 – to a classroom of baying intellects? Christ – I was happy to be part of the third tranche, even if at the back of the pecking order. "The whale is representative of revenge, of adversity turning its heel. Don't you see Arnold, Moby Dick carries the suffering and anguish of the little man and therefore must one day strike. Whereas you.....you are a modern-day *can* of anguish and – some would argue – scant justification for the fight ever commencing.'''

'She said that? Ormerod said that?' my mother immediately cried.

'Yes.'

'Well I wish I'd known. I wish I'd have known, Arnold.'

'Why?'

'Because I'd have grappled with her or something....at the parents' evening. Taken her dusty attitude and.....well, you know.'

Ignoring her rather defiant and charming response and my own intentionally ingenuous questioning, I found myself slightly amazed by her recalling the name of my English teacher. My housewife mother, now 'resting' from the part-time bar work which had previously occupied her time, was obviously indulging herself in the academic archives of her two sons. Behind the floury hands of this domestic wanderer resided a freelance librarian, a chronicler of events little known but significant.

'I knew *before* the Moby Dick thing though. What I'm trying to say is, it feels like I can sense evil in a person – however diluted.'

I had her stumped for a moment. The gregarious manifestation that is my mother, halted by a semi-religious assertion. Eventually though – 'Sometimes I wonder which son turned out the way we intended. James – so sure and business-like, yet understanding. Or you, my son Arnold, with your growing, unwritten crusade. Because I see it, you know. The railing against things, the change in your general manner. It isn't a bad thing, but you do have to be careful, Arnold. Your father – he learned to bite his tongue, be more....philosophical about things. The man you see now is less confrontational than when I first knew him. Other qualities have risen out of him: patience, consideration, generosity. Let me show you something....'

Comfy in one of the brown-patterned chairs now, I watched as she rummaged around in the cupboard at the base of the bureau.

'Here....here it is.' She sounded pleased, almost jubilant. Certainly excited by the find. Thrusting a scissor-sculpted photo into my palm, she waited patiently for my reaction.

It was my father. The man in the photo was my father. His pose was almost a classic one – sat there on a pebbled beach; his arms, short yet strong, gently holding the neck and collar of our first family hound, crouched before him. He wore a blue cardigan, a similar coloured winged shirt and beige pants. The socks, very evident with thick vertical and horizontal stripes, seemed to lead down to what appeared to be a pair of black leather trainers. I had never seen my father wearing trainers – just slippers and shoes; at least during the last epoch or decade. This picture therefore, this image of him, seemed to permeate some of my long-held assumptions. And looking at his face, with its blue stubble, munificent side-burns and flicked hair – none of which had carried him through his forties – a slight sense of compunction or remorse hit me.

Had I misjudged him? Had he somehow tried to tie his external appearance to his steadier and responsible mind? Were me and James indirectly party to the snatching away of his trainers? Had we been helpless fledglings in need of regular sustenance; fledglings with a razor blade astutely positioned behind our tiny wings? And now – in the twilight of his playing days, did he envisage a return, a pilgrimage of sorts, to a side-burns Mecca or ebullient stronghold?

I wondered. I considered the fact that my father was perhaps a living parable; one of Melville's more sophisticated constructions. I looked towards the ceiling knowing that his feet would be the other side of it, buried and indeed assuaged by a pair of thick-furred slippers that for now at least represented his level of wildness.

'He looks different,' I offered, or rather spluttered in the direction of my mother.

'He wanted a family, same as me, knew his limitations, and agreed to walk a steady line.'

I imagined my father being randomly breathalysed at home – made to walk the front path from door to gate, and back again; a slip or off-balance stride leading to his detention and the calling in of the S.S. More importantly, I imagined what could have been: a man less willing to inscribe the words 'Clearance Sale' on his knowledge at the implicit behest of the middle classes that visited the house with their broken TVs; a man less likely to cower, or rather accept, the mighty opinions of others simply because the topics were outside of his normal jurisdiction, and therefore somehow disqualified his probing.

But then, I would never have known him. I would never have seen the bruising humility that became his ally.

CHAPTER 3

'What do you do on Fridays?'

The question seemed to fall down in front of Pendlebury like a dark drawbridge, imploring him to walk its merciful path, yet at the same time adding fearful shadows of objects and things that no longer existed. I hadn't been sure of quite how to phrase the opening sortie, and so had opted for the least possible ambiguity at the risk of appearing blunt.

Stood there only a few yards away from the bus stop or our proverbial Russian/Polish border, I waited for a response now that he had committed himself by ceasing his stride. Locking his gaze upon me for a few seconds, and then turning away as if steadfastly assimilating and dissecting me, he seemed undecided over whether to venture an answer or not. I noticed his sweep of the entire area – not just me – in an effort to perhaps confirm the anonymousness of our 'discussion'. 'Safe', his left eye appeared to register, whilst his right was more intent – almost misanthropic – concerning the surroundings.

From him there evinced a quietude if one looked deep enough, particularly when set against the gangling concrete structures – central to the carriageway – which held fare over the terraced vicinity. Speaking positively, the early evening hum of traffic, and somehow its smell, seemed to serenade Pendlebury into acquiescence.

'Why do you ask?'

The words were soft, endearing – close to shattering. I was taken aback by their celestialness.

'Because something changes you. The others might not notice, but I'm quite perceptive. And it's more than the prospect of simply not mixing with these...' - I gestured towards the old church – '...halfwits for two days. I know it is.'

'It is, is it?'

'I think it is,' I replied, feeling slightly embarrassed and somehow younger.

'Let me ask *you* something…'

'OK,' I agreed.

He looked serious now. Gone was the apolitical generosity. 'Why didn't you help me?'

'When?' was the instant response, but I knew when.

Pendlebury lifted his eyebrows. There was a quiet insistence to them.

'Nobody wants to be on the outside,' I ashamedly acknowledged. The traffic partly muffled my words and I was forced to repeat them after seeing Pendlebury cock his head: '*Nobody* wants to be on the outside.'

He looked at me, unsure. His stare was slightly more comfortable now I felt, particularly as the unspoken words hadn't choked me the second time round.

'But some people don't get a choice. Right?'

'It would seem so,' was my dejected answer.

'You're the Court of Appeal though(?)'

'I…' I couldn't quite grasp whether Pendlebury was telling or asking me this. His words were both rhetorical and quizzical. At the same time, however, I managed to loosely gauge the coalition thread silently swinging my way.

'It's OK,' were his words. 'You're not ready – I can see that.' Crossing into Poland, he hesitated, before – 'Perhaps you'll knock on the door Friday…'

There wasn't time to answer. No time for the rush of blood to my face to offer a bluff or at least gracefully come clean. Pendlebury's gothic façade had seemingly transmuted into a bat and before I knew it he had gone, disappeared, vanished.

Stood there next to the hard concrete, I felt wiser, yet isolated. So isolated and alone. One of the tutors – predisposed to leaving fifteen minutes after the apprentices – drove past me in her low, classic car, honking wastefully due to my audible reticence. Something had partially shut me down. Something had declared me non-nuclear, yet so vital and no longer surplus. I breathed in the toxic air as it shimmied its way across the tarmac. I surveyed things with less faculties, yet I was rid of the fat. Searching, visually, for an anchor, I seemed to lose coordination, as if a lack of direction was somehow more noble.

More cars rushed past, but all I noticed was the blurred light emanating from the metal, set against the blackness of the quickening night. I shuffled forward a couple of steps – immediately stopping due to the haze before me. I was in a dream, yet so conscious of the tangible surroundings. Reaching out for a lamppost a few yards from me, I stumbled awkwardly, feeling oddly intoxicated and galvanized. Despite the strangeness of my predicament, I felt......reconciled to the truth – to the all-inclusive menu of faux pas, humility and grandness.

If people noticed me, then they carried on. I was not significant or noteworthy, but simply wobbly – psychologically sheared by Pendlebury's brief words. That my actions should not be lauded nor lambasted was only right. I was merely a little erratic and such behaviour ought to be bracketed, allowed – overlooked.

Eventually, I held my arm out, managing to bring to a halt a passing bus. Stepping on past the shushing doors, I showed the driver my pass. He seemed indifferent – perhaps shattered and worn by the cubicle which cornered him; which smothered his vagrant designs and philosophy. I walked on, down the spine of the bus to my seat, ignoring his marked hostility. Bowing my head slightly, I shut my eyes and lapped up the kingdom inside my head.

Stood on a misty playing field, part football pitch, part running track, I cast my eyes over a girl perhaps one year younger. She wore a navy skirt and same-coloured sweater; apparel from school, yet still adorned late into this spring evening. Fourteen or fifteen – that had been my age, my calling, alone with this marvel from the other side. She had appeared, suddenly – at first with a younger sister or companion, and my friends had cantered away. Then, offering us the entire expanse of exquisitely fenced in field, the companion had sauntered off – perhaps to join the gossiping cluster that had developed. Now, a few feet apart, we barely managed to lift our respective chins in order to maintain eye contact. She had been beautiful – a reverential picture of near womanhood. I, unfortunately, had been diffident to the extreme – still perhaps wrapped in the teenage code of exclusivity. Alas, to this day, her face danced inside me – poignantly, evocatively, unsettlingly. I had foolishly walked away – declining to even taste the meal before me; churlishly tossing the cutlery to the floor. I would not, months after, even permit myself to peer through the thin glass of the restaurant door through fear of embarrassment or acute poverty on my part. She had been from a lower social stratum, and yet later, it was I so bereft of fine garments and direction. Che...

The driver shuddered the bus to a halt having misjudged a traffic light. My eyes, thus, remained open for the duration of the ride – taking in, absorbing the cartilage-like strip or road, with its broken fences, wandering mutts and garishly-painted houses. At least two barren petrol stations seemed to stalk the proceedings with their boarded-up, balaclava faces – eyes in the form of screws and nail heads harking to the urban echo; the painted strip around the forecourt roof partially blow-torched, like a worn head band around the temple of a veteran marathon runner.

Five minutes on and I was greasing my shoes across the grey flagstones that led down to my, or rather my parents', house. The door was partially ajar – my mother's hand gripping the inside handle whilst evidently speaking on the hall phone. Clearly she had been caught between watering the plants in the porch and subduing the ringing of the plastic intransigent. But then, perhaps she simply didn't wish to exclude me given that my brother James was on the phone, and had therefore nudged the door open as a welcoming gesture.

I walked through, past my obviously joyful mother and into the back living room. My father would be at least an hour. I remained stood up, in an effort to absorb the surroundings more coherently. The carpet was a criss-cross brown and beige with intermittent hoops that shattered any symmetrical intent. The walls were covered with an age-old wood chip paper – itself the victim of a cream-laden, paint brush molester. Everything, in fact, appeared to have a hint of brown, including the wooden structures of the suite and the display cabinets, neatly positioned in the semi-alcoves of the room end. This was not to denote or consign the room to a laughable or staid level – because I, personally, blended in...felt, somehow, safe – yet it undoubtedly acted as a repoussoir in shifting the occupant's eyes out into the garden through the chrome patio doors.

Here, the final stop, before the roving fields and golf course, animals had been buried, apple trees had offered early promise and badminton nets had been strewn above the lawn between the secure points of the garage and a wooden trunk. I looked out now, amidst the naked winter show. The soil was hard, the shrubs somehow defiant and the fencing tired. Into the distance, the story became more opaque: my grandfather's cottage, one of three just beyond the practice green, way up on the other side of the course. Incredible really, that we were together – my mother, father and I beside the 8th fairway, my grandfather pitched at the angle of the dogleg 3rd, and, well, James in the Midlands – one hundred miles south of our Lancashire pocket – in his second year at university and getting skinnier by the week. But opaque – hard to understand – it definitely was. My grandfather, being on my mother's side, wasn't part of the Debrito family tree, and yet, in terms of pure militancy and nihilism, he scorched a path which often made those around him uncomfortable. I would hear bits of stories concerning his doggedness whilst sat amongst my parents: his defection from the local Conservative Club to Labour based entirely on his misogyny which had "boiled over in the early eighties"; his blatant disregard for designated parking spaces – particularly at golf clubs – because he had sickened of such "bollock prejudice" during his WWII days in Delhi. My father, whether serious or not, had christened him "Castro", yet was notably pliant whilst in his company. Their relationship was in many ways like a meeting of A J Cook and J H Thomas; one stubborn and preacher-like, the other less demonstrative – open to negotiation.

Turning away from the sequence, I shifted myself closer to the hallway in an effort to overhear my mother in garrulous mode. 'That's good,' I heard her repeat – the intonation filled with semi-pride and wonder. 'Just four more months,' she continued, offering a form of benevolent reassurance to my often lonely sibling. 'And then summer.'

There was angst from the other side – the other end of the line. My mother's hurried words presumably filling in James's silences. One suspected too many numbers floating around in his head at times, and insufficient rest and food; the commerce and accountancy undergraduate, the family protagonist, quite supine from overwork. Speaking relatively, I supposed him to be in Beirut with its fractured support system and harsh living conditions.

'Perhaps this weekend,' my mother continued. 'No – *definitely*. This weekend,' she echoed, with a grainy kind of staunchness, referring no doubt to their visiting him – food parcels and all.

'I'll have your father check over the car Friday night,' she went on, with timely grace and efficiency.

The mood of the conversation then seemed to pick up once more – James clearly appeased by the knowledge of their imminent arrival. Hope. Light. Sustenance. My mother was all three. 'Arnold? He's fine.' Pushed a little more, I heard her deal him a synopsis (her voice manifestly easing off the decibels): 'There's something of your grandfather in him. Unmistakably. And I don't think it's simply a teenage thing that he's likely to grow out of. He seems to be....what's the word, James....re-ca.....Recalcitrant – yes. They say prisons are a breeding ground for crime. Well, Arnold shatters that theory instantly. His breeding ground is his own mind.'

I was flattered rather than insulted. The concern in my mother's voice, if negative, did not warrant any compunction on her part, but instead prophesied – through duty or accident – my relationship with Pendlebury. I hadn't, of course, mentioned Pendlebury to anyone, through fear of misunderstandings. But my route in life – its face slowly unmasking – seemed more solidified than at any previous time.

'We step out of the fast-flowing river and find that it was tricking us all along!'

'Jack!'

My father had returned and my mother's appreciation of him was obvious. Still in the back living room, but aware of the new presence in the house and James perhaps combing through his balance sheets once again, I sat down and pulled a newspaper close. Seconds elapsed and then my father wandered in.

'What news then, Arnold?'

'Nothing. Nothing much.'

'College?'

'They're sending us for interviews in the spring.'

'Good. That's good.'

I watched as he struggled to maintain the upbeat tone. Something in his demeanour balked at the hypocrisy of what he had said. His beatific show was, alas, tragically ephemeral and weightless.

'Fixed many TVs?' I asked, in an attempt to restore a sense of reality and harmony.

'A few. Just a few,' he stumbled.

He seemed to be…out of gas, but more candid because of it. Slumping into the chair, his heavy arms padded against the sides. Exhausted. Forty-six and exhausted. Those were my thoughts. I imagined him, my father – Jack Debrito – counting backwards from eighteen and a half, dreaming of relaxation.

'I was a radio man when I was younger, you know.' A smile clawed its way onto his face. 'TVs became the job though.'

'Jack? Two or three?!' my mother shouted from the kitchen.

'Two,' was the flat response. And then, looking across at me, he added: 'I only deserve two.'

Sometimes he wasn't my father. When the self-pitying came in, I preferred him not to be. Stoking the earlier chatter, I continued its line: 'How old were you?'

He jumped up and began to pace the room. 'Eight or nine as I remember. Hearing – it's enough, you know. Keeps the brain sharp…concentrated. Let's you think.'

'I agree.' I felt as if I was agreeing that television should be outlawed; that my father's profession should be condemned.

'Good things make few demands on you. It seems that there's a kindred politeness…'

His sentence tailed off and I was left to pick up its abandoned shell: 'Thirty years in the profession and you're having second thoughts?'

He was stood at the patio doors now – looking out, avoiding eye contact. Providing an answer to my question wasn't possible whilst simultaneously being judged. I waited. He coughed a couple of times. He then raised both hands, seemingly to wipe his tired face. My mother shouted us in at this point – into the kitchen-cum-dining room. My father hesitated – frozen by something, some aspect of the scene before him perhaps. I couldn't go. I couldn't leave the room until he'd turned around, however perverse. My mother called us again – angered by our reticence and inertia. Jack Debrito immediately turned, and sped out past me without saying anything.

'Long day, Rose. It's been a long day,' I heard him pronounce. But I had seen his red eyes, his unnecessary embarrassment.

I slowly walked through to join them.

CHAPTER 4

The old church felt unimportant Tuesday. I observed a lot of what was around me: the white-stained walls of each room; the clumsy management debating worthless concerns; fellow apprentices with physical and verbal habits both spasmodic and eruptive. This wasn't an educational establishment, I decided, but rather a human zoo. If I had, fatefully, led these....these ragamuffins, by way of a bank job, then the outcome would have been termination of life; a boot camp of lackadaisical encumbrances. That aside, however, my concern was Pendlebury. Seeing him still humiliated, I looked on like a toothless embassy. Unable to directly affect or bedazzle the inner sanctum of the operation – the self-acclaimed petty officers – I plotted the downfall of a fervent follower (someone to perhaps replace Pendlebury). He was too keen, too easily swayed, that I felt it my duty to undo him. As I examined his cushy laughter and barbarous asides to the POs, I noted his obvious character flaws; weaknesses and defects which a child would have pointed out, yet the sum of which were now vital as part of a tactical offensive. When a man cannot breathe – or as he should – then aid him, whatever the unusual methods. The words somehow blanketed my insides and instilled in me a sense of purpose, if necessary hypocrisy.

I looked across again – this time with a reined-in circumspection. It had to be now, otherwise the wider circle of buzzards and vultures would be upon Pendlebury – each clawing away at a given piece of him.

'Oye! Twig!' There was no doubting who my words were aimed at; my continued stare foraging ahead of me into the well of his eyes.

He looked back, initially, in what seemed absolute silence, yet the murmurings soon surfaced. His face was pale – a shocked, pale brown; his relatively long, meagre body poorly hidden by mock rappers' pants – more so than at any previous time. He was off balance – clearly stung by my opportunist bellow. I watched his mouth as it ticked over – each vital second one push from the inner sanctum's core. I waited – expecting a retort, a blast of some kind.

Nothing. Nothing at all, and so I allowed the verbal cavalry to bugle its way to the front: 'Yeh. You! The remnant of autumn. The twig on the ground...'

People began to laugh a little – still unsure as to where this would end up, yet content to lather themselves in the ephemeral froth. I was not a supporter of Pendlebury, they seemed to exude, but rather someone with an uncanny eye for similarities. He *was* a twig – a frail, spleen-like human who had risen the ranks, much to the discomfiture of the POs. And such failings had to be remedied at once.

The sniff of air immediately turned dank. My job, albeit brief, was evidently done – signed-off, enveloped and semi-heartily archived. A quiet respect seemed to float across, clutching at my available senses. The POs were actually grateful, as if in the presence of a double agent or inside mastermind (but, thank God, did not want or expect my allegiance). Their new-found vilification of their once begotten steer, however, both alarmed and repulsed me. Cornered somewhat by his former associates, 'Twig' was subjected to racist insults and personal attacks: 'Gollywog'; 'Horlicks Boy'; 'The Ripple Man'; 'Black Hoochy Cooch'; 'Drumstick'; and so not to ease off the expletives completely – 'Chimney Sweep Twat'.

He looked perturbed and slightly concerned or disoriented by the rebuffs, yet also more hardened by the experience; ready to save a little face.

'Honkey bastards. Snowflake mothers!'

The physical retribution was swift. Four versus one. And I had caused it. Fists I barely tolerated. Feet were cowards' instruments. Somehow the ante had been upped significantly though and the random acts now before me I felt were being initiated by my own body. Enervation ran its fingers over my veins. Fecklessness stroked my brow. I hadn't considered the undertone of my brief sortie nor the simple edict that I had unwittingly released. Pendlebury was surely safe – given a reprieve perhaps; that was the only thought driving me. As the noise lessened and the air of animosity diminished, I gauged the faces around me.

It was a school. Despite the otherwise glorious claims, I was sitting in a school. And it would always be like this, no matter what the age. Things carried through – found themselves at the bottom of a balance sheet and were brought forward. The same nefarious acts existed irrespective of the environment and the level of maturity. Quite what I could do to alter this course or destroy the pre-destined scripture, I didn't know.

Subsided by the now flat aura of non-conflict, the faces and their lines of vision seemed to converge upon myself. I had become a spectacle, a source of intrigue to their vacant minds. There were clear expectations as to my future behaviour. I was worth watching, if only in the corner of one's eye, because I was liable to flip out or entertain. The humiliation of 'Twig' was merely a harbinger to other, more pernicious, acts and therefore I was the latest novelty.

'Boo!' I felt like roaring, with a rehearsed vehemence, but I sensed that the irony would be lost within the folds of their savvy.

The attention gnawed at me. It was more irksome than the insatiable middle classes that hungered for titbits whilst collecting their TVs from my father. 'No news,' he would often proclaim, if in a playful, obstreperous mood. To which, their reaction would be one of attachment. How many of my father's words, or how much of his demeanour, was guided by the need to earn though, I wondered. I recalled my mother talking of 'foreigners' and me instantly picturing a swarm of Chinese, Indian and Pakistani men, TVs in their arms, restaurant and shop takings in their pockets, pleading for my father's assistance.

As I was later to learn of course, 'foreigners' – by definition – meant that my father plundered his remaining energy whilst jeopardizing his livelihood. 'No – just family and close friends,' my mother would endlessly repeat down the phone line, in an effort to legitimize my father's obviously heinous actions. Except, our family, if measured by lack of space around the house, was dilating by the week; the electrical item of a cousin's friend's brother typically sat quite precariously on an overloaded shelf or windowsill.

My thoughts returned to the crowd before me. A lesson or class was due to start very soon. The more conscientious individuals began pushing their plastic seats back; the stragglers emitted inaudible noises and stared at the floor. Pendlebury, at the far end of the room, away from the hub, caught my eye. A faint nod was dispatched by him – so brief and subtle that it transcended the politics of the room. I immediately understood its meaning, but more importantly yielded to its Zen-like projection.

Divisive and full of protestations, I visited my grandfather later in the day. His cottage offered solace, with its décor unchanged since my grandmother's passing away. The sweet trays were as prominent as ever – littered with Uncle Joe's, Uncle Luke's, Mint Imperials and Bassett's Allsorts. The expandable tables lay untroubled by human intervention (my grandfather having no inclination to entertain or offer buffets, as my grandmother had done). The sturdy, Dralon-covered sofa and chairs looked dependable and inviting. The ticking clocks – all seven of them – suggested a deep preciousness to life. Only the contents of the kitchen cupboards had altered – tins of tuna and wholemeal bread ('both in the enemy's camp') making way for a small collection of paperbacks, including biographies of Gandhi and Desmond Tutu.

Swinging open the gate and crossing the cobbled courtyard, past the now disused, coal bunker, I waited after lightly ringing the bell (a modern invention that my grandfather planned to 'disarm before long'). He slid off the chains, turned the key and in a matter of seconds was before me – dressed in natty, grey pants, brown cardigan, slippers, shirt and old braces.

'Arnold! Arnold, my boy!' He offered his hand, to which I promptly engendered a robust shake. 'Come in...'

We wandered through the thin kitchen, down a step, and into the back living room. The front of the cottage which overlooked the golf course, and from which my parents' house was visible on a hilly pedestal, was only used between March and September. We thus sat in the 'winter' room, complete with wooden fire – my grandfather's pipe lying dormant on the table next to his rocker.

He immediately leant forward and threw an extra piece of wood on the already magnificent fire. I had never seen him not do this, as if the plumbing of courtesy was still uppermost in his mind when his guest was of the right ilk. Perhaps, I laughed to myself, he took a piece *off* the fire when my father visited alone.

'The fridge is well stocked, if...' He gestured back through the hallway – 'Lemonade? Kestrel?'

I strolled back into the kitchen and his expected utterance followed me in – 'A small tipping of the book end would be nice, Arnold.'

The book end, rather than being an ornamental chunk of wood, was actually a rectangular and rather weighty thick-glassed bottle of whisky stood next to Gandhi et al. A sterling job it was doing as well; my utilitarian grandfather clearly bolstered by its highly lamentable disguise.

I tilted Gandhi to stop the other books from falling, poured the bourbon, plus a shandy for myself, and then replaced the 'condiments' from where they had come. My grandfather's neatly positioned fingers were already hovering above his chair arm when I returned. It took him back – no doubt – to Indian hospitality, to a momentary feeling of being cared for.

Releasing my grip on the small glass and passing the Constable print in the centre of the wall (opposite the fire), I watched as the initial swig seemed to glide over his lips. A deep, refreshing, yet rasping sound bounced out of him. He quivered a little, but this was soon wrestled under control by his bodily vigour. I sat down, across from him, and lifted the larger glass up to my face. I felt extremely young as the liquid surged towards my mouth; like a ginger beer Prince sat with a blues maestro or learned dissident.

'So what's on your mind, Grandson?'

It was a simple yet rather clamorous question given my already inharmonious state. I reminded myself that I was now with a kinsman, however, and that wariness was to be short-changed as a child would be with a poor head for figures. Before I could respond though, my grandfather piped in with a typically intuitive and plenteous sentence.

'I used to think that people could read my face. That they should – even if they were only half-intelligent – be able to understand my viewpoint and ruminations, *without* any input from myself. Certainly no plain, obvious banter.

'One's expectations aren't always met though. Most of the time people require communication in the manner of a chip shop owner to his customer. You can't simply – however much it disappoints you – assume that people have that....that discernment. Or even the spur or time to want to figure you out.

'Small circles. Ultimately people will be effortless with family and close friends. The rest of the time they expect or know to give something else – something quite awkward perhaps, but easier over time. If there were more everyday philosophers and psychologists out there then the playing field would be less verdant. But we know that not to be the case. We've seen and are aware of the brutish modes that exist.

'I'm not asking you to give up your sullen or esoteric manner, because – Christ – some of the genes were passed down from me (and they're bloody beautiful...they are). But – how can I put this without being a traitor to my own beliefs – smile more. No, don't, just let the fuckers think that you're content. Be absorbed. Not in a public relations way, because that sullies the general good, but by your own fervent designs on life.

'What I'm saying, Arnold, is that I'd hate for you to be ostracized. Or indeed, so disheartened with life, that you become a recluse like Salinger – in self-imposed exile. Because that's no way to live. People need people. It's just a case of finding the right ones. Not easy when you're car-less *and* a Luddite.'

Some of his final paragraph was personal. I could see that. And yet, I had never viewed my grandfather as vulnerable or needing company. But rather, as an indefatigable warrior of sorts. His Datsun Cherry had long since been sold / impounded, only months after becoming a widower ('In the latter days it was really only ever a conveyor belt for vanilla slices. Your mother did an awful lot for us once we retired – too much in fact.'). And the phone – my grandfather used sparsely, damning and lambasting people's reliance on it: 'Sophocles would never have used it.'

For some reason, I now recalled my grandmother showing me a telegram she had received during WWII. It was their anniversary, March 1944, and my grandfather had sent a strictly worded message from his stationed position: 'You are more than ever in my thoughts at this time   61.' Number '61' had been his choice, like a Chinese meal. Sartorial alignments or tailored constructions were simply not permitted in case they were intercepted by the enemy, and too much had been given away concerning the troops' state of mind, tactics or positioning. And so '61' he had plumped for, in an effort to best encapsulate his feelings.

I remembered seeing the other one hundred and eighty eight choices on the reverse of the C & W telegram, and thinking then – as now – what an apt and wondrous selection my grandfather had made. Not all the others were relevant of course, yet to home in on such a tear-rendering and acutely solicitous composition was…was divine. How much of that consecratory substance had I inherited, I now selfishly pondered.

I examined the man in the chair opposite me – the bourbon still romancing his lips like the tide refreshingly and wreckingly sweeping over a sand castle. His words were deep-seated and too long in the peripheries. I wished to harness them, bind them together in a chemical fusion, and then spit them at the enemy.

I lifted my glass once more, took a swig of the shandy, and then continued our discussion: 'How am I to know that *you're* a philosopher? That being a hermit is the wrong path?'

He smiled at me forcefully. 'You're not.' The delay was well-timed and resonant, before: 'Except that I *am* a hermit, and therefore aware of its truth and destruction. Truth is mostly gleaned from silence, you see. And so, a dichotomy exists where you're going back for more of the drug to facilitate your wider inhabitance. Not such a bad thing, but like anything, you must get a good balance.

Too many people out there, Arnold, who are afraid of silence. No enrichment therefore. And when these people rise the ranks of the world we inhabit, their limited minds skewer and defile the others, who are judged to be less dependable.

'I'm the opposite. I need more visits from you. From James. From nieces and nephews. Otherwise......'

He hesitated, and it concerned me. I scrutinised his face and all he had said. There was an immense aura to his logic. I could see how he had crafted it, yet how it was now in danger of crafting him. Of pushing him too far along its cylindrical tappet.

'You're OK?' I half-stupidly, half-caringly prompted.

'Of course I am.' It wasn't said with malice or enmity, but rather in a reassuring, should-know-better, mature tone.

I suppose it was what I needed; 'Castro' to be unflustered, unflappable – true to the implicit contract between grandfather and grandson: 'Zero politics, complete composure.'

It felt awkward for a few seconds, but I allowed him to believe that his maturity had swept over me, that my young mind was perhaps less enquiring than it actually was. He seemed to look through me now and then into the very cornea of my eye – alternating, dipping his focus like a car beam. I had seen such a gaze before, lasered into my grandmother – the former occupant of the chair. The look was somehow filled with a wanderlust of the mind, with a beseeching calm and solace.

He was missing her. The completeness that she, my grandmother, had brought him was unable to be replicated. Nor would he want it to be, given its unabridged pre-eminence. She still walked the vault of his skull – quite patently. Still harnessed the grey matter that sponged his interpretation of the world. Age had not lessened the grief, but had instead siphoned the effusiveness.

'The other room...do you mind if we go in the other room?'

It was perhaps an attempt to shed the sensations that had welled up, and so I indicated my accedence with a shake of the head and a puffing of the lips. The fire would rage with no one in attendance. It would flicker with less shadows about it. Yet not everything could be placated.

I followed him in. Into the summer room, two months early. The furnishings were softer. The room was slightly more spacious. An unused fireplace stood to our right, the copious windows to our left – curtains not yet drawn. In here, there were smaller, framed pictures: family; memorabilia; another Constable. The lack – or sparsity – of wood somehow made it more inviting, more summery, attuned to a softer and invigorating melancholy.

We didn't sit immediately, but instead looked out over the trimmed grass beyond the garden and hedge; my grandfather dimming the light to banish any reflections in the window. The only visible incandescence was from the street lights weaving their way through a former field now civilised, named and part of a bus route. The bourbon still hung at my grandfather's side – a mere trickle left, yet the gripping of it a form of salvation.

'I see a lot from here, Arnold, during the day. Different birds. The tree heads swaying. People playing the course…You remember when we used to play the binoculars game?'

'I do. Yeh.' It brought a smile to my face – his reference to the early days, maybe five or six years ago, when my grandmother was still by his side.

'Two…five…three – no, four. Seven! We never said two hands.'

I would slip into my parents' bedroom, during a lull in the day, slowly pick up the receiver and phone him – my grandfather – whose cottage was visible with the naked eye. He would instantly know it was me due to the chuckle and my fine, rehearsed sentence of: 'How many?'

I hadn't known at first – for perhaps a month – that he possessed a pair of binoculars, and so a blind faith had gripped me that he could, over the distance of a golf course (say, one mile) make out how many fingers I had up.

There had been something bewitching and enchanting about it. Something unaffected, even on the day that my mother had purposely stayed behind, whilst my father had driven me round to the cottage. The subsequent phone call – which I had been encouraged to pick up – leading to my mother taking my role, and me my grandfather's.

'How many?' she had asked a second time, after my initial wild guess – at which point my grandfather had passed me the magic instrument.

I should have known all along. If I had been scientific then I would have been able to cut through the mystical sheen. If I had been scientific then….fascination and wonder would have stayed in their boxes, never to visit me.

The day I discovered I had been duped wasn't in any way tragic, although I sensed caution on the faces of those around me, but rather….flattering. An elaborate effort had been derived for me – for my gratification and pleasure. That is why I continued weeks after, I suppose. That is why I introduced a second hand – to pitch the odds, ever so fractionally, against the loving perpetrator.

And he didn't mind. Although now, the interactions of old seemed unrepeatable. Today, was less glorious – empty in many respects. Crater-like in its self-bombardment.

'I like it when one of the chaps uses the practice green. He'll hit forty or fifty from the bottom, up towards here. A seven, eight or nine iron depending on his age.'

He started to think. He looked pensive – intrigued.

'There's something in the flight of a ball that hypnotises me, Arnold. Its arching, its trajectory – so replenishing.' He turned to me. 'Have you considered it?'

'A couple of kids in the street play. It's crossed my mind.'

'I've an old set of Swilken in the shed – still up to it. Have a think. Get back to me. You'd be a junior you see – no waiting list.'

It distinctly sounded as if he had already made a few preliminary enquiries. I imagined him stepping into the local club, walking into the members' bar and signing my golf adoption papers over a couple of whiskies. Was I to scupper things now, they would come looking for me – the sand wedge mafia.

We continued, looking out over the course or my soon-to-be homeland. My grandfather was more sanguine, his expression more animated. He pointed to the outside plots and in doing so described the history of the area; the fact that it had been a farm with chicks on it that he had tended to and where the greenhouse had been positioned before.

I recalled him clipping the hedge with the sun on his bare back – the rest of the family pottering round assisting or sat taking in the early afternoon heat over an iced drink. Full is different to empty, I thought. Roles are replaced, temporarily aborted. And then, the next cycle....the next killing field.

CHAPTER 5

'**Y**ou'll be OK? And you're sure you don't mind us leaving tonight?'

My mother's questioning was the epitome of benevolence. She was deserting one son for another and it didn't quite fit with her family politics.

'He'll relish it, Rose,' was my father's reassuring hors d'oeuvre.

'It'll be good to spread my arms and legs. Don't worry.'

My father opened the passenger door and hastened my mother inside – conscious of the time, her doting and his weary frame.

She looked out through the glass and then wound the window down. 'We'll try and be back for Sunday lunchtime. OK?'

My father followed this up with something which I couldn't quite make out – him being on the far side.

'Stay longer,' I enthused – 'James is hungrier.' (Hinting at their UN-like status.)

I caught the flash of a smile from my mother and then the straightened arm of my father hard against the wheel as he sped away. I remained there at the end of the drive until the colour of the metal had gone. I looked around briefly, at the grassy, circled grove to the left, and at the square, British Bulldog 'arena' to the right; both childhood dens in and around which cycling and running had taken place. Often farcical and sardonic games, yet light and simple.

I checked my watch, strolled back inside and then sat down – staring at the wall or into space. Pendlebury's invite hadn't washed itself from my mind. Neither the colour of its summon (a pale red), nor the palliative kick which it implicitly promised. Clasping and unclasping my hands, I looked up now into the corners of the ceiling. I expected to see something – if not just the closed symmetry and finiteness of the room. Something telling and exhibitive; a manifest message which limited itself to the four corners of where I was sat. Nothing. No exaltation from the Gods. No piped murmurings. I laughed. I was being drawn into a self-revelatory mould which I had no concept of. It was too early, if not unequivocally foolish of me to think that I was an English Dalai Lama or any such sacred being.

I remained in the same position for the next thirty minutes – nervous of the calling to Pendlebury's second home. Winded by the magnitude of knocking at the temple-like door. It felt like a date – something I had never been on or tasted, with the exception of the meeting on the field two years ago. Perhaps, in light of that, this was a further trial – a marching in of the jury. Each race ready to pass its edict.

I got up, on my feet, made a thorough check of the house (locked windows, doors etc.) and then exited. It was after nine o'clock when I arrived – stood opposite the semi-detached haven. I expected people (somehow more than two) to be loitering near the front window, watching out for me – ready with a smothering device of some sort. Eager to baptize me in their ways. Nothing though. No obvious presence. No car on the drive. No flicker of a TV screen against the pale wall.

I approached the door, still apprehensive, yet willingly solicited by Pendlebury's image. The knock, was at first, light – gentle beyond comprehension. I maybe wanted to rap a couple of these, before kidding myself that there was no one present. As I reached for the door a second time, however, it opened – acutely aware of my attendance. He looked down at me, seemingly pleased – Pendlebury, with his old-man haircut and brown sweater. There was nothing too theological about him, but rather a roughish demeanour sprinkled with a Friday casualness.

'Hello. I'm glad you came.' He indicated for me to come in, leaving the door at my mercy and walking on ahead, rather than enveloping me.

I entered, more confidently than I had expected. The inside of the house was dark, except for a light at the end of the hall. There was a distinct smell, not of incense, but of tobacco fresh from a pipe. It reminded me of my grandfather, with its tortoise-like intimation and contrived laggardness. I stepped into the room at the rear of the house – the source of the smell – seconds after Pendlebury. In a soft, leather chair at the far end of the room, next to a green banker's lamp, sat the same magnanimous fellow I had seen only days ago. I looked at him, without any reservations, and he immediately smiled at me.

'This is my uncle,' Pendlebury proudly announced.

'Nice to meet you,' I responded, without any reaction from him, other than a continued smile.

I turned to Pendlebury, partly for an explanation and partly for a clue as to the evening's agenda. My quizzical manner prompted an immediate rejoinder.

'There's a room at the back of the house upstairs that's quite salubrious. We can talk there.' He gazed in his uncle's direction – 'We'll see you later.'

Uncle P nodded gracefully and this was our cue to wander upstairs onto fresh land.

'He's deaf. Not mute, but deaf (from birth). His voice is – shall we say – different. He's therefore only comfortable with people he knows. No offence.'

'How long......' My sentence seemed to trail off – somehow bruised by Pendlebury's candidness.

'...have I been seeing him? Have I known him? Since the local authority told me of his existence five years ago.'

'But didn't your parents....'

'I don't have any parents. I'm fostered.'

I found it difficult to pry any further, but then I wasn't being impertinent looking at this objectively. It was Pendlebury, somehow caressing my sails, guiding me along a certain course, without worry on his part or recoil. No diplomacy. No concern. An anachronism. The Pendlebury I first saw myself in.

'I thought…'

'You imagined him to be perfectly normal. Better than normal. Deity-like almost. Well he is. I tell you he is.'

It was becoming awkward. Pendlebury was making assumptions about my knowledge, my thought-patterns – my very reason for being here.

'I imagined the two of you chatting away – yes. And not in a staggered fashion. I imagined there was something here which I could latch onto…something different, searching.'

'And now you're not sure?'

'No – that's not the case.' I looked around for something to inspire me. The room was sparse in its decoration though – almost sullen from its semi-nakedness. 'I was sure – *am* sure – of you…this. But I thought there'd be more people. A membership of some sort.'

'Others to disguise our fecklessness?' Pendlebury followed this with a laugh – an unexpected snort.

'No. Just to bolster things. To enact whatever theories we have.'

He was silent for a moment, before: 'The only theory we have….is live by simple means.'

He gazed out of the window now, as if in a trance – as if pillaged of his physical presence. I wanted to ask him about his parents, about life on Dickinson Lane, about a thesis he might be slowly and secretly working on. The moment somehow demanded my silence though. It held my tongue in and begged me to watch.

Pendlebury's eyelids fell, yet his head remained in the same position. His lips parted two or three times without extolling any words. Finally: 'My uncle blows leaves. By definition, he's a leaf blower. That's what they gave him. He neatens things, you see. Helps others walk a steady path. It can be rewarding – when the bags are full. There's a sense of completion, I suppose. When he finishes, it's not only an uncluttering of the paving stones and ground, but also….his mind.

'What are you, Debrito – by definition?'

I was still taking in his words. Playing them back and forth. Pausing them. Trying to notice the nuances throughout. 'I guess I'm – or will be – a computer man.'

'For what reason?'

'The same reason as you, I suppose.'

'Oh, I don't intend to…'

To what? To see it through? To finish the course? To write the next life-changing computer program? I sensed Pendlebury's departure, having only known him for a few minutes; his single-mindedness on a par with his greying hair.

'…I mean, it's what you do, isn't it. Bowl yourself into something which you don't fully comprehend.'

'So do you comprehend it now?' I asked.

'I do,' was the immediate, assured response.

'And what about your history?'

'That's…' He wavered, as if never asked such a thing before. '…a little different. There are more layers.'

'How?'

I could see him becoming agitated, yet I pressed on, aware of a turning point. 'How is being illegitimate in the eyes of the college attendees different to having no parents?'

'Because the former doesn't matter! Because it would flatter the perpetrators to suggest that they were anything other than one-dimensional, one-layered fiends.'

It was unchartered territory – me riling him. Yet given his normal composure, I had to press on, if only to discover something which would otherwise remain concealed or protected. 'Their behaviour's conditioned though, isn't it? Some would consider no parents therefore better than poor parents?'

'Such people ought to have a surrogate framework around them for the first twelve years of their lives then, and no blood relatives. Such people should be thrown into a foster home from birth – completely dependent upon a stranger's random kindness and whim. They should be made to eat separate evening meals of inferior quality, like a canine would, all the while aware of the finer food being dished out later.'

'This happened to you?'

'It did. But it's gone. And I don't want you passing me tokens of sympathy, Debrito. None of that left-wing conditioning theory either. I'll buy it to a degree, but after that – well, the individual has a duty, a responsibility to follow their soul, their personal god.'

A hush descended now. We had exhausted part of something which had been building up for a couple of months. I wondered whether Pendlebury's uncle – the leaf blower – could sense the mood in the air from downstairs, despite his audible penury. I wondered which of the two of them – Pendlebury or him – was the leader of this radical cell. Because there had to be a membership, of which this was the nucleus. There had to be a following, even in the wake of Pendlebury's earlier reticence on that very subject.

'Your uncle. Can we spend some time with him now?' I prompted.

Pendlebury looked slightly alarmed. 'No – that wouldn't be a good idea.'

'May I ask why?'

'Because it was a mistake inviting you here. I don't want him infected with your apathy or insouciance.'

'But that's....'

'Please leave. Please leave at once.' His stare was somehow calculated – cruel yet superficial. I had no option but to absorb and respect its manipulated construct.

I bounded down the stairs, shut the front door behind me and then ambled away. The experience had affected me. I had unearthed pieces of him which, although only partly unravelled, were both sensitive and political. Nearing the end of the close, I gazed over my shoulder, and viewed – as expected – Pendlebury's silhouette stood solid in the front upstairs window. I looked ahead almost immediately – down the line of my journey home – all the while tracing his darkened shape in my head. Nobody knows. Very few people know what life is. He is one of them though, I thought. He has a handle on its ruggedness and folly.

I continued – thinking while walking leisurely. My life, in its cavernous state, streamed through my mind like a binary code or dual-atom, abstract pattern. There were contradictions in everything, even from an early age. Numerous personal landmarks passed through me: age six; age ten; age fourteen; and now. Bits of history flew at me, almost in a rage. Sacco and Vanzetti. Neil Armstrong (the Chinese people weren't told). McCarthyism. Ngo din Diem.

I stopped. Breathed deeply. It was too much. The puzzle was too large. The weight of its pieces seemed to load my shoulders with a philosophical grain. I had to burst the bags – allowing the grain to spill onto the earth where it belonged. I couldn't monopolize the seed, or even attempt to think for everyone. Yet that's what was coming to me more and more – a divine awakening, pouring itself into me, imbuing me with its celestial righteousness.

I walked on, semi-ignoring the ten o'clock fair in all its promiscuous glory: random drunks; short-skirted ladies; verbal tirades; gaudy architecture. I didn't feel, in any way, superior to these protuberances, but merely different; melted down by an internal structure. Dodging their ill will, I ventured forward – neglecting the opportunity to hop on a bus half way. This was an evening for seeing things, however depraved. For walking past realities and in doing so, trying to understand them with a fleeting glance. I had four miles left. Four miles of scanning, rather than openly questioning people and events with my eyes (so not to be thwarted). I would return just before midnight, to an empty house, to a hollow eager for company.

The sights became less welcoming: fourteen-year-old kids partly pissed up on cider, dancing in the road in a hardened fashion; mid-twenties stooges running from shaven-headed, bouncer-like, behemoths; tramps staggering around from the scraps of a good Friday night; vociferous exchanges seemingly ricocheting off the cheap neon signs that blanketed just about every pub entrance.

This was normal, I supposed. It was the human race in all its filthy splendour. It was a release – an emancipation of some kind. From what? I asked myself. From the mundaneness and wretchedness of factory life, of bland office concerns, of little hope or guidance. I was seeing before me a slow secularization – a lack of faith in anything. As I watched, I wasn't hoping that pews would be filled or that reverends would be made to feel powerful again, but rather that this pocket of the human race would interact wholeheartedly with each other – with others. Tomorrow they would wake up, on a stone floor, on a mattress, or on a couch, and persuade themselves that they were on the right path. That this was somehow the only permissible route, or clutch at sanity, given the vaporous oppression around them. After their fry-up, their incongruous wolfing of a chocolate bar, or morning swig of spirits, they would gear themselves up for another riotous outing (with little or no physical memory of the exact moment one opens one's eyes (and throat) – bar the glorious tales of torpidness).

Perhaps experience – any experience – was better than bowing compliantly to the authorities in exchange for a modicum of comfort. Perhaps defying the norms was a commodity of sorts – a saleable unit. But then, what if the authorities had noticed such a paradigm, a grand formula – our repulsion at extreme behavioural ways. What if they realised that WE – the majority – were the ones that REALLY needed keeping in check. What if our fear of becoming what we assumed to be the 'undead' drove us on – made us readily accept the hegemonic powers which arched their tentacles around and within us.

I had considered such a theory, on and off, since my final year at school. I had examined, from afar, the mannerisms and ways of tramps and the like. Were they paid to lie at the side of cash points, to endlessly consume soup, to look disheveled and reek of life in all its staleness? Were they actually operatives from the seemingly dethroned upper classes, with a continuing clandestine hold on society – imploring us to idolize the suburban sameness they had constructed for us? And what of the occasional minds, the true dissidents, that see the prosaic culture for what it really is, despite the backdrop and threat of impoverishment? Are they singled out for scrutiny, for cognitive correction? That was the beauty of the system: such measures weren't necessary. The individuals either folded after time (glad of a sense of normality and re-acquaintance with their mediocre friends). Or, they were divested of everything and sucked into the bile of homelessness (an acceptable state of affairs prompting an underclass civil war which the state could not lose). There, they would scramble for the surface once more – realizing their predicament was not as first imagined – or if completely devout and strong, fight on, in hell itself (perhaps wage a campaign against the staged poverty before them). The devout were few though, and the 'super' tramps were many. Looking at the latter now, I could see that they were not feeble – that beneath their rags were pistons for arms, and dynamic limbs. Whether or not I could confirm such an outrageous hypothesis would mean trailing one of them; trekking into their ungainly den of viaducts and hostels.

Perhaps in time...

CHAPTER 6

The knocking came hard the following morning. It was 7.50am – minutes before sunrise. I struggled out from beneath the covers, perturbed by both the intensity of the noise and also the insomnia which had gripped me throughout the night. I thought of my parents – their returning early maybe. Of my grandfather, wishing to see the sun from this side of the course – appearing as it did seemingly from the foundations of his cottage. Finally, I thought of Pendlebury – seconds before I cautiously opened the door to him.

He stuttered: 'I was taken aback by what I thought to be your mini-interrogation. I'm sorry.'

'It's OK. Come in,' were my slight sentences, in the midst of yawning and mastering my body as a cohesive unit.

'You have a window at the back?'

'Yes. A patio one.'

'Good,' was Pendlebury's response, before swooping past me, opening the curtains, and positioning two armchairs so that they faced out – over the fields and golf course. 'Please,' was his simple invite for me to partake in this civic enrichment by taking a seat.

Sitting in the chair to my left, he opened: 'There are no clouds, so we're fortunate. Just describe the feeling – that's all I ask. Let it bask you...tell me what it means.'

Silence. Just silence at that point. As if alone. As if wedded to the hillsides and foliage. I tried to concentrate – forget the roughness inside me. My mouth was dry, my stomach wavy. Something implored me to disengage though – to extricate myself from physical concerns.

Within a minute the colour began to creep upwards. It was a

supreme yellow which dominated the horizon. I imagined the world's animals responding – powered out of their mass stupor due to this single light force. Given to tribal expressions as a means of revelry. And we, their human superiors, no longer commanded by such a primitive stimulus. Wanton to respect nothing. The sun – that wrecker of parties – what did it ever do for the human race? Christ! Humans had their *own* radiation. Lots of it. Beautiful, beautiful stuff.

'Anger.' It was my first word to Pendlebury and one left isolated for some time. I expected him to interrupt, as I did most people if mute for what was considered a questionably long period. He didn't though. He merely intensified his focus.

'We forget, don't we.' I looked into the colour as it increased its prominence before me. The circular crown was somehow eminent and bespoke. 'There's no appreciation. And appreciation...can only come through nature. Life needs to be symbiotic.'

The words seemed to trip through me, as if commencing a manifesto without me – as if ignorant of any controls but their own. The final word I had never used before, yet it favoured my tongue and so I had to deliver it.

'So any plans beyond the spring? Beyond the interviews – your imminent fate?' Pendlebury was as acute as ever. He had stirred something which somehow had me shackled with its holistic bite.

'I don't know. That's just it – I don't quite know.' I gazed down for a moment, along the line of the garden.

'We're both young. Incredibly so.' The succinctness was built from the lips of an older being – surely. I looked at Pendlebury in an attempt to seek affirmation of this. The premature greying hair – yes. The subdued dress sense – yes. The rest of him – unfortunately not. Why had I met this person? I asked myself. Why were his words, each time, like a sealed invitation – something which, if I dared to unbar, would own me a little.

'How is it that you seem to know all the answers?' (I decided to buffet him, be direct, until something gave.)

He smiled, as if suddenly more human. 'Far from it. I just allow things to wash over me more. I listen to the messages inside. With others, I merely canvass what was already a bud.'

'That's quite political.'

'Everything's political, isn't it.'

I had him. 'So I'm a prodigy of sorts, and there *is* a membership?'

He waited. Delayed. Procrastinated. Until the right sentence fed itself into him. 'Oh, you're more than a prodigy, Arnold. You're well....' He seemed to catch himself at this moment, as if governed by another source, as if nervous of telling me too much.

'What?'

'A deliverance.' It was said rather flatly, fearfully – in a way which seemed to vanquish the loyalty and staunchness we had built. It was also said with a distinct sorrow; Pendlebury looked, amazingly, distraught – guilty, like an assassin pushed into his profession.

'I don't understand.' And I didn't. For once, my brain had seized – its three-tiered kingdom of thought, memory and emotion had shut its doors. My very comprehension of where I was sat even seemed to have a mist to it.

'We're missing the sun.' He pointed ahead of us in a weak effort to change tack. I felt his desperateness, yet also his diligence in attempting to regain composure.

'It's an eight-hour film. We can revisit it later.'

'No. No it's not.' His faith in himself seemed to return. 'This is the aurora. Dawn. Daybreak. The first hour is everything. You can't examine it for five minutes and then come back in the afternoon. That would be....foolish – the act of a fool.'

'Maybe. You're digressing though.'

'Not really.'

'OK. Deliverance. Why am I "a deliverance"?' I was insistent.

'Because, like everyone looking east right now – everyone on this side of the world – you're sharing something. We're all part of the same atom. This is a multiple birth. Part of you has changed. You just don't immediately know it. And that's good, because not everything should be grasped straight away. This is a double vodka before the breath test. It may take someone else to register it.' He looked away, seconds after the homily, out of guilt, or annoyance at my failure to understand sooner.

I didn't feel like talking much more anyway. It was early. Today was a rest day. I suddenly felt conscious of Pendlebury's awkward frame and not so much the magic which poured from him. I was disappointed that the membership I knew him to be harbouring was actually a collection of anonymous individuals merely performing the same functions as him, elsewhere, at the same time of the day.

I wished him gone. I needed time alone. Time *not to think*, but simply idle. I couldn't tell him though. I couldn't say 'piss off' or 'please leave' as I would do a foe. He was more than this – much more. Yet still, somehow, not a friend.

I noticed him lodged in the chair – the brown early-eighties upholstery partly sculpted around his similar garb. And my robe / dressing gown, beginning to wear on me – hedging closer and closer to an inappropriate time of day. I needed to get dressed, but first relax with a bit of breakfast. I couldn't eat in front of him though – have him extol things while I concerned myself with hearty matters. I obviously wasn't the complete disciple or student, but more a part-time heathen given to selfish feasts.

Pendlebury, far from the pedagogical mantle and closer to the circumspect crown, seemed to sense my unease. He stood up, suggested that he roam the fields and edges of the golf course for two hours, before returning at 10.30. I duly accepted and then watched the back of him as he strolled through the gate.

Gone. His frame disappeared from view before I could sleepily execute even three blinks of the eyelid. I sat down again and thought of the field. Its history. Its occasional symmetry. Its joining with the flattened paths which cross sectioned it. And then the perfectly trimmed golf course. Was that its border, or was it the other way round? To a golfer, the ruggedness of the field was merely 'rough' – somewhere to avoid. Somewhere capable of upsetting the fluency and fluidity of things. Yet, to a walker, the svelte curves of the course were terribly 'pretty' – the perpetrators and enforcers of conformity; a nauseous and quite villainous cousin.

I stood in between the two – confused, yet contented with the polar face off. One day, the rough. The next, a forged carpet. I wished to roam on them both. Something, however, was insisting that I choose. That I favour one and castigate the other. I couldn't though. No matter if the voice trumpeted from the Pearly Gates themselves. My mother, Pendlebury and his uncle were somehow the decorous and sculpted ones. Whereas my father and grandfather were, and would always be, deep-rooted wildcats. And James? I wasn't sure whether or not I really knew him anymore. He had always seemed....clever. He had had a more fulfilling youth in terms of friendship and social bashes than myself. He had done the identity thing by wearing trilby hats and lipstick in keeping with the bands of the time. He was, I suppose, 'a player'; a player of the game. He had accepted the structures around him and was now sourcing the most agile route forward. That he was bound to meet charlatans and intellectual prostitutes along the way, and have to smile in their company, was part of the forsaken journey. My concern – my only concern – was whether he would become one. Not consciously, but through a steady, corporate transfusion of sorts; a plasma swapping defection.

I had him now, in my head, as a relatively tall, ungainly person or brother; one able to be polite, however and disarming in a strange, manageable sense. He could remember things, with or without a system. And that was powerful, if not necessarily sagacious or inspiring. Those qualities came later. Not in a pure sense, but one honed to fit the business agenda, along with its steered cachinnations. He would, eventually, walk into rooms, and command respect through his calm manner and past cases. He would rarely talk of his experiences with me, however, because he knew I was different. Recalcitrant. Poor, in the grand scheme of things, because I was too selective. I was not willing, nor tolerant. I had allowed marginal influences to stalk me and scupper my sense of what was real. I was dangerous. Not the kind of brother to readily invite if celebrating something. Celebration was beyond me. Out of my capacity, jurisdiction. I would never celebrate whilst the flag-waving apotheosis continued across the Atlantic; its smiley cant both unsettling and inharmonious.....

STOP. I pulled myself from the voices that raged and battled for my loyalty. Too young. I was too young for anything to pick me off, dismantle me in part and then build and repaint me according to set criteria. Autonomy, it seemed, wasn't universally attainable after all, but rather something which was handed out (in a post-21 full membership way) to a narrow band of sharks. The dorsal fins of the human race, of course, manifested and morphed themselves in different ways: through the cementing of the occupant's ears; through his/her disengagement from grass root concerns; and through the inbred corporate laughter which scrubbed the faces of the minnows clean. That was it. We were dirty. Specimens that should harbour a smile just by being in the same room or near to these...maestros.

I wasn't even there yet, so how did I know? How could I judge? I could read, feel, sense. I was aware of forces – gravity-like dogma spilling over, encircling James' campus and also the wider commercial sect. I could see the reddened arms beneath the sleeves of the many suits; Beelzebub traits which were passed off as the by-product of a worthy venture. Roll up. Roll up. Get your tail and horns here.

'Thinking?'

He had returned, and I had dressed and eaten in between thinking and pontificating. Pendlebury looked rejuvenated – lifted by his crisp, morning exercise.

'A little. Yes.'

'Any conclusions?'

'Just that I'm quite different from my brother.'

'Perhaps that was intentional.'

'How do you mean?'

'Sometimes you need to see the opposite to know who you yourself are.'

'I suppose.'

It wasn't an explosive observation, but it was enough. Where the chatter would go from here though, I did not know.

'It was a good walk. You're fortunate to have all this land to the rear of your house.'

I nodded.

'There was an old man the other side. We got talking. I was intrigued by his thoughts.'

'A resident or just another walker?'

'Oh. A resident. I helped him remove his door bell. He was quite anti-technology / self-sufficient, which I found heartening.'

'So what did you chat about?' I said this, thrown slightly by Pendlebury ingratiating himself and tinkering with what was obviously the mechanics of my grandfather's cottage.

'Golf. Gandhi. And globalisation. All the Gs really.'

He smiled, but I wasn't having it. Something was amiss. Did he seriously not know who the chap was? Was he playing with me? Pendlebury didn't operate this way. He was candid – nothing else. Deception didn't know him. And he didn't know it.

'What about them then?' I was forthright.

'Golf he longed to play, but he was too old now. He watched it though – quite studiously so. Both on the course and on TV – just the majors. I told him I didn't know anything about golf and didn't wish to know. He laughed, but I wasn't sure why.

'Gandhi was his hero. A man whose country he had seen. He marveled at his simple possessions: spectacles; loin cloth; moccasins; and toothbrush. He was eager to clear his house with such a great minimalist approach in mind. I had to agree with him on this, and said so. He smiled this time.

'Globalisation he denounced as a huge mothball hanging in the wardrobe of the West – repelling the third-world moths from the giant suit that adorns us. I thought him a genius for saying this. He thought me impressionable.'

'I don't understand.'

'Which part?' he enquired.

I was dazed momentarily. I looked at him and tried to gauge his facial tweaks and his general integrity. There was nothing coming back. Nothing of substance. Nothing that hinted of mendacity. He was being straight. He knew no other way.

'Globalisation. I've not heard of that term before.'

'You will in a few years time.'

'So you and m....the old man, are privy to the future?'

'It was *his* word, but I understood it. I suppose we must be privy to reverie and contemplation.'

'But what's it mean? What does globalisation mean?' I had an idea, but I wanted him to slug it out intellectually – to dissect each of the thirteen letters.

He paused. Stiffened his expression. Played for time. Before – 'It means opening everything up. Linking the world, the globe, through time, culture and trade. Except the playing field already has a number of indentations… nicks from the big economies. Bias chairs the interactions with a condescending grin.'

'The giant suit then – it not only adorns us. It was actually put together by third-world hands? They stitch our comfort and their own harshness?'

'Yes. In a way. To a degree. Perhaps that's what the old man expected from me.'

Pendlebury looked in awe, as if my grandfather had cut some of the lingering chains from off him. He looked buoyed by what he maybe thought to be a human panacea.

'He asked that I return – visit him again...' The sentence seemed to hang, as if Pendlebury was seeking my approval. He couldn't be though. He didn't know. He couldn't see the blood. It was my imagination. It had to be.

'And will you?'

'It's a long way. I don't know.'

I asked myself now why I wasn't letting on. Why my grandfather's identity was so precious – so esoteric. To be kept from Pendlebury. From the one man I would gladly introduce to him.

It was opportunity, I suppose. The chance to see a fuller being because of my supposed impartiality. The chance to observe a neutral commentator mulling over the traits of a man two generations ahead of me.

'For what reason would you go back?'

Pendlebury looked at me, as if not sure himself. And then, with his impervious barrier somehow shifted, he answered: 'Context. Understanding. When you're younger you're little more than an automaton – an apparently happy one, but all the same, *unaware.* I think of myself at the age of twelve, getting on a bus to the sports centre from school. The only thing on my mind – table tennis. Perhaps there were other minor concerns. The odd bully. Girls. Exams. Generally though, I may as well have been in a wind tunnel. I didn't know or understand, or have the capacity to interpret *everything* around me. Now, however, I feel like I'm getting close to this ideal. I'm not learning for learning's sake any more. It's a different tenet I'm a part of. One which craves the whole – the complete workings and interconnections of life. Being around the odd sage helps. Particularly when they're not in too plentiful a supply.'

'So the old man allowed you to live. That's what you're saying?' I probed.

'He stoked my appetite. Something which is strangled by everyday banality – its neck constricted by moribund pursuits. I felt at peace, luxuriated, in his presence.'

The solace I understood. My grandfather, when on form, had a habit of exuding a certain stillness and comfort. If you were in his orbit then he unashamedly offered his all. If you were outside of the curved path, however, then you were ignored, treated with reticence; a plight more grave than being verbally speared against a wall.

'What was he doing when you first saw him?'

'Collecting…searching for golf balls. In and around the lodge at the side of the cottages. He had an old bucket with him. Why?'

'I just wondered.'

Pendlebury's thick eyebrows leant downwards causing his forehead to furrow. He examined me, aware of an agenda of some sort. 'Nothing more?' he enquired.

'No,' was my guarded response.

'Well. I have things to do.' His body motioned towards the hall.

I had expected him to stay longer. Somehow implicitly coach me for my new role in life, whatever that was to be. But then perhaps I was ahead of myself – cheated by my own egotism.

'OK,' I plied.

'Soon.'

'Yes.'

Soon. What did he mean by such an inviting, yet cruel deferment? What did he intend to rummage from my mind? I caught myself. Nothing. Nothing at all. It was innocuous. A one-word nugget used to exit places. To leave.

CHAPTER 7

I attained an 'A'. James a 'B'. In mathematics. Numbers had been somehow manageable. The keepers of secrets. The stalwart hoarders of fractions and decimals through roundings. I figured that these 'bits' were still around us – searching for a home; longing for their creator. And until they were appeased or harmonized, the world would lunge awkwardly, off centre, scraping other planets in its tracks.

Pendlebury was the quarter in 2.25, yet with a minus sign draped over him. He was, by now, unrecognizable to his parents, and they to him, I assumed. It was upsetting to know someone who lived without backup – without unconditional support. Yet it was also inspiring to witness a summoned strength which rose from the charcoal wreckage of absence. Pendlebury had been without air, without proper ambience for years, and had still managed to push aside the charred mass and climb out. He was me, but with a doctorate in life. Me, without the fear.

James. James though, in this one discipline, was a lesser man. Maths. I had edged him. For what though? How had things transpired? He was in the trenches, only months away from a larger prize. Just a little more gunfire and semi-starvation. And myself? I wouldn't be flying. No. I was rooted. I felt the earth around me – reluctant to lessen its grip; contractually-bound by an intangible high priest.

Commerce. Accountancy. What was it really? Did it profess to hold the key? Would James wield his soon-to-be power for the general good? There were grave doubts. Rudimentary principles shone upon him in a haunting and duty-bound fashion. Follow. He would have to follow the paths chiselled before him; occasionally glance at the flea-ridden insubordinates tilling the soil, but then walk on, along the designated highway, head bowed to the majority hymn.

My own hymn had undergone a subtle form of mongrelisation. I was becoming more and more attuned to computers and their workings. Figures, numbers, found my head to be ideal practice ground in which to limber up. And business: my briefing in this area had been of a tertiary nature, yet one that had given me a hat trick of O-levels. English, however – my dearest friend – had decamped. Whether the space in the tent had been unsatisfactory, or the beans too cold, I did not know. Either way, she had marked me down for an 'E'. I had walked away, knowing that I was incomplete; one short of the necessary set. Capitalism would know I was capable, yet think me an inarticulate fool. The job market would taunt me – listen to my cackle and Byzantine tongue, and then renege on the slightest of promises (an interview, a shot, a job).

That was then, though. 1986. Before the summer months of July and August. I had re-fuelled, restocked during those nine weeks; something not entirely under my own direction, yet a hybrid response to my new, college environment and the adult world I was now a part of. I had more time in the evenings – time to reflect on who I was and what I wanted to become. I wouldn't know either, an inner voice reminded me, without discovery – without assembling bits from books which suited the slow-gathering moral framework in my mind.

I didn't know where exactly to begin. My father had rows and rows of encyclopedias – good, stocky, well-bound publications, yet they were not inspiring. They spoke of precision, not philosophy – certain events and developments, but not causes. I needed the battle cry of the oppressed, the marginalized – not simply the imperial nobleness of latter-day giants. I had wandered into the town's library with this in mind, and had at first tried to find my own bearings; a through road to the truth. It felt futile, as if a set of conspirators had seen me at the entrance and subsequently ridden off with the potent texts. The books I picked up and glanced at were little different to the ones at school. They were books which communicated only with themselves. Didacticism and dogma held fare. These establishment scrawls were responsible for me only knowing numbers. Sentences, I had decided, were in the main, ugly – the conduits of worthless droning. History and English, as a result, had been the enemy – stockists of superfluous pap. The former I hadn't even carried through to my final year. And so here I stood, naked of belonging – sterilized by the educational barons who were supposed to have taken my hand, not my hair.

Eventually, I asked. At the oval counter stood a grey-jacketed gent in his mid-forties. He appeared thorough – sedulous even.

'The books. Are there any alternative ones….I mean, different takes on the world?'

I could see that I had wounded him, as if he himself chaired the committee that decided upon the library's content. He looked up from the printed, dusty scrag which was occupying his time.

'Alternative?'

'Yes.'

'Due east, down the steps, and out – out into the sickening fold which stalks the streets.'

From the slow-paced delivery and the coming together of his teeth, I interpreted his sarcasm and caustic tone to mean one thing: that somewhere inside the library there was a bungalow where he resided; a flat, insipid construction which whispered its mighty ruse during the early hours.

I left, and within days signed up to re-take my English O-level at night school. There were a couple of chaps – both Asians – from college, travelling down the same road, eager to put the secondary school thing to bed; both prepared to give up one evening per week for the sake of a balanced CV. And the classes – they weren't bad. There was a semblance of refinement to them; a code void of compulsoriness. We were there because we needed judging again. It was a re-trial of sorts. And this time the jury would be kinder, more discerning. They had to be, otherwise….we were doomed.

Books *had* blessed me before the September start – socialist and Muslim schools of thought mainly; recommendations from my night school and apprentice college counterparts. I found them narrow though – some way from the pure doctrine which I hoped would fasten itself to me. This had the result of inhibiting our friendship – of awakening the race issues which weren't quite unfrosted at that time. I was a white boy who knew only how to shop. I was one of Allah's toy soldiers and he would knock me down with one breath should he see fit. I told them, in jest, that Allah was working in Bradford as an ice-cream man.

This wasn't the whole story. Now, four months in – January'87 – and I had grown. Immensely so. The classes outside of college had given me a slight presence – through listening to book readings which were significantly more advanced than the ones I had heard at school. *Animal Farm. England Made Me. Of Mice and Men.* They were written by giants who mattered. Maybe it wasn't the texts themselves. Perhaps I *had* heard similar vehicles before. The environment though. It was more heartfelt, and consequently things stuck. Words. Book covers. Faces. People of my age enunciating sentences in a more individual fashion. No barracking in the wings. No sniping from the roof tops. Their concentration and effectiveness was somehow ours. Luck would unfold itself further should we respect what had gone before. There seemed to be a unanimity to this – a belief, that were we to take even the class dunce seriously, then our own work would be blessed.

It worked well. Despite the blind faith in some that all TV was fact. Despite a naïve blur occasionally hovering over us. There was togetherness – quite noticeably. There was anything but the breathless tarmac feel which seemed to permeate the modern day secondary school. Here, at least, things were less dictatorial. The tutor appeared relaxed, even if frustrated by his own treadmill-like progression in life. He was, quite honourably, the characters we read about rolled into one: George Minty I.

He warned us of the people we were likely to meet over the course of the next twenty years. And if, by the age of thirty-seven or thirty-eight, we hadn't 'sussed it', then it didn't matter. None of the people in here, he regularly announced – waving a random book in the air – had made it to the celestial homeland, and they were all the richer for it. If you're sacked for having fight and conviction by a bloody-minded fool, then take it as a compliment. This was his opening sortie after the Christmas break. Without an introduction of any kind. Without context. Without reason. Yet beautiful because of its appearing on the landscape, somewhat unclothed and disarmed. You will meet piss pots, bespectacled traitors, women and men so ordinary that you'll actually see the hole in them, and others – some kind, some truly nauseating.

It could have sounded bitter – so very easily, like a catalogue of personal experience (some very recent), yet it avoided this fate through tone and expression. His face was somehow anchored to a glorious shore which allowed the odd, vile speedboat such excursions. Commanding us beyond these occasional fillips was easy. I suppose this was so because of the very enactments which he undertook. He had gained our respect through controversy and truth – through a bold manoeuvring with his limited power.

Four months. Seventeen weeks. The pickpocketing of time had been remarkable, yet all too easy. This was a snippet though – merely a caption of the current grand scheme. My apprenticeship was the hub; an inadvertent lesson in tolerance and strained human interaction. Things would change, however. The middle of the year would signal a new track: job; exam; familiar, pristine walks along the course. I would hurdle or fall; bite next to the lip of the hole or smash a five-iron against my shin.

The night soon rolled in. I lay down for a while in its sable shroud, thinking. My physical presence seemed to eschew scientific norms. I was neither aware of being fully conscious nor being in a dream-like state. Before long, I was walking. Through the ostensibly deserted streets of town. Through a life folded in on itself; the music and cacophonous bawling now crunched up into matter and placed between the cracks in the poorly mortared buildings. Nothing, so it seemed. Nothing to interfere with the rotations of one's mind. I was walking, inter alia. I was concentrating hard on what this meant. On why I was here – out of hours, outmoded in some sense.

And then, the answer – like an unfinished pattern deciphering itself into a mural: a human shape shifting from its squat position, absent of emotion, not perturbed in any way. I watched over it, him, her, without moving – protected by shadows whose sole duty was that of clemency. He (no woman would extrapolate her indifference with life in this way) managed to stand, helped by the sides of the shop entrance. There was no staring straight ahead though, as if such a luxury was strictly the domain of workers making £30,000 p.a. No. The head, the gaze, remained tilted, like a golf flag on a windless plain, or a mourner staring into the coffin of an esteemed friend. He nudged himself forward, without looking up, careful to grip firmly the rags which were his house, his car's upholstery and his lover. He took short steps, half strides, as if wary of random elements which might interrupt his progress, as if not entirely trusting of the bare streets before him. I followed, with difficulty, knowing or expecting him to tilt his bedraggled brow upward and then isolate me with his stare on what was effectively *his* land and parlour. He either seemed slowly and blindly determined, or purposely contented though. I couldn't be entirely subtle in my tracking of him, yet not once did he pause, cogitate, or show learned concern over my 'threat'.

He continued, down the long, main street – always inches from the shop fronts and away from the kerb. His garments were the same as all of them – creased, thick and without true colour. Perhaps they were mass-produced. Perhaps they were the uniform of the undead. I chanced that they were conditioned by the same environmental factors: sweat; noise; annoyance; dirt; rain; insects; and filth. His body, however, despite its continual stoop, looked neither undernourished nor wretched. This was my theory – finally manifesting itself before me – and I now simply had to watch and wait.

He turned off down a concrete ramp – so slight in gradient that I could still make him out once he was half way. I then shuffled across the road and stood next to the cheap, urban foliage that masked this neglected end of town. I watched from the top of the ramp as he made it onto the flat; thin, stony paths, rough grass verges and a semi-polluted canal dancing beside him. And above him, an arching viaduct frowned – the hour not suited to a new age of trams or trains.

He stood there. Next to the corroding brick. Silent. Statuesque. Like a pulped or hollowed-out trunk. All movement had ceased. It was as if the rags had been inhabited by a spectre. Nothing. Not even the fidgeting of a small child.

And then, a hand on my shoulder. I turned. 'Not a very safe part of town, sir, at this time of night. I'd suggest you head into the centre and get a taxi or something.'

The garb *seemed* to fit. He *appeared* to be a policeman. But ... I resumed my original watch. I looked down at the grubby pocket of land, filled as it was with the earth's fancy dress. Nothing now. Damn! Just the vacant path where he'd stood. Definitely nothing.

The same hand gripped my shoulder. 'I'd seriously suggest you move along, sir. There are too many miscreants to mention in and around this vicinity. Your face could easily come to mean something other than a lost citizen to us.'

I sensed the subtle threat from his steely expression. Repeating an instruction wasn't something he particularly enjoyed. I looked at him coldly and could see that his Roman eyes knew nothing other than conflict.

I walked away – back into the centre, back towards home. He shouted after me: 'You chose correctly. Now move along, move along, sir!'

It was the language of a master to his horse. I should have resented it, turned around and thrust a hand signal in his direction. Something stopped me though. Something told me to pity him, to work through my mind the whole machination of what I had seen. Was he a coincidence, or instead, a supporting mechanism? A man on duty, bored, yet somehow lifted by society's woes, or a seed, a plotter and protector of secret goings-on? I didn't know. I couldn't know. Without assistance. Without harvesting a fuller image in my mind.

Where was the tramp now, I thought. Behind an artificial wall? In the belly of the canal? Beneath the scrub of grass? I hadn't heard anything. Neither a splash, nor the sesame-esque shifting of brick. I knew him to be close, but that was all. Amongst a hidden breed of kings whose collusion was perhaps charged daily by a uniformed guard. Or hiding from his persecutor, the very same guard.

CHAPTER 8

'**D**idn't you think to tell him at any time?'

Stood, in the winter room, my grandfather with his back still to me (we had barely entered), I asked what had been on my mind for most of the night. It was now just before noon. I had left the house wanting to ensure that I was out before my parents returned.

He moved to the left, took his usual seat closest to the door, and looked up at me as I wandered over to the window. I felt uneasy provoking him, this 74-year-old man with all his experience and astuteness. I felt stupid, like a court typist questioning a judge. I expected him to curse me, to admonish me for my slack tone. But then, during these last few minutes and seconds, I had forgotten who my grandfather was and somehow what he represented.

He smiled, as if in the company of a baby lion; one whom he respected for its forthrightness though, and its toothy growl. 'I did, if I'm honest. I thought about it several times. But – and you know this as well as me, Arnold – there was an intersection I would have had to pull up at if I'd....let it be known we were related.'

'So instead, the green light stayed on, you drove on through and the milometer clocked up a few more miles of deception?'

'It wasn't quite like that...'

'I think it was though. You acted like a spy, a mole. There could have been private things said about me for example, on the basis that you were *un*related.'

'Curiosity led me on – for certain. I can be a little wily, I suppose. But Pendlebury – he wasn't a fool. He understood where the line was.'

'That doesn't matter. Like you said, you drove on through. You *didn't* stop when it was clear who he was. When...when was that anyway?'

'Almost immediately. It seemed somehow ignorant *not* to shake his hand. Doesn't happen often, but there was something...incandescent about him. I had my head down collecting golf balls at the side of the lodge, and then...he was there, up above me. I wandered up towards him. He was quizzical, endearing. Things simply seemed to flow. I chatted about golf. I asked him if he lived nearby. And that's when he mentioned yourself. Just by first name. I looked at him, his age and I knew. What followed just confirmed things.'

'What followed was improper information gathering. What followed disappoints me.'

'I'm sorry – really, Arnold. But there was nothing that you could call *sensitive*. Believe me. Mostly, we chatted about the world at large.'

'Didn't he ask about *you* though? Didn't he enquire about your family?'

'Funnily enough – no. He didn't. He didn't actually come in the house either. Just disconnected the bell, mostly from the outside, bar the necessity to lean inside the door frame to pull out the wires.'

I could see that he thought me paranoid. I could see the wonder in his eyes and the deft control he had over it, so not to be intrusive. I had awakened a curiosity in him – about my relationship with Pendlebury, about my life as a whole with all its chambers and vessels. Despite this, however, and despite Pendlebury's taciturnity or wilful silence regarding family, I had to cross-examine my grandfather; I had to lift the 'Castro' veil and forget, momentarily, our blood line.

'It doesn't spare you, nor exonerate you though. Pendlebury's being discreet is *his* saving. You had intent, irrespective of the other party. You acted like a spy. You *are* a spy – what's more, a communist one.'

It sounded foolish, labeling the grandfather that I worshipped 'a spy'. The momentum seemed to come from outside me though. I was saturated, imbued, with a chemical composition – a lingering opus which grappled with my senses.

'Now that's your father talking, Arnold. A communist indeed! I despise large-scale planning. It's the modern curse – the world's nemesis, whatever the ideology driving it.'

'But...' I had run out of both steam and a credible picture of events. I wilted, knowing that I had brought it far enough though – knowing that 'Castro's' next line would be a revelation or betrayal.

'Your father's the spy. Or very nearly was, at least.'

He went silent, careful not to say any more – obviously cautious of the ramifications, despite his standing.

'What do you mean?'

He looked down at the floor, unable to meet my eye. 'Nothing. It's an irrelevance.'

'No. Please. Go on...'

'Nothing. It's nothing.'

There was a stalemate – an impasse which neither of us were prepared to fight. I, because my grandfather was worth more than a pious victory. And my grandfather, perhaps because of the already-strained relationship he had with my father, his son-in-law.

'What if I ask him? What if I ask general questions about his past? As a matter of family history...Every son wants to know where his father came from, what he represented, what he did. Maybe not at my egotistical age, but later...always later.'

'Then wait four years. Wait a few years.'

'But why? Isn't precociousness allowed an early pass?'

I could see I was reneging. My mind, instead of coming to rest, instead of laying down its armour, seemed to want to continue the jousting – like a half-battered pygmy.

'Respect my earlier words, Arnold. That's the last I'll say on it.'

It was a side of my grandfather which I had never before seen (largely because I tended to be in agreement with him). It fitted, equaled even, the abstract descriptions of him put forward by Debrito Snr, my father. I had clearly been naïve, ingenuous, in thinking that my grandfather could be pure and entirely faithful or steadfast to my needs. He had his own quite separatist thoughts, be they prohibitors of openness or regular, defined themes.

I sat down. Rocked in the arm chair that for so long had bent to the contours of my grandmother's frame. I hoped to quash the atmosphere which had built up. I hoped to look my grandfather in the eye and let it be known that I was clutching, desperately reaching out for an adulthood which was slowly unmasking itself before me – promising, somehow, to cast me in a central role.

He exhaled what was half a cough. He then spoke. 'We all know part of a person which is unique to us. Not ubiquitous, but unique. Now, that person may have moved on in one sense, may have shed what was evident before, but it's still locked in the mind of me, of you – in the mind of whoever was around during that earlier era. We won't have necessarily seen the same thing, even if we witnessed it together, but a take, a snapshot, a lingering impression will have lodged itself within us. And if we choose to keep our little piece of truth private, then that's perfectly fine. More than fine – it's commendable.'

A line had been drawn in the sand – very much through the heart of my castle. It conceivably meant that I could no longer build inexorably. It meant compromise and concession, understanding and estimation – things I had assumed to be the vehement enemies of truth. I didn't know quite how to respond, or how to counter such factions. And so, I walked out.

They were there, when I returned – victims of my mother's over-anxiousness; back in Lancashire for Sunday lunch. My father looked tired, but refreshed – full of heartening tales and updates espoused by my brother James. My mother, perhaps less concerned with the business side of university and James' reason for being there, seemed pleased, yet mindful of his health.

I opened: 'So how was he? What did you all do? Why back so soon?'

Although directed at both of them, my mother answered, as always, as if given the role of speaker when taking their vows. 'Your brother was a little off-colour, a little grey, but excited. What's the word? Trem...'

'Tremulous.'

'Yes, Arnold – anxious, yet filled with the prospect of his life changing. The degree is important to him. I only wish these educational people had some appreciation of the physical pitfalls. Jack?'

'He's strong. He might not look it, but he's strong.'

My father's words clocked in for work in their usual, succinct manner. Over the years I had noticed a pattern – that for every five words my mother delivered, my father would usually chip in with one. Such consistency was surely destined for a hall of accolades.

'He's focused. There'll be plenty of time for nourishment later on. Business meals. Restaurants. Home cooking, if he finds himself a wife. What about the three of you though – did you go out?'

'We did. Of course we did. Wandered around the city during the day. Visited art galleries and little cafes. And then, your father drove us to the outskirts last night. To a lovely pub in the country for a bar meal.'

'Did James pay?'

'Of course not,' my mother retorted, before picking up my sardonic tone.

'He's learning all about the wheels of industry at the moment…'

Unlike my mother, my father sometimes sought approval and vibes before continuing with a point or half-story which was ladled in his mind. On this occasion, he stopped, hesitated.

'Go on, Jack.'

'It's the side of his degree which veers away from the usual balance sheets, profit and loss…all that. There's room for debate apparently…'

'Concerning what?' I asked.

'Industry,' my father replied, looking somewhat miffed at my continued questioning.

I took a breath and then sighed. 'So which side is he on?'

'Side?'

'Yes – right or left?'

My father appeared bamboozled, despite his occasional, brilliant proverbs, and despite his trumpeting of the oppressed. It was as if his grasping of a simple, political concept (one which had only recently shown its face to me) was somewhat insoluble.

'I don't think it's like that, Arnold.'

The words were defensive – purposely enigmatic and ambiguous. I wondered about my father's state of mind, his lost bearings and outlook.

'Right.' It was all I could say, although the word seemed to act as both acknowledger and inferrer. I looked away, around the room, beyond my mother's protective stare – out into the garden for comfort. There was nothing to put me at ease though – nothing to clothe me from this surreal and absurd thunder storm.

I got up. Left them to it. Missed lunch. Thoughts encircled my mind. I wondered when the change would come; when the weight of skin which currently bound me would drop off – leaving something more defined and sure. How, also. How was one to know that contradictions had ceased – that one's personhood was complete and without elementary failings. There would have to be questions from every side – interrogative rumblings between each fissure of doubt.

My thoughts dispersed. Drawers slid open in my mind. I lay back on my bed and allowed the contents of each to bid for my attention. It wasn't hard. My price had fallen off. The swoopers clawed, rushed and thrummed my brain. James – I should telephone him. See how he's doing. My grandfather – let him sculpt me a little. Introduce me to the golfing fraternity. Pendlebury – now I knew him a little, we had to move on. Out of the mire which seemed to plague us. My parents – was I slowly losing them? Following a carved path which wasn't to their liking?

Concerns washed their algae against me. I seemed to be a docking station for often rootless anxieties. Something was speaking to me, but not others, I felt; my autonomy slowly deteriorating, yet my sovereignty strangely whole. I looked out over the fields from the bedroom which was now mine. I examined the semi-landscaped playing areas; former dens of intrigue and curiosity which had been passed on to those younger than myself. I maybe wanted those days back – their easiness and unthinking beauty.

I gripped the handle of the bedroom door, and then peered out onto the landing. Things had subsided. Whatever conversation had started up after my departure was now dead – inanimate. I wandered down, gently connecting with each step. The house felt like a vacuum – the opposite of only minutes ago. Turning into the living room, with its fuscous mood, I immediately caught sight of my father – alone, seated, with his solid arms as companions.

He looked up and nodded. 'Your mother's gone for a lie down.'

I acknowledged him, muttered a 'right' and then sat down myself. I felt somehow traitorous – a let down to his thirty years of graft. I felt indebted to him; burdened by a nebulous demand.

'I still don't know which one you are…' my father suddenly

pronounced.

'Which one? From what…who?' I enquired.

'The shoe man and the fish peddler.'

I looked confused and so he continued: 'Nicola Sacco, born 1891. And Bartolomeo Vanzetti, born 1888.'

'*Should* I be one? Is it a family requirement?'

'For my sons only – yes.'

As much as I liked to hear their names – Sacco & Vanzetti, Sacco & Vanzetti – I hadn't read anything about the two. For some reason I had relied entirely upon the storytelling skills of my father. I had trusted and kept dear the basic injustices of the trial – political intolerance and racial bigotry – yet I had no knowledge (no real knowledge) of the backgrounds and personalities involved.

I deflected things slightly. 'James. Which one is he?'

'He *was* Sacco. But being an undergraduate of commerce disqualified him.'

I supposed I knew why, and so I declared myself the other: 'I'll be Vanzetti then.'

My father smiled. 'Vanzetti was the lonelier of the two. Didn't marry. Read a lot of books. Had a huge moustache. He was older as well.'

'So I become older than James?'

'I guess so.'

His words and expression hinted that, in some sense, I *was* older. That my mind had sped past James's – eluding the narrow, cordoned-off, educational tradition.

'Perhaps I'll grow a moustache.'

'That would be interesting,' my father retorted, aware of his own successful forays – evidenced by various photo albums.

'History seems to smile and fascinate when it's been brave.' The sentence carved itself through me, before I knew I had delivered it.

'You could be right.'

'Anything that you look back on that stirs you?'

'A lot, Arnold. The birth of you and James. Marrying your mother. Other, more public events. The landing on the moon. The Cuban Missile Crisis. I'd only just turned twenty-two when Khrushchev and Kennedy were slugging it out. And Vietnam, of course – in between.'

'All American-related then?'

'Yyyes. I suppose so.'

We both thought about this, as if British history was dull – as if its subjects no longer looked *inside* for attachment, but rather *outside*; in the process becoming conditioned citizens of a country just turned 210.

'What about Britain? Were you part of anything significant…let's say in the last ten years or so?'

'I could have been.'

There. There it was. 'Castro's' seed. It had to be. What was disconcerting was that I hadn't planned it. There was no slow manipulation or contrived spiel. We simply had to reach this point. It was a summons – an arousing of fossilized information quite pivotal to Debrito history.

'Could?'

'Yes. But I declined.'

I waited.

'1976/77. You might remember me being away from home for nine months. I was lecturing in Cheltenham. All quite grand for me, but an experience I couldn't pass up – a change to be educating people instead of simply having my head in the back of a TV. I used to come home and see you all at weekends.

'Anyway – towards the end, a few of the chaps or TVBs (television boys), including myself, got wind of a government office expanding in the area. It wasn't what you'd call a normal operation though. It wasn't part of the town hall or anything. They were hiring frequency listeners – people with experience; TVBs and radio men. Nothing was advertised. This wasn't public. Instead they were poaching from the local colleges and schools. I think there were five TVBs approached from my college. Yes. Four plus myself.'

He went silent now. Almost bowed his head. I had a rough estimation of what he was referring to, of what part of history this belonged to, yet I needed him to spell it out – to provide a lucid picture.

'There wasn't the usual three interviews or anything. They simply *knew*...from files, from speaking to the right people, from intuition, that we were the right candidates. One interview, fifteen minutes in length – that's all it took. I remember us agreeing to drive down together, because the interviews were staggered over one hour on the same afternoon. Five of us in a Vauxhall Viva! Quite an appropriate car really.

'We arrived there, at the end of a dust track, to be met by two guards – one either side of the entrance. Both were wearing camouflaged hard hats like military personnel. There was wire meshing and barbed wire all-round the site or compound. Beyond the entrance were a few indistinct buildings, blanketed by trees and foliage – mostly foliage. Arching above them though – above everything – was a huge satellite dish. All of a sudden, we felt quite in awe – serious. The guards asked each of us three questions: our full name, date of birth and place of birth. We then waited for them to check everything in what seemed triplicate.

'Finally, we got the nod. The barriers were raised and we were told to drive very slowly – not more than 10mph – to the top, where someone would be waiting. Other aerials, antennae and satellites were evident as we approached. The buildings began to take on a mystical edge. There were a few other cars dotted around – nothing special by any means, in fact less than average. One of us spotted the interviewer or contact at this point. He was stood at the top of a path next to the main entrance – just waiting whilst scanning us. No effort to walk to the car or anything.

'He was very nondescript – staid I suppose. Bald with glasses – quite rotund. We got out of the car, all of us quite restless, and raised one arm in acknowledgment of him. He nodded back, very slightly. It was all pretty dignified. We honestly wondered at this point what the hell we were doing there. A couple of the chaps stared at me as if we'd stepped into a Mary Shelley novel or something.

'Anyway, we wandered on up towards him. He seemed a little more human as we approached – introduced himself as Webster. Didn't say whether that was his first name or last. He would be interviewing us, asking us to sign the secrets act and then passing us each a dossier which would tell us everything and anything we needed to know. The offer of a post would be made the following day, to which they needed a response within 24hrs. So we were basically two days away from changing our lives completely, which shocked a few of us.'

He was getting closer. I had never heard my father speak consecutively for so long. It was as if this one tale, this redolent feast, had been fermenting for years. And finally, someone had prompted its consumption.

'You were offered it then? The interview went well?'

'I got the impression that the interview was quite irrelevant, academic – that they'd already decided on us. There were no real, penetrating questions from Webster's side. It just seemed like an opportunity for me to probe a little.'

'And did you?'

'I asked "Is this operation directly connected to the Cold War?".
To which he replied "Yes. We document the unremarkable but
significant. Anything deemed potentially crucial to British and
American intelligence.".'

The Cold War. My father. The two seemed, somehow, polar
opposites. I wasn't even sure that I approved of this pre-
Thatcher/Reagan ideological harbinger. The operation was, in
one sense, an apologist or kit man for the nuclear arms race
stalwarts.

'Did you want the job?'

'It was a chance to see things, I suppose.'

'But you declined?'

'I did. I phoned Rose, your mother, the next day, after receiving
the offer. She.....wanted me back in the north west. Didn't want to
move to Cheltenham. That had been our unofficial deal, you see.
Nine months of 'play' and then back to the family home – our nest.
A steady engineering job again.'

He sounded disappointed, but it was the showing of this which
seemed to prioritise my firm grasp of his history over and above
the potential sensitivity of my mother. Thirty-six he had been.
Part of him corpsed. His mind spinning like a naked axis in a
junkyard.

'The others. What happened to them?'

'They all accepted.'

'Are you still in contact with them?'

'No,' was the immediate, wistful response, as if he had been
savagely cut out of the Viva 5; his unfortunate choice pilloried,
not by the TVBs' collective voice, but by their new lives and
implicit politics.

I left it. It was cruel and brutish to continue. I would revisit the
subject when we were older, closer. I looked at him – read other

things in his face. There was a crushing stupor around him – one which had partial control of his expression; his jaw, cheeks and forehead. Thoughts had lodged themselves inside him, and now pushed and prodded the wrap of skin around his skull which purported to be under his own jurisdiction. I felt for him. The tweaks and awkwardness emanating from his face were Pendlebury-esque. This was physiognomy striding forth and revealing things which my father would rather remain private. It was a bruising humility, back again – fighting alongside him.

I turned away.

CHAPTER 9

College seemed pointless. I left the house and stepped on the bus as if heading there, but I rode an extra stop. Standing now on the pavement, open to the Monday cry, I gazed at the traffic as it passed; its occupants somehow programmed to participate in the haste. Slowing down, or even stopping – as I had done – was shameful, reprehensible and anachronistic. It didn't belong. *I* didn't belong – in the mode I was, not blindly pursuing industry's cocktail, nor bowing to avoid its cursed wings. I should justify myself – my actions, my thoughts. I should wait for a cloaked figure, to authorize, to give permission.

But then, who is this being? What gave him or her a higher calling than myself? Why does he or she remain faceless and therefore more compelling? I dismissed it – them. I ignored what I thought to be a societal premonition. Beyond and after my parents, there should be no one – no loose fiend shaking its staff. Too many are afraid – cordoned in by others' reputations.

I thought of them, my fellow apprentices, soon to be interviewed – some laughably so. Wasn't this the first swinging to of the prison door? Weren't we all to be disappointed upon working for another? I pictured Pendlebury in amongst the horde, perhaps safer now in the old church, even without my presence. He had been so sure of life beyond the college – old, in the sense that he knew our current endeavours were nothing more than a frivolous game. Pendlebury's uncle – the leaf blower – would perhaps be home now – arraigned by the harsh January Ice Lords of pampering to their seasonal enemy, Autumn.

In my randomness, I was just over two miles from the house. Yes. I had to see him. Isolated – away from his nephew. His deafness concerned me, as did his unopened mouth in my presence (albeit after one fleeting visit), yet I knew I could dig. And, as with my grandfather, be passed the proverbial spade. Tales and insights surely ran across the senses of those that wanted them. Or at least inhabited the finer minds of the next worthy crop.

I walked on, oblivious to the noises which were vying for life's pulse. Straight, turning, hurriedly, slowly, I went – still magically immune to the decadent clamour. I ignored everything, reciprocated nothing. My purpose seemed to exceed even food and water. I desired little – just information and new stories which would metamorphose the thin track I was on. This man. This blower of leaves. Perhaps he was the beginning. Of what, I could not begin to surmise, yet there was something pulling me. Pendlebury, my grandfather, James, my mother, my father – they all seemed like pieces of The Leaf Blower's face. And now, having known them, I was to meet their fleshy anthology, their garnered, iconoclastic-speaking titan.

'I'd like to talk. Come in, if I may.'

I was there, facing him – not really understanding anything, yet content. He waved his arm, his hand, invitingly, and then walked ahead of me. The manner was Pendlebury's. The lack of encirclement was the same. I closed the door – nervously so. I was with a stranger, in effect, but one whose frame knew nothing other than serenity.

The same leather chair as last time came into view – alongside it the banker's lamp, switched off. He had positioned himself in the chair already – eager to conduct my walk and have me sit opposite. I did so and what words, sentences, I had stored seemed to flee, as if embarrassed – as if thrown in the ring with a huge thesaurus.

We stared, at each other, and at the surrounding room. I thought of my father – how he valued his hearing more than anything, and here I was with someone deprived of such grace. Here I was, unsure – stripped of etiquette – yet comforted by The Leaf Blower's mellow gaze.

'I don't normally offer up my voice to people I've seen little of. But with your goodself – the friend of my nephew – I must be whole.....guileless. I cannot lessen our chatter with this.

'I...cannot...lessen...our....chatter....with....this.'

The repeated words were digitized, synthesized – a speech

automatic mouth. They emanated from a humble speaker I now noticed to be lodged into the base of the chair – one obviously connected to the tiny keyboard on the left-hand arm. Pendlebury's uncle could hear neither. Not the spoken words he dared to entrust to me, nor the machine's effort on his part. He had, over the course of many years, presumably begun to understand each expression's impact yet, as with the clatter of a spoon against a cereal bowl or the more salubrious singing of a bird, he would never fully interpret their weight.

I re-loaded his initial words: normally; goodself; friend; nephew; guileless; chatter. They weren't in any way artless or stultified, but actually beautiful and mellifluent. Not retarded nor foreign, but better because of their challenging sweetness. I wanted to communicate this to him, because I knew he relied on others, just as others relied on the media. It was more so though, due to his inability to hear the evidence in its purest form.

'Well – I'm flattered.' I followed this up with a modest smile, to add tone and facial hue.

'Where do we begin then?'

'I'm not sure.' And I wasn't. It simply felt calm and benign sitting here.

'How about we begin with the irony of this banker's lamp then? And after that move onto a flood of subjects that interest both of us...'

'Yes. Fine.' I couldn't not be in agreement.

'I have a theory that we're heading down the wrong track. That something or someone will intervene. Maybe not in Britain. But somewhere – in the Majority World perhaps. In the world's landfill sites. Rubbish (both metaphorical and not) as defined by today's masters, will turn on them – its creators and conditioners.'

I gazed at him as he talked. He sounded revolutionary, yet polite – nihilistic, yet convincing. Art had somehow occupied his bloodstream, his body, and was now petitioning the sewage which continued to dominate the waters. He knew who he was, even if only 40% of him was there, in the midst of an eternal conscript-like rain.

'The bankers and money men will return to their roots. Of duty and humility. Not continue along this sodden path of avarice and irresponsibleness. They know now that the status quo or an intensifying of this is wrong, madness, yet they're all in the game. Well, I aim to help in the tipping over of the board. I aim to build something other than a meritocracy – something which doesn't *exclude*.'

The final word seemed to chalk itself in the air again and again. It seemed to pick at my own consciousness. I was running down the road of exclusion more and more, and only on reaching its depths would I be useful to the membership; a membership I still had no evidence or insight of, but one which surely now existed.

'How will this come about - this tipping over of the board? Aren't there too many pieces weighing it down – securing it in place?'

'There are a lot. A lot playing the game – that isn't in doubt. But only a few of these would stubbornly resist. If we defy them...well, we don't *play* anymore, but begin to have *purpose*. I'm not advocating the closing down of parks or the prohibition of laughter. This isn't 'play' in the wider sense that I'm talking about. Nor am I suggesting an Act of Parliament closing down all the theatres. Christ – I am not Charles I. No, Christ. This is about knowing who we are and demanding change – change which is reverential and mindful of modern folly and insidious divides.'

He was rolling – swaggering in a subtle, yet necessary way. The play / purpose contrast seemed elementary yet marked. It squeezed the juices from the over-ripe myth of there being no alternative. And his touting of British history, not its unsettlingly precocious daughter, America, was refreshing – enlivening even.

'I've heard similar lines from Pendlebury. How will this...this angst be channelled though? What's in place already? I need to know – know more than the generalisations being espoused.'

He looked at me more carefully now – perhaps wondering

whether to cross the line, to risk rupturing what he had built. 'My nephew is like an apostle or disciple. His history is rare, but important. If I tell you a little about his background, then things should become clearer. Maybe you'll retract the thought that I'm trying to obfuscate you.'

I acceded with a nod of the head, not wanting to interrupt his flow.

'Pendlebury's mother died after giving birth to him. She was haemorrhaging immediately upon him entering this world. Her blood failed to clot or coagulate as it should have. Ten thousand to one. Stupid, stupid odds of such a thing happening, but it had....'

He paused. I felt depraved for prompting such a personal story – worthless under the weight of his tumultuous emotions. I looked across – examined him. He appeared, all of a sudden, exhausted and lethargic; there was something of himself wrapped up in the tragedy.

'His father – my brother – found the experience impossible to bear. He couldn't focus, think or understand any of it. He didn't simply put his head in his hands. He shut down – quite acutely. Pendlebury's mother had somehow allowed him to be normal. She was the acceptable face of their relationship – one in which he masked some of his more extreme ideas. Without her, he was alienated – locked away from society. He knew this and so pre-empted his fall. It wasn't an *asylum* he voluntarily walked into, but more of a refuge – a small and rural private hospital. After three months there, he disappeared...two days before I was due to see him.

'I don't think it was a selfish act. What you have to understand is that they had been together for thirteen years. From the age of eighteen to their then same age of thirty-one – just a year younger than me. We were all still scrapping for our route in life. We were all unprepared in some sense for such devastation. Adapting would have been the credible route – the glorious offshoot of something so terrible, but.....'

A heavy strain entered his face. His history – his family's history – was onerous, difficult to muse over, difficult to find vindication amongst its wreckage.

'I wanted to take him. I said so. But the deafness….they said it would make things difficult. How would I hear him crying? How would I tend to him properly? I didn't fight their questions. I bowed – became compliant.'

There were missing dabs and areas to the painting. I felt I knew the Pendlebury history almost as well as my own, yet obvious questions surfaced in my mind – questions which I undoubtedly *had* to exhume and get answers to via The Leaf Blower's worn brush.

'You didn't see your brother again? There were no grandparents to bear the weight? You didn't visit your nephew?'

There was silence. His head and body appeared to vacillate – alter from their quite motionless state. I wasn't sure whether he had managed to lip-read my words and was choosing to ignore me, or whether his skill or art had momentarily failed. I repeated myself, guiltily – unwillingly.

'No. I haven't seen my brother since 1970. Grandparents? All now dead, but at the time in failing health on our side…one deceased, one in a home on my sister-in-law's side (she herself an only child). The authorities implicitly told me that a completely new network of people would be better for Pendlebury's welfare. There would be a stronger chance of adoption later on without any 'claimants' in the picture. I adhered to that – stupidly, fecklessly. It was only when Pendlebury's own questioning became intense that they crumbled. That was five years ago. Difficult to believe that he had been in the vicinity throughout…'

I didn't empathise – not in the verbal sense. He needed something different than a soft, yielding locution. I thought of the banker's lamp, his original non-meritocratic talk, his unrest with the current world order. He craved politics, ideas, discussion, solutions. I would ask him for specifics – enquire again as to his status within the membership or movement, before putting forward my own cerebral, plus somewhat effusive line. I knew his 'brand', his flavour to be partially driven by the past, yet I also interpreted in him foresight and knowing.

'I need to be made aware of what it is you believe in. Now. In the wake of Pendlebury's guardedness.'

'Level Four.' He was frank, disarming. I let him articulate the two words in their union – their jellied confederacy: 'We speak from the shade. We're not sun-dried tomatoes void of plumpness, of juices. We don't allow ourselves to be wilted by the acrid air of modern politics. The name was derived from a person's typical cycle. Level One – greed, want. Youngsters, I suppose, can't help but be unfamiliar with altruism, sacrifice. When I say youngsters, the age probably reaches twenty-two, twenty-three – time enough for them to have seen the world in its chaos. Level Two – a desire to change things, physically and intellectually, having seen the straightforward cruelty and incongruousness of life. A change of job, a different attitude, a slowing down, a tapping of one's consciousness. This of course doesn't last, for the majority of debutants. Two, maybe three years I would say. Pressures soon re-exert themselves, others 'overtake', albeit in a monetary sense, and the soul is left torn. Level Three? An effective return to 'the game', but this time with no dreams beyond that space, no beautiful notions or illusions, however misguided. Level Three is disheartening, because you're older, voluntarily stoical, bent and shaped by the wishes of others. Not family, or close friends, but what seems like an odour, permeating you – cancerous in its suffocating or eating away of your deeper thoughts. Conquest. Slaughter. Famine. Plague. That is the effect.'

The last few words were clearly apocalyptic, yet my identifying this perturbed me having no knowledge of religious education, or revelationary texts.

He continued: 'So there it is, Arnold. One, two, three. We offer Level Four – a leap across Three's rapids. We're a modern day Christianity in that our movement is an immoderate challenge to today's Roman Empire: market forces. We're protectionists, and I say that not as a gangster but as someone that values equality, sanity. We don't ditch the lower intellects. We actually harness their slow-working minds. It's the same with blind people, those hard of hearing, those disabled and without limbs. We're a ragtag band of communists when all is said. And I must stress our slant on this, because I'm certainly not Joseph Stalin. We hold things in common – our banishment from the decision-making processes, and more outrageously our neglect by the media eye. In one sense, we need a messiah. We're close though – perhaps only a few years away.'

I found his talk of a messiah slightly obtuse – clichéd by hundreds of years of desperate faith and scientific antipathy. And yet on hearing him more, I understood his desire to have someone 'shout' the opposition down – someone to convene and inspire the ranks.

'How do you know you're close? That's ludicrous, isn't it?'

'Pendlebury knows.'

'How?'

'We entrusted such a mission to him. The movement was born with his appearance five years ago.'

'Would the movement still have come about without Thatcher and Reagan?'

'You're inquisitive...'

'Would it?'

'Of course. Yes.'

'You're certain?'

'I've just said so. There's no reason to lie. The world started to slide after 1968 when America's air quality and natural resources began to suffer. The charge towards worthless goods was monstrous. Society was effectively plundered. The knock on effect to other countries was obscene.'

'But I still don't get it. Besides solace, rallies, meetings – whatever the fashionable communist methods are – how does your movement, your membership make a tangible difference? Aren't the people still swimming in Level Two and Three? It's a part-time masquerade, isn't it?'

'Like Sacco and Vanzetti?'

'What?!'

'Sacco and Vanzetti – Pendlebury mentioned them.'

'What about them though? How are they a masquerade?'

'It's not my place to enlighten you. But they themselves aren't in any way a sham.'

'Tell me. What is it you mean?'

'I....can't....go....on. I'm...sorry.'

The digitized words broached my annoyance. The Leaf Blower's vengeance had been swift but unjust. What did he mean? What was the reference to? To mention something through retaliation, through enragement, suggested a weak leadership. It was edgy, surly, surprising – because I had thought Pendlebury's uncle to be almost God-like.

I looked at him now. Tried to see through his obstructive demeanour. He failed to register my gaze – instead choosing to close his eyes and dream. I seemed to penetrate his eye lids, however – circumvent the physical barriers which proffered a steely 'Game Over'. In his eyes, his very being, I read weariness and fatigue – things synonymous with others, but not him. He was ordinary – that was the mural inside of him, despite my elevating his soul and presence. The vigour of only moments ago had been withdrawn – perhaps permanently. And yet, in the wake of his enervation, I somehow felt omniscient. Former grey areas peeled themselves before me. Family faces swept across my line of vision. I appeared to know the reasoning of others. James – why he had chosen accountancy / commerce. Why he aimed to tread the corporate path. Because he wanted to achieve things which would lead to comfort, and that was barely possible fighting from the other side. My mother – why her kindness largely transcended her own needs. Because she sought popularity – a suitable haven from her long-diminished personal dreams. My grandfather – why he had chosen me to play out his golfing desires. Because people were dying on him – people of his generation – and walking the course was a way of accessing any final bits of silence, of truth, Finally, my father – how his bruising humility had come about. How…

The Leaf Blower opened his eyes, as if reading this point in my thoughts, as if aware of a sudden oscillation not representative of the last few years. 'I… have …. a … book …. about … the … philosophical … anarchists.' He pointed. 'Over … there – middle … left.'

In him was apprehension – alarm almost. He was offering me something vital, yet uncomfortable. He was reading part of a map, tentatively and inconspicuously, in the hope that his abstention and neutrality would remain. He couldn't afford to tell me what I was about to read, because that would be like steering the ship; that would be rendering himself complicit – the architect of gloom. And I knew it to be gloom.

I found the book via its spine, pulled it from the neck-high shelf and remained standing. I opened it – flicked through speedily at first, noticing the dates in the margin. I had been expecting a write-up of the 1920s (the key dates being Sacco & Vanzetti's 1921 trial and 1927 execution), yet this covered one hundred years. 1880. That was the start – the first historic attachment, the earliest tremor of what was to come. Large-scale immigration had begun. Italians were arriving in the United States like ants crossing a puddle of water. Among them were anarchists. Anarchist – it was huge word; a word which resonated of physical combat, of hurt, of shocking deeds which caused distemper; deeds which were often random and therefore heartless in their execution. But then anarchy had two principal definitions. It spoke of the former – people causing disorder and upheaval, people killing in the name of politics and injustice. It also though – and the book emphasized this – spoke of the anarchist's desire for voluntary cooperation rather than government, for a social system void of anonymous might.

I read on. At the back of my mind – seemingly trapped – were thoughts and echoes of Level Four plus a watery image of my father's face. My knowledge of both was embryonic – usurped, to a degree, by ignorance and naivety. Against this insecurity, however, were a flood of dates and happenings beginning to grapple with my intellect. 1886. The Haymarket Affair. The explosion of a bomb during an outdoor anarchist meeting (the meeting itself a protest against police brutality). Eight policemen dead plus a number of civilians. Anarchists, themselves, to blame – four of whom were executed. For the final decade of the 19th century, Boston – over one hundred years after the infamous Tea Party – was to be the centre point for anti-alien and anti-radical movements. America was slowly becoming xenophobic in the face of a class war. Whilst not on the same scale as the War of Independence, turn-of-the-century activities, all the same, were altering the landscape and environment. Italians were spearheading the fight against what they deemed to be the severe inequalities of capitalism – a huge fissure in its make-up. Most Italians had been receptive to such a fight only *after* witnessing working-class life in the Land of Opportunity; a melting pot that not only pitched everyone together irrespective of race, but also tended to sanitise the nasty striking habits of the oppressed by whatever means.

The word 'assassination' now jumped out at me. 1900. Anarchist Gaetano Bresci left America to kill his own King, the colonialist, Umberto I. The following year Leon Czolgosz killed William McKinley, the imperialist, and 25th President of the United States. Politics were taking hold – setting man against man. The underdogs were refusing to bow to militia men and organised government groups intent on strengthening the system. 'In the past man has been first. In the future the system must be first' – F W Taylor, 1890. A lot had preceded Sacco & Vanzetti. They had only really arrived on the movement's 28th birthday (1908) and it had taken them four years to grow and understand their surroundings, before committing themselves to what they thought a worthy cause. The extent of this commitment – be it abstract or practical – was to be their downfall, their grim reaper.

I thought about this: man's decision to act now in the belief that thirty, forty, fifty years on, perception would alter, power would shift – vindication would open its arms to his foresight and courageousness. To not live in the present – the present as defined by the great forces above – must have been hard. To be divisive in the eyes of those you know to be pernicious and plutocratic must have been insufferable. Two generations though

– perhaps three. That is what entered my head when thinking about altering life's course permanently. Sacrifice, altruism over fifty, sixty years from everyone, or at least the vast majority. To be hailed in history books, but to be without now. Was it manageable? I didn't know. I knew, looking down at the book in my hands, that efforts – however misguided – had been orchestrated though. Duets had been forged *before* the one central to my history and the very direction of my blood. Condensed over the course of a decade, up to 1920, their names rang loud – if not louder – than *my* stalwarts, my family's exemplars: Ettor and Giovannitti (strike leaders falsely accused of murder – 1912); Abarno and Carbone (entrapped by police in a plot to blow up St Patrick's Cathedral in New York City – 1915); Salsedo and Elia (anarchist editors detained by the Department of Justice for 'freedom of expression' – 1920…the former beaten and thrown to his death). And publications, all prior to the 1920 arrests / 1921 trial: Luigi Galleani's *Cronaca Sovversiva* (1903); Aldino Felicani's *La Gioventu Libertaria* (1914) & *La Questione Sociale*; Vanzetti and Felicani's *Cara Compagna* (1919).

Vanzetti! Unlike my brother, James 'Sacco', I had been involved in editing, in sending out an alternative message to ordinary people; a message which pilloried the government mechanisms of the day. I was, of course, at this point, picking – running my eyes over bits of the text before me. I couldn't hope to grasp fully every strand, connection, loop and interplay. I couldn't hope to make concrete statements without holes. I needed to wander in the dark though – shine a light on the more non-contentious points. History was bombarding me with undisputable data relevant to the mood slowly brewing, whilst the activities of Sacco and Vanzetti were becoming ever clearer. I read about the importance of both Luigi Galleani and Aldino Felicani – the former very much the pre-1919 linchpin and the latter, during the course of the trial and the years that elapsed up to and after the executions on 23rd August 1927, wishing to keep the legacy of Sacco and Vanzetti, and the hypocrisy of America in the public eye. Anarchists *respond* – that had been their message. They don't initiate worthless acts.

Galleani, who advocated revolutionary violence, had been on the scene since the turn of the century. He had seen from afar the Ludlow Massacre in Colorado in 1914 (a 'them' and 'us' act of horrific proportions – striking workers and their families attacked by the militia). He despaired of the owner of the mines, John D. Rockefeller, for his hubris and monopolizing. Sacco and Vanzetti had become disciples of Galleani between 1912 and 1917 – *Cronaca Sovversiva* 'pushers', fundraisers and strike agitators. In 1917, after years of internal unrest and splendid isolation on America's part, the adopted son Galleani and his Galleanisti (comrades / followers) fled to Mexico. March had seen the beginnings of the Russian Revolution and in May military conscription was afoot in the United States. Very much anti-war, the Galleanisti (made up of Sacco, Vanzetti and some sixty-odd Italian anarchists) had to ensure that their liberty remained intact, in full anticipation of a revolution in Italy.

It didn't happen. And five years later, *Il Duce* (Mussolini) took power. Exile wasn't in the blood of the anarchists – its separation from the cause making it impotent – and so the Galleanisti returned to the United States; Sacco, later on in 1917; Vanzetti, the year after. By now, America was wising up – injecting an arbitrary power into its veins. Woodrow Wilson introduced a host of immigration laws – their brawn designed to be used against alien radicals. *Cronaca Sovversiva* – seen by many as "the most influential anarchist journal in America" and the guiding hand of the 'fight' – was suppressed (Galleani and his co-editors / supporters arrested and deported the following year (1919)). Into this vacuum seemed to step Felicani – arriving in Boston in 1918. And what was to follow was twelve months of turmoil – very much the shoehorn to Sacco and Vanzetti's fall; the dates 1 May 1919 – 6 May 1920 imprinting themselves on my mind.

I paused, blinked a few times – turned my head away from the text. There seemed to be stages to my understanding and assimilation – junctures to my taking in the nature of these people and their surroundings, realities. Immigration / tension: that was the first port, the first loop to this journey. Cultures were destined to clash. The 'home guard' would mostly be desperate to teach, but not learn. The aliens were there to 'shovel the shit', not contemplate what a democracy should look like. Action: alien 'miscreants' or non-believers dishing out violence in the face of suppression and 'do not step on the grass' lecturing. Reaction: the chosen ones marching and hauling back into line the fresh faces of their 'banana boat' lackeys. Increased stakes: the lackeys using symbolism through assassination and steadfastness – wanting to pull down their 'other' status by destroying the upper layers of repression before them. Manipulation: through law or whatever means in an effort to damn and lambast the alien upstarts hankering for more.

The headings read like a male / female relationship; a simple affair of cat and mouse. Tension. Action. Reaction. Increased stakes. Manipulation. Except, there were other stages and levels – a heavy artillery of riots, bombings and murders; arrests, indictments and sentencing; appeals, fresh evidence and defence committee posturing; executions; and something else – although I appeared blind to it. I looked at Pendlebury's uncle. It was strange to be here – unravelling that which was central to my being in front of him. He knew some aspect of it to be consecratory, however. The people, the radicals, the anarchists – they were different to me, to us. Their taking of a life, not casually, but brutally all the same, was like killing oneself in my mind. It was abhorrent, unacceptable, but worst of all destructive, out of control and an encroachment upon the sanctity of life – any and every life. How far Sacco and Vanzetti had gone, I didn't know. I expected restraint though. I expected self-abasement. Reading on was like discovering the secondary school grades and careers of my unborn sons. And what I didn't want to hear was: 'Assassins. They should both make good assassins.'

I sat down. Continued the assimilation whilst level and opposite The Leaf Blower; his bushy eyebrows and slightly pockmarked face still anxious and puffy with foreboding. 1 May 1919 – May Day riots in Boston and most major cities. 2 June – bomb explosions throughout the United States, including at the house of Attorney General Palmer. Palmer's name was to attach itself to American initiatives or counteraction (depending on how you defined the first blow). 'Palmer' raids shocked the country – up to 33 of its cities – in November 1919 and January 1920; the aim, to weed out all alien radicals. Between these dates was the first, more innocuous, shoe factory hold-up at Bridgewater; a botched robbery with zero casualties. Four months later, however, on 15th April 1920, a decisive and critical blow was made: robbery of the payroll at a shoe factory in South Braintree, Massachusetts – both the guard and paymaster killed.

It was the moment – *the* moment – when everything changed. What had been largely dissent from afar was now a magnified killing – a killing of two innocents. Within twenty days, five of the Galleanisti not already deported, were interviewed or arrested (for reasons relating to support of *Cronaca Sovversiva*, the Bridgewater hold-up, the South Braintree hold-up, or all three). The names walked before me: Coacci; Buda; Sacco; Vanzetti; Orciani. I wished to erase the third and fourth because nearly sixty-seven years later their very mention had the effect of underpinning my history – not necessarily in a truly strengthening fashion, but maybe one in which sophistry was rife. I instantly thought about the two men's jobs or vocations. "The shoe man and the fish peddler" – my father's very words. My brother, the shoe man. And myself, the fish peddler. Both hold-ups at shoe factories. Surely such an incidental link had no bearing on one's guilt or innocence. I dismissed it, although *my* guilt, *my* culpability seemed to lessen the more I read. I was a sacrifice, an obedient Adam, a deliverance. Someone had labeled me the latter, but I couldn't think. My brain refused to be pored over. Vanzetti and I were one, split by a different era, separated into atoms whose nuclei had been heading for adjacent centuries. In the wake of Coacci being deported, Buda disappearing after being interviewed and Orciani being released because of his watertight alibis, it was left to myself and James to carry the weight, the burden, of crimes which needed pinning to someone if only to appease the law's masters. That is the impression I was now gleaning – just one page on – just one page after fingering my brother through footnotes of ballistics tests and Defence Committee minutes.

'It... doesn't... make... easy... reading.' The interruption was from Pendlebury's uncle, and I sensed that he meant the injustice now hawking its frame over me, as opposed to the fluency of the book itself.

I looked at him. 'No,' was all I could say. I had to read about the indictments, the trials, before coming back to him, or committing properly. Even then, I wasn't sure I would be in a position to judge, to decide, here in this house.

"...They themselves aren't in any way a sham..." The Leaf Blower's former words seemed to have more meaning, but still retained echoes of another dimension – a posthumous reflection perhaps. I turned my attention back to the text, while the icy weather outside rippled against the panes of glass behind my companion.

Four dates haunted me: 11 June 1920 (my indictment for the Bridgewater hold-up); 1 July 1920 (my being convicted); 11 September 1920 (James and I indicted for the South Braintree hold-up); 14 July 1921 (our being found guilty). I played with the dates in my head. July was unlucky. It was a tale of two of them. Set against August though – the impending 23rd August 1927 – July was merely abstract; a shell collecting words, sounds and intent; a billboard boy announcing imminent events via his ladders, paper and glue. I was frightened though. I hadn't known *when* we would be taken from this earth, just that motions for a re-trial would be put forward over months, years. I was a cat, in the sense that I had lost my first life on being found guilty of murder. My other eight lives were motions – all denied. Enemies and friends had lined up throughout. Unfortunately, I had counted the former at seven and the latter at six, although five days after our indictment for murder a fellow radical, Mario Buda, had been instrumental in the bombing of Wall Street (revenge, I understand, for what he thought to be the wrongful indictment of James and I).

I supposed then, that in many quarters, my dignity was applauded – and also that of James. What never got out, however – at least from my side – was the fear underneath the etched and solemn face. I had arrived in America in my twentieth year, full of hope and promise – not of hate and premeditation as some would have you believe. Certainly, unemployment changed me, as did the drudgery of low-paid jobs, yet paranoia and disappointment do not make for murder. If that were the case, there would be no people on this continent. I undoubtedly acted suspiciously on the evening of my, our, arrest. I was surrounded by pistols, ammunition and anarchist literature, and my tendency had been to lie because of concern regarding my beliefs in the eyes of the authorities. I wished to disassociate myself from eight years of radicalism. I wished to avoid their sanctimonious stare, following the slightest admittance. I wished to be free again – or free, not behind tangible bars – and so I rebuffed their simple claims. In creating this 'consciousness of guilt', of course, I added to my woes – I fingerprinted an extremism in me which never existed. The initial trial, too – my lone trial for the Bridgewater hold-up – I had succeeded in persecuting myself by not taking the stand (my stance again centred around not being labelled a radical).

How could it be though? How could democracy crank up and amplify one's actions – strip away one's 32nd birthday (11 June 1920) with an indictment aimed at staining my character in readiness for the second jury (the murder trial)? Listen now please Stewart, Thayer, Katzmann, Vahey, and those that would come later (Proctor, Fuller, Lowell): I was selling eels on the day of the crime. My countrymen attested to it – more than twenty of them. But, no, because of their origins, you chose not to believe them. Whiter Americans, however – prosecution witnesses afforded more faith – had powers undoubtedly borne at the golden door; powers more than eight years in the making which enabled them, when present at a crime scene, to deduce that the perpetrator must have been a foreigner "by the way he ran". Vahey! You were supposed to be *my* attorney, *my* defence – *not* a collusive friend and future partner of the prosecution (Katzmann). Thayer! Call yourself a judge! An upholder of the truth! You wanted this conviction. You needed it because of the Red Scare. Yet…I forgive you. I forgive…you all. Even the police chief that entrapped me - Michael Stewart.

I run through even now, in my mind, the murder trial. How Thayer and Katzmann followed up their abnormally high 15-year Bridgewater sentence with the death penalty: execution; electrocution; my ceasing to be. South Braintree. Again, it wasn't me. Yet you needed a couple of Italians for the shoot. You asked Captain William Proctor of the State Police to perjure himself, to testify in effect that the bullets were ours. You stoked up a court room of invidiousness – had us guilty of anarchy, atheism, alien status and not fighting in WWI. Worse than this, Thayer, you gave free licence to Katzmann's vicious and prejudicial tongue – the body politic of which knew nothing other than governance *of* the rich, *by* the rich, *for* the rich.

I had friends throughout the six or seven years – fellows close, distant and not known to me. Good people from whom different skills surfaced. They were the six fighting the seven mentioned: the old warriors Aldino Felicani (treasurer of our defence committee) and Carlo Tresca (advisor and all round radical stalwart); Fred Moore (our attorney for four years between August 1920 and August 1924) – a lawyer, used to assisting industrial workers, who sought to prove that the prosecution had a hidden agenda, namely its collusion with military and federal authorities in seeking to suppress the Italian anarchist movement (Moore had been a tireless publicist both inside and outside the court, and the chief reason why our names transcended local politics thus bounding onto the international scene); William Thompson (our attorney for the final three years / Moore stepping down at James's request) – a liberal Hindu, Boston Lawyer and necessary 'respectable', keen to defend the well-being of Massachusetts law and in turn the very lives of James and I in the face of patriotic fatuousness; Felix Frankfurter (a law professor at Harvard) – a solid campaigner in his efforts to win over the non-radical, 'sensible' crowd, the pinnacle of which was a pro-Sacco-Vanzetti article written for Atlantic Monthly five months before our deaths (his phone was to be tapped by the State Police because of his involvement); and Celestino Madeiros (a member of the Morelli Gang which history would point to in relation to the South Braintree hold-up) – to many a procrastinator, our nemesis, yet his confession on 26th May 1926 (albeit fourteen days *after* the Supreme Judicial Court decided to uphold our conviction) was brave and redemptive.

I know all the above to be true because when I died I was handed 'the book'; passage after passage of inky scribblings somehow indexed, ordered, yet rich with random beauty. I also know that the Governor of Massachusetts, Alvan Fuller, after much public pressure, considered clemency for James and I (although only *I* signed the petition). The resultant committee he appointed – named after Lawrence Lowell, the president of Harvard – took two months to reach its conclusion. Two months of pacing a cell. Two months of pleading mercy, silently, for something that had occurred in my absence. When the recommendation came back, when Fuller saw fit to slain us with the full might of its no-more-recourse toxicity, I cried. Not outwardly, but through the withering veins that languished inside of me. I felt, finally, overcome – bankrupted at the feet of a machine whose reticence had wounded both our physical candour and our ability to reason. The weight crushing down on me was intolerable. Its luminous hand seemed to slap and beat me. It assumed that my living half a life was satisfactory – not tragic and calamitous. No corner of the world felt sacred. Nothing was left to protect me. The indignation I should have sculptured fell flat, shapeless, void of indentation – even after having whispered in my ear that I had been a radical "watched from the very beginning"; a comrade of the man responsible for bombing Attorney General Palmer's home in 1919. That had been it from the outset – retribution, however oblique or skewed, my conviction tantamount to elimination. The 'movement' had polluted a high-ranking official. Carlo Valdinoci had pissed with the wrong man, even though his dismembered body at the bomb scene preceded their vengeance. And *we* had paid. *We* had been caught in the sweep – the filthy revenge of a government with crimson hands.

Madeiros was electrocuted with us, at Charlestown State Prison. I cannot tell you how the final seconds of my life felt because the memory was smuggled from me by a greater good – a kind, serving force which seemed to blanket me as soon as the pain hit. The writhing image you may have of me sat in a wired-up chair *was* an actuality, however, the dehumanizing act would always fall harder onto the souls of those that wrought it, rather than my own fretfulness. The days and years that followed, I watched with interest and incredulity. Felicani continued his great stand, publishing for a further forty years until his death in 1967. Gutzon Borglum, a renowned sculptor, had a plaque of James and I refused by various State Governors what seemed like each decade after our passing, until Boston Public Library finally 'conceded' in 1979. The month after our cremation, ending at Forest Hills Cemetery, all Hollywood newsreels of us were ordered destroyed. America had attempted to take away our birth certificates, our identity, the visual mien which was in danger of tainting others. 1959 though. Thirty-two years on. The age at which I was first indicted. Perhaps I had missed it before. Perhaps the heavens had seen the irony and kept me from the glorious entrails of man's equitable lot, not wanting to rush my higher baptism. I could see it now, however, and whilst my vindictiveness was contained, the divinity I felt was unguarded – abundant. The Republican Alexander Celia had introduced a bill asking for our posthumous pardon and whilst the petition was denied, it was to maybe elicit our exoneration eighteen years on, on 23rd August 1977 (the fiftieth anniversary of our passing). The Governor of Massachusetts, Michael Dukakis, proclaimed it

Sacco and Vanzetti day... Debrito and Debrito day.

We had been forgiven. No – reprieved. No – pardoned. It was the only word. One in which our glacé consciousness seemed to pick off its own icing and offer it around. To the doubters, the shortsighted, the bandwagon foes. There were some that still refused the sweetness, the dulcet taste of history turned over, of chaff set alight, yet their blinkers would undoubtedly remain – in judgement of others as well, proving them untenable and untrustworthy. The crux of this, however – the truth now blinding me with its incandescent force was that the year had been 1977. I wasn't Bartolomeo Vanzetti. I was Debrito. Arnold Debrito. And that very year...

'Father!' I threw down the book and dissolved into a heap at the foot of the chair. I had been lied to – given a history, an attachment, on the understanding that our faith had been autonomous. Not supported by someone in office. Not rubber-stamped by Dukakis and therefore the community at large. Beacons of hope? Liberators? My father had disgraced himself – pulled me aside only weeks after the pardon and pretended to know only the events up to 1927. It was too much of a coincidence to be otherwise. For God's sake! What had he been thinking? Playing with the mind of a seven-year-old as if the accumulation of years wouldn't threaten him later on.

'Why the hell did he do it?' The words were directed at The Leaf Blower, who was still sat opposite me – watching, knowing from the turned, strangely curative pages how much I knew.

'I don't know. Only he can tell you.'

'What *do* you know then?! What do you know?' I was impatient, inflamed. Stripped of religion, of fatherhood – *real* fatherhood – I felt worthless and forlorn – renounced by a book whose pages had encoded in them my own downfall. I was now shivering slightly – drawn away from everything holistic into a world where my father's face was replicated before me as pop art; his blue stubble the remnant of a dubious harvest and his thick black hair cellar-like in its subterranean furtiveness.

Pendlebury's uncle met my starkness with a stodgy riposte:

'Arnold. Now is your chance. To build on adversity. To really start things.'

'Wait. Wait. What do you mean? It's the opposite. Ten years of deception. It should break me. I've been done over...'

The faces flew around me – expressionless and harsh. I blinked them away only for them to return – come at me – with an extra dissonance and severity. I was becoming feverish in the space of a few seconds – exasperated by the cold climate, both immediate and distant. I closed my eyes – shut out the semi-detached reality that I was in. Attempted to move my still body with my mind alone, ignoring the coordination of limbs. Everything seemed to darken before me – move at a pace that transfixed me, at least for a while. And then I was running, into town. To its outskirts. Down the concrete ramp that had kidded me, that had partook in the class war. I stood, on the stony path, moved my neck and head violently in an attempt to catch sight of anything animate or alive. The corroding brick seemed to crumble ever more in front of me. The polluted canal seemed to voice years of neglect and industrial warfare. In the mesmerizing sadness of both, I missed the rush of bodies at me; policemen, full of bulk and aggression, not hitting me but pulling me to the floor – pinning my arms, length-wise at the side of me and holding my feet together like an act of crucifixion. One, two, three, four of them, uniformed against the blackened sky – their silver buttons glimmering occasionally under the moon's esteemed light.

'Not again, boy! Didn't I help you the last time? Didn't I separate you from the miscreants...'

It was the one from before – the Roman, now talking with a ratchet-like hauteur; his manner exaggerated all too clearly by the numbers around him (companions whose existence, whose very business was playing on or obstructing the desires of others).

I was more attuned to confrontation now, however. I was filled with sixty years of dust, ashes and others' wrong doing. And despite my rib cage being forced into an acutely convex shape, and my vulnerability being harnessed, I spoke back: 'You gave credence to my suspicion. That is all. And so now I'd like you to direct me to them.'

'Them? Who might *they* be? Figures in your mind….your rotting head?'

'The miscreants. They aren't real. They're your masters.'

'Listen 'ere.' He screwed his face up close to mine. 'I don't *have* a master. What do you think I am – a *serf*?!'

'However you define it doesn't matter. *They* exist. I know they do.'

He pulled his arm back as if to hit me and then splayed his fingers on the ground at the side of my head after feigning the follow through.

'We have room for you, you know…' The words were like a semi-admittance and instantly changed the complexion of things. He followed them up. 'It's like this though: once you're in, you're in.'

I knew he wasn't lying now. I had somehow developed a sense of people's veracity. What could I say though? How could I gauge properly the world I imagined without glimpsing it or indeed perusing its folds? But then, what if this 'mafia' were to envelop me as he'd stated?

'I need to know some things before committing.'

He shifted his weight from me and indicated to his colleagues to do likewise. They retreated next to the wall, allowing me to get to my feet again and stand over the canal with the Roman.

'We don't 'fill you in'. This isn't the Round Table. You get an instinct for what we do beforehand and then stay or walk away.'

'My instinct tells me that there's a caste system within your enterprise. Just the two grades. Not wanting to be a copper, however – where does that leave me?'

His original demeanour returned. The way he thought me too complex for his 'x' and 'y' world. The way he looked at me as if I was disruptive and purposely obdurate. Black and white. Black and white. No grey, because to search or admit to it would flatter us with time.

He called them over – the rest of the coterie. They held me roughly and put a bag over my head. Initially I felt asphyxiated, but then I realised suffocation was neither their aim nor their love. Steadying my breath, I heard their witticisms and quips, their attempts at self-amelioration: 'he's a bloody Lord'; 'no, a *toooooff*'; 'he built this country up – didn't you know'; 'fought in both World Wars'; 'a teenager – the forgotten Duke of Carlisle'.

'What *is* your name, boy?'

I had no reason not to tell them. 'Debrito.'

'An Itai. And you think you're our fulfilment? You're ready to lead us – replace what we have. Is that it?'

'No.' My answer was flat. I wanted out – away from these provincial hucksters. Only the thought of Vanzetti – his dignity and courage – kept me upright.

'Then what are you here for...' It was rhetorical. Their brand of patience had ended and I was guided through a multitude of walkways and doors. I heard murmurs along the way, but nothing definitively upper class. I wondered throughout where they were taking me. And then, an injection – in my upper arm. They sat me down. There were no convulsions, just a soft, sleepy afterglow; a feeling of warmth and heaviness. My eyelids acted like bread bins, my jowls like a mashed heart. People left the room. I felt alone, yet did not have the energy to remove the bag which still arrested my view. More seconds turned and then I lost consciousness – fell from the blackened plate.

CHAPTER 10

'**H**e's coming to.'

'Yes.'

I awoke to hear voices – tones which were somehow reverberations of a surrogate family. I listened more – held out for concern and attentiveness, although my motives were clouded. I felt worn – hindered by a bout of information recently assimilated. Finally, I opened my eyes – took in the two faces before me.

My words were ingenuous: 'You only stay here at weekends...'

'I asked him over especially,' came the reply from The Leaf Blower.

'But what about your guardians?'

'They're fine,' Pendlebury eventually offered.

'And so are yours,' The Leaf Blower assured me by intervention. 'They know you're here.'

'Right,' was all I could say; the facts of the last few hours struggling to register. 'What day is it?'

'Tuesday.'

'No college?'

'Not today – a rare exemption.'

'OK.'

It felt surreal, yet uncluttered. The bad seemed to fall at the door of my mind the more I looked about.

'You were shifting, twitching – having nightmares I think. You slept right through. I went up at midnight and phoned Pendlebury this morning.'

'Somnolence.'

'Twenty hours we estimate. Are you hungry at all?'

I thought about this. My mouth wasn't as dry as I would have expected, but it did require juices of some sort. 'More…thirsty. After the fast.'

'Fast?'

'Yes. It's still with me, I think.'

I was saying things before understanding them. Handing out messages which were transcribing themselves in me.

'For what reason?'

'Why, the only reason…' The words eluded me temporarily. '…having no father.'

It seemed to shock them, or at least do something which I didn't fully comprehend.

'When will you stop?'

'Stop?'

'Yes.'

That part seemed simplistic. 'When it's resolved.'

Things went silent now, as if I had shot through their wisdom, as if their respect for my loss had muted them quite commandingly.

I got up, went to the kitchen for a glass of water, and then left. They just watched me, allowed things to unfold – didn't in any way attempt to persuade or obstruct me. There was something fateful in what I was doing, and so beyond that everything appeared extraneous.

The call to 'Castro' seemed right. It was the precursor to the showdown, the moment when I would look at my father differently, pensively, upon his return from work. When I would declare him no longer that, no longer blood nor homogeneous.

I arranged to meet my grandfather outside, next to the practice nets – away from the clusters of people and interference. He seemed elated at my suggestion, not knowing my formula or game plan – unaware of my recent lesson in family history. Golf was what infused his mind. Finally, his chance to breathe again, to live out the course with its roaming origins of heights and streams.

He raised his arms on seeing me – wide and high as if greeting me on Christmas Day. His smile seemed to polish everything dull or hazy on the horizon. And his clothes – they were redolent with sporting intent.

'The clubs are in the locker room. I'll get them.'

'So you've already signed me up?'

'I anticipated this day. Sorry if…'

'It's fine.' I was somehow mellow, now I had heard the worst. Unaffected by tiny indiscretions like my grandfather forging my membership of a 9-hole golf club. It was, all in all, humorous – something I could play on at a later date once his reputation at the club was glowing, and therefore precarious.

He returned with the clubs – the silver Swilken he had mentioned. He pulled one out – a five iron – and proceeded to swing it, shaving the grass before him.

'We should get you working with the medium irons first. There's a bit of them in both the long and short game, you see.'

He was like a boy. Coaching me had the effect of invigorating him. And although it was my grandfather's money, understanding and effort that had got us here, I felt pleasantly altruistic –

charitable in some sense.

I took hold of the iron and stepped into the net. 'Castro' placed a ball in front of me on the grass-like mat and then moved to one side. I looked at the white shell before me – its circled indentations affording it traction and grip; its coating hard yet supple. I didn't interlock my hands while gripping the club as most did, but instead chose a simple baseball grip. As I swung the club back a couple of times to gauge its weight and feel there was no advice from my grandfather – just a concentrated gaze. He wanted to check for raw talent – see me unaided, before stepping in, before honing what I had. I nudged forward a little – lined up the club with the ball. I flexed my knees because I had seen it somewhere and turned the upper part of my body into a rotator or axis-like mass; my arms forming an upside down 'V' in front of me at an angle of about forty degrees from my thighs. When, finally, I felt right, I swung the club back keeping my head poised and still. The follow-through seemed to shift the energy from my shoulders, down the shaft of the club, and onto the sweet spot of the ball. The net bulged outwardly, my right leg and 'welded' hands seemed to denote the direction of the ball and my neck shifted to allow my eyes to follow the trajectory.

It wasn't like being on the course. Everything was cut short by the protective net which offered solace to the high-handicapped waywards. Judging from the brief flight of my debut ball, however, no solace was needed – just a stretch of prime grass and bunkers. I looked at 'Castro'. He seemed dumbfounded. He was still looking ahead, down the flight path, down the five metres of grace.

Eventually: 'You have the basics. Your technique's a little unorthodox, but then so is that of Mr Ballesteros.'

I thought about this, about having the basics of anything, and being able to do *everything*. It diluted life. It gave answers which hadn't been worked for. It misled.

'I want more than the basics. I want a detailed briefing before setting out.'

He sensed something in me – something which meant we weren't quite here. 'Of course.'

I took four or five balls from him – lined them up on the mat and then bore down on them with my club. Each shot seemed wilder – more hurried – than the last. My body's poise was deteriorating; its serenity slowly folding.

'That's not it!' my grandfather shouted, appalled at my capitulation.

I carried on though – lashed out at the final two balls. Something needed hitting, my body needed to expunge the source of its angst. Around me was no longer a golf course, but a hilly purgatory, an open-air factory – at the top of which was my parents' house.

'What is it?' he asked.

I didn't stop. I just swung the club at nothing now – guided by a rage within. Being next to 'Castro' seemed to unblock the emotions that had clung to my insides.

He lunged at me – my 74-year-old grandfather; brought all his weight to bear in an attempt to contain me, to stave off the demons. We both fell to the floor, the surface of the mat, and there I started to kick out and attempt to free myself from him.

'Not to your grandfather, Arnold. Not to me,' he gently espoused.

I took his words in and stopped my shifting, my youthful display and manifestation. I was exhausted, panting and woven by a heavy air.

'What is it?' he repeated.

'He…' I faltered. I couldn't speak beyond the pronoun which was explicitly him – my father and apostate. Any mention or denotation was intolerable.
'Who? Tell me who…'

'He…' Again, I couldn't muster the words beyond the tacit identity. The second word simply jammed in my throat.

'Slow down, Arnold. There's no hurry.'

We sat up, with our feet and legs over the edge of the mat touching the bark surround; my grandfather's arm on my shoulder and his face leaning in enquiringly. My body was arched, sullen and slumped. I felt without something, weak and vulnerable.

'They weren't our liberators. Not his. He knew, you see. He knew...' I trailed off, awash with vehemence and distrust. 'Castro' watched me, but remained silent.

''77. The pardon. He had to know.'

My grandfather pulled his arm away and put his hands up to his face. 'Christ,' he muttered.

I looked at him. 'What?'

His expression took on a semi-culpable air. His eyes shielded themselves with a vacant and lost countenance. 'I knew it would come back. I told him.'

'Everyone knew?!'

'Only because he would say their names over and over again to you, in any context. We wondered who the hell they were. And so he told us.'

'And when you questioned him?'

'He.....didn't seem to think the pardon mattered.'

'No! That can't be right.'

'It's true.'

'So he's dumb, instead of a disgrace?' My father is dumb?!'

'Anything but.'

'Then why?'

'Because he needed something. He had no intention of *not* telling you about Dukakis, but it got harder. The more you latched onto the names and his original words, the more difficult it was.'

'But the seed, the original seed, was tainted. He told me....Christ, the exact words aren't there, but...'

We both went silent. I was sick. Sick of rhetoric and twisted truths. 'Castro' was defending him – the man he had always had a notable grudge against, the man whom he had so few words for. Was that it? Was the birth of the grudge Sacco and Vanzetti?

'He couldn't have thought it – that the pardon didn't matter. Why are you blockading the truth?'

'I'm not. That's what he thought, said. And I admit, it does seem implausible. You have to understand your father though – Debrito history was important to him.... more crucial than a governor's proclamation.'

'Not if that had a bearing on his telling me. Would he have hailed them *without* the pardon? It's bloody central to everything. Would he have risked our family name on a couple of dago nihilists? Because if he didn't, then the underdog is dead.'

My grandfather stared at me. There was little he could say, except: 'I've never asked him that outright. I've just assumed.'

I stood up. 'You all do it to me, don't you. Keep me in the dark. Pass over the responsibility to someone or something else. Pendlebury's uncle. And now you – my own grandfather. How could you *not* ask him? How could you let his discursiveness blow you into the gutter? Am I the only person on this planet that demands forthrightness?

'You fought over it. At some point you fought over it – I see that in you. Don't you think I notice how you speak to each other? When was it? Soon after? Three, four years? Tell me.... please.'

He looked down at the bark. He appeared stoical, yet full of emotion. 'Let's not allow this to fester, Arnold. We shouldn't wreck things - a family in its prime....'

'When, grandfather?'

'Six months. It was just six months after he told you. I thought he was weak. I told him so. There was an incredible forbearance to him though. I took it as apathy at the time, but thinking now, maybe it wasn't. Perhaps he didn't feel the need to defend himself. Perhaps he trusted something else.'

'Like what?'

'I was hard on him, Arnold. I had more spirit then – some of it blind and assuming. Your father – he was twenty years into his profession. He gave short change to big personalities. And I *was* that, I'm afraid. I was...'

'But what did he trust?'

'The divine. The ineffable. I don't know. Something outside of your everyday events.'

'God?'

'I don't know. I honestly don't. Your mother knows the man. I'm afraid I can't say the same.'

'So where now?'

'That depends on what you want to say and do.'

'I want to see him. Not today though. Not anymore. I need to be fresh. You'll let me stay?'

'Yes. But I'll phone. You were out last night as well?'

It came across as an afterthought; a probing one though. I met it with a simple and open reply: 'At Pendlebury's uncle's.'

'Is he anything like his nephew?'

'I think he is. They both seem.... honourable. Part of me seems to have awoken upon meeting them.'

'That's good. Try not to shut the other doors though.'

I didn't respond. I couldn't. Justifying myself or offering a retort seemed wrong, apprentice-like. Doors were creaking and swinging each day and only on seeing their motion live was I able to decide what was true.

'Castro' got to his feet, pulled a club from the bag, and started to swing it flowingly. 'Life is a battle to be humble. That's what I've come to reckon. All the power and ephemeral gains mean very little set against family. We're microcosms, not the dominant invincibles scientists like to think of us as. We're the earth's guests, not its masters. Your father understands that. Pendlebury understands that. Not many do though – not nearly enough. Even this golf course has its roots in control.'

Control. The word lingered – jumped at the gates of my mind. The only way to survive it was to let it batter you. The dominants – they actually believed that their reign was physical, that by possessing property and resources their hold on the earth was more convincing. Worse than this was their belief that the 'small' wanted to be 'large' and the 'slow' wanted to be 'fast', and because they weren't they needed deriding and training in *how* to look envious. Because if they didn't show resentment (not pity), or jealousy (not stupefaction), then the whole structure of life, of the last three hundred and fifty years in particular would be in danger of folding, of collapsing from the inside. They – the minnows – *had* to admire the suited 'braves' before them, the chemical-laden air around them, because it was *their* reward. Political lies too – concocted in the interests of the 'little man', for if he knew too much, life would surely be unbearable.

We returned the clubs to their locker – avoided talk where possible with the regulars eager to verse me in club mythology. I perhaps appeared rude, rushing my grandfather, wanting to get home and sit it out, to think of Wednesday and nothing more. But he knew, both my need and preference, and so waved away middle-aged efforts to entrap us with folklore and sculpted history.

We walked up the lane, past the pub in the dip and on. I still felt relatively empty from the fast, yet with only hours left I had to see it through. 'Castro' didn't know. The subject of food hadn't been mentioned. I thought of his book on Gandhi, how the division of a country and the pointless fighting that followed was a happening worthy of disgruntlement. And mine? It felt small, insignificant, yet important. There were different fasts – fasts during daylight, fasts *with* liquid, those without, fasts central to one's religion, believing that 'to be without' shows great effort and empathy. But protest fasts – they were sporadic and unbidden. Their quality was in their bending, their suppleness, their ability to strike when the need arose – alert the opposition of its inadequacies. And if it didn't work? Then you died, thought better of it or succumbed to compromise and family input.

That night I ignored the lemonade *and* the Kestrel, and pulled two small glasses from the cupboard. Tipping the book end, I looked into the syrup-like spirit, saw its richness and warm glow. Why not? I thought to myself. Why not seek comfort in the reliable? Sitting across from my grandfather, he watched me – my pathetic attempt to swallow naturally and the burning which I felt. 'It's not the way out,' he said – 'merely a look through the window.... a chance to pause.'

CHAPTER 11

I felt raggedy the next morning – uneven and nebulous due to the 'Castro' medicine. He had lit the fire. I could tell because the heat warmed the floor beneath the bed. I looked across, at the ancient clock hung on the wall. It read 7.45, and so I slowly turned the cover back and stepped onto the rug-laden surface. I sat there, my hands on my knees, the pale furnishings somehow soft and agreeable. My father's face instantly swam in front of me – its sideburn-less complexion twisting and helpless; his mien lost, yet aware of my imminent wrath. Was I to put off the showdown, the confrontation, due to these fears – fears of him shutting down or collapsing? I couldn't possibly, because it would ask again, in later years – my consciousness with its looming shadow and insistent air.

I ran the taps in the bathroom – both hot and cold – and cupped the water onto my face. It had the effect of softening me, refreshing me – providing a newly-built highway for my thoughts. Downstairs, I could hear my grandfather moving around – shuffling through the motions and perfunctoriness of another day. The noises were small and comforting – like echoes from a deeply thought out documentary. I wanted to be down there, in amongst the simplicity, and so I dabbed my face with the worn towel and descended the high, thin staircase.

He was there, in the winter room, when I opened the door – fully dressed in official senior garb: brown pants high above the waist; lime-green shirt; tobacco-coloured cardigan; episcopal socks; and wonderful, over-comfy slippers. I wished him a 'good morning' and took a seat at the table; the various marmalades and bread positioned before me in the manner of a war game.

'How do you feel?' he prompted.

I had no definite or sure answer, because I felt marginalised here in this 'retreat' – overly safe and bizarrely insulated. If anything, I suppose I felt embarrassed – foolish for being away from home. What I had to trust though was the now peremptory voice inside me which talked of parental duty and factualness.

'OK,' came the flat, yet resonant response.

He buttered himself another piece of toast from the rack. Not that he particularly wanted it, but it kept him occupied – it lessened any awkwardness. I soon finished *my* lot, of juice and more juice, and then gazed from the summer room at my parents' house, wondering how to approach him - my father, Jack, Debrito Snr.

I dressed slowly, methodically, giving myself no time to wash properly. Given that there was only one toothbrush – belonging to 'Castro' – forgoing brushing my teeth was obligatory anyway. I said goodbye in a tired and soporific way. My body seemed to take on an invisible load as soon as I stepped outside of the cottage. And the walk – all fifteen minutes of it – appeared to add further burdens, resulting in a slower passage, a delaying of me being there at 8.35 as planned.

I knew he left most mornings at a quarter to nine; the straightforward drive down the hill and into the back street of the main road shop or TV emporium, where he would park up and push to the door of the workshop which housed his bench. Some days – 'giant lulls', he called them – he would sit there *without* work, *without* the opened back of a TV, and just look around – at the tatty shelves, at the hard floor, at the permanently-live TV which was hinged high up in the corner of the room (its flashing glare pleasing my father's less able, but more passionate work mate).

I was concerned now. As I approached the house, turning onto the straight from where I would be able to view the end of the drive, I desperately looked for the front of his car (my father reversing into the drive each evening so as to make his morning exit simpler). Yes. It was there. The blue Toyota estate. His company car. My watch made it 8.44. I sped up, not wanting to miss him, not wanting to lose the momentum I had precariously built.

The front structure of the house rattled – my father's arm, angled behind him, firmly sealing the gap between frame and door. He hadn't spotted me – his mind perhaps elsewhere – and so I had to shout, do something, before he ducked into the car, started his day.

'Dad!'

'.....son...' He looked stunned, even confused as to what had befallen him. There were no words beyond his simple address. We were frozen – him unable to step inside his car and myself still feet away from the drive's different texture.

Finally, he walked towards me. 'You OK?'

'I need to talk.'

'After work then?'

'Not really. I'd prefer...'

'What is it, Arnold?'

'I need some of your time.'

'But...Hang on.'

He walked back down the drive, opened the porch door and then that of the house and called to my mother: 'Rose – tell them I'm sick. I won't be in... please, just do it... nothing, just a chat with our son...'

The house door suddenly shut with both of them out of view. I tried to listen, but nothing made it through the thick wood of the door. It was two, maybe three minutes before my father appeared again. He suggested that we drive to somewhere neutral, pleasant, conducive – somewhere away from his work and customers.

I got in – moved the seat's contents before sitting down. It was like this with a company car. There was something poetically magnificent about being surrounded by clipboards, meters, fuses, casings and the like. The smell as well – of blankets, electronic parts and velvet cushions used as makeshift polystyrene. It was old, comforting and workmanlike. And the bear-like forearms now at the side of me, horizontally hoisted up to the steering wheel, merely added to this feeling – merely added to the panic inside of me.

'Your mother's worried. She thinks it's something she's done.'

'I'll reassure her it's not.'

We were moving – driving out of town, to the outskirts, the country, to the hills that paraded so proudly. Some of my father's sentences made it easier for me, unlike his physical deportment which retained a certain brusqueness. The two, in fact – his words and physique – were sometimes in harmony, sometimes not. When they were, it was a question of which side you were on; whether you matched the soft humility that mostly exuded from him or whether you were able to be blunt, sullen and defiant.

'I don't like this, you know. However much the job irritates me – and God knows it does – taking a day off, skiving, isn't me. It's not a part of me that should be coming to the fore. Rose – your mother – 'll give me a dressing down in her sweet way…'

'But the 'giant lulls'. Isn't what you're doing now roughly the same?'

'No. Because I'm not there. I'm not *at the bench*. I'm on *my* time, not his. We have to be *seen* to be waiting – expecting work. There, on hand – a shout away.'

'And watching TV while you wait, looking around at everything and nothing – that's *necessary* is it, because TVs are the business? What you're doing therefore is admirable, keen, pioneering?'

'No. No – it's not. Where d'you get all this, Arnold, because… I don't remember bringing you up this way. The words, the sureness, this… temperament.'

'I see things. I question until the truth gives itself up. I wait for it to gladly raise its arms and come out, not harassed, but emancipated. Is that wrong?'

The car shuddered a little. My father pulled over into what

happened to be a gravelled parking area with a view of the roving fields and sparse cattle. 'It's... what I was before.'

The whistling, blanketing, semi-silence of the winds on the fields now seemed to cover us momentarily – request that we think, philosophise internally and dragoon any doubt or fearfulness away from the encounter. I looked down, at my father's clothes, as he stared ahead into the open and across the many caverns. His Hush Puppy brogues, lightly chequered pants and conservative sweater spoke of middle age, yet beyond that there was nothing – nothing to gauge or understand the depths, the unchartered mass that sat within him.

'Can't you be it again?' I asked.

'I'm forty-six, Arnold. Truth isn't a smooth, sailing ship unfortunately. Along the way I've had to put a few anchors down – satisfy demands that didn't always meet my definition. Work, marriage, family, social interaction – they all add shadows to the white beneficence you try to give out.'

'There's still a line. There must still be a line though?'

'Yes. And you try to see it. You.... try to uphold what you started out with.'

'And Sacco and Vanzetti?'

My father reacted with a dull, expressionless silence. Seconds after he opened the car door on his side, stepped out onto the gravel and routinely closed it after him. He stood with his back to me whilst looking away, perched against the bodywork and window – seemingly unperturbed or insulted by my question.

I remained seated in the car. I waited to see if he would return, across the short but testing boundary. His body, poised as it was, was somehow acting, as if rehearsals of this scene had been on-going for months, even years.

Stepping back in, he immediately put a name forward: 'So Castro has finally given you his version of events?'

'No,' I protested.

'What then? Who?' There was no anger in his voice – just the need for reconciliation.

'A book. I read a book.'

'But something, someone directed you to it?'

'Yes – you. Implicitly. Every day.'

'Good. That's good. So you've finally learnt our history.'

It didn't seem real. I had been expecting a larger defence – a wall of ironclad soldiers with swords and spears; something that would mercilessly speed things up and therefore avoid a combing of the truth.

'You don't see anything wrong with what I've discovered?'

'Wrong? That depends how you choose to interpret my knowledge at the time.'

'How should I interpret it, Father?'

'You expect me to tell you? You expect me to turn my dignity into putty?'

'I expect a straight answer.'

'Tell me, Arnold – who was your favourite? Of the characters you met – Felicani, Tresca, Thompson, Galleani – who was the one that stole you, that gripped your mind?'

'Moore. Fred Moore.'

'Without hesitation?'

'Yes. Absolutely.'

'Moore is interesting, you see. He did everything possible to help Sacco and Vanzetti. Everything. But one thing didn't please his comrades – Sacco most noticeably. That was when he offered a reward for the *real* South Braintree perpetrators. 1924, I assume, because that's when Thompson stepped in.'

'I read that. And it added to my seeing him as a remarkable man. Up there with Felicani for challenging anarchist ideals.'

'But doesn't such a stance undermine everything he stands for, namely client confidentiality?'

'No. I don't think it does. Because murder has to be the exception. Nothing can stand in the way of knowing the identity of a killer.'

'It's a whistle-blowing culture, surely though, isn't it – albeit with an extreme example.'

'Enlightenment I prefer.'

'You think you're objective, my son?'

'Put like that – no. But I'm aware of you evading my original question.'

'OK. 1977. I was disappointed at having to turn down Webster's offer. I needed something else – something to make you proud. James, as well.'

'You finished college in the spring. That was about the time of the job offer. The pardon was in August. But you only told me of Sacco and Vanzetti in the autumn. What am I to believe?'

'It doesn't look good, does it…'

There was nothing. No effort or robustness – just open acceptance of the ambiguousness. I understood my grandfather's frustration, his accusations of weakness toward my father. But then, why should my father dissect five months of his life as part of a trial not of his making? Perhaps because he had to be Fred Moore and William Thompson *himself* (along with the Galleanisti), yet this time win out – walk his clients free of the chair.

'There's something Jewish in your...' - (I thought of my grandfather's word) – '...forbearance. We're all shooting you, walking you to the gas chambers, yet you remain tolerant as if something higher will step in... take your spirit.'

He looked at me now with intent as if during the course of my rambling I had finally verbalised what he had been hoping for – waiting on. 'Is that so bad?'

Despite my own spiritual awakening, I suppose I wanted my father to have none of it – to prioritise human justification at the expense of profundity. More importantly, to prioritise me rather than a god. 'If you dispel the need to explain yourself then I can only interpret guilt.'

'Humanity's greatest flaw: speaking for the silent. Thinking it – above all else – has the answers.'

I felt distant now. Pushed away. Culpable in some sense. I assumed my father didn't feel the need to tell his own son of events crucial to his upbringing. Humility had seemingly got the better of him. Indeed, it had embarrassed him whilst metamorphosing into sanctimony. I had expected him to rejoice somehow in my keenness – take delight in my staunch interest. But no – I sensed none of this. Worse still, he appeared intent on wrecking parts of my understanding, my interpretation of the particulars of the case. It was as if Sacco and Vanzetti now represented something he could no longer aspire to and, because of that, pieces of the defence such as Fred Moore had to be lambasted.

Suddenly, from the silence encircling the car, my father spoke up again: 'Why would I keep mentioning them? Why would I say "Sacco and Vanzetti" eight, nine, ten years on if I wanted you to forget... if I would rather bury the wrong, the damage? Do you think by repeating their names I stood a chance of erasing such history? I was lodging it in your consciousness almost every day.'

I hesitated. 'You're still asking though. I need you to tell me. Just tell me – give me the dates. When did the Sacco and Vanzetti seed enter your head?'

'No. You're getting nothing more. Understand, Arnold. *Bloody* understand.'

I was afraid of an elaborate bluff. Repetition had the potential of merely compounding the original, lank, pretence. I couldn't possibly say this to him and so it sat there, still, in my mind. I started to breathe more heavily. Fumes from the previous night fired themselves up through my throat. I felt dirty and hungry – disappointed and hollow. All my thoughts of the last two years – the more weighty, finer concoctions – seemed to disband and run free from my mind. I was no longer seventeen. Instead a post-pubescent scrawl occupied my head and dallied with my efforts at intelligence.

'You've been drinking with him?'

'Who?'

'Your grandfather.'

'Yes. A little.'

'A look through the window?'

'Don't do that. Don't make him out to be a clichéd caricature – an old, left-wing bastard. You don't know each other…'

'You're right.'

He could be calm. Most of the time he was calm, yet it was somehow more galling. I wanted to reach the end soon, but this placidness merely subverted my drive forward.

'Why am I right? Why are you bowing out?'

'Because it's already become something I didn't want it to.'

'Control. I never had you down as needing it. I assumed you were happy to let the show run at its own pace…'

'I have discipline, Arnold, and restraint. They're not the same. Can we end this now?'

The question strengthened his sense of fairness. It hung in the air politely hoping that *I* would escort it to its rightful partner. 'Yes,' I obliged, not wanting to go on – not wanting to sever the family ties that I knew were already threadbare.

He drove home. Conversation became a cipher – a nonentity or tacit transcript between our respective facial twitches. I half admired the view outside whilst having him there – my father – in the panoramic sweep before me. I caught his expression exuding a ghostliness and pallid disfunctionality. I felt, during the course of the moving minutes, that my actions had somehow pillaged him of his entrails or hollowed him out in a way quite unthinkable. I attempted to speak, to show a courteous hand, but my body whimpered – unable, through its deportment, to execute the slightest concession. I knew my thoughts and temperament to be wayward and intractable, yet something had lifted them beyond everyday compromise. It was as if there was a guiding or destructive hand orchestrating, choreographing; a hand fused with my mind and its polymorphic understanding of the world.

Upon stopping, outside of the modest semi-detached home that was my parents', my father asked kindly if I would inform my mother of his intention to go to work. I acceded and then stood on the pavement while he drove away quite sombrely. The meeting or confrontation hadn't thrown up what I had hoped for. Instead, it had seemingly darkened every corner of the relationship between my father and I. I concentrated on this while walking to the door. I tried to extract a semblance of level-headedness from the political mix. And then – my mother's face came into view. Her angst-ridden look demanded something which I wasn't in a position to give.

'Where's he gone?'

'To work.'

'Will you tell me what…'

'Not now. Please. Later.'

I bounded upstairs – didn't wait for a further cue. Removing my outer garments inside my now sealed bedroom, I immediately felt lighter. Turning the cover back, I rolled into the single, Trappist-like bed and then covered everything but my face. Staring up at the ceiling, I felt protected – shorn of possessions, yet complete. The cool linen beneath me transcended the discomfort of the last two days. I was home, albeit semi-incarcerated, yet the planet's energy and information output seemed manageable. Yes. It was manageable from here; here, as if a personal coma was capable of halting the useless churn of traffic, machinery and lies.

Two or three hours in, I heard knocking – the rhythmic tap of my mother's bent forefinger. She slowly opened the door and entered cautiously with a tray full of soup and bread. I instantly thought of my fast as she placed the food on the cabinet beside me. I also thought of the worry that she projected – of its inability to rest or wander leadless; the need it had to find reassurance and serenity.

'I thought I'd rustle us up a small winter dish.'

'Thanks,' was all I could say, as if in the presence of a nurse – as if a form of temperance had gripped me.

'You'll take a spoonful while I'm here?'

I sensed in her a desperate need to see me eat, a motherly hue which had maybe been coloured by 'Castro'. I didn't resent it. I couldn't possibly resent it. And so, I took hold of the spoon and shifted its brimming contents toward me – my arm acting like a crane swinging across a deserted scrubland.

It felt good. It tasted wholesome – pure. I followed it up with a lunge of the bread into the tomato red pool now before me. I was grateful to them – 'Castro' and my mother – for showing tact, for not barnstorming my head with urban regulations.

'Good. Good,' my mother said. 'I'll leave you in peace then.'

Seconds later I heard the pips of the phone. I imagined her and my grandfather talking easily – confiding in each other, showing relief. I knew she wouldn't phone my father because he would have to step out of the workshop and into the front; he would have to leave the relative privacy of his bench for the no-man's-land of invasive ears and customer parsimony.

I eventually placed the tray back on the cabinet after hurriedly but somehow tentatively finishing off its contents. I then closed my eyes, dreamed – took great delight from the mid-afternoon wanderings of my mind. The feeling of completeness was unparalleled. It seemed to suspend any sense of worry or anxiety, whilst clothing my omniscient silhouette in fine, radical garments.

After a while, the thick black line dominating my vision seemed to melt – fall down on me as if dissolving into my bloodstream. I lay there, strangely ready, strangely prepared to face my fears – knowing that I could return to semi-unconsciousness, to an innate garden of delight.

CHAPTER 12

We were walking, to college. Pendlebury had surprised me by calling round – anticipating my eagerness for routine. He talked, of nothing much, of the spring – our future. I told him, of the careful manoeuvring between my father and I – the polite exterior which had developed but could never last.

'My uncle says keep a log. Of everything you now do. Not specifically in relation to J.D., but so that your future, your history matches the non-meritocratic mould. People may need to know one day. They might want to pin a certain asset or defect to a key decision you made. What direction you took. What you decided to read. What films you grew to love. What character traits you admired in people. What music you listened to. What politics – if any – you had….now have. What countries you wish to visit and why…'

I listened to him, his extrapolation, his heedful words. He continued in the same manner until the old church came into view – the college which we were affiliated with. He then, upon seeing its granite exterior, descended into self-consciousness.

'Everything OK now' - I nodded – 'in there?'

'Better. A little better. I'm still ignored though. Par for the course.'

'Just four months, aye.'

'Yeh. You don't mind if I….'

The request in his eyes was that he walk on ahead – enter the building without me. I was surprised that his non-diplomatic finery had been evidently infiltrated or purged. 'No,' was my automatic response, my rejoinder, yet behind it chagrin and disappointment stalked and wandered.

I followed him in. Left about ninety seconds between us. It felt stupid, unnecessary – everything I had been turning away from. The mustard-coloured plaster met my eyes instantly. I walked past it and along the outer corridor of the main rooms. It was still early. I arrived in the common room with fifteen minutes to spare. There were six or seven people dotted around – each unerringly positioned with their chairs facing the entrance. They looked at me with an intimidatory squint – an expression sculpted by boredom and E-laden foods.

'Here he is,' one of them announced.

I recognised him straight away as one of the POs or petty officers. The very same member who had taken my cue in denouncing 'Twig', thus shifting the focus from Pendlebury.

'Where have you been, Debrito?' another one asked.

'He's been to London to see the Queen!'

'Yeh – the Queen… or *queen*.'

It was whimsical, capricious – almost rehearsed. Their ricocheting words seemed to induce an acrid laughter among the ranks.

'Let this court begin,' the taller, evidently sturdy PO pronounced. 'Escort him to the dock.'

I was stood a few feet from the entrance, reluctant to take a seat, reluctant to move at all from this vantage point. 'I'm *in* the dock,' I replied firmly, as two cohorts approached me.

'He's *in* the dock,' the SPO voiced with a certain irony and indifference. 'Let him be.'

They backed off – didn't attempt to question the edict of their 'leader'. Had they grabbed my arms, I sensed I would have done something, but the thought passed through my mind at haste.

'OK. Silence in court… Arnold Debrito - you are charged with a crime against your fellow man. A terrible crime which warrants the highest form of punishment. As such you will not be afforded a defence team.'

The kangaroo court was beginning to oil its wheels. I remained standing – my inertia complying to a degree with their 'show', their shockingly semi-erudite performance.

'Bring in the first and only witness!'

I turned to face an adjoining door to my right. It swung open and through it came three individuals, the middle of which was Pendlebury. They had handcuffed his wrists behind his back, tied a neckerchief around his open mouth and head, and draped a pink, feather boa around his shoulders. I felt sick. I wanted to dive in – wrestle the bastards to the floor – but I knew it would be futile. And so I watched, intensely – my face almost unmoved, yet my mind jarring itself against my skull.

There were hoots, jeers and cackles directed at him – Pendlebury. It was ugly, uncontrollable – everything one fears when in amongst a group of bandits and charlatans. Finally, after the ridiculing - the prosaic and degenerative screams – the tertiary charm of the SPO surfaced once more.

'You, my man – you're counsel for the witness? You'll speak on his behalf?'

The question was directed to one of Pendlebury's 'gaolers' who, in this farcical setting, also happened to be his brief or adviser.

'I will, your honour. But what I have to say isn't easy.'

Further laughs erupted. It would have been easy to overlook the malevolent and baleful thread which gently pierced each part of the room, yet it was here – real; its ragged cotton burning against the limbs of Pendlebury.

'Take your time,' came the SPO's response.

'Yes. Well. It's pretty straightforward. My client would like to say that this man' – he pointed to me – 'buggered him on Monday night.'

'Why might he – the innocent man – be bound then?'

'For his own protection, your honour. We fear an act of revenge.'

'Wise. Debrito! Could you run through, for the court, the foreplay that preceded this?'

I was speechless, statuesque. My whole bearing railed against the tired game before me.

'Debrito!'

Two fingers on my right hand suddenly twitched and so I simply raised them in the direction of the SPO, all the while silent and perhaps mercurial to the expectant group.

'If you won't show willing or beg for pity, then you must suffer…'

I looked ahead into his eyes, but it was as if he was addressing those around him. In a matter of seconds he had signalled something to them.

'In Middle Eastern countries they stone the accused. Here, we have a different slant.'

Each cohort pulled a book out from beneath his chair – mostly hardback – and clasped it between his hands while now standing. They then seemed to position the base of the spine between their fingers and thumb – the book itself at an angle.

'Last chance,' the SPO warned.

I could have reversed, ran – after all, I still had a clear exit behind me. I could have attempted to divide the followers with an impassioned and suitably brutish speech, yet the only thing that filled me was a strange listlessness – a bequeathing of my reactionary impulse.

I *did* protect myself. When the swirling books came at me, I naturally covered my face and head. I found myself moving closer and closer to the throwers as it continued, until… I faced one of them – just twelve inches between our noses. He looked unsure, but then drew back his fist – his whole body – and launched his compressed hand at my cheek.

I took it. The bitter pain shot through me. And then, a word –
certainly not of my choosing – surfaced from my insides: 'Again!'

He repeated his action, this time a little more hesitantly.

I moved myself – shifted my body – around the group, imploring
each cohort to hit me. 'Again! Again!' They did – some of them
two or three times – but I seemed to be draining them. Each hit at
my battered face seemed to entrench them in a muddied
conscience; a state further on than their original blindness. As the
pain began to take effect and the blood appeared before my
eyes, I caught a last swirling look at the group. They were partly
encircled around me, each looking in as if curious of the effect of
their actions, yet also culpable and apologetic in the same gaze.
All except two; two of the nine bodies near to me which had to be
restrained because they were intent on proving their worth, their
obstinacy by wrestling with pacifism itself.

Pendlebury had disappeared from sight. As the last throes of my
awakened mind ebbed, I made out the SPO being held back,
spitting with rage and fury – his tertiary charm now a casked
prisoner bereft of influence. And then – nothing. Just darkness. I
seemed to swim above my body – only the whites of the eyes
below me visible, through the anomie of the room. I stayed there,
watching, trying to understand the moving incandescence
below, the interaction in the ranks of the specious 'cool'.

There was panic – a desperate need to reverse the damage, to
make everything light and innocent again. The different voices
each clamoured for direction: 'Fuck – he's out'; 'Christ – do
something, man'; 'What?! What do we do?'; 'Roll him on his side!';
'Unkymmm...' The latter murmur was from outside the circle.
'Pendlebury! Get the cuffs off him! Let him help out...' '*Where's*
the fucking key?' 'Here!'

I couldn't make out who was who. I couldn't see myself, probably
because my eyelids were closed. Something moved though and
then bent itself in the centre of the room. I assumed he –
Pendlebury – was attending to me, assessing things, weighing up
what to do, although I felt nothing. My body was weightless and
elsewhere – here above them. He spoke: 'An ambulance... call

for an ambulance. *Now!*

The spatial scene altered. The planetary eyes passed through black holes and then formed a different elliptical orbit. There seemed to be gases in and around them – atoms too weak to hold their position, to guide this collective and ramshackle group toward saving me.

Pendlebury though – I recognised his presence now, his steadiness. He had come to replace the SPO. He had stepped into the centre without the need for sublimity or honour. His body language exuded grace and maturity.

The others finally stilled themselves. One of them announced that the ambulance was on its way, after being followed in by two of the college staff. What occurred next perhaps didn't interest me, because I drifted away – no longer within earshot, no longer above them and myself. I imagined – quite vividly – the remonstrations from within the group after the inevitable witch-hunt or vilification from the adults. Who was responsible for this horrendous attack? Who would even contemplate such terror? If not one of you, then *all* of you.

Of course, this went beyond the walls of the old church. It was criminal and proceedings would maybe follow. As to the extent of those proceedings, my survival was at their hub.

CHAPTER 13

Hazy. Unclear and hazy, apart from the prominent clock on the whitewashed wall. I blinked several times but the fuzz or semi-concussion wouldn't leave me. I knew there to be four bodies or people sat around me, yet their identities remained translucent and shadowless.

I felt two of them immediately move and then within seconds a rush of lighter images strode towards the bed. 'Arnold? Can you hear me, Arnold?'

The words echoed around my head. I knew that I was supposed to respond, but it was difficult. Tentatively, I raised my eyelids again – my heavy eyes and sore face flinching slightly, preferring the blackness of sleep.

Still, the distorted view tested me. It asked that I hold and wait – slowly build up one face and then another. And so I did. I concentrated my weak stare on the near image to my right – the standing presence of what appeared to be a woman. I immediately focused on her eyes and as I did I caught a softness in her through her smell and light touch. I wished that I could wake to her each day – her concern and genuineness. I wished a lot of things as her skin roamed across my face and neck. If one was to fall ill only once a year, then this – she – was ample reason to serenade life again.

'Take it easy with him.'

Her words lingered longer than her physical bearing. They introduced me, in part, to my family camped around the steel edge of the hospital bed. I could now make them out: my mother, father, James and 'Castro'; the latter two at the foot of the bed (my father to my left, my mother to my right).

'How d'you feel, Arnold?'

I looked at her, my mother, and around at the others. They

seemed to hang on me producing an audible note of any length or deportment. 'I ache,' was my succinct reply.

'You took a hell of a beating,' 'Castro' commented.

'It's over now though. And we're pulling you out. No son of mine works in a mad house.'

They tried to stem their obvious intrigue, their propensity to reach a swift conclusion via a volley of nimble exchanges. The silence that followed my mother's words was for me. It covered us all like a shell; the entrapped vacuum of wind somehow able to describe things beyond its own locality. I listened briefly and watched. Of particular interest was James. I was able – through the beseeching silence – to concentrate and understand his actual thoughts as he sat there pensively. I had inconvenienced him. There had been a deadline, an essay and my 'setback' had proved to be a vexation. He appeared restless – pleased in one sense, yet pressured in another; slightly indignant at my mother's expectant summon.

I caught her now – her face upon him as if aggrieved by his 'wanderings'. She signalled for them to stand and move over to near the door. They did so, politely, leaving my father and 'Castro' looking lost and uncomfortable.

I overheard their tete-a-tete, their private pourings: 'What is it?' 'Nothing – I've just got quite a bit of work...' 'But this is your brother.' 'I know it's my brother. I know.' 'Then just a day or two. James?' 'It's difficult – there're deadlines. Things like this don't hold any weight.' 'Well they should do – has the world gone mad?' 'No. Yes. Perhaps.' 'So you're leaving?' 'I could lose a year. If I don't get back, I could lose a year.' 'You could lose a brother.' 'He's OK. He'll be OK. Don't play that on me when you know it's not true.' 'It's still early. The doctors have to keep a watch. Concussion can be erratic.' 'I *do* have to go. I don't want to, but I *have* to.' 'What you're doing isn't right...' 'No.'

Following James' onerous admittance, he stepped back across the ward to the bed, leant over and kissed me on the forehead. He then muttered a doleful 'Sorry' in my ear and was gone. I looked at the remaining family members. Each had their own thoughts on the 'desertion'. 'Castro', I sensed, understood. My father didn't want to be seen as railing against my mother and so gave off an expression of hurt and despondency. And my mother – for all her words and sincerity, I sensed disillusionment not with James but with the wider structures of life.

Later (I didn't know the day and had not bothered to ask) I awoke to find them splayed out around me – each attempting, against the odds, to find comfort in the plastic chair beneath them. My slight movements, my aches, seemed to disturb them. 'Castro', my mother, my father all looked up and I had one question for them: 'What happened to the people that did this?'

'People?' my mother responded, as if surprised. '*Person* you mean?'

'No. People. There were seven or eight. What…'

'But… it was…'

'Castro' stepped in. 'Pendlebury was taken. He didn't deny his involvement. The others did.'

'But that's him. Don't you see – that's him. He hates diplomacy. He tries to let the truth struggle on its own – without assistance, without intervention.'

'But the police – they seem sure,' my mother attested. 'There are witnesses.'

'I'm the only valid witness. The others are… Christ, I thought they'd learnt something.'

'We need some clarity here, Arnold,' my father asserted. 'You're saying that Pendlebury had no involvement?'

'He was the reason… the reason why I took the beating. They tied him up and so I offered myself as a target to appease them, to deflect their efforts.'

They looked at each other quizzically. 'Well – he's due. The policeman's due – here.' They checked their watches. 'In fifteen minutes.'

It was Sacco and Vanzetti all over again, with Pendlebury inducing a consciousness of guilt. And I? Who was I? I tried to think. I was the paymaster, dead, with no recourse other than the stench from my rotting corpse. I was one of the twenty Italian witnesses who had seen Pendlebury on the day of the first crime selling eels, only for my testament to reek of bias and collusion. Finally, I was Fred Moore, exhausted by too much truth in a world turning increasingly to public relations – image packaged as legitimacy.

I thought of The Leaf Blower now – his obvious deficiencies when dealing with the establishment, his sad history following the death of his sister-in-law. And Pendlebury – to lose him again would finish him. I pictured him at the station, in the cheap, wooden parlour which you begged to get beyond, which stood at the base of the snakes and ladders board. There, trying to communicate with a head of short, bristled hair whose priority was liver pate sandwiches.

'One of you. Please go. Pendlebury's uncle – he'll be at the station. He's deaf. He may need help.'

'Castro' immediately got up. 'What about his parents?'

'*Guardians*. I don't know. His uncle is the blood line though. Go to *him*.'

'I will. I'll go.'

I expected a modicum of protest from my mother, something about mixing with the accused, but it failed to materialise. They sat there – her and my father – like the only two people left in a bomb shelter, waiting, waiting.

Eventually, he came. And when I saw the face, his Roman eyes, I felt nauseous. I blinked. I had to be wrong. Again, I looked, but the same face pirouetted its way towards me.

'Mr and Mrs Debrito. Arnold.' The greeting was pleasant, but then I would have expected a guise marinated in fake benevolence and oniony professionalism.

My father stood up and offered his hand. 'Jack. Rose, my wife.' His introductions were respectful and well-meaning.

The Roman pulled my father to one side without the slightest effort, as if schooled in organising people and their tacit desires for the wider good. He spoke softly of the need to see me alone initially – to try and glean some sense from the 'unfortunate event'.

My father, of course, bowed out. He signalled to me that he would be outside, down the corridor. There was no reason to doubt the silver-buttoned law man before him, no reason to think that he may be at the hub of a power conspiracy.

I looked up now, as he approached the pillow-end of the bed. His frame seemed to dominate the whole room with its doom-laden presence and castigating armaments.

'I don't want you this close,' were my words, before I'd thought of them.

'As you wish,' he replied, backing off with an intentionally neutral smile.

I waited. I decided not to commit in any way. He seemed to weigh up the surroundings, develop an unusually keen interest in the cupboard to my right.

'They're not ideal, are they. Hospitals.'

I said nothing. I would hear him out – see where he was going.

'I mean, the same, same, same in the wards. The ubiquitous furniture. The labelling of everything now. Then again, it helps to universalise things.'

I could see that he was content – content to push an agenda which suited the few. His use of the word 'ubiquitous' was almost ugly – contrived days, even weeks before the incident, and begging to be uncaged.

'Are you in the former or the latter camp?' came his *raison d'etre*, his assured juxtaposition.

I ignored him and simply stared in an effort to unsettle him.

'That's part of the problem, you see. Silence. We can only construe it as subversiveness. Pendlebury isn't helping himself. You're not helping him. What am I to think?'

'Were you selected for this case?' As I said it, I saw in him Michael Stewart, the Bridgewater police chief. What if Pendlebury and I were deemed modern-day anarchists. What if the whole college thing had been orchestrated by this, this... Roman, sixty seven years on.

'We're not Scotland Yard, Arnold. Chances are I'll be involved in most local fracas.'

'You think this was a fracas? You don't think it was premeditated in some way?'

'I was hoping you'd tell me.'

My hope was that I was wrong. That my mind had been dancing with paranoia, for days, even weeks. The Roman – all I had on him was his warning me off from an unsafe part of town, his steely gaze which was standard for the job. It was nothing. My dream, of course, had tunnels and people being forcibly drugged, yet it was just that – a dream, a blind projection.

'We know each other,' I prompted.

'From the other night. Yes.' His reply was sure – undaunted by the surface suspicion in me.

'That doesn't have any bearing on this case?'

'No. Not at all.' Again, his answers were quick, textbook-like, almost Pendlebury-esque in their equanimity.

'You can't really think that my own friend would have done this?'

'The problem is I can't assume anything. Pendlebury, in particular, was thought to be a loner by the college staff. To think otherwise would be to broaden the picture.'

'And loners are naturally dangerous. The very word is pejorative – the noun regularly trodden on by our glorious six o'clock bulletin.'

He hadn't missed it – my caustic aside wrapped up in a dissenting skin. In fact, his words seemed to play along: 'Loners should be judged in the same way a family man would be. I certainly won't be encouraging or even standing for any victimization or vigilante-ism.'

'We should broaden the picture then.'

He pulled out his notepad and I began. I told him of the awkwardness from day one – how Pendlebury had been excluded from even the slightest cultural bent within the walls of the church. I told him of my own fecklessness in seeking acceptance rather than standing side by side with the public pariah. And then I told him of the meetings – the chinwags which we thought to be clandestine, the chinwags which far exceeded the dried up spoutings of youthful cliquishness. I added my obvious disappointment that teachers largely seemed to be a breed of callow, insular Punchinellos.

We talked further, about subjects I hadn't anticipated, about life in all its furore. I hadn't expected it. I hadn't envisaged the man's desire for detail – truthful detail. He seemed 'of the day' – very different to when I had first met him among the cold shadows of town. In the end, it came down to an off-the-record comment (his pad now firmly embedded in his jacket pocket): 'How far do you want to go with this?'

'I'm not sure.'

'It's like this, Arnold. Pendlebury is released as soon as I radio through. As for the others... speaking professionally, we should haul them before the courts – shit them up a little. They've got slight provocation, but nothing else. As for the real world which you may want to go back to, well, I'd expect your standing to be that little bit higher. I'd also expect a kind of immunity to fall over both of you after what's happened. I'm not saying forget their actions. I'm saying that this has bought you the higher ground. You're Gandhi, for god's sake. When they next look at you and realise you rode it – the whole thing – they'll wonder what kind of armour you have.'

The talk was a little bit bullish, expectant, but I understood. 'Four months,' I shrugged.

'Good. Good,' he countered. 'I'll try and tell your parents.'

I heard the expletives coming from the corridor straight away. I knew my parents took scant comfort from psychological warfare or prudent analysis when the suffering was their own or that of their family's. The word 'horseshit' seemed to trundle through again and again. My father was clearly agitated, refusing to run the strategic gauntlet. 'Concussion,' he bellowed. 'You expect me to sit on this knowing that a mob of eight youths... well, I won't!'

The conversation became muffled then – the Roman leading my father closer and closer to the hospital exit. My mother, I could see, remained. She looked on as they disappeared from view. Entering the ward again, she approached the bed. 'He's unusually tense over this, Arnold. I don't know quite what to say. Are you sure what the officer's suggesting is what you want?'

I looked at her – all 125lbs. She was clearly torn. It was Ormerod all over again, except this time she knew and was in a position to act, to force a little retribution. My father soon followed and immediately stood at her side – his woollen sweater brushing against her.

'It's down to you, Arnold, but I hope you'll let us prosecute...'

I sensed in him a compensatory gesture, an attempt to wipe out the grey area in relation to Sacco and Vanzetti. Had he or hadn't he known? The thought still choked around inside me. 1977. Spring. August. Autumn. The telling me came last. But the seed – when?

'I need to talk to you alone.'

He hesitated. 'Is that OK, Rose?'

'Of course,' my mother agreed, looking slightly wounded and rejected.
Once she had left – wandered to the drinks machine – my father opened: 'What's this about, Arnold? Why exclude your mother?'

'I'll prosecute if you tell me.'

'Tell you what?'

'I think you know.'

His face displayed an instant pallidness. He was uncomfortable, discomfited. 'I thought we'd agreed not to revisit this.'

'I know, but it's holding me back.'

'This is manipulative though. It's the wrong way of doing things.'

'I don't see a good or right way. You refuse to give me my history – say whether Sacco and Vanzetti had been a sure bet or not.'

He knew that more words would compromise him – further the debate when he had already decided its end point. And so he simply watched me – looked above me and around at the walls.

I continued. 'The reprieve needn't have been given. It didn't matter. History could have judged them guilty. I just needed to know – *need* to know – that it was foresight on your part. That you were committed.'

'I can't do it. You're, in effect, suggesting that I'm a TV man fundamentally instead of a radio man – that my silence is somehow visual and manifest. Understand, Arnold, that my view of *you* is on the line as well.'

'I confess to not having thought about it that way.' I didn't know whether my words were meaningful or sardonic. They seemed to unfossilize though – scrape themselves from an imaginary rock face and suspend our chatter with their sagacity.

There was no way forward now, except for me to break something that was already tenuous. I could see that my father was still concerned for my health and so he unpretentiously pulled up a chair and sat in silence, on an empty frequency band. My mother would follow shortly. She would be perturbed that Jack had not gone in search of her, but that was small indeed to the reaction I expected from her tomorrow or the day after.

I would tell them of my leaving – the necessity I felt in wanting to 'take to the road'. Not in a literal sense, because I didn't feel the Kerouacian pull, but .... Addressed to them both, I would mention the imminent job and how I wished to attempt independence with its rigours and rewards. Privately, to my father, I would tell him of my need to find a history – one which I could see with my own eyes and have no doubts over; one which didn't rely on a dubious vicariousness. Whether he would be offended or not had to be discounted from my thoughts. The salient concern was ten or fifteen years on. The long term. The future as architect of a benign history.

CHAPTER 14

When I asked him, in the winter room, if I could move in, 'Castro' at first eyed me curiously. 'This is because of *them* – the anarchists. Your father refuses to play ball?'

'He does. But it's more than that. I need space. You're somehow more... neutral.'

'This makes things awkward, Arnold. I have a daughter who happens to be your mother. Have you told her of your plans?'

'No. I've told no one.'

'Then tell her properly – be courteous – and make an appointment with me afterwards. I won't have it said that I came between mother and son. I can't offer anything for certain, but if you're intent on this course then I'll listen to the full facts – facts which include your parents' emotions.'

'OK,' I acknowledged, suddenly aware of my polygamous-sounding stance, aware of the semi-treacherous hold I had.

'Castro' began to pad the end of his pipe with the pouched tobacco to his left. It was ritual, calming and without it his grandfather status risked decline. He then struck a solitary match and hovered it over the nest-looking creation whilst seemingly slapping his lips against each other and the pipe's slender mouth in an effort to start the fire. It began to smoulder and so he blew out the match and threw it onto the side table. 'This Leaf Blower fellow. I like him,' he commented, after his first drag.

'Why's that?' I asked.

'Because of what he does. I mean – blowing leaves. To some, it would seem futile. To him, however, it's a craft – therapeutic and melancholic all at once. In a way he's grappling with nature's autumn speech – its epitaph. Yet in another sense he's helping to bury its dead – take the fallen and crisp foliage off to recycling or wherever. Clean paths though. Give civilisation its 5%. No more.

'He smokes as well. We can compare pipes. There must be twenty years between us, but... bugger it. He's a good man, I sense – much better than me. He said I could walk with him if he's in the area. Not just the leaves you understand, but does tend to work on his own whatever the job.'

There was a renewed excitement in my grandfather – one which was slowly finding its feet again five years after my grandmother's death. 'I'm glad,' I said. 'But don't shut the other doors.'

He looked at me in full appreciation of the irony. His expression seemed to suggest that the other doors had been wide open for years, yet no one had bothered, or when they had seen him his occasional obnoxiousness had come to the fore thus etching out his lonely fate.

'I talk to her, you know, Arnold – your grandmother. I'm not ashamed to say that. Everyone knows that she softened me – gave me a contentment which is irreplaceable. I'm not one to speed through mourning really. I think...'

He blinked a long blink and I saw his eyes changed and watery. He continued so not to forget his line: 'I think haste is man's biggest crime. Rushing to nowhere. To mammon. We're all beginning to feel it, but I see the new generations filled with an ugliness that I can't describe.'

All I could do was listen, because he had articulated part of what I had already seen. He had fired one of the many warning shots which would serve as harbingers or be blanketed and ignored. I left soon after. Went home. Sat at the dining table with my parents intent on telling them. I was fearful though. I preferred normality – at least within these walls. I looked at them. Each had a different happiness. My mother, quite patently, celebrated the family. Our very presence was enough because it filled the room – it offered safe tangents to her functions within the house. My father, besides his continual courting and worship of Rose, had his radios – the kindred politeness of their airwaves. I would often catch him, eyes closed, listening – letting Radio 4's audible refinement sweep over him, almost push him into a different world. But then – flashes of light, TVs like daleks; his consciousness semi-drowned by the sensory overload, the mauling of people's minds with a vapid set of pixols.

Thirty years. It was hard to evaluate. He had had the soles of his shoes fixed last year by a man in the market place who limped. "29 years," the man had said to my father. "I've been doing this for 29 years." They had immediately struck up a rapport – a rapport which was to fade, because despite their sameness, their equal commitment to their respective professions, my father no longer exuded happiness. Three decades had pilfered his soul, unlike the sanguine shoe man who corrected people's walk, their deportment even. My father, introspective and pensive, had thought about this. What did *he* correct? People's ability to have their minds asundered or usurped. He had to tell himself that he quashed the loneliness of old ladies by re-engaging them with the world's goings on – events too distant for their frail bodies to reach. 'Just try and stick to the news. The news and documentaries,' he often told them, unbending himself from the box in the corner of their living room and in the process breaking his employer's code of ethics: thou shall not pass opinion on the preferences of others. 'Daytime TV will kill you,' he often smiled, with the double-bluff of a man wishing to cover his tracks, wishing to softly pronounce or indeed *de*nounce the nefarious leanings of television.

And so now, with everything I respected about my father – and everything I adored about my mother – I had to tell them. Tear up and destroy the remaining thirteen years of an unofficial contract my father didn't expect me to see out, but certainly hoped I would utilise until the age of twenty one or twenty three.

'I've decided to move out,' I hesitantly scripted, in between my mother passing round the desert bowls for 'afters'.

'What do you mean?' she instantly replied, in an unbelieving fashion which assumed I meant a weekend at Pendlebury's or somewhere else with the word 'permanent' gouged out of its handbook.

'I suppose I want to become an adult.'

'But you can do that here. You can do that here, Arnold.' Her words were almost shaking. They sounded wretched and inconsolable. 'Tell him, Jack.'

My father partly opened his mouth, but failed to conjure anything up. I suddenly noticed he was more emotional, more fraught than my mother. His face began to twitch. He removed his commanding hands and forearms to beneath the line of the table as if unable to keep them still and calm. I noticed the disappointment in my mother – the questioning stare as if my father had let her down, as if he had missed their one chance to 'retain' me.

'What are your plans?' he eventually asked.

My mother's thoughts chimed out: you're moving it *on* a stage. Such a question concedes the early ground. Jack! You're losing it! You're losing us the fight – our son!

'Nothing definite yet. But I think I'd maybe like to stay with Grandad for a while. He needs the company.'

'So this is purely a charitable act?' my mother pointedly asked.

'No. I just think that some valuable time together would do us both no harm.'

'And college – what about that?'

'I'll return in a few days.'

'Arnold! The risks. You should be here. There'll be something else.'

'He's decided, Rose, that he's old enough. We have to stand by that.' My father's words were sure, yet somehow traitorous to his real convictions. He appeared steadier, but absent – impaled by the stubborn line he had taken with regard to his knowledge of Sacco and Vanzetti.

'Give up then. We give up? Let him get beaten again. And live like a gypsy. We need you here, Arnold. Don't we, Jack? Don't we…'

My father hung his head and shook it marginally from side to side. He wasn't signalling a negative response to Rose, but rather his cul-de-sac thoughts, his despair at the situation.

'Does my father know you're planning to colonise his house?'

'No. He doesn't.'

'So if he doesn't agree, you'll stay?'

'I don't know. I hadn't thought beyond the cottage.'

'But you must. You'll need a nest egg. Something to start you off. How else will you afford it?'

'Let me speak to Grandad first.'

The desert remained untouched – a fruit flan whose server was effectively on strike until my future was resolved. I looked at it - its shiny apparel and moreish base – wishing that everything was normal and that we were devouring it slowly.

'You can't play us off like this, Arnold. You expect me to sit here until your grandfather gives you a yes or a no. I'll phone him myself.'

She got up with the intention of walking into the hall, but my father put his arm around her midriff stopping her in her tracks. 'We can't demand certain things of him anymore, Rose. Let him think it through. Don't intervene.'

'But he's too young. Look what they did to him.' The bruises and cuts on me were still apparent; their manifestation increasing my mother's anxiety. She started to rap her clenched fist against my father's thick shoulder. 'We'll lose him next time, Jack. I know we will.'

I hadn't realised how much she had been affected by it all. I became slightly ashamed of my hurried plans. What if, I thought, there was a compromise. What if I could somehow wait – appease my mother's concerns.

'I'll ask Grandad if I can move in when I start the new job. Until then I'll stay, but I *have* to go to college. The slightest fracas and I agree to pull out.'

They looked at each other – my mother searching for some sense along the contours of my father's features. He gripped her more tightly, reassuring her, silently confirming that I would be OK.

'Why now though? That's what I don't understand. Why now, Jack?' she asked, with her face turned away, speaking of me in the third person.

My father looked at me in full knowledge of why it had to be now, but his words circumvented the true issue: 'Because... because he has to grow. Find his way. Just like James.'

'I'll be across the golf course. I'm not leaving as such,' I added, but my mother had welcomed in silence and Jack indicated for me to leave the room, the flan, it all.

I walked out and upstairs. I gazed through the window at the black, sodden grass that stretched onto the horizon. I could just make out my soon-to-be 'digs' / bedroom, 'Castro' willing. Around it were the steep lodge, cattle fields, electricity pylons holding hands and the orange, ember-like dabs of street lights swerving up from the right. I could be there, here, anywhere, but it would root me out, abolish the mild designs that I often permitted to infiltrate me. It would insist that I change the very landscape, the impoverished harvest which leant its stark philosophy against the backs of the masses. I would do something, perhaps great, and... it filled me with dread.

The weeks ambled by. I played golf – practised when I could; allowed 'Castro' to verbalize his years of perfected theory. It did me good and I was able to work on him, evince my parents' emotions as he had requested. He soon agreed, although by then my mother knew what his answer would be, from her visits, from her not having any desire to 'block me' anymore. She grew closer to my father, not in a neglectful way, but in a way which understood that life had moved on.

Eventually, I was put forward for a job which seemed to match the criteria I had listed as part of my periodic apprenticeship review. Top of the list had been 'good with numbers' and so a financial advisor outfit had been approached with a view to take the right candidate for the final year of his/her apprenticeship. Exiting the main office in the old church, I froze for a moment after discovering that my only challenger would be Pendlebury. Not the usual five or six candidates for the job, but just the two of us, paired together by what seemed to be the mind of a sick Roman Emperor. We were gladiators due to fight in an arena of their choosing and my momentary lapse, my trusting of the Roman was at an end. It had to be orchestrated. It simply had to be. The fact of our imminent 'clash' was enough. I hadn't quizzed the principal of the old church concerning the unusual basis of the selection process because I knew; I knew there to be two or three stronger contenders than Pendlebury. Even taking into account the computer skills of each, Pendlebury was fourth at best. The principal had appeared straight forward and matter of fact, yet surely the tentacles of the wider conspiracy had him – both his thought patterns and his limited communication network.

I talked to Pendlebury openly, before the others – disinterested as they were – because I could. The Roman had been correct in one sense in that we had indeed inherited the higher ground. Pendlebury too was no longer reluctant. His words were many and his decibels higher. I asked him what he thought but he seemed unfazed by my implicit suggestion – impassive even. 'Let's have the interview and then try to unthread it afterwards,' he countered politely.

'But…'

'Arnold,' he interrupted. 'The day *you* leave is the day *I* leave, so in a way it doesn't matter. There won't be any open warfare. We won't fall out over this.'

There was a note of semi-defeatism in his words, a thin rejoinder which knew the future. He was saying that I would leave first, that I would become a financial man for 'x' amount of years. And he himself would then walk out on the college, ignore their structure, their plans for him and maybe in the process undermine their utopian vision.

I drove to the interview. I had bought my Mk.II Escort the week before from an uncle – the brother of whom was sat in the passenger seat now as I meandered through the streets with my 'L' plates on. My father waited – sat in the car in a back street while I walked across town to my third floor interview. Entering the building I passed a couple of individuals on the stairs – suited up yet confusing in their expressions; neither dogmatic nor munificent.

It was the home of a provincial conglomerate that I was entering. Not a sharp, city outfit, but a modestly furnished and far from the centre of the world operation. The floor below where I now stood housed insurance clerks and bosses, yet the planning and structure of this company was such that the investment arm had to be at the top. Even then, as I discovered while being escorted across the floor, an obvious and more acute power hierarchy was in place across the sixty square metres that I now inhabited. Past reception came two offices which were hired out. Next came the dulcet faces of the life assurance clerks, seemingly content and without fiery ambition. Then it was the stern and unyielding pomp of the pension behemoths – clerk being too lowly a word to define such fervour. And finally, my future 'home', my necessary calling if Pendlebury was to be understood and believed: portfolio management, or speculation as the more wily and visibly irreverent individuals preferred.

I sat outside one of three offices on a cobalt coloured leather sofa, at this the far end of the largely open plan 'L'-shaped floor. It seemed like an exclusive hovel, the intimidatory mouthpiece of a small conglomerate which generated profits of £2-3M per year. Through the vertical glass pane at the side of each office door, I made out a presence inside; a balding man with thick glasses, a man his very opposite in terms of ostensible aesthetic appeal and finally a group of six or seven individuals communicating, turning their heads and bodies, gazing at screens plastered around the room.

To my left were what seemed to be secretaries and administrators to the core 'talent' of the operation, yet they appeared unduly ordinary – jumper-laden women with inappropriately large necklaces and gaudy skirts. 'Without them I'd die of boredom. Feminists are what a man needs!' a voice suddenly boomed.

A few faces looked up at him, others carried on with their work seemingly fatigued by the cursory interruption. He walked over to me, intent on sharing his thoughts with someone. 'Who are you then? One of those youngsters with dreams? Think you'll reach the finishing tape in super quick time?'

'Warwick – don't taint the new blood. Come in, Arnold. Come in.'

I got up, walked past Warwick and into the office of The Balding Man. 'You've caught me on a good day,' he instantly said. 'Won the medal competition with a 67 net at the weekend. First victory for ages. Accused of banditry now though.'

I gave him what he wanted which was incessant golf talk mixed with a few financial market morsels. In many ways it seemed ridiculous that I was here. I knew numbers and the basic workings of a computer, but this was something different – a hybrid of bonhomie and unctuousness. Still, I was able to display an enthusiasm – some genuine, some spun via an internal loom – which satisfied the man's porous demeanour.

'It comes down to this, Arnold,' he slowly elucidated. 'Man is liked and not liked. Shall I show you around the floor?'

I nodded. Acceded to his offer. Shook a few hands. Smiled a few smiles. Generally induced laughter among the middle-aged ranks because of my youthful exterior, my effort at adulthood. Finally, he took me into the third office, the epicentre of the portfolio management operation. The room was twice the size of his, yet it occupied not one but seven – soon to be eight – individuals. I looked around stupidly for *my* space, an inconspicuous corner, the placenta and blood of *my* beginnings. The faces looked back at me with suspicion and friendliness, curiosity and neglect – one, and then the other, dependent upon the data shimmering from their screens, dependent on the reds and blues. Warwick was at the hub of the bodies – head forward and occasionally down. He wasn't interested in me now. His demeanour suggested that sharing a stage with anyone was awkward – particularly when it was The Balding Man, a currently more 'powerful' executive, yet one that failed to inspire him. The clown-like jacket belonging to Warwick hung over the back of his chair – its coloured stripes running vertically and almost blending with the 80s brown upholstery on which he was sat.

'Everyone! This is Arnold Debrito. Possible new recruit. Bill – I'll let you take over. A mini tour if you've got the time…'

Bill, a man somehow grazed by life given his tendency to cower unlike the others, tapped the 'space bar' on his computer and offered me a seat to the right of him. 'Two things really. The software to look at the portfolios – segregate them. And the software to conduct our research. I'll show you the first.'

He called up what he described as a 'new' portfolio or client. Bottom left of the screen was the total cost of the investments. Bottom right was the value at yesterday's finishing point or 'close'. They read, respectively, £50,000 and £47,632; a difference, or rather loss, of 5%.

'That's normal,' he said, now the only face on me in the room. 'We take 3%, the fund manager two.'

I asked him how that was justified. He talked of professionalism, expertise, marketing, strategy and time.

'1% for each?' I enquired.

'I shouldn't think so,' came his curt response, before telling me how they were regulated – everything being above board and fair.

A couple of snorts then lacerated our pained chatter. 'The boy doth question our sincerity? Show him Webster's, Bill…' The screen changed – flickered with a different account whose investment cost was £400,000. And the value: £1,310,245.

'What are these?' I asked, referring to the ten lines above the total, themselves split into five columns.

'Unit Trusts.' He pointed at each column. 'Date bought, manager, fund name, cost and value. In America they call them mutual funds. Each one has a basket of shares.'

'Chosen using the fund manager's expertise?' I probed, half seriously, half sardonically.

He nodded and in that split second I looked at the dates and descriptions of the funds. 1984. 1985. Gold. Australasian. Precious metals. Repetition upon repetition of 'deals' done two and three years ago – each one in gold or the half-cousin of gold. And the rich return: +200%.

'Shouldn't he sell – use the money wisely?'

There was instant laughter, even from Warwick who conjured up his own sentence: 'On the back of what piece of analysis?'

I desperately wanted to say 'the analysis of enough being enough' or 'the analysis that leads down the road of philanthropy', but my diplomacy kicked in. It strangled the idea that I might have been on Level Two. It sliced the genitals, the release system, off of my heady, incumbent self.

'Stupidity,' I said, like a well-disguised but floundering soul.

They laughed – all of them now – almost as if I had purposely galloped towards them on a Trojan Horse, as if I was no less of a capitalist than them (my green and red steer washing off its colours to reveal a tattoo of the Bank of England).

I left soon after, following the realisation that they would both trust and entrust me quite easily. And that had to be my exercise, my learning curve, to understand fully the mechanisms of this pious world. On passing the cobalt sofa, I indicated to Pendlebury that I would wait for him at the bottom of the staircase, at the foot of this inverse heaven and hell. It seemed illogical that we were both here, fleetingly together for a moment on the runway of this asset manipulator. Pendlebury, in particular, resembled a giraffe, a normally able seer, caught in the kiln of this leafless world, this computer-dominated stronghold.

I stood there with my arms folded, feeling slightly awkward when people passed, yet exuding a certificate of possession, belonging – an impression of rightfulness. I thought of Pendlebury with The Balding Man, with Bill and Warwick, and I was aghast, devoid of sufficient imagination to play out their chatter, their general interaction. I could only compare such a scene to the meeting of Thatcher and Scargill, Reagan and Fritz Schumacher; impossibles that would never come about, that would never make it through the highly contrived set up around us.

When he showed, in half the time I had had, and looked at me with difficulty yet purpose, I knew I would be coming here again. Pendlebury's expression afforded me a god though – it allowed me, for a few moments, to set my stall higher, to bypass the need to give valuable years away strictly in the interest of seeing the 'other side'.

'Level Four. I want it now. Tell your uncle please.' There was panic in myself, the victor. There was a renewed sense of desperately wanting to tread through the promised land.

'I can't. It wouldn't be the same. It would put in jeopardy everything. You need to see this because of who you'll become. And Level Two – that will be easier.'

I didn't understand. I was somehow ignorant of 'the pull'. 'You didn't want this job then?'

'I'm afraid I have no wish to see this world except to pull it down.'

I wanted to demand an answer as to why *I* must play it out – act as the begotten stooge in a questionable production. I wanted to approach The Leaf Blower now and ask him to re-write this stolid affair. Instead, I went silent – enough so to prompt Pendlebury's departure: 'I'll see you around then.'

'Don't you want a lift?' I asked, somehow thinking that this was the last I would see of him.

'I only travel on tracks, where there's less harm. No tracks, then I walk.'

'But I've only just bought it. Surely…'

'I'm sorry.'

And with that, he ventured off. No talk of the interview. No mention of the future, our friendship. Just an exit, and with it a signal of some kind, a foreboding – not of something bad, but of something different (a changed landscape). I looked up, at the many windows above me, and thought of the faces staring out in their majesty. Not for long, was the echo inside my head, given off through Pendlebury's lips. Not for long.

CHAPTER 15

That same afternoon it was confirmed that The Balding Man had chosen me. Because I played golf. Because I was diplomatic. Because I didn't have greying hair and an odd set of clothes. Mostly though, because providence had wanted it that way.

I was to start in two weeks, preferably with a tie hung around my neck. I was to report to Warwick who would laugh at my inadequacies where and whenever possible and constantly remark on the fact that I would not have been *his* choice. Such hauteur would give me leverage though – an understanding of Warwick's needs and therefore his weaknesses.

I bought a few shirts over the next few days and had my mother – who had resigned herself to my 'loss' – run up the legs of two new pairs of trousers. I would come home after my first day at work, indulge in a special tea or dinner, and then pack – allow the transition from parents to Grandfather to occur without delay or embarrassment. My father would help me with my cases, my belongings and then wave, perhaps regrettably, as I drove to 'Castro's' in my yellow jalopy, my T-reg Escort.

On arriving I would leave the cases in the long hallway and sit in my grandmother's old chair – opposite 'Castro' and his pipe, opposite the well-built wood and coal fire. I would then muse over the future, extract from my grandfather his remaining visions and dreams. I would maybe discuss my first day in the financial cauldron – how suited or otherwise I was to the number-etched existence which appeared pivotal to almost every facet of life. I would pour us both a whisky, 'celebrate' Level One, and then retire in earnest ready for day two, day seven, day eight hundred and fifty three.

And my thoughts concerning Pendlebury? I supposed they would fade. I supposed his absence would test my conviction, my being drawn in the direction of otherworldliness. What if the false gods gripped me, however? What if I began to gauge life using graphs and vacuous terminology? Then I would have failed. Allowed popularity to mask itself around the sacred designs not yet known to me. Permitted a torch of Corinthian conception to be lit, thus killing salvation and leading us down a remorseless, darkened path.

I had to feign it though. I had to be a pseudo-capitalist. Only then would I see the inside, the freshly scraped misgivings at the floor of Warwick's mind. And the others – their borrowed tenacity sauced in a scabrous laissez faire. Who were *they* underneath their wondrously silky camisoles, their perfect shirts and smell? What did their skin speak of? What did it cloak? Because if there was nothing behind it, then my job would be harder – importunate.

Weeks in, now summer, and I knew the basics of the world I had joined. There had been distractions like me having to open the post on the floor below with the new 'bodies' in Insurance (an exercise meant to humble me), yet in the main Financial Times' had been spread out before me, a deluge of graphs and tables had been loaded up on my screen. I had examined all before me – the people, the products, the windless hierarchy – and concluded very early that the whole thing was a game similar to my brother's; a manifold atom on the investment horizon.

Warwick, I noticed, had habits – the mispronunciation of 'proven' being one of his more foul crimes (said as if the two syllables were independent rather than harmonized by the letter O's ability to invisibly breed or remove its crown). Such mannerisms were meant to lift him though – place him firmly above The Balding Man, if not in salary terms then in intellectual or highbrow stature. Other examples of his tomfoolery (I didn't know it to be this, but I guessed) included his car, parked narcissistically at the side of the building; its private reg. moulded into the word 'G 1 A N T'. Those who couldn't see his triple irony tired of him, I noticed. They denounced his sexist, jovially dogmatic culture as being that of a cynic. Warwick, however, repeatedly stressed that he was not a cynic but a sceptic, there being a considerable gulf between believing the worst in people and simply questioning their motives. 'A sceptic is today's hero, Arnold – its benefactor and battalion,' he would tell me, usually after three gins.

The pub was to become our insurrectionary pallbearer; its

anonymous and hazy depth allowing our chatter to bend and rebel, turn away and defy, but then ultimately cross the point where the serious brigade resided – walk us through the exit in corporate rags, moribund shoes and make-up. Here, for a couple of hours at least, there was no weight on us – neither The Balding Man's occasional ask nor the dripping fervour of the floor. Around our fourth or fifth visit we caught each other's gaze as if we knew, as if we were allies woven together by a largely unspeakable fulcrum. Warwick would continue his 'clown' act, lavish his own ears with the outrageous, bison-like mutterings that parted his lips. He would talk of mock fascist worlds where nay-sayers (those above him with more power) were rounded up and thrown in a special wing of the local prison for crimes against wisdom. 'Crepuscular fools!' he cried, at least once a week. 'Run the business like bloody actuaries.' It wasn't so much ethics he was seeking like myself but a world in which people understood they were nothing, that conviction was wasted in the majority of professions. And I was comfortable with that. Not a laughter which extended beyond fundamental comprehension, but one which belittled procedure, smoke screens and insidious puppeteering.

Warwick liked to place his cards in front of you, check your reaction and then ram home the beauty of each. He loved transparency. He loved knowing the occupation of every single client. Because without them both, the job would be unbearable. He would be a cipher – a carrier of other people's opinions. He would be a barren, humourless machine; an employee whose head was not his own.

I told 'Castro'. Of my mistake in initially disliking Warwick. Of my enmity toward professional people, a few of whom it transpired 'knew how it was'. He approved of my beer-laden rants, balanced with a strange, new tolerance, yet questioned wholeheartedly Warwick's tipple, gin. 'It's a woman's drink – mother's ruin. They used to take it in an attempt to abort their unborn child. Warwick has thoughts which can never come out and so he tries to abort or purge them.'

I laughed it off. Spirits were spirits and as long as Warwick lubricated his oft domineering mind then I knew his triple irony was still there; its carriage hoisting pleasantly forward the

Gentiles. 'It's an odd world. Trying to understand people's set ups. The reality beneath the layers of skin.'

'Castro' looked at me. 'Culture. Some people let it breathe. Others stifle it because they're afraid of its radicalness.'

~ ~ ~

Mid-August, I took the morning off and walked up the steps of my now only college – night school. A printed piece of paper was pinned to a board behind a sheet of protective glass on the ground floor of the building. My English O-level grade was on it; my re-take; my future within the unpredictable folds of the business world. Familiar faces darted around: the two Muslims aggrieved at my denouncing their edicts; followers of Greene and Steinbeck; and my tutor, George Minty I, clearly buoyant and welcoming.

'Have you seen it, Arnold?' were his words upon noticing me slowly treading the old, tiled vinyl floor.

'Not yet. Have you?'

'I've memorised them all.'

I was glad that he had memorised them. I was glad that he had approached me, because surely such a happening would not occur had I failed. If he was audacious, however – somehow twisted – then...

The possibility had to be discounted – pushed to the floor, the margins, and trodden on. He was a good man, certainly not prone to smiling at the scene of another man's bankruptcy. I looked ahead through the glass. His eyes bored into me as I nudged past the loose bodies. Finally soaking in the list, I found the line – 'Debrito, Arnold   C'. It was as if it had been stencilled by me – the barely worthy pass mark which would serve as a launch pad for higher, more defiant and recognisable work. A 'C' was a compliment. It shot through churches ringing the bells without consent. It lay in ditches and behind fences in full view of the world's hind quarters, themselves flailing like a pantomime mare. It somehow marvelled at the judgement synonymous with it – the assumed mediocrity and forced cough which together acted like a town check point. It was two grades higher than my first effort twelve months ago, yet in many senses it was no better; simply a ragged effort put together in a decrepit gymnasium.

'You'll make it,' George Minty I heralded, now at my shoulder and eager to interact.

'You think so?' I asked, not at all concerned now I at least had a ticket for the fair – capitalist candyfloss and all.

'An 'A' wasn't you, you see. Too much conformity.'

I enjoyed his logic, his mellifluent and cogent feed. But then I thought of my mathematics 'A'. What were the implications? Had I not seen it all as I should? Within minutes we were separated. I doubted if I would see him again. This was the far end of town and I had no reason to return other than to develop things beyond the student/teacher niche. I felt my name being called elsewhere in any case – its first two syllables chiming in my head... de-bri... de-bris. Perhaps that's what I was; fragments of something destroyed; rubble before it had begun. It? What was I meaning... alluding to? What was it that had my mind so ensconced?

'Come and look, Arnold,' Warwick exuded upon my return. 'It would be remiss of me not to show you the new decision makers now you're equipped to understand.'

He led the way – walked down to the Insurance floor and along to the far end among a group of huge, potted plants. Through the discreet leaves and a few feet ahead behind a sheet of glass sat seven individuals – each absorbed by The Standing Man at the head of the rectangular table.

'Here they are. Ready to kill us with procedure. Ready to crush the innovative flair we might possess. The E.M.T. – that's who they are. Executive Management Team. Quite how they got hold of the reins I don't know. That's the thing to remember about corporations, Arnold – it's only ever the no.1 that knows. You're probably only a day behind me yourself when it comes to the grapevine. And now you've got your English O-level, perhaps a half.'

He threw a mock smile my way. It seemed to encode five or six meanings. Given that I knew Warwick less when he was gin-less I simply acknowledged his observation by way of an ambiguous facial contortion of my own.

'We're being slowly sterilized, Arnold. These chaps are nothing more than a Health & Safety militia. We may as well begin sharing a desk with the government's regulatory arm.'

At that point – and I knew it might come – The Balding Man (one of the E.M.T.) stepped out of the room we were monitoring. 'Warwick! Anything I can help you with?'

'I'm giving the boy a grounding. He needs to understand the internal hierarchy.'

The Balding Man pulled him away from me. 'Not this one, he doesn't,' was the firm whisper.

Warwick seemed to shake him off and in the process open up the private forum. 'But the boy has his English O-level. He passed. Reward must follow, otherwise…'

'Excuse us, Arnold,' The Balding Man intervened with, this time escorting Warwick into a side office.

I read his lips, his first sentence as he stood inside the executive cubbyhole – opposite Warwick and his nihilistic juices. '*Are you pissed?* came the direct accusation, to which I couldn't see or hear the answer but merely utilise my growing omnipotence. They both shrugged and gestured, pointed and intimated. Eventually the door swung open and Warwick led me back to the top floor.

We reached our office (the seemingly former epicentre) next but one to The Balding Man's and he immediately ordered everyone out. There was an instant disquiet – cacophony of manicured voices, a deluge of precise mutterings. Warwick stood firm, however. He blanketed their cries, their pronounced syllables with a fitting paragraph: 'There are six of you. An audience of two and a doubles. Do something that doesn't involve a screen. Just until my consultation with Debrito ends.'

A couple of them looked at me – wondered what it was that a seventeen-year-old could possibly have on their boss. Drink, I nearly testified. Its ability to seek out the gaps. Pull from a person that which isn't diplomatic.

The door closed. We found ourselves both seated. For a moment it even seemed natural – to be surrounded, just the two of us, by graphs, flashing statistics and office paraphernalia. As long as we had the controls. As long as we weren't secondary. Then maybe we could make enough – to sit on, earn interest off; a small ransom which would buy us years of planning and then action. Because I sensed he could come with me. Despite Warwick's bent, his capitalist aptitude and marauding mentality, he had the makings of my first convert. To what, I was still unsure, yet Pendlebury would tell me or I would develop without realising it. The glint inside of me would eventually form rays – lucid streaks which would serenade all before me.

'This industry, Arnold – it's built on a quite precarious science. The prediction of markets. Markets themselves being an embodiment of greed and fear. I've been to conferences – god knows how many – spoken to fellow advisors and the conclusion is much the same. We make informed guesses. The information itself is often obtuse and open to being railroaded by media outlets. In many respects that is what we have become – interpreters of an interpretation. Not a vision with the naked eye. Nothing wonderfully empirical. Because truth suffered a relapse despite it being trumpeted otherwise. Truth wandered into the desert when we were busy globalising each segment of the world. So now we have a network of people who choose to ignore that which is of most concern to them: society. The image from the top is not an image that is relevant, yet it continues to be given an implicit credence by the very fact that people don't choose to dig. You'd be amazed by some of the myths sloshing around. My job, it seems, is to visualise the lie in all its glory – a lie which inevitably makes people money – and short it, sell it, at its high point. Because it does come unstuck. Not always at the point I imagine, but with time.'

It wasn't as I wanted it. To remove six people and then line me with a mediocre polemic was unacceptable. I expected stories, meaningful lessons – not general statements nor the carping from an old financial dog with personal disappointments wrapped as society's. In one sense it paralleled my theory concerning the bogusly dethroned upper classes, yet where it fell down was critical: Warwick wrongly assumed that all counter-forces were dead, without energy or compliant. He talked of lies, not realising the biggest one of all – the structures which surrounded the media, politics, the country. The 'super' tramps had forced his hand, his decisions in life without him realising it, without him cursing them, their private acreage, and their rich, salubrious culture. How I would tell him, I didn't know.

Perhaps not telling him though was Level One. Perhaps by understanding his quips and annoyance I would move on.

CHAPTER 16

When it came, like a stork dropping a baby not into the neat folds of a mother's blanket but onto the rough fibres of a household carpet, Forson Watshaw were ill-prepared; the October 1987 Crash swept in as they were unconnected, moving desks, nudging the hierarchic playing field towards Insurance. Two months of talks had ended with the E.M.T. deciding that Investment was no longer deserving of the top floor, that their steadier income stream from monthly premiums warranted more respect. And so they had wandered in on the back of the broken souls of their staff and the overnight news from Japan and Hong Kong, ready to salvage something, ready to sell out now – lose a quarter, rather than a third. But the desks, the computers, the paperwork – it was stacked high in three or four corners of the unfamiliar expanse of floor. They had prioritised the swish look of the now mightier Insurance arm – which stood above Warwick et al with a certain gleam and polish – yet had disbanded temporarily the behemoth that was Investments with a noticeable irreverence.

The men responsible for this, the weekend tillers and gents of great girth, had merely taken their cue from the E.M.T. or satraps. Their return was scheduled for 9am; 9am on this the final day of their three-day job; a Monday, a seemingly bland day – the poorer cousin of the others – yet one developing an African skin. It would be known as Black Monday – the cursed enveloper of everything hyped and oversubscribed. Between the now transparent holes of the world economy Black Monday would send a shot of ink – stain and drown out the parasites, the blind bandwagon hoppers.

'A desk! I need a desk! Where the fuck is he? *Where is* the little shit?!'

Warwick's first words were met with dumbfoundedness and so he rampaged through the statuesque crowd, up onto his former floor. I followed, along with two others. We watched as he meted out more undiluted words, more unassailable truths.

'Very swish! Very swish. But what about us? What about the paper napkins of the operation – the mouth wipers, the catchers of *your* drivel?' He raised his voice now to a furore: 'Ladies and gentlemen – we have a falling market! One which should hopefully lead to a few job cuts up here. Now, can anyone tell me…'

They opened the door of their ornate dwelling – the E.M.T., The Balding Man, The Standing Man. 'Warwick – we've had a meeting…'

'A meeting?' He was incredulous, stupefied and astounded.

'Yes. And while we appreciate the timing of the move has been bad, we think the situation is not beyond the mire.'

'You do?' Warwick was suddenly calm. 'May I ask which one of you gave express permission for this move to go ahead without informing everyone?'

'We work as a unit, Warwick – *you* know that. Now can we please remedy this? Begin to act.'

'We're twenty plugs down. It appears as though the Insurance arm didn't have much call for technology. And so we're twenty plugs down.'

'Then…'

'Improvise, yes? Understand the chain of priorities? Oh, indeed I will. But I still need a name. One person who is accountable. The kind of reckless halfwit who would fail to stress the importance of having *ALL* our computers up and running on day one.'

'This is divisive, Warwick. You're out of your depth.'

'No! Clearly *I am not.* Clearly one, if not *all of you*, are.'

'This is preposterous,' The Standing Man half-bellowed. 'Simply get to work, Warwick!'

'Not until our beloved family here has a name.' He swept his arm around the room to include the insurance clerks in their new den, plus myself and a couple of wily speculators.

'Who can do his job?' the E.M.T. then muttered to themselves, not so circumspectly. 'I don't know. Bill? A couple of the senior dealers...?'

I watched, transfixed. My loyalties were undoubtedly with Warwick, the steamrolling inadequacy meter. He started up his machinery again, this time with added verve and purpose.

'What message does it send? When you try to oust someone who possesses noise and angst – someone with the company in mind rather than a network of cronies? All of you are guilty of engendering corruption and hesitancy. That is unless you have a name.'

Warwick knew. He understood that they would not break rank, but rather push home their insolent supposition, their oligarchy-weaned drum roll (expect disunity from the minnows, yet stand firm themselves). It reminded me of my father and his inability to give me a date. *When*? And now – *who*? Each hankered after a critical piece of mass, an elixir which would lessen or completely dissolve the anxiety prevalent.

'Let's take this into the boardroom...'

'I'm reluctant to do that, chaps,' was Warwick's reply, yet his cards were running out, his ebullience was receding through necessity rather than enervation.

'This represents a difficult position for us as well...'

'Five minutes,' Warwick replied, allowing *them* to lead the way, giving their choreographed stampede some of the prairie.

We looked in – through the thick, semi-soundproof window – at the bodies now more demonstrative and forceful. Prominent foes were The Balding Man and Warwick, The Standing Man and Warwick, The Pension Man and Warwick. All, it seemed, against Warwick save the flying rats outside.

'Do this now then,' finally channeled itself to me from the lips of The Balding Man, difficult as it was with their frames side on. I needed The Leaf Blower at my side as experienced interpreter and the gabbing around me to stop.

Warwick signalled something to them – a delicious swan song and timely epilogue. It appeared to consist of severance, ideas on how to run the ship without him, permutations of staff and software which they would probably ignore. It was all there – in his partly keeled over, yet forbearing face. Two minutes later he was out (door flung open for effect) almost as if we had imagined the scene. The faces behind him seemed unsure concerning the outcome, but relieved that harmony – a strictly vetted one – was now combing the floor, restoring the neo-liberalism which had been rudely severed.

'My hearing. It seems to have lost something,' Warwick communicated to me as we approached the top of the staircase. 'I've always had different feeds, but now it's unbearably quiet almost as if my sense of the world has diminished.'

We returned to the lower floor. '1801 – that's when it all began!' he bellowed. 'Well we have right now our very own 1929! It's been a long time coming... savour it! Plug points please! Desks and computers in place. Anyone outside of my team is this morning a labourer – not just any old labourer, but one that will prevent our demise!'

He turned to me then, away from the strident crew and the semi-raucous faces. 'I leave Friday, Arnold. Perhaps a gift?' He winked and was gone – the bowling of himself into the sea of bodies depriving me of understanding. A gift? Did he mean the whole thing was a blessing, that his public spat with the E.M.T. had merely prompted a wondrous coup? Or that I ought to purchase something fitting given his imminent departure, given that his birth year had effectively come around again?

The area of desks specifically arranged for this one selling spectacular now stood, after much shouting, rancour and glee, like a modern pyramid; Warwick's desk not where it should be due to the plug shortage, yet along with the team's, positioned at the heart of 'pension country'. Individuals stood, lined up against the wall, ready for the bell, ready for the intrigue which would sauté their minds, teach them that they were in fact nothing – that their jobs were an appalling amalgamation of the public's fear, class obsession and greed. Warwick began to hand out sheets to his team – simple bullet points that he had drafted ensuring that no one went astray or overcomplicated the task at hand. The jobs were simple: sell the non-staple stocks; switch the life and pension funds into cash and short-term bonds; and then wait, assimilate the intervening data, and phone the fund managers at 9am (see if they were 'playing ball' or if they'd decided to utilise one of their contentious clauses thus freezing 'x' billion pounds worth of assets). As much as Warwick used the fund managers, his distrust of them had always hinged on the redolence and colour of their unkempt air, their shadow playing and au gratin posture. 'They will levy you because the uncle of one of their administrators had a heart attack.'

My position, although not central, felt sufficient. I had a seat and desk whereas some of the senior pension figures were forced to stand and watch – catapult their thoughts within the cranium of their very being. My job, besides 'listening out' for news relating to the US trade figures which had largely caused this investment avalanche, was to watch and learn – report back to Warwick any deficiencies at the end of the day which I viewed with concern or even amazement. I did so, unbeknown to Bill and his colleagues, at the risk of my guise slipping, my only loyalty within this putrid, provincial 'vestry' becoming known. Before then, however, the day had to begin – run its ancient steed to the starting line; jump with tight hooves into the air before the bell.

And then... silence; a watching of the synchronized clocks – their analogue and digital manes blowing closer to that vertical repository which would signal the beginning. Yes. Go. Away with you. Warwick lifted the grey plastic which had been sweating beneath his hand. 'Sell! *Fucking* sell!' he boomed. 'Sell what?' came the firm intonation. 'It *all!*' he replied with gusto and vigour. '500/- ICI.' 'Two out.' 'Fine! Fine.' He scribbled down the price, understood that the book was 'thin' on the buy side and moved on. 'Si' down!' he then roared at the pension 'stiffs' lined up like toy soldiers against the wall. 'If you're not bidding me, then SIT DOWN!' Most of them heeded Warwick's filthy words. Those that didn't shook their fists thus invoking Warwick's approving smile. He held his hand over the receiver – played with them while on hold. 'You want some?!' They turned away, slowly retreated in full, bar two pros who knew him, who catalogued Warwick's rage under 'N' for nursery rhyme. 'I don't like it,' Warwick suddenly voiced with not an ounce of sincerity as one of his stable hands asked him to close out (sell) a position – 'What's your T-date?! How many days 'til settlement, you *fucking otter?* When the answer didn't wing its way back *before* his final word, he lifted up a set of trays – balanced them on one finger – and let them crash to the floor. Disapproving looks encircled him. Some of the female staff attempted to decamp, only for Warwick to shout after them and point: 'You! Get me a barley orange. You! A tray of mini éclairs…' It was incongruous, absurd and probably the last time I would witness such sheen, yet the portfolios were being offloaded, some of the losses weren't as bad as feared. I could see the weightings on the screen before me – simple minute by minute pie-charts dissecting the revised portfolio assets (risk, sector, country etc) – the cash 'shading' increasing with every call.

Culture in its purest form was not this, I supposed, yet Warwick was somehow a conjuror, a man in his last throes making light of his profession which was neither that of a surgeon, a farmer nor an architect. He saw the movement of money as one of bluster, as the crowning of the rich not in their full regalia but while holding the bottled sweat of the masses (to be sold back to them as wine). Warwick understood that his being born in 1929 had given him destiny, yet in recent years he had begun to ask why. On seeing the immutable etchings around him – the faces of The Balding Man and The Standing Man in particular – he had begun to return home each week day with an odd feeling that seemingly besmirched him, left him cold and derailed. His face, however, was out there – imprinted, packaged and contracted. People expected his enormous mien to jump on its horse each day, gallop at haste and then wave a hearty but critical farewell. Should he extinguish such turbulent play then he wouldn't last – there would be others ready to fill the vacuum; 'inept youngsters' who actually believed in power as if it was an alchemic force, as if it enhanced their respectability. They had no knowledge or intention of 'coming clean' at the end. They wouldn't bow to their underlings, suggest as part of their epilogue a revamped way forward, admit that it was thirty years of building a pension pot as opposed to actual belief in the system. No. They wouldn't humble themselves so that others could gain fuel nor jeopardise the climactic guffaw with a seemingly insipid, yet oddly radical speech. Such 'acute benevolence' and ultimate betrayal could never be allowed to surface, could never step out from behind its Hijab.

And so Warwick had written off the final years of his working life, negotiated with a quite hardened crew, namely the E.M.T., over the terms of his departure (pension: they would contribute for four of the remaining seven years; leaving speech: a three minute maximum; memos: strictly none; company car: to be left in his 'contract space' Friday) and was now seeing out his last Monday with Forson Watshaw. People, he could not buy – bring to his 'retirement home' and interact with – yet the need to mix, not become estranged from society, was foremost in his mind. The Domino Club he would continue to frequent (he had always had a penchant for becoming its President). The crowd or 'regulars' were what he liked to innocuously call 'dullards'. In among them, however, were generally three or four saved souls – patterned individuals rather than gregarious types, full of depth and harmony and capable of rounded, iconoclastic chatter both *at* and *away from* the white and black spots. Also, he planned to increase his visits to The Reading Club; a place where as many as twenty people would sit – chaired up – in a circle, each reading five pages at a time from a democratically-elected novel. A good read, Warwick bestowed, took three minutes per page and so each season they would gather for an extravaganza or marathon wherein they would – between them – read for fifteen hours (a whole novel) without stopping. '*Fifteen hours!* The stock exchange opens for eight – *six* in some countries,' Warwick would often chafe, amused by the incongruity, the myth that financial employees had it tough. After that, after his two prime leisure pursuits, he would reckon out the remaining hours – attempt to understand when he needed to be alone and when such a pastime was capable of harming him, of depositing in his mind a pernicious shell. Daytime would initially be the hardest, him having no wife and therefore no sounds that could act as instant comforters. Other sounds he would hear – the residue of society's often futile, yet binding industry – but these would be torturers and persecutors, reminders that he was inert, quiescent, somehow worthless and forgotten. If that were the case, if such a feeling permeated him, then he would start to catch the train at rush hour, feel the thrum and thrust of bodies massed together within a machine; a machine heading for work and perhaps mental and physical sunder. Except, he would be permitted to smile, listen in to their anxious chatter and then follow clusters of people even to the very entrance of their place of employment. Wherein, he would shake his empty briefcase quite merrily and make his way to the city library to take his seat among the more serious students and the prematurely retired. Looking around he would perhaps wonder at the extent of the indoctrination within the buildings dotted around, particularly the tertiary 'salons' or primary schools, right up to the professional brigades which blessed their 'armies' with taut footwear and mind-altering helmets.

Yes. That was it. He would open a 'small school', a teaching establishment which excluded orthodox teachers and pedagogues. There would be no ranks under his, or the group's roof – only elegant, magical titles devised by him firstly, and then two of them, three of them, and so on until full (enough men and women poached from discontent into chimeric joy). He would at first go into schools and naively announce that he wished to interview the unhappiest individual there. After a period of minutes and then the realisation that he was actually serious, the secretary or deputy head of the school would curse him for his audacity, his brazen effrontery. They would then escort him off the grounds and Warwick would proceed to place eye-catching ads in prominent papers which would unsettle not one of their employees but a good percentage. Of course at that point Warwick would be forced to filter out the frauds, the steady 'yes men' who were symbolic of everything he was working against. They would try to persuade him otherwise – insist that their tacit compliance was radical at heart, that without it their day-to-day existence would have been oppressive and unbearable. But that was what Warwick hoped for – individuals who had openly waged war against the sanitised layers around them; sufferants choked by the deleterious words of the petty bourgeoisie, now ready for a merely imagined deliverance.

I watched now as Warwick gave a sublime coherence to the shouts and messages on the lower floor – weighed inside his mind the importance of each call and news update. He seemed, or appeared, relaxed – perhaps encouraged by his imminent 'escape'.

'The dollar continues to weaken!' I furnished my floor compatriots with, feeling self-important and momentarily at the hub of things.

'Weak is good,' Warwick muttered, gazing through me. 'Weak is good.'

CHAPTER 17

Half a decade changed many things. People I had expected to be close absconded in a temperate sense. Pendlebury's absence was the hardest to bear, despite his words ringing in my ear daily ("...because of who you'll become."). I had it on authority from 'Castro' that his uncle had gotten him a post at Lake Vyrnwy, blowing leaves and tending to the general landscape. This, I found honourable – almost generative in its skipping from uncle to nephew. I had always known that Pendlebury would be freer than the average man – destined to roam whilst devising a Thoreau-esque philosophy – and yet I imagined him at night in his small cottage missing civilisation's husk, its facile layer which allowed one to cheat and assume grace.

His uncle – Pendlebury's uncle – visited my grandfather less and less, maybe aware of the manifest interference, of the overbearance which threatened the gods, or rather their time-laden plans. A belief permeated the air that the more benign cousin of neglect – evade – was necessary in assisting a speedier societal change. The theory went that individuals had to learn alone, then come together years later in order to quilt their disparate, yet fraternal cloths. Even Warwick, whom I had expected to keep me informed concerning his ventures and spare time, had drifted – lifted his anchor and failed to call out in panic once the waters became choppy. It was because I brought him old tales now – stories which had occupied his bloodstream for decades, for too long. And any mention of The Balding Man simply angered him – gnawed at the new slides he was attempting to create; slides which promised a fecundity greater than the price of gold or the asset value of 'a rapacious portfolio'.

As for my family – my incumbent friends – 1992 brought a harsh, potent sadness. The fact of my grandfather being one day short of his eightieth birthday when he collapsed and died elucidated much of the despondency I still had for the world. Consoling my mother, who had prepared the largest surprise party in Debrito history, was disquieting – insular in its terribleness. Losing the one man that implicitly adored her was unspeakably crucifying.

His departure both silenced her with a haphazard induction of grief and affected her ability to see out a normal existence. The first week, still, in bed – save Jack's assistance readying her for the funeral – was understood by all, however the continuance of this 'mode', this muddied wallowing was, if not frowned upon, then incomprehensible to some – those that would place a limit on mourning, an average, a par.

'Tell them that my wife, Rose, is *not* an average! She is in no way unexceptional!' my father had screamed one evening to a relation intent on stressing or accentuating the future. 'And if you don't understand...'

That had been it – as far as my father could carry it without breaking down himself, evincing a deeply-wrought emotion which pounded the austerity sweeping down the phone line. His duty was to now lie with her, retire his own interests indefinitely and beckon her needs. For her needs without a channel of some kind were likely to be drawn curtains and water, darkness silhouetting my grandfather's frame. Our meals in the meantime would consist of careful measurements from leaflet recipes – exact ingredients rather than the instinctive and swift manoeuvring of food by the lady now absent. The house across the golf course would stand empty until I was sure of returning – as a tenant of my mother and father rather than my beautiful grandfather.

My own thoughts on the subject – the death of a great nihilist and remarkable friend – were overshadowed by the sympathy I felt toward my mother. In amongst the nooks of the blaze, however, I felt an awful emptiness – a boat filled with water, overflowing as if saddled with extra weight. The heaviness persisted, but then the wood would crack each time the pulsating angst became too much. I wanted the noises to stop – any noise, from the odious cries around me at work to the synthetic sounds outside which went against nature's chorus. I found it hard to think unless lay in bed – *really* think; aware of our shrunken family. There was a shrillness to everything, a discordant, giant kettle on the horizon coming to the boil – penetrating my senses and making me want to bow out of society's turmoil, its infernal and inexorable grip. I didn't appear to see people any more, but rather a gargantuan process void of creativeness. The beings I passed and interacted with were somehow shorn of understanding and therefore had no conviction, no fight with which to build an alternative. A great force seemed to push down on them almost as if the sky was merely a tantalizing celestialness and not the glorious entity they had been taught when young.

But my grandfather – his face, more than ever now, wandered in and out of my mind. Particularly when it was dark. Particularly when the world seemed to slow. He simply gazed upon me, unable to speak, yet proclaiming everything because of it. At first I ingested only the bleakness of his non-tangible state – my inability to touch him, pass him his whisky, secretly crave his paternal warmth. The manner of his exit, his passing, then began to burden me. A collapse. Coronary thrombosis. His blood flow halted like a mini revolution. Although he talked of understanding, of purposely blunting his acerbic tongue and dampening his spirit due to its judgementalness, such an outcome – death – he had not contemplated. There had been a renewed excitement to him, a sense of immortality or at least another twenty years. To cut him down now, even if sparing him a long, drawn out and pernicious cancer, was…. cold, viciously 'corrective' and unjust. Whichever god had ordered it, I would demote, sail out of heaven and ask for an answer from. If the whole premise had been to make me stronger, fit for 'office' with a more autonomous baggage, then they, he or she had acted callously, unmovingly – it was ignoble to judge my mind better than I myself could.

What did they hope to assail? What was this heaven that purported to trace the years of one's life, unwrap its eddies and then strike? I had no knowledge of it, yet it had entered our family heartland and poisoned the rivers – pushed our clan into sickness. My own reasoning was being slowly dissipated with time – over days, even hours. I wished for my grandfather's pipe almost melodically shifting opposite me – his ancient-springed chair rocking with grace and perception. And the Constable (my grandmother had thought the print worth something) now ownerless – its landscape somehow barren and leafless despite the greens and browns. In the future I would ponder things in the summer room, alone – allow the prismed light of this sure season to warm me, push me into thought or oblivion. The bookend, I would have to swill down the sink, or else be tempted by its rich façade and ruinous fire.

It was decided. Through the circumstances that had plagued us, I felt at overwhelming odds with the world, and so I would escape, take a sabbatical, basically leave my place of work. More than four years after Warwick's departure, I would follow, sit it out – observe. My mother's needs would take precedence and relief would be given to my father whose retirement was closer than mine and therefore not worth jeopardising with a prolonged absence. Everything I had accumulated – including my meagre savings – would have to last. My investment knowledge, built up and refined on an often potholed pitch, would hopefully see me through a final stint elsewhere, leading to valuable comparisons and the great mourning of Level One. I would have four or five months of cooking, baking, cleaning – time with positers of the soul. It would cleanse me, educate me in tune with the seasons and re-invigorate me for the long haul. *Would* – because I somehow knew what was next. I somehow understood the blackness – both its figurative and actual dimensions.

When it was settled. When The Balding Man surprisingly regretted my moving on, I met with James. It was at *his* request – the '88 graduate and now successful chartered accountant; my brother and estranged family member. It was a country pub in which we met – one closer to my parents' house, yet still fifteen miles away. I drove there in my polished VW Scirocco – the modest successor to my crumbling Mk.II Escort – not quite in the midst of a dusty wind, yet reasonably hot skinned and prostrate. I felt wary of his attention, coming so soon after my – our – grandfather's death – the funeral of whom he had attended, yet in too routine a fashion as if contracted 24hrs a day by diary entries and clients.

He greeted me with what appeared to be a manicured hand. His words were firm and without emotion: 'Arnold – I'll cut to it. Here's a cheque. £2,000. I know what you're doing and it's... honourable. This should see you through.'

I looked at him incredulously. 'You've been appointed?'

'Hurr?'

'Appointed family treasurer?'

'No. No. I simply want to help out.'

His body was shaped ready to go. He had actually driven ninety miles and was seemingly prepared to leave without even having a drink with me.

'Why didn't you post it? You're intent on scarpering and I've only just arrived.'

'That wasn't my intention. I promise you. Things seem to have caught up with me though.' He pulled out his diary and showed me an entry. "Monday 3.15 Smithsons". 'I used the pub phone while I was waiting. Spoke to the office. They've re-scheduled. Nothing I can do unfortunately.'

I was bemused. 'Why pick a Monday then? Where are Smithsons based?'

'They're ten miles from here. Ten miles back on myself – south.'

'You know all the good joints then – the respectable public houses?'

'Yes. I travel. It's encouraged early on in the career. All aimed at getting a big desk.'

A thought addled my senses. That I was quite secondary to my brother's concerns. That this philanthropic gesture was aimed at clearing his own decks – those strewn with black and white photographs and ancestral pangs. I took hold of his diary, held loosely in his hand and opened it. 'I do get an entry then...' ("2.00 A.D.," it read). 'A full hour maybe. Give you fifteen to get to Smithsons.'

'Well – fifty minutes. The roads...'

He hesitated, yet I now knew fifty minutes to be my worth. I wondered about what we would have chatted. Had he not been re-scheduled. Had I been early. Not even a drink – it rankled with me.

The cheque which I had disregarded still swung from his right hand. He tried again, this time manifestly squeezing it into my palm. I let it drop to the floor and he instantly bent down to save it from ignominy. At that moment a rare thought choked me. I nearly brought my fist down on his head; the words '*Don't you get it?!*' ready to parachute from my lips. Instead, I simply mumbled: 'It wouldn't be right.'

'I understand your reluctance, but this'll give you more time with her.'

'*Her?*'

'Mum.'

'And what about *your* time, James. No price?'

'It's the career. I have a career. Once you're in, well... expectations build. Once I have the big desk, then...'

'How many years?'

'*How many years?*'

'Yes.'

'Five. Ten. I don't know.'

'Did they not tell you?'

He threw his shirt sleeve back and examined his watch. 'Arnold. I really have to...'

'That's OK.' It wasn't OK. But I excused him. I gave him a clean deck for the journey south. I had seen a minor part of his world through my provincial wanderings at Forson Watshaw. I had witnessed pressure of a kind – a sombre awakening which seemed to trap one's erudition with endless promises. James had been let in. Into the grand marquee with its fake chandeliers. And he now had to make it to the centre. He now had to taste the punch and understand for himself that it consisted of rotten fruit and putrid beverages.

'I better go then. Send my regards... love.'

I felt his eyes pierce into me as he strolled through the exit. I was an enigma – something he *could not* categorise. His accounts were chaotic with me as a part of them, and so I expected to see him next in perhaps two years' time - maybe three. I wouldn't mention the cheque to anyone. It would be lost in the unwritten annals of Debrito history.

CHAPTER 18

I played golf during the next few days. Walked the course. Attempted to rationalize the epoch I had entered. I was poor. My swing was undisciplined. The green I saw ahead of me on each hole was somehow cataclysmic in its finality. I didn't wish to putt – give fuel to my scorecard. I merely wanted to hit and hit until I found him. Stride forward until he showed himself. There could be no slowing, no lining up of gentle rolls. The close, neat cut of the 'end' grass was at variance with my unfettered thoughts.

And so, I played through – over each green and beyond; the brushed intensity of the fairway locking me in and affording me fluidity. I soon reached a couple ahead of me – retirees snailing onward like wavering tenpins. Would they fall or stay upright, manage the bumps or hobble off course? I pulled a three-iron from my bag, swung to limber up, and then knocked the Titleist over their heads – it slicing terribly in the process. They heard it land, perhaps thirty yards in front of them, and turned around appalled and indignant.

'Oye!' was their retort, their pithy battleship. 'What the hell...?!'

Some of the sentence blew away on the wind, but I understood from their re-directed and plinth-like bodies what was next. They walked towards me severely and methodically. I stood with the three-iron still in my hand.

'How long have you been a member, son?' they both seemed to pillory me with, almost in unison.

'Five years,' was my instant, sodden answer.

'And etiquette – you know what that is?'

'I'm just trying to find him,' I pleaded. 'He was here. Around here.'

'*Who?* Who was here?'

'My grandfather. This is his garden.'

'This isn't anybody…'

'Wait. Wait…' The other man put his arm out. 'It's Fidel's boy… Jeee-sus.'

They re-adjusted, gazed upon me attentively. Their whole demeanour softened as if in reverence to something. 'I think he's resting, Arnold.'

'You saw him finish up? He was out here earlier then?'

'Not exactly.'

'Then I'll carry on. Do you mind if I pass?'

'Arnold…' The Other Man partially stopped me in my tracks. His mind seemed clouded, yet full of approbation. 'No. No – we don't mind.'

I put the iron back in the bag, marched on parallel with the lodge and arrived at my ball. This was the furthest point on the course from the clubhouse. If he had wanted solace then surely he would be around here – on the bench at the side of the green or in the attaching fields which acted as perimeter (full of cowslips and primroses). I looked around, but nothing. Lifted my hand to my head to shield the sun. I felt more frantic now – cheated by an omniscient power. There was a well to the right – a dispiriting and out-of-service contraption with no roof or sides. It appeared menacing and hazardous – the nemesis of all around it. No attempt had been made to board up its gaping hole and so it stood like a vertical tunnel – the swallower of things unaware or un-engrossed.

I cautiously looked down its neck. It occurred to me that my grandfather might have tripped. Whilst looking for golf balls for *me*. Whilst being altruistic and capturing the enemy's fodder; its play jewels; golf's capitalist bullets which we had vowed to exorcise before using. I failed to see anything. Just the darkened air which blockaded the tube-like run. To see beyond, into the well's core, I would need light, a torch, something medicinal in its conviction.

I scurried around, quite desperately. There appeared to be no immediate answer to my problem. The sun was high, yet it failed to reach the inner walls of the well – the splayed shadows of scraggy bushes blanketing its rim. Moving onward, although cautious in their stride, were the retirees – perhaps ready to holler or assist me with their goods. I waved them forward in wonderment of their possessions, both tangible and cerebral. I hoped they would add cohesion to my mild frenziedness.

The Other Man spoke first – his associate seemingly more presumptuous and heedless. 'What is it, Arnold?'

'I'm worried that he's fallen. The well, *over there*. It's difficult to see down it though.'

They looked at each other; The Other Man slightly holding sway over their joint expression to me. 'The greenkeeper's obliged to check that each morning, Arnold. It's top of his list... certainly until the funding's there to start it up again or block it off.'

'More likely block it off,' his associate concluded.

'That's what – 8am though. We're six, seven hours on. *Today*. It could have been *today*.'

There was pity in their eyes – a Eucharistic allusion I didn't understand. It seemed to imply loss – privation of some kind. The Other Man eventually spoke: 'I've a small torch in the bag. Let's wander over.'

We walked the forty yards without his friend's presence. Reluctance had somehow permeated him, made him stand and watch with a gritty exterior, a semi-disapproving countenance. On reaching the well, The Other Man stopped for a moment. Rather than immediately reach for the torch, he attempted to get my full attention. 'Do you really not know, Arnold?' came his sombre, ethereal sentence.

'Not know?' My eyes were level with his, almost pinioned to the pronouncement that echoed from them.

'Your grandfather…'

'Shine the torch, please! Shine the torch.'

'He's not in there.'

'But you came across. You offered to assist.'

'I wanted, needed to speak to you alone. I felt it best.'

'Alone?'

'Arnold - your grandfather passed away. Three weeks ago.'

'No. No. You've got it wrong!'

'A few of the chaps from the golf club attended the funeral.'

'You're mistaken. You're deluded. I know I haven't heard from him for a while, but… he's around.'

The Other Man placed his hand on my shoulder. I shrugged it off straight away. To leave it there was to grieve something I *did not* recognise – bemoan the passing of a perpetual life.

'It's true. I'm very sorry, but it's true.'

'You say it's in the bag. The torch?'

'Yes. But…'

I leant down, zipped open the bottom section of his golf bag and managed to find the compact torch. Immediately switching it on, I pointed it in the direction of the well. The flood of light was poor until held below the surface or rim. Then the darkened air made way for old mortar, fungi and half a bike trapped between the circular wall. Further on the detail became less sure. I could make out floating objects – canisters and the like – yet the discoloured water harboured secrets whose unveiling would be difficult. I needed to see the bottom. Cast my eye on a weighty object half in and half out of the water; something which would indicate depth and therefore my grandfather's absence or potential presence.

The Other Man shouted: 'There's nothing! Come away.'

I lifted my head. 'Wait. Please.' What I was now looking at was round in shape, slumped in the corner of the well, although *every part* of this brick construction, at the bottom, was a corner – a clever angle. It was dirtied with the putrid filth that resided here. It looked like a face, turned away and motionless. 'It's him! God! Christ!'

I was pulled away. Both of them gripped me now – tried to restore my sanity and judiciousness. The Other Man held onto me longer while his associate shone the light on what I had seen.

'It's a football. An old leather football. There nothing in here except for scrap.'

'That's a slight! It's him I tell you.'

'Get a grip, boy! I'm being real – very real here. I have good eyes. Your grandfather is dust. I hate to say it, but he's dust... cremated. We have friends who saw.'

'Why? Why like this? You must be part of the conspiracy. They've taken him in – haven't they! He was 'Castro'... an English Castro. He's been restrained, I know he has – taken underground. They're depriving me. Of his final years. His knowledge.'

'No. He's gone, boy. The service was deeply respectful. You were there. Don't you remember?'

My answer was slow, ponderous: 'No. I don't. It's gone. It's been swept out of me. Why is that? Have I done wrong? Am I culpable? Tell me – you must.'

He walked over – joined The Other Man. 'You're grieving. It plays tricks on you. Smothers events. You've done nothing, except ache. And understandably so for he was a great man.'

'What do the others know?'

'That he didn't care for rules. That he drove us insane, but he had something – a duty – that wouldn't leave him.'

'He was decent then? In the end, he was decent?'

'He was. He was… Fidel.'

'That's good?'

He didn't answer. Only nodded. As if wrapped up himself in death's embrace. As if part of a coterie whose badge I had not seen.

'Come. We'll take you home, Arnold,' The Other Man insisted. 'Home.'

We hauled the bags back to the locker room. They then held the door of the car open for me. The drive was a matter of two minutes up the hill and around to the right, yet it was needed, required – my persona flagging and almost in complete surrender to the earth's manacles. When the metal contraption stopped, when the brake pads prevented the tyres from rolling, I looked out, down the short driveway and at the front door. My eyes then lifted – noticed the curtains still drawn in the front bedroom window; their heavy material out of season yet efficaciously securing my mother's dark thoughts. I pictured her behind them, wrapped up with little desire to enter the world again. What, after all, was the point? If the years rolled on and then the gods decided to take Jack *before her*, she would be ruined, embittered – quite worthless to the wider world with its vivid maquillage. Her dubiety would come to the fore with simple questions of stateliness: How do they do it? Carry on? Where does their strength come from?

I exited the car at this point. Asked the retirees if they'd mind *not* escorting me to the door. They assented, told me that they would watch my locker – no.33 – until I felt fit to return, which they hoped was soon; soon being twelve months in its current laboured state. I entered the house – its quiet air immediately murmuring and droning around me. Beyond it there was life, yet I felt I had to savour this pre-evening hour, draft all my reserves and sit not far from the sky's harmonious show. It reminded me of Pendlebury, when he implored me to look east, when he was here in this very spot suggesting that we were all part of the same atom. To watch nature's movements, its plucky resolve, was to understand, to counter the forces below it which purported to know and caress what was right. Each of us would look one day with absolute, synchronistic flair – see and behold the mighty heaven with its drawbridge at our feet, its master telling us not to despair, but rather see the passing years as spiritual vanguards. No temple or church would accord such a privilege, no robed sire would be permitted to extrapolate that which he did not see. It – the truth – would simply ask that we consider it such – kneel before us until our mind was satisfied, rid of amalgamated centuries of puff. But then with no more randomness, with everything known, with one fount only, wouldn't life die? It would be a step on from now. Such order could then be given folds – ambrosial grooves in which one's preferred play took a hold.

'Arnold... I didn't hear you.'

My father had walked into the room – discovered my dreaming presence. I looked up and loosened my pensive features. 'I was thinking.'

'There's more of it when someone is lost.'

'Yes. I suppose there is.'

It hadn't completely gone – the chasm between us, the Sacco and Vanzetti debacle – however five years had assisted, restored a polite kinship.

'I start back Monday. I told them today. Are you sure this is what you want?'

'I'm certain. I think we'll *all* benefit.'

'And money. You're OK for money?'

'I'm fine. Living modestly pleases me.'

'The job. You won't miss it at all?'

'No. Too many directors strutting around. Without Warwick it became... an exercise in aggrandizement.'

'Prestige *does* seem keen on monopolising life. Maybe something'll fight our corner.'

'Do *you* ever think of it?' I probed.

'I'm soon to be fifty-two. I don't think fifty-two-year-olds put up too good a fight.'

'You're not part of the establishment though. You never have been.'

The appreciation in his eyes startled me. I had known his priorities to alter permanently fifteen years ago, to feed not on the unique endeavours of his own soul but rather the scraps of light from his children, yet this level I was now witnessing, this surrogate wanderlust, truly shocked me.

'Maybe,' he mouthed, half-embarrassed and contented, yet clearly eager to move on and not delve.

In that moment, with silence at the fore performing a soliloquy, I took a sweeping look around. What struck me was the accumulation of electrical equipment – TVs, transistors, toasters – perched on the sides. He couldn't possibly fight anyway. Not with so many 'foreigners'. Not with his mind as an exemplar of diligence. Carefulness had entrapped him – not in a rotten way, but in a manner which required his unflinching steadiness. The middle classes would be waiting. For their goods. For the affirmation that Jack Debrito was still willing. Willing and poor. Poorer than them. And such an unfolding would propagate their love. Jack would be their *source*, their *contact*, their *own* extended knowledge; a branch of *their* created world. His own metaphysical musings would be umbilically defunct.

The phone calls, aside of consolation and sympathy, had been surprisingly low on demands. 'You said two weeks, Jack. I'm missing important programmes. I know I can still record *without* it, but things are beginning to stack up.' What Jack thought, what his *own* code of conduct and ethics hinted at was never expressed. His occasional slips while with a customer at work ('Documentaries, ma'am') were nullified completely when on his own patch, almost as if his non-dogmatic self roamed more comfortably when out of the 'Pale of Settlement'. Obstreperous he could still be, but officious – no. It wasn't in him. He listened too intently to others. Perhaps questioned the madness around him, yet played along. Because he was older. Because Rose had subconsciously passed on such a desire. Because it was an inadvertent gift to one of his sons. Myself. A double helping. He wanted me – not through planning or intent, but rather generational fate – to carry the flag, to beckon the lost souls with words and profound gestures. I was beginning to understand even though nothing had been outwardly professed. I was listening to corridors of thought which had suddenly awoken in me.

Looking at my father, the extent of his promises tangibly evident in the form of electrical goods with their 'hoods' removed, revealed a calmness. There had to be twenty jobs, perhaps forty owners, yet the exacting pull each morning, afternoon and evening seemed to fire him up rather than impinge upon him. The scrap yard feel to the house appeared to bypass him and simply deposit with it the understanding that his boss and his boss's wife would not be able to dine here for a while as they did on a bi-monthly basis. Pending jobs were usually banished to the spare bedroom / work room, but there were now too many to covertly move. There was an overhang, a shadow, which promised to lay bare his 'heinous' sideline, his 'weekend treats' kitty. Rose's condition permitted him to rebuff any random visits by his employer, however – ply the doomed family script with full elasticity. And not seeing his boss on his home turf. Not buying in fancy nibbles from the supermarket with his salary that rose *less* than inflation *every* year, was somehow poetic; the tenure between them smiling and being disengaged.

I moved upstairs, pleased. I then sat at my mother's side in the darkened room. Waited. Wondered.

CHAPTER 19

Towards the end of the summer I started to apply for jobs. Prompted by boxed copywriting. Marshalled by my mother's recovery. Some applications on spec. Others tailored by company criteria and strict rigidity in the form of three-page testimonies. It was the former method which inevitably offered me a chance, a window in which to convey my thoughts.

And so I arrived, at an out-of-town slightly Victorian building. Greeted by a man with possibly the blackest hair on record. His manner was that of someone tall with a fast metabolism, a little ungainly yet confident. He offered his large hand which seemed to suddenly appear from out of his jacket's sleeve like a hedgehog's head encouraged by the silence around it. I gave a pathetic squeeze of his hand, an uncorporate salute by way of my seemingly tethered language. 'How yer doin'?'

He didn't pull back, however. Nor did he show restraint. There was something classless about him – caste hating. As I would later discover, he had worked his way up from sweep hand in a factory – passed intellectual tests on the job rather than exams. And after hopping from profession to profession found himself advising people on what to do with their money (taking a fat percentage in the process, yet never questioning such entitlement). People were prepared to pay and they took from him a worldly insight plus a feverish disregard for birthright and privilege. In him was the fight of a family man (wife in the medical profession, piano-playing daughter, amorphous yet beguiling son) and his sharpness seemed to unhinge his lesser counterparts. To have a tale such as his was crucial, edifying. It brought him into contact with an array of similar 'scrappers' – people with money who trusted 'their own'.

Despite this, despite the role offered to me – its non-hubristic definition pushing me closer to Level Two – I saw in it a blind spot. Black Hair's confidence, his penetrating eyes, saw the world in its flat guise. He seemed to ignore or be ignorant of the prop hands altering the stage quite subtly – a stage which he failed to realise had been in place since the outset (the birth of himself, the birth of me, the birth of *all* except those in adulthood *prior* to the executions, prior to 23rd August 1927). And of those who had seen life naked and overt, yet hadn't dared speak out against the new world's mask, its coming force, age had silenced them – stored their bones in the ground or laid waste to their eighty and ninety-year-old minds with the threat of bringing them in for sedition.

Here, now, sixty-five years after the mauling of Sacco and Vanzetti, I was sat at an oak table surrounded by pleasant beige walls and the bodies of two men. Black Hair had brought in his departmental head – a green-suited, overworked drudge with impossibly arrogant brown shoes. Arrogant because the man, five years my senior, continually had his right leg crossed while swinging his shoe rhythmically via his foot – intruding in my space, almost grazing my leg. There was clearly a tension between the two. Green Suit's reluctant stride down the stairs to be here in attendance perhaps conflicting with the need to complete a batch of work.

'We're sacking a man to make room for whoever it is we employ,' Black Hair announced.

'May I ask why?'

He indicated to Green Suit to speak, of his disappointments with the current 'crop', the immature resolve which threatened the smoothness of the business should it not be weeded out.

He did so: The man... boy... boy... man, has become a little complacent. There's too much on my shoulders and so I really need to ease the load.'

I would have imagined him happy at the prospect of a new co-worker, yet evidently not, maybe in light of the time it had taken to get to this point. Something was in the air, and the rocking shoe – despite its justifications – was beginning to disturb me.

'What do you see me doing?' I said this not with complete disregard for my predecessor whose seat was still warm, yet in a curious manner – one which understood that this would hopefully be my final Level One undertaking.

'Admin'. Market and commodity watching. Some systems stuff. We're a small outfit, so whatever comes up really.'

'Looking at your C.V., Arnold, it should be similar to what you've done before,' Black Hair offered in an attempt to reassure me or bolster their game.

'The decision making. Who does that lie with? Who gets to meet the clients?'

'Myself... and the other two directors. Your own input isn't ignored though. It doesn't go unnoticed.'

Back office. Myself and Green Suit would be the back office. Hidden from view. Quasimodo-like in our shame, our non-social grace. My role at Forson Watshaw had been of the same order with the exception of the final few months. When I had been thrown into the bear pit. Made to sit alongside our 'convincer' or salesman. Witness him in action. Read the client.

I had come out of these meetings, these 'torturous sessions', in an uncomfortable state. To sell was to die, to hock your entrails. Everything was seen to have a price. The known world in its entirety was malleable – nothing sacred.

'Is it your long term aim to meet the client?' Black Hair asked.

'No!' I instantly responded, perhaps too loud, too quick off the trigger. I prefer to judge these types from afar, I felt like adding. I only wish to meet up with people as a way of interacting naturally. Business puts a curse on this.

Green Suit smiled. And before his nostrils had settled above the gilded curve of his mouth, Black Hair had left us. Torn away. Business. An emergency without blood.

'I do this job out of necessity,' he proffered, now barren yet forthright. 'I sometimes cry behind the steering wheel on my way in.'

'Why do it then?' was my only prompt, my salted nicety.

'I don't think good jobs exist. I intend to include in my retirement speech "I leave here a dumb wreck of a man. Thank you". I work on such lines almost every weekend. To date I have sixty leaving poems, ten polemics and fifteen essays.'

'How long until you retire?'

'Thirty-seven years.'

'I imagine the choice will be difficult by then. Which to use. Youthful vigour. Middle age defamation. Or senior brilliance.'

'I don't expect the youthful vigour to ever pass the baton.'

'Leaving you where?'

'In a dank cell of my mind's making.'

Less than four weeks later, we witnessed Black Wednesday together. Britain's pulling out of the E.R.M. Interest rates rising to 15%. The stockmarket half beaten up – black, but not blue. Green Suit, although with savings linked to the monster's shaking of its tail, plus an embryonic pension still deep in the soil, managed to smile. He enjoyed unpredictability, whim, caprice – anything which unsettled the accumulators of money. Listening to the news, it was as if the whole country had been ravaged. The archetypal picture of a braces-laden, city executive with a phone at each ear meant not so much a juggling of sales, but rather a medium term grocery-cutting exercise for the small investor in the aftermath. They had been suckered in. Told of the riches. No one actually *worked* anymore. They played. The markets. That merry rejoinder which supposedly bore baskets of fruit when asked only for a solitary grape. Thatcher had taught them well, from the extracts in her Pinochet bible. How to prize unrealistic expectations. How to unfairly climb over your neighbour on the way to the well. Life was for the vociferous – those with mouths that demanded everything be marked down. To do this was to barter, haggle – kill unnecessary premiums. Culture and art could wait. Until the finer elements had been destroyed. Until the world served them as it rightly should. Only then would they have shows, plays, recitals. Yet *without* actors, for actors were a scourge – part of the negative concentration which jeopardised the business 'whole', which undermined its roving might. There needed to be a single party, a single machine which crushed the ungrateful, taught them science, with particular regard for the Second Law of Thermodynamics – made them *real* whilst gutting them of foolish notions. There were too many dreamers without a hard understanding of life. Those that championed Burma with its doomed spiritual plan.

We watched. As the panic set in. As the phones rang seeking answers, understanding. An articulate brief, however, was not forthcoming. Language somehow failed to recognise its own world. The contrast between the calm, outside walkers and the rushing interior bodies behind glass and brick was startling. What had been a divine right (namely profit) – at least since the last crash five years ago (Black *Monday*) – was now a shredded pulp.

'Ha, ha, haaaaa!!!' Green Suit laughed, seemingly not present in October 1987 and therefore eager to daub his thoughts on the day, his apocalyptic debut. 'People should understand now. They're funding a blind enterprise. An enterprise not given to helping the whirling earth. What their money does is come back at them in the form of fat cat policies.'

I was inclined to agree, yet there was something more – a further rung which hadn't been grasped. The critics of this world were rarely inspiring, their words sautéed insufficiently.

'You think I'm prosaic, Debrito. I see it in you. You think I'm dull. Well – listen. Hear Kierkegaard...'

And then, he reeled if off – something imprinted in his mind, something central to him; his entire philosophy taken from another man's tongue:

"*One sticks one's fingers into the soil to tell by the smell in what land one is: I stick my finger into existence – it smells of nothing. Where am I? Who am I? How came I here? What is this thing called the world? What does this world mean? Who is it that has lured me into this thing and now leaves me there?... How did I come into the world? Why was I not consulted?... but thrust into the ranks as though I had been bought of [sic] a kidnapper, a dealer in souls? How did I obtain an interest in this big enterprise they call reality? Why should I have an interest in it? Is it not a voluntary concern? And if I am compelled to take part in it, where is the director?... Whither shall I turn with my complaint?"*

He breathed heavily. Looked for a better response in my eyes. I nodded. Its conclusion "where is the director?" had plagued me for years. Because of this, because of the bent authority which prevailed, conviction had deserted us. And without it we were but a heavy race of miasma-ridden mortals. God had been either crucified, stoned or ignored. The latter because the modern world was unable to tolerate or worship anything other than a scripture bearing his name. To have a physical presence, a living deity, was ungodly – outrageous. Like the blacksmiths who had laid down their tools in order to follow Jesus – an act far from convenient to the Romans – modern government and nation states could not conceive of a more deadly act. To think, pause, consider – affect for a moment the nation's tills – was ruinous, anachronistic. Gods didn't just show themselves in human form, despite Jesus's well-known 'foray', despite the teachings of sages. No. They were now contracted to sit in political minds – espouse that which reviled and repulsed them.

'Say something!' Green Suit demanded.

'There's nothing I can say, except... yes, you understand.'

'But what? Decipher it. You seem to know.'

'I don't know. Not yet. But this is part of the pilgrimage. Not a walk, but a visitation... into the dens of those that don't see.'

'But in here, in *this* den, you only really know me. The others – who's to say what thoughts they have?'

'I've probed them. Quite circumspectly. And their position is very clear. They stand undecided while no alternative exists.'

'Well, create an alternative. Because this low culture is demeaning us all. Some who don't know better – buyers of tabloids. Thirteen years now since the bitch got in and two years of Major has done nothing. I don't give a damn even if we have a dictator. Someone to lift us from this malaise. Someone who I agree with 80%, yet am prepared to sacrifice the remaining 20% because I admire them. I haven't admired a politician since Tony Benn.'

'And politicians are just the flannel.'

'What?'

'Nothing.'

'No. What did you say?'

I was reluctant. I had let no one in but Pendlebury (himself responding with impassiveness) and now, through a desire to press home something other than a raw generalisation, a selection of unedited words had leapt from my mouth.

'There's a deeper network. The upper classes – they're still in control.'

'What?! *Who* says?'

'I do. And there are myths all around us to prove it. Tramps – none of them are real, except for the dissenters that have fallen fighting what they know. Windsor – the debate about us becoming a Republic is rolled out every few years just to polish the mask. There are forces behind everything that we see. The Falklands War – it wasn't Thatcher's call. It was the call of a faceless demon. We're all – each one of us – a Frederick Douglass; chained but with no official law or manifest Gulag to rail against.'

'But when I'm at home at night – what then? This isn't an Orwellian world. There aren't any picture frames with cameras.'

'I don't know what exists in full. I don't yet know their inner workings. I simply *feel* the conspiracy. There are things which are unsettling. As with any power though, failings which continue and aren't attended to raise suspicions. Those, for me, are inequitable elements – the speed with which things are conducted. Time has become the friend of profit, yet the enemy of accountability. We're heading for a society which will allot fifteen minutes each day to disputes, queries and grumblings. I suspect this will be between 5.30 and 5.45pm – outside of peak business hours. Even with general interaction amongst neighbours a silent code will prevail insisting that they are tolerant of wrongs or slights against them, or even nuances which they formerly – somewhat gleefully – complained about. Society will become a smiling piece of hypocritical rock – a collection of people persecuting each other through an implicit code, a horrendous taboo not of their making. And when the negative forces are allowed out, the gabble will be so acute, so desperate in its unleashing, that few will be heard. The pseudo-dethroned will take great delight in policing the neighbourhoods, cities and phone lines when 5.45 chimes. To the point where people will reconsider whether to stop utilising even this small window for fear of mumbling concerns when the chimes sound (the intentional deliberations of the big company stooges shifting the minutes with ease; the complainers eventually resenting the semantic warriors before them). Eventually, of course, negotiations will squeeze the allotted period. Faceless leaders will voice concerns on behalf of their 'subjects' that whining creates unease. As a gesture, however, they will retain a minimum five minutes for equivocal feelings and emotions – aspects of humanity still deemed to be unscientific and therefore unreadable. This 'puff' or convoluted chorus will crash against the sky each evening. Act as a momentary catalyst, but then die – submissiveness ensuing, creativeness a plasticine colonised by the new order.'

'And once we understand every tentacle of the shabby compromise of modern society – what then? Who will our battle be against – the hidden kings or the apathetic masses?'

'Always the kings. Despite my ambivalence towards the victims of dumbing down, I believe them to have room enough for what will come. Popularity will fall from its horse and diversity, celestial minorities will ride again. There will not be a cold worshipping of that which is big – namely countries – but rather a world of hamlets, profound in their identity yet linked harmoniously by a few core values; inviting and benevolent yet with conviction.'

'So when? When do we raise our proverbial swords?'

'Soon. Quite soon now.'

CHAPTER 20

On the morning of the day I left Green Suit – wrapped up another piece of history – I had been awoken by a multitude of singing birds. They were my cue, my prompters, the dominion which rarely left me. I imagined them being sent by Pendlebury in readiness for Level Two – my desire to change things, myself, the thought patterns which traversed the invisible runways around me.

Green Suit would continue with his polemics, his poems, his weekends of soul saving through the text of yet another letter of resignation which would not reach Black Hair. The impetus behind such effort was clear: without his repertoire, he was a herder of other people's ideas and constructions – a fallow depository. He would interview for a replacement, cross his leg again and swing his right, arrogant brown shoe up and down, down and up, until his mind had edged closer to an understanding of the right candidate. He was recruiting not just someone suitable to assist him, but a future ally – a neo-Luddite who would join him, us, at a later date. Revolt. Attempt to reverse the dilution of culture.

When I had said my farewells, when I had used my spare holidays as the normal notice period (so that colleagues were unable to fully question my plans), I immediately posted the form. It had on it my course selections – all six of them. I wanted to be educated, or at least witness to university corridors, lecture theatres and seminar rooms. The vicarious understanding I had built up of power, erudition and privilege had to be set against that which was partly tangible. I could not begin to formulate a justifiable cause until I had stood shoulder to shoulder with the rucksack hordes and their tutors. This, after my dallying with finance, commerce, Black Monday and Wednesday, would ready me – strengthen the developing bastion within.

And the courses, the establishments? English was predominant. I had grown to love its bending, fruitful grace. To spend hours with blanket and hamper along its winding river was sacrosanct. And the others? A humanities degree and a speech therapy degree – the former a dip into kindness and mercy whatever the social discipline; the latter a whim of sorts, an ambitious desire to bring forth thoughts compromised by neurological deficiencies. I would stay local due to both monetary constraints (I had saved a living expense kitty of £4000 while under Green Suit's wing and did not wish to burden myself with London's expense) and an overriding impulse to study in my grandfather's house. Either Lancashire or Greater Manchester would act as host to me – feeding my mind and introducing me to people I would normally perhaps be wary of and quick to categorise. This would, however, be *after* the acceptance – something I had no control over and something which was yet capable of snubbing my comparatively poor list of academic qualifications.

The weeks were quick to run into the spring of this dappled year: 1996. My days consisted of gazing and thinking (my golf membership having run out due to a lack of funding). Every man, woman should be permitted six months of absolute leisure every four years; time in which to reconsider fundamental beliefs – themselves forged at too fast a pace. Books existed to be pored over slowly – absorbed, rather than abused in a state similar to infidelity. A snapshot 'dance' of promiscuous leanings, a juggling of two or more texts between journeys to and from work was perfidious – criminal in its disrespect. Upon buying a book you instantly owed it every virtue known plus a comfortable shelf on which to rest. Its contents were picked at only by non-aficionados. Those that knew – really *knew* – used their evenings and weekends, bathed with it, sought a whiff of its printed pages. When touched, taken, moved by a smattering of words, they momentarily brought harmony to the spine – pushed together the pages into their original state and looked out, around, in the knowledge that they understood art (that its carvings had not eluded them).

That was it really. Once you gave it time then you had a chance. And if that led to an understanding, an affinity with art – the high priest of truth – then you were in, ready. You simply read more until the day came. I, myself, was shepherding something absent yet full to that point. That is what I felt – that one day I would speak to a large crowd; infuse them with a body of ideas (circuitry both latent and avowed and present within them). I would be a white

Martin Luther King Jr. I would quiver, show emotion and only shirk from the pulpit in the event of my demise, my deliverance.

Christ! Deliverance! I had heard the word before. In the company of Pendlebury. He had talked of looking east. But what if he was being tactile? What if my life was somehow the key to *theirs* – the making of a renewed existence? I swallowed hard. The day had been leisurely, yet taxing. My mind had wandered off track. Yes. That was it. My thoughts had become fanciful – disparate in their waywardness. To think of myself as somehow honoured, like a charger at the core of a battle, was to destroy the paradigm I had maintained. *No one* had the right. To apotheosize. To claim others' minds as if tasting the air – as if knowing which way to go.

When the first rejection landed on the cottage floor, I didn't think anything of it. I knew the old school establishments to be strict with their entry criteria and not always forgiving to those without A-levels. They had to have certain standards, guarantees in place, and I was a risk – the potential water in their whiskey-like debates. When, however, course selections two, three, four and five swiftly followed, I developed a fear. That no one would test me. That the Romans thought me dangerous the closer I got to their nucleus and so had intervened unfairly – rubbished my character to each dean. But then would they not want me more knowing that they weren't to select me? Wasn't that in their nature – their recalcitrant bones? I had no answers. I was simply tiring of the white slips with their formal paragraphs intoning defeat.

The one which remained, the one whose star still glistened, was at a former polytechnic or 'the land of the dumb' as the callous description went. It had been the only 'joint' to interview me, to peer over university spectacles at my stupefaction, my academically naïve frame. And when I had stated my aims, my desires, the humanities co-ordinator had tried earnestly to push the economics mould upon me.

'Your choices are English, Politics and Sociology, I see. One or two of which you'll carry through to your finals. I'd have thought Economics though was the natural route for a man of your leanings.'

That was the misapprehension, I professed, with initial difficulty, despite a photocopied testimony sitting before him which I had written as part of the application process. Numbers aren't enough. I'm good with them, but where exactly do they lead you? To mammon? To a 'home' similar to that which James was building? To a non-polysyllabic world full of procedures, apathy and moneyed culturists? If you gave it enough time, enough years, you lost all sense of distinction. The big desk became everything. Reaching its surface, sitting before it, was the great panacea – a whirlwind utopia. Holding the pen and looking down on lesser beings was deemed magnificent, glorious – the final calling before you were cast in stone and worshipped by subsequent generations.

'You may have a point,' he slowly voiced. 'Even though, it would seem, *I* myself fall prey to your 'big desk' critique. I heartily welcome a cross section of candidates for this course however, particularly those attempting to shed a skin they feel is no longer suitable.'

That is how he left it, with nothing definitive. Yet I was glad he had seen me, I was glad that my educational 'demand' would be processed more healthily. And now, I could only pace the floor. I could only gaze at nondescript golfers from my grandfather's former bedroom. The world had me cornered – dependent upon its occupants' judgements. I was sure there were hundreds like me – escapees wishing to take their next step, yet temporarily marooned until the deliberations, the turning of minds had mechanically and cerebrally reached their climax.

I continued to look. Outside where life continued. Where the sanguine colours of golf attire brushed uneasily with nature's purer forms. The roaming bodies seemed to multiply each hour as the day became finer. Spring was crisp, light – mottled in its brazen canvas. The singing birds which led its procession, its carnival, were tireless, sacred – the trumpeters of intricate patterns, of Gaia. Without them, without their darting flights, their colours and their vocal insistence, life was shallow, dead – a network of manmade coarseness.

Before I knew the day had ended, I was awake, ready to commence another. I slipped on my bathrobe to bolster my fragile morning state and wandered down the high cottage stairs.

I needed grapefruit, toasted bread, marmalade and all the other grandparent-induced breakfast items. I would sit at the wooden table – uphold tradition and mull over a new day. Through the hallway, into the kitchen, I spotted it: the final yes or no in its brown apparel; an envelope whose contents would see me lifted or bedraggled. I bent down, took a careful, respectful hold of the light, transited paper. Even holding it, unopened, brought me closer to its clandestine message. The face of the humanities co-ordinator or admissions tutor seemed to jut out of the seal imploring me to discover my fate.

Earlier words from the one paragraph they (UCAS) afforded you upon rejection still stung my brain, still hampered my optimism:

Dear Applicant

Your application for admission to the course(s) indicated has been carefully
considered by the institution(s) concerned but I regret it has been unsuccessful.
If you have applications outstanding at other institutions, I will inform you of their decisions in due course.

Yours sincerely

M A Higgins
Chief Executive

It was the fold – the fold in the letter which killed you; "Dear Applicant" visible, yet the rest not. Such a fold had been discussed at length apparently – ruminated over as to its fairness, its not wanting to unduly excite. And in the end, they had decided that a delayed negative was better than an immediate negative; that "regret" and "unsuccessful" were better than "unlucky" above the fold. Of course, they hadn't allowed for the printing machinery which would sometimes stray off course and thus include a further eleven words above the fold; hinging on the word "carefully" which in any context always seemed to be the bearer of bad news.

This one now – this one I was opening, however, didn't have any of that. Two words rippled against me: Unconditional Offer.

Saved. I had been saved. By a simple letter from Cheltenham; a pocket of Gloucestershire which had promised my father so much two decades earlier. And he had reluctantly said 'No'. Such an answer was not an option for me. But then, I was not a father of two. I did not have a wife to consider. All I had was Level Two – the desire to change things, a belief that grafting my mind with literature or the wisdom which was at its core would propel me somehow. Who I would meet at institution MMU on course Y400 was less certain. I imagined them younger than myself, perhaps less diligent, yet definitely with greater natural intelligence. In my head I was still in the third quartile – at the very back. Ormerod had imprinted beneath my skull the position I would supposedly occupy for the next fifty years. As an adult she had lacked sensitivity and therefore was a risk to developing minds. She was not entirely to blame for my stunted appreciation of English, however, at no point had she sought my comprehension through lateral methods or a profound intuitiveness on her part. Choosing to castigate me in public had been her ploy, her only device. And for that she was not worthy of picking up a book.

I was not bitter at what had gone before, because the naysayer that she had been in the presence of my effort at reading Melville was one of a corrupt chairperson, an odious pedagogue. And the soft folds of her cream blouse did not compensate for the barbarous sounds which emanated from her. If only she had done battle with my mother. If only I had had the ability to lock horns with her intellectually. The outcome would have been momentous, pivotal even.

But then, this movement I was planning – whether overtly or not – was possessed with a will to save rather than defeat, overcome gargantuan obstacles rather than lay into them. Eventually, I would welcome in those who didn't understand, those who acted like Corinthians, those who sought to question my intent and sincerity. It would be *after* though. After the pseudo-dethroned had dethroned.

CHAPTER 21

'**T**oday is the 10th of November. Don't you know? Don't you know? This is 1996. One year on.'

I looked at the fellow, stood, on campus, as he exuded word after word of a subject I had no knowledge of. His arms were thick with black hair, his face partially bearded and, although Asian, he had the attire and body language of an African or Caribbean. He continued his one-man show, surrounded by dramatic posters fenced around him half-octagonally depicting ordinary Africans, desolate villages and colossal gas flares: 'We know the Atlantic, therefore we should know Africa – its leaders, its history, its despots. The one I talk of today. The one I immortalise because of his brutality is Abacha – general, General Sani Abacha. This man would disrespect Mandela, Tutu – the living greats. Why? Because he doesn't understand genuine accomplishment. He doesn't wish to move 'his' people on, forward; Africa's largest country which goes by the name of Nigeria.

'Look at posters one, two and three which give you most of the story. Poster one: the before and after – Niger Delta's golden egg, Oloibiri. Oloibiri – giver of oil, the blood in its veins. Nearly four decades have passed since oil was first struck. Oh, this is long before Abacha, but it is the seed. Not much has changed – poor vegetation, tatty homes, dirty water. But that is the point – the oil companies promised civilisation, a flood wall, schools. Nothing was done. Forgotten, because they are weak. Raped and *not* re-clothed.

'The Ogonis in poster two were stronger. They had Mr Ken Saro-Wiwa – poet, articulate steer, prominent speaker central to the Movement for the Survival of the Ogoni People. MOSOP. So prominent that when Abacha's military cheated the elections of '93, almost within a year they had framed, arrested and incarcered Saro-Wiwa. On the 10th of November last year they hanged him and eight others.

'So you have both an image of the evil that still stalks Nigeria right now as we approach the 21ˢᵗ century; an image which surely can't tie in with the pleasant surroundings in which we study – quietly, peacefully. And you also have an image of Saro-Wiwa – someone who dared contradict the self-imposed government, embarrass them with words (if only they read). And for doing so found himself mercilessly eradicated, abused in a fashion which belongs to the dark ages. Incidentally, the trap door failed. When they brought him out to the gallows, the trap door failed. They kept testing it and bringing him forward, until... How would that make *you* feel, knowing that your liberty had been taken and was almost being played with. Played with, I ask you! A man's *life*. As if in the hands of a German officer during World War Two – the officer inconveniently running out of bullets mid-genocide with a shackled Jew lay at his ankles. And then re-loading his handgun while the Jew excruciatingly watches – counting the moments before...

'We move on... to a piece of symbolism: the gas flare. Poster three. Who constructs these? The oil companies – loving consortium partners. What do they do? Burn off excess gas while pumping out oil. And their effect on communities? Basically an environmental assault (this interspersed with military assaults): a poisoning of the atmosphere, the destruction of wildlife and plant life, deposits of thick, black soot eventually washed into the soil by what is already acid rain, pollution of water courses, noise, toxic smells, respiratory problems for the locals, poor diet, cancer. Whatever we in the West say about the necessity of oil can be countered incorrigibly so by the stark misery which unfolds as a result of its exploration. And I haven't even begun to go into the business and politics of it all, because we all know that most people in these arenas are beyond the pale.'

Silence. Then a couple of applause. Three or four. But nothing beyond that. No radical seed. Simply students passing through. Pleased, or rather, entertained on their way. Not stayers though. Not ready for commitment or discussion. Enough of that *inside* the seminar rooms. To commit in everyday life was surely foolish – one less beer.

Over I walked. Waited for the solitary few to take their leaflets. I then offered my hand: 'Arnold Debrito.'

He waited. Questioned my genuineness. Finally, on reading my face, he proffered his name: 'Ragavan – dealer in posters. Why the interest?'

'You looked as if you meant what you were saying.'

'I did. It's what should draw a crowd, but...'

'They're apolitical. If the beer stool doesn't rock them into an upright position, then they trust such fatalist vibes.'

'They trust the easy life. It's good to them. Every part of them... except their conscience.'

'You'd rather they were here?'

'No.'

'Why?'

'Because I don't understand applause. I don't understand what each set is saying.'

'They're saying we're with you.'

'No. No. On that you're wrong. Applause are political also. Different pressures behind each set. Pressure to conform. Pressure to be altruistic – help out the fool who chose to speak about a subject most ignore. Pressure to help out a brother.'

There was still no offer of a hand and so my outstretched arm had found itself retracting slowly during the course of our interaction. I had never 'chatted' to an Asian before. In twenty-six years such an opportunity had strangely eluded me.

'So you *do* understand?'

'No. As I said – I don't. Pressures are many. I have but a few examples. I really have no wish to understand the privileged.'

'And Saro-Wiwa?'

'What? What about him?'

'Does he not need the backing of everyone?'

'No. I don't think he does. Now – I really must go.'

He hastily folded up the sizeable, half-octagonal stand behind him, gathered a few papers on the table before him and then slowly made his way out. Past me. Through the doors. Without a farewell of sorts.

Ragavan's creed interested me. What he was trying to do seemed brave, even if risible to the wider world. I sensed in him a tinge of racism, a bizarre and contradictory stance given his support for minorities. I had never been confronted with such an implicit accusation, particularly as most saw in me a desire to fight the machine, the clumsy, bureaucratic manifold around us. But then, I had not seen the world with *his* eyes. From behind his darker skin. And perhaps he thought me fatuous because of it.

Whatever the implications or inference, I would pursue a friendship with this man, this Rag-a-van. I would fight his preconceptions, his subtle diatribe. Quite why, I thought I knew, yet my mind seemed to trip up at each juncture – offer a Job-like explanation, a crucial bringing together of the races, a class-killing formula. Ragavan, the Poster Boy, was to be, somehow, a nemesis whose successful conversion was upon my shoulders. And while not obviously one of the Romans or 'others' given his Saro-Wiwa stance, there was something present, something awkwardly kicking within him.

Level Two, in light of this, was not as I had imagined. I had thought it smoother – less cumbersome. My first six or seven weeks at university had resulted in two friends – both of which I had little in common with, except for the angst of a freshman along with the willingness to double one's normal effort. Because of this, because of my slim pickings which would or would not develop with time, the Ragavan episode seemed at least 'challenging' – worthy of a new mental plane. (Unlike the grinning barons before me who, while not intelligent or unintelligent, simply exuded the worst kind of symptom: prosaicness.)

The first chap whom I had 'happened' across whilst sat at the introductory lecture had a quite nebulous face. His shaking of my hand had been welcome given that I knew no one, however it soon became apparent that he was a serial greeter with little room for discernment or predilection. He simply 'had friends' – none of whom offered him a particularly deep loyalty. His ambitions beyond university life were sketchy although inclined toward politics. His mind was a lower 2.1.

The other chap, in a sense, was more steady. He had a girlfriend from his college days – now a medium-distance relationship given her decision to go to Sheffield. His physique was that of someone concerned with vanity and fitness yet not overtly so. And his chosen career (which threw me somewhat) was that of a policeman. Quite why he felt the need to complete a degree in order to pursue this aim I did not know. A fast-track application was a possibility I supposed, yet given our time together thus far in lectures I had come to glean an understanding of his cerebral 'level' (his handwriting and spelling equivalent to that of a ten-year-old child). Perhaps such 'minor' points were irrelevant. Perhaps being a Detective or Constable was about one's ability to make a moral 'call' or uphold the law. I sensed, however, that this 2.2 mind – nothing more, nothing less – was destined to pound the streets for a while, quoting and re-quoting "….anything you say may be…"

It was full of them. University. People I hadn't expected to be here. But then, this was a former polytechnic – an establishment still seeking its stripes, its initial fifty years of respectability. A First here, it was said, equated to a 2.1 elsewhere – at one of the blue chips or red bricks. Such proclamations were spread, however, with the luminous desire of betrothing the old guard with a Dalit-like status or untouchable cadre. The tutors at institution MMU, in my estimation, were hungrier than the red brick souls whom I imagined still churned out archaic reasoning; they waved their *small school* licence in the knowledge that the breadth of their research went largely unchecked and therefore offered undergraduates an extra highway of thought. Such talk was of course representative of the minority of tutors – say 25% – as with any grand claim. There were undoubtedly elements within the recently built walls of this magnificent, yet simple cube-like structure with its huge atrium, visible walkways and deep-socketed lecture halls, that lacked the ability to inspire or enliven the minds before them; politics tutors heavily steeped in right-wing dictates; sociology tutors lacking the grace to permit discourse when the subject matter concerned one man (their belief that even Martin Luther King Jr cannot, alone, steer or affect societal change). Fortunately, in my third discipline, English, I found the stone of radicalism – minds not fixed by questionable standards and a piqued bias.

My tutors were a spectrum of talent if ever there was one: an Irishman whose madness had increased with age resulting in an indefatigable candidness which, to a first year student, was like the blessing of a Sunday crowd; a short, plump lady who, prior to being a Doctor of English or the arts, had watched old movies during the daytime for ten years whilst unemployed; a fuzzy-haired professor whose father had been a senior figure (Englishman) in India – the early years of the son thus involving man servants obliged to carry him around until the age of eight (his limbs not properly developing until his late teens as a result); a black-haired beauty who despised Kerouac's work like myself and, although not qualified to lecture, freely exhumed her past during seminars – the grease and adversity of working in McDonald's for five years still partially evident in her face; finally, a working-class loner who contested life itself, whose agenda was probably too much for the inexperienced foes he found before him in the form of first year students. (Nevertheless, he had something – a non-aesthetic, almost ascetic and Pendlebury-esque desire to level things out, kill class differences completely and start again. For this, he required two generations of people to sacrifice everything; a difficult project, yet one admirable in a sense.)

Each tutor I found to be in disagreement with the others, if not publicly then in a way which leant itself to the grapevine. A significant, earthquake-like fault line had developed upon the Professor (somewhat new to the institution) being asked to unwittingly share a room with his working-class counterpart. Tired of viewing copy after copy of Brendan Behan's *Borstal Boy* while marking his work, the Professor adorned the wall with the flag of the Orangemen – the Protestant opposite of everything Behan stood for. Subtlety was the usual battle clothing of the Professor and so to be met with row after row and poster after poster of what he deemed to be naïve propaganda, his tactics had had to change somewhat. For his working environment not to be conducive to mellowness and cordiality was tragic – everything he had fought against on his way to the apogee. The response to his Orange adornment had been quite apoplectic, verbal, tirade-like – everything, in fact, the ascetic one was attempting to redress. That had been the irony, the Byzantine twist – that a seemingly inflexible colleague had rejected the very basics of what he chose to teach; that the 'ponce' before him – together with his creed – would perhaps take more than fifty years to 'educate', to be scoured of their genteel, but miscreant nature.

It was decided that in the interests of campus harmony they would be allowed to 'divorce', that another room would be found for the Professor and that the book collection of the ascetic one would be permitted to breed. Attending the lesson of one man and then the other was like being purposely lied to and then promulgated with the truth. Which piece of information to trust, or who to place one's faith in, was decipherable only in the mind of the individual – not necessarily now, but with hindsight upon entering the real world later on.

CHAPTER 22

When I next saw Ragavan it was, strangely enough, the second anniversary of Saro-Wiwa's death – the 10th November 1997. Quite where he had been in the intervening three hundred plus days I did not know. A different course. A different life. A different institution. All the possibilities presented themselves before me. The only thing that raced through my mind now, however, was the physical appearance of him, the mannerisms which bowled themselves from him like heavy armoury. His beard had thickened – conquered new land. His arms had somehow got broader. And his demeanour – it was difficult to tell. He certainly appeared less confrontational, less wound up by the white man's ignorance and permissive clover. But then, there were more posters than before – pictures of grinning, duplicitous politicians which acted as attestations of shame. These people had met Saro-Wiwa's son *before* the hanging. They had shook his hand, hinted at assistance and then – upon the junior envoy leaving – had immediately turned their back. Photographs represented their cheap history, their saunter across another tomb. Made still, life was as they wanted it – courtesy of an ephemeral smile and an attempt at meaningful dialogue.

Oil's mouthpiece, its spokesperson was seemingly everyone – everyone with a job, a family or an expensive habit. The willing colluders, aiders and abettors were on every corner, licking its whiskers, its dumbfounded face. Meanwhile, the crude manifestation took delight in its lewd poisoning of people's lands – far enough away so as to leave its beneficiaries undented and therefore merrily blind. What I was viewing now was striking, telling – Ragavan had exorcised his first anniversary bluntness and replaced it with a semi-Machiavellian gallery. The throng of people was intense, Ragavan's language carefully crafted. Mumblings and interactions ricocheted around the tight rectangular space. The big arms at the head of this flock were conductor-like in their guidance, their ushering of thoughts. Although the words mostly passed me by, I noticed this time – the faces, the eyes acquiescent and drawn. Ragavan's annual fair was voluminous, tragic and yet necessary. For all its cogency, it – in the end – spoke of neglect and torment – humanity fighting itself because of constructed needs.

I waited. As I always did. Ragavan shook a multitude of sweat from his head as he bowed, almost sardonically. The crowd thinned. There were no leaflets this time. No proverbial 'nibbles'. Just a summoning intonation from the bearded giant: 'Go!! Take with you Abacha's face – his portentous skin ruddied as it is with oil.'

They left. Wandered away. There was to be no analysis of what had gone before, no close up or lingering question. They seemed to understand his need for an unreserved privacy, a deity-like rejuvenation. All except me. Myself. I faced him as he folded his mammoth pictures together – their impressive compositional elements almost alive and mocking. What he had brought together was a flatness now synthesized into art; a one-dimensional fair now breathing.

He eventually lifted his head. Looked around. And then in my direction. Upon 'scanning' me, feeding my image into his mind, he at first appeared confused. He was somehow at odds with what he saw. Within seconds, his expression then changed. He looked anxious, almost guilt-ridden, yet stricken. The pictures in his grasp fell to the floor. And at once, he took flight. I could not believe it nor understand it. That he would run from a simple stare, that he would choose to see me as a threat, I found appalling.

My instinct was to follow him. Run. Flee from the campus like a blue-collar impostor. I did so – strode down the steps, looked around hurriedly and desperately. He was there, to my left, walking fast now rather than running so to lessen the attention. Myself – I did not care. I immediately broke out into a run. Pounded the paving stones with my waxed boots, unsuitable as they were to a detective, gumshoe-like role. He gazed, over his shoulder. The anxiousness, I could see more starkly in his eyes. *What, who* did he think I was? An assassin? An establishment figure fresh from the shadows ready for my debut kill? With each stride and then burst of speed, I felt like a wrongdoer, a transgressor. I had to catch him though, talk to him. Because if not now, then it would perhaps be another twelve months. If at all. Ragavan's frame, despite its participation in public sermons, was elusive – almost nonexistent and chimerical. I wondered, while in pursuit of this broad-backed behemoth, whether in fact my eyes were trustworthy and sure – certain of what they had seen.

As I trailed the Poster Boy - this purveyor of hardened, yet piercing images - the street population seemed to become more dense. I was getting closer, yet having to swim around people in order to retain my bearings, my proximity to him. I pushed, nudged against the hordes, assimilated faces which threatened to stop me in my tracks. Through, finally, a pocket, a cluster, I sped though. And upon coming out the other side I noticed he had fallen. Ragavan had tumbled to the floor and was now shifting himself backwards while sat on the ground. Afraid of me. Too flaccid to stand. Pointing. And then words: 'I know who you are!'

'What?! *Who*?' I was dumbfounded. The ability to express myself appeared, all of a sudden, to dry up. There was an aridness to my vocal cords, a thrust back, away from reality.

'I've not forgotten Lepanto – the Battle of Lepanto. Where you harmed my Ottoman brothers.'

I did not know what he was saying or what he was referring to. I could only observe the fearful and somehow retributory face of Ragavan with its evident bent on history.

'Lepanto?' I questioned, ignorant of his statement's roots.

'Ha! The white man's mind. Centuries do not matter. Only decades. And then he would struggle with more than two. Don't you see?! Don't you see – that is why we are *here* at *this point*, now.'

He seemed to wail, ululate following this cryptic drawl. His body's motion ceased – replaced with a slump, a static and unbecoming pose.

'Who am I? What is *this point*?' I semi-demanded.

He lifted his head. 'All so immediate. Now. Ephemeral. Transient.

Evanescent. No time for discussion, understanding. That is the fissure – don't you see? You don't allow the beauty to permeate you slowly. One cannot demand. One must earn. But no – we must rape the lands, set up our structures, *claim* everything including that which is not ours… all in the absence of a god, an omniscient heart. And so we are here.'

'Where?' I asked, still swirling, still bewildered by Ragavan's mental transcript.

He stood up. Those that had been watching intensified their gazes. 'I'll teach you where,' he offered – his expression emulating the total sum of conviction I had experienced before, his fear and nervousness dissipated or at least assuaged by an inner switch.

'But I *have* teachers,' I responded, in an effort to provoke or understand more of this man, this Muslim hybrid. I have Pendlebury, my mother, father, 'Castro's' spirit, The Leaf Blower, George Minty I, Warwick, Green Suit, I thought. Through university there was the potential to meet other such mentors. So why another, why crowd my latter-day memory?

Ragavan leant forward and whispered in my ear: 'There aren't enough for the table though.' He then placed a card tight in the centre of my palm and was gone.

I shook. In front of the remaining watching faces, I wavered, looked around embarrassingly, sheepishly. I felt a hole bore itself through my organs, the very gravity which stationed me here. I was light, almost airborne, but sick – sick with a feeling of apprehension and disquiet.

'What did he say?' came a voice. Others added to this – repeated the question in an effort to satisfy their insatiably perverse inquisitiveness.

'Nothing,' I refuted.

'*Nothing*?!' they harmonised, in a rude, expectant manner. 'Nothing? But his mouth was next to your ear…'

'He uttered nothing. Those are my final words.' I was suddenly full of conviction, repose.

'Well that isn't enough.'

They began pushing me, from one 'corner' of their human circle to the other. Again. Again. I allowed it without resisting – gave them unlimited clemency. Their aggression at first heightened. The pushes became harder. I felt my body recoiling inside, yet its physical mass stuttered – gave licence to the blows and taunts. Eventually, I fell – hit the ground; the weightier bundles of skin at the top of my arm softening the landing. My instinct was to curl up, despite the resulting humiliation. I protected my head and face. To the people stood around me I was obviously weak, feckless, a pathetically warped appeaser.

They moaned, laughed, criticized. Their disgust lasted for a further two minutes. Their epitaph for me upon dispersing came in the form of a swinging boot which jarred my rectum. I reeled, felt the pain instantly, placed my left arm behind me to support the soon-to-be bruised area. Odd as it may have seemed, lay there like a whimpering fool or victim, there was something redemptive about my plight. Not in an atoning sense, but in a fulfilling, bottom-of-the-pile, nadir-like way. Here, lay on the pavement, open to the elements, I was at the core, the essence of life – witness to its fundamental urges. There was no hell below me because purgatory had been washed out by the rains of the earth.

Opening my first eye, I saw the clouds above me – their translucent, rich clothing intensely seraphic and unattainable. And then, a girl, a woman – her words lyrical and concerned: 'You're hurting…'

I opened my other eye. Took her in. Tried to understand why someone would stop for me. 'Che…' I nearly blurted out the name of my only love. She seemed instantly comparable, this presence before me twelve years on.

'I'm OK.' She helped me anyway – her Egyptian-like eyes scanning my contorted face as I stood, partially placing my weight against her.

'You didn't fight back,' came her exclamation, her seemingly ambivalent take on things – events.

'I…' I stuttered.

'I think you're brave,' she observed.

Her cheeks became an almost inflamed pink. Her demeanour seemed momentarily stifled. She quickly surpassed such inconvenience, however – continued her short thesis of me: 'Pacifists are very few these days. When spotted they should be adorned in silk.'

I smiled at her humour. Beyond that I struggled to interact though. Most of what I crafted was passed from one part of my mind to the other – not released and shared (particularly not with women). And so I smiled again – upon her turning to face me – like an incorruptible, yet bland driver's mate.

'I have enough money for two coffees if that interests you.'

She was fascinating, patient, yet would surely begin to question my credentials should I not add to my three-word tally nor match her social decorum.

'Yes – it does. But… allow me.' Together with my hand movement indicating that her stride should take precedence over mine, the words seemed sufficient. We walked to a Bohemian-type café that we both knew wherein we each took a seat at a corner table and ordered the same drink. It soon became very easy to talk to this fellow student, this lady if ever there was one. A few sentences in we realised a proper introduction had passed us by and so exchanged our Christian names; my 'Arnold' for her 'Josie'. I was enthralled, enchanted. That a person existed who still held naivety and nostalgia at the fore, believing them to be venerable, was improbable, outlandish – beautiful. Josie, it transpired, was in her final year at the university next door studying theatre. She appeared bright, sensitive, yet humble. Her sentences spoke of the future as if her dreams and innermost desires were unshakable – circumventers of everything average and crass. Asked what she would do upon graduating, she looked deeper into the well of my eyes, before: 'I'd hope to produce or direct. Perhaps a small theatre group and then… well, we'll see.'

There was still the girl in her. Quite plainly. Not the youthful self-centredness of a mild delinquent, but the clutching brief of one seduced by possibilities rather than a deadened reality.

She asked me about my first year and where *I* was heading, to which I was unable to provide a firm answer. This seemed to please her, as if not knowing was a form of pre-cathartic greatness, a last stand against the bloody waterfalls which would ultimately rage against me.

'You're about my age…' she eloquently pried.

'Twenty-seven,' I responded.

'Good. We're the same then.'

By 'same' I was sure she meant a legion of non-numeric associations: principles; opinions; build; ardour; zealousness; desire. I examined her. The fact that no mention or rather detailed questioning of the earlier incident had come about made me think. I could not shift my mind onto the next subject until she had an understanding of the crowd's motives and Ragavan's gestures.

'Before, when you stumbled upon me…'

'Yes. You were the victim of an erratic mob. I don't think they were students. I'm quite certain, in fact.'

'But…' She had thrown me a little. I had no idea. My being pushed around seemed less acceptable because of it. '…I was going to reason, for you, their motive.'

'Their motive – people like that – is always the same: fun. They must roam around in groups because to be alone is to invalidate their worth.'

'I see.'

'And the man that left you. You haven't met him before?'

'Ragavan. Yes. A year ago. I wanted to ask him. About Nigeria. About his background. He ran from me though.'

'He *can* be unpredictable. But I think he means well. He's quite an obsessive.'

'You know him?'

'There are a few of us. We meet once a week. We discuss world events. Politics, I suppose. Ragavan is a great knowledge base.'

I had to ask it, despite my reluctance, despite my wish not to add malady to the trust I had quickly established with Josie: 'I'm not part of an elaborate recruitment drive then?'

'I don't think so,' she quickly answered. 'Although…' she tittered. '…I see your logic. Curious Muslim fellow as the bait. Crowd of sympathisers. Me there to sweep you up.'

The subject matter then changed. Josie seemed to engage her mind with Ragavan's background, his initial appearance two years ago. 'I first met him a few days after Saro-Wiwa's hanging, you know. There were seven or eight of us in the union building. We used to meet – we still meet – for two hours each Wednesday evening. A kind of socialist HQ. I prefer 'splinter group'. Anyway, we were chatting about the birth of the W.T.O., its sinister role in world affairs… then came the big knock. We could see him through the glass. This huge frame. He looked like something imagined by Mary Shelley. Of course, we couldn't turn him away. The bosom of socialism awaited him. He entered. His first words were "This desk and paper won't help. Whatever it is you're discussing should be out there propagating justice". We looked at each other, slightly bemused. He pressed on.…'

She seemed to have revised Ragavan's maiden speech word for word. I listened as she pulled each syllable from the barrel organ of her mind. '..''In Port Harcourt, Nigeria, nine people have just been hanged. Blood drips from the hands of suited devils… oil executives, foreign ministers, people that would willingly dally and forsake innocent lives. *Five hundred days* they had! Saro-

Wiwa was incarcerated on 22 May 1994. And then on 10 November 1995, Abacha's henchmen took his life. So you see, my socialist comrades, there *is no* international community, no true support system. For every customer of Shell, every one of its oil-needy car owners, I put it to them that their part in this most horrific of military crimes is one millimetre of the noose tightening. The rest, I must stress, the ever-decreasing diameter of the rope is, in my estimation, the contemptible and tacit fault of an oil company porridged by its own share price".'

Stories. Parables. We all had them. And they alone – conditional upon our choice – had the effect of pushing minds together. This one, this more recent event that Josie clung to, was *her* Sacco and Vanzetti, her focus, her semi-didactic guide. With its telling some of her veneer had dropped away, however – and I was sure of this: despite the dirty knowledge which permeated her, she continued in good spirit – fought her way through life not with a sword and whip, but with a sharpened understanding. To smile among the difficulties and drama of the world's stage was not moronic (unless excessive), but forbearing – just as 'Castro' had described my father upon me doubting him (something which, in recent years, had blown away yet had an air of unanswerableness).

The ending to Josie's speech ("share price") seemed to beckon my experience, demand an insider's perspective, a compounding of our suspicion of business and how its softly-regulated playing field was wrecking all around it. I knew the Third World's masters to be mostly in support of resource-stripping and self-enrichment (more so than even the West), yet something else skewed the picture, the human understanding – something invisibly spiritual, something laden with years of misappropriation and inexcusable sunder.

At that point I recalled the card Ragavan had squeezed into my palm. I pulled it from my pocket – gazed at the simple etching. It had on it his address and name. No phone number or allegiance of any kind – just the necessary basics; enough through the old methods of communication to follow things through, assimilate his teachings, his assessment of 'where', exactly, humanity stood. I chatted more to Josie, even though she had seen my toying with Ragavan's card, his calling. We discussed Wednesday nights.

She pressed me to come along, make an appearance, if only when the hours were up to collect her, take her on a date. She stressed that her 'splinter group' was a body of contrasting ideas and people rather than a militant wing sure of everything – beholden to a strain of megalomania. I kissed her hand and then left – agreed to meet her two days later. As I walked down the road, away from the campuses and throng of people, a voice pushed itself into my head. It was low, whisper-like, quite indistinct. I barely caught the gabble of words as they fired through my mind: 'not... we will not.... partner.... not permit a partner... consent to it....'

I stopped. Attempted to shake the intrusion from my mind. The whispering continued though. I felt like a canister, a shell. How dare it, I thought. How dare this voice make judgement on my life, my preferences. Hadn't I given it twelve years of abstinence? Hadn't I, since meeting Pendlebury, believed something intangible was out there – soaking up my thoughts, adding resonance to my already-alienated self? I had *given*, and for that I wanted affection, love. I was not strong enough to continue without it. I did not wish to bat to and fro my own thoughts without interaction, without devotion.

CHAPTER 23

'**C**ome in, Debrito.'

I had arrived, at Ragavan's small, terraced abode – the inside of which was immaculately clean, impeccable in its structure, the space it gave to books and files whilst retaining a softness, a comfortable 'through road'. I sat down whilst Ragavan toyed in the kitchen. I stared at the art work glinting back at me. Nothing was out of place, crooked or wrong. Ragavan had arranged the contents and furnishings of his dwelling in such a way that one felt warm – party to a landscape of preciseness and immutable history. The books, which covered two walls, were in the main by majority world authors – Urvashi Butalia, Eduardo Galeano, Vandana Shiva, Satish Kumar, Edward Said, Desmond Tutu; people I was just starting to discover through magazines (collections of slowly-conceived polemics, essays, stories) and BBC2. Other titles by Wendell Berry, Rachel Carson, Naom Chomsky, Thomas Cahill, Lewis Mumford and E F Schumacher seemed to complement their neighbours' efforts – drive home the need for reasoning, sensibility and patience.

'I'm a part of every book you see before you. If ever I go astray then please remind me.'

He passed me a bowl-like cup full of a brown liquid and then sat down himself, placing his drink at the side of him. I sipped the offering. It was the perfect temperature, thickness and taste. Of what, I couldn't make out. I shifted my mouth ready to ask what it was I was drinking, but Ragavan was keen not to dwell on such trivialities.

'I've just commenced a new list. I'd be interested in your opinion...'

I nodded in accedence even though his word "new" implied an existing knowledge on my part concerning his interest or work. A list, I thought – of what?

He returned with a file marked 'WARS'. He then sat on the couch next to me. 'It's only the last half a century, but it helps.'

Helps? Some of Ragavan's gesturing, his language, was loose, open – almost intentionally so. It was as if the discernment of his visitor was being tested, challenged. I didn't speak. Instead I simply combed through the wad of printed paper – casually examined its contents.

'Things need collating. History. Happenings. We can't trust governments and so... what you see before you is an effort at the truth – a history of the Left in many respects.'

'When you raged at me earlier, you mentioned Lepanto. Why?'

'Please. The list. I'll work towards Lepanto, but that's another three and a half centuries.'

'But you know. You know without having to document it.'

He lied: 'Not really.' He then seemed to ache physically.

'Josie says otherwise. You're a "great knowledge base" it would seem.'

'Josie doesn't know. How did you meet her? She doesn't know...'

He seemed deflated, cursed somehow by me quoting him and then Josie. The mood of the house had altered seismically. I decided to offer him some respite: 'After the lists then, we talk about Lepanto and your Ottoman brothers. Because truth, part of which you are documenting, cannot be selective.'

He looked at me, at first unsure. Then, through his eyes only, he gave me his consent, his promise. We turned the pages back to the first paragraph of his dossier. The initial line, clearly designed to grab the reader's attention, talked of politically-related deaths in the twentieth century. And the figure that Ragavan had placed next to such a volatile statement was one in twenty (5% of *all deaths*). I *did* gasp to myself. It was a shocking expose of the strife which had plagued nearly ten decades. The figure for some reason I seemed to trust instinctively. Ragavan's work then moved on, to wars with hundreds of thousands of military deaths: the Korean War 1950-53 (1.2M); the French-Algerian War 1954-62 (160,000); the First Sudanese Civil War 1956-72 (100,000); the Vietnam War 1965-73 (1.2M); the Biafran War 1967-70 (100,000); the Iran-Iraq War 1980-88 (850,000); and Afghanistan 1980-89 (150,000). The numbers were small compared to the near-30M total of the First and Second World War, however their overriding theme was one of mass individual suffering – minds abolished, thoughts unplugged forever. If this was me, if one of these was me, then I would be saddened that I had not been allowed to develop, interact with humans who knew a change had to come. I would be utterly despondent if in possession of the knowledge that my family had lived on not knowing every bit of me.

Ragavan paused at this moment. 'Of course the real tragedies exist when peoples suffer under their own leader. When civil society is massacred and replaced with terror networks and a non-primary truth. de Salazar, Tito, Suharto, Mengistu. Many, many years of sadness. Between them, one hundred and eighteen.'

He went silent. I read on. Picked chunks of text from the file: contested areas which he had chosen to highlight; differing means of affliction (concentration camps, terrorism, dissident executions, starvation, battlefield casualties); 'democratic' head to heads (American Revolution, French Revolution, Spanish-American War, Anglo-Boer War) although not during the stipulated period, but between 1775 and 1901.

The papers became heavy then. And so I asked him 'Why? Why do this?'

'I told you. History. We need to collate things. Lists can be powerful.'

'But behind that. For *you*. Where is the satisfaction derived?'

'I like knowing things. I only seem able to read serious news, data, stories. Laughter – I do try. But then I return to what I know. It justifies occasional action.'

'Action in what?'

'Wait here until it's dark and I'll show you.'

I did. Ragavan prepared a light tea or dinner in the meantime. Continental cooking of which I approved. Ratatouille with bread and wine. I made a mental note in my head not to forget about Lepanto. I would ask him later. After the proceedings. Whatever they might be. Wherever they were. There was clearly much to discuss – theories and thoughts which I would pull from him and then dissect. The heavy burden which encircled him would be split apart – cleaved and severed.

CHAPTER 24

'**I** am a hypocrite of course, when the lists have been drafted and everything appraised,' Ragavan spoke, breaking the fresh silence as we sat in his company van apparently far enough away from 'the cameras'. 'Look out – ahead,' he continued. 'The advertising hoardings are partly *my* work, privy to *my* fastidious pasting. I am an intellectual prostitute, a pusher of capitalist values – one of its ailing henchmen.'

I looked at him as he said it and then ahead, as directed, at the boards before me with their night lights on and consumerist faces. Ragavan, although self-critical, seemed to enjoy the release. As if planning a next move. As if somehow in full harvest.

'The banks I prefer to target,' he openly admitted. 'When I'm putting up their gleeful lies during the day I feel rotten – ashamed. Companies that would seal their doors in poor countries, pilfer local savings and then move on – continue to showboat in the West – I deplore. The collective memory of a people is almost challenged. "I deposited $1,000 with you." "No. I am afraid you didn't. If you still insist that you did then please speak to your government. They are the ones with the answers. *We* are not accountable."

'At night it is not me. Not the man from before. The Poster Boy. I drive to previous jobs. Leave valuable days in between. Other people's jobs as well – their pastings, their jigsaw making. The one ahead of us, in the middle, I put up twelve days ago. Always twelve days when I come back. I like the number.'

The advertisement, wordy, yet unglamorous touted cheap flights abroad. "Break. Relax. Spend more once you're there." The language was encouraging, beguiling, celebratory.

'This one I'll edit now,' Ragavan enthused. A worried expression seemed to coat him, yet his lists and his planning mitigated the risk – rubbed out his slight angst and soon replaced it with steadiness and purpose.

I sat there. Watched as he marched towards the wooden structure with a spray can and set of small ladders. It was somehow fascinating seeing his mammoth frame take over, tame and control what he deemed to be a modern evil, an amnesic entity which spurned the future for the sake of instant gratification. The words began to appear slowly: EACH BIT OF SAND YOU KICK SMOTHERS THE WORLD'S LUNGS.

Ragavan slid down the ladders like a hoarding connoisseur. He then strode back, casually and calmly. The back doors of the van were opened and the equipment replaced. 'Ten words is a big job. It feels like you're in the 'vault' too long. I shan't be doing it again. Three or four is the norm. I was showing off, which is stupid. Stupid!'

He was genuinely annoyed with himself. The threat to his conscience-salvaging forays was quite real and potent.

'This work, this spearheading of a higher truth – it steers me away from self-pity though, however nefarious our 'masters' claim it to be. I sometimes feel that we must all go to jail at some point in our lives, otherwise history will disown us.'

There was no question in amongst Ragavan's sentences, no affirmation-seeking prompt. His words simply hinged on the library of thoughts he had at home and ones which to a large degree now rested in his head.

'You've heard of Eta?' he probed.

'I have,' I replied, a little uneasy.

'Well, let me show you Etc.'

'Et cetera?'

'I suppose so,' Ragavan responded, quite delighted with my acronym expansion. 'The unspoken... the miscellaneous... the 'so forth'. That's who we are, isn't it?'

'I don't know,' I said, although feeling a connection with

Ragavan's direction and grace.

'Perhaps when you see the innocence of what it involves, you'll back me.'

I remained silent. He didn't expect any words until the next destination, the next neo-Luddite task.

We arrived. This time in an area more dense. Filled with row after row of terraced houses. It was now 2am and a sweeping echo seemed to fill the streets. I wondered for a split second what I was doing here, who I was actually with. But then I knew the initial uncomfortableness would pass, I knew Ragavan simply possessed conviction and a steadfastness – qualities walked away from by most in an effort to 'fit', remain inconspicuous.

'The End terrace campaign – I founded it three years ago. A lot of things began three years ago. Wait here and you should understand. Perhaps you'll even read its symbolism.'

He got out of the van. Pulled a different set of equipment from the rear this time: ladders – taller and expandable; a liquid – perhaps simply water; a metal stripper. I watched, like I had all night, like a movie-goer, a vicarious thrill-seeker. Ragavan was swift, his arms like pistons against the poster. He was a human destroyer, a wrecker, and yet I was beginning to understand what Etc was about. End terrace. End terrace. It was an effort against the consumerist colonising of people's habitats, their very homes – the plastering of adverts on the brickwork of one's retreat, his or her safe haven. Implicit in such a common practice was humiliation and dominance. That an amorphous piece of 'art' should adorn one's dwelling was degrading – it was a paganistic swipe at genuine civilisation. And now, as I watched the mulched pieces of advertising fall, I knew Ragavan to be a warrior of sorts, an honourable steed. What cemented his efforts was his tidying up – the collecting of the damp, screwed-up paper on the pavement below. And so, just blank. The canvas was blank. His silhouette, set against the dim street lights, returned. We drove away immediately, parked up in an anonymous spot, and then he talked.

'You understand now?'

'I do, I think I do,' I said. 'You're a kind of saviour. You prefer people's homes to be daubed with craftsmanship, not commercialism.'

'Yes. But I'm not happy at what I leave. Even the wooden frame is perpetuating the cycle – this belief that minnows can be exploited, insulted. I have never seen a large, detached property with a toothpaste ad' on the side of it. Or a castle with a car ad'. Just end terraces – just the comparatively poor. For now though I simply remove the 'glass' after committing my crime and campaign to councils to outlaw such a practice. One day they will see the connection. One day I will be caught returning from what I believe. Each time I return I imagine them there on my doorstep – a line of police. That is why, in part, I detract from my most strident issue by defacing hoardings not under Etc's jurisdiction. They have my name, my address though – they are able to find out where I work. I am sure it will not be long.'

'Your employers – they'd lay you off?'

'Without hesitation. That is why Etc remains a quiet, diplomatic operation – conducted only through the privacy of local councils. A percentage of my employer's business is at stake here, so, yes, my dismissal would follow were they to find out about its existence – myself being the founding father or even a disciple. Money before honour. Always money before honour.'

We sat there in the dead of night. I had other questions, yet their release seemed neither pertinent (fundamentally) nor useful. Ragavan's guise had been revealed. He was not a student, an undergraduate like myself in the second year of his degree, but a worker and part-time campus player – a tapper of minds afforded a three-year sabbatical in life (and through this an unofficial attendee of Wednesday-night socialism and the odd lecture no doubt).

'The Saro-Wiwa thing. That was money before honour too. There's much that hasn't been told – facts withheld from my speeches for fear of altering the tone, making them too personal and bellicose. The public have a dislike of the truth in its most raw form. I'll tell you now though. I'll tell you here, away from everything...'

I listened intently. Ragavan immediately rhymed off the names of what he called a 'Last Supper of Dereliction' – twelve individuals who, in his mind, were party to Nigeria's crimes: Brian Anderson (Shell Nigeria's Chairman and Managing Director); John Jennings (Shell's International Chairman); Steve Lawson-Jack (Shell's Head of Public and Governmental Affairs); Eric Nickson (Shell's International spokesman); Mr Achebe (spokesman and colleague of Anderson); Lieutenant Colonel Komo (Head of Rivers State); Major Paul Okuntimo (Internal Security Task Force Head); Major Obi Umahi (Commander); Captain Tunde Odina (part of the military); Thabo Mbeki (South Africa's Deputy President); George Nene (South Africa's High Commissioner in Lagos); and General Sani Abacha (butcherer and embezzler).

'Oil represents ninety percent of the Nigerian government's revenue. 90%! One seventh of Shell's barrels are currently from this huge African country. But let's ignore the numbers. I wouldn't like to be judged by statistics myself. Instead let me tell you of the hurt...'

He talked, of Saro-Wiwa's brother, Dr Owens Wiwa. How he had met with Anderson six months before the hanging. How he had sought medical assistance for Ken and indeed this had been forthcoming (for the first time during his eleven months of incarceration). A second meeting had then followed in which Wiwa asked Anderson to use his influence. The response had been "stop the international campaign and I might be able to do something". Wiwa, at this point, stressed that he had no such power and that the campaign against Shell would reach a natural end should it use its conscience and prevent the trial or tribunal from happening. Anderson had been eager, however, for a press release denying the reality of environmental devastation in Ogoniland. This, Wiwa, thought incredulous – particularly as the world had known of such happenings since 1990 (when the Ogoni people's "anger had coalesced into a protest movement" galvanized by Saro-Wiwa). Finally, a letter from Ken was passed to Anderson during a third meeting with Wiwa. It stated two scenarios over the coming months: Ken Saro-Wiwa's death, thus turning him into a martyr; Shell doing the "right thing", using its close relationship with the military government to the advantage of all those that would laud human rights thus ending the illegal detentions (mature discussions to follow and an ostensible end to the international campaign). Anderson had been unable to accept the gist of either in his mind – perhaps through self-delusion or a fear of his status within Shell declining. He informed Wiwa that no more discussions would take place, that he would be travelling frequently, however a colleague by the name of Mr Achebe would be on hand. Numerous phone calls to Achebe merely resulted in messages being left due to *his* absence – Achebe, it appeared, had caught the travel bug as well. He was in Germany, then Abucja and then Port Harcourt. No effort on his part was made to return Wiwa's calls. All the while, Ken Saro-Wiwa's trial was getting closer – hastening, counting down each day.

Ragavan paused. 'So Wiwa turns his attention back to Anderson – the M.D., Mr Big. He phones him at his office and at home. At first he is told that Anderson is at a cocktail party. Then, on a separate occasion, he is having lunch. Then, he is not available… not around. He has basically become the Scarlet Pimpernel! The lives of *nine men* are at stake and he is in hiding, avoiding his civic duty, sipping cocktails with his 'corporate junta' pals. How does that work? How can such a man look at himself in the mirror?'

I thought, on the back of Ragavan's boiling anger, that this was Sacco and Vanzetti squared, that the three deaths sixty-eight years earlier (1927) had simply multiplied. A trial of nine in the year 1995. Would a trial of eighty-one come about? And then on, on… When would it end? When would the kangaroo courts be set upon – become a target of rampaging truth-seekers?

Ragavan continued. '*The others.* Do you wish to know what their roles were?'

I nodded.

'Well, I have a list – of each person's crimes. A list, my friend, young Debrito. If not mouthpieces of Shell, then they speak from a Hell. One and the same? Should such a question even be posed? If it gets out, then *we* – *we* become vulnerable… followed by the surrogate sons of money… maimers, killers, people to whom a life is nothing… an unsacred collection of skin.'

Whilst holding the list – the list with a dozen names upon it – Anderson's face (what I imagined it to look like) sauntered through my brain. I wondered whether the choice had been entirely his – to discuss things with Abacha's regime, to calm matters and negotiate with an iron hand the release of the Ogoni Nine. He was the Chairman – that power had been his, surely. Thoughts of Warwick's days plagued me though. How his seniors had used their collective will in an attempt to negate individual responsibility. How they were *together* and in this state thought themselves beyond reproach, not able to be pinned down.

It was more callous. It had to be. Placing personal 'survival' above human lives. Ignoring ethical considerations by sewing executive jackets together in a united, but misguided front. There was a level, a 'No' sign, beyond which even a zero-conscience individual knew not to tread. The Balding Man and Standing Man, and now Anderson, had chosen to flagrantly ignore it though. They had bathed in a myopic selectiveness. And so, we were here. In Ragavan's company van. Discussing life's folds – its testing of human fecklessness.

I looked at the other names and at the comments Ragavan had written alongside each...

Jennings – what is the role of an International Chairman? Surely it is to oversee and intervene where appropriate in the larger activities and decisions of his company's worldwide network. Isn't there something structurally and cataclysmically wrong when such a man's finger is not on the pulse?

Lawson-Jack – principally an inventor of oil spills designed to enrich himself and community leaders. Sought to appease local rebellion through bribes and the re-directing of community development money.

Nickson – openly admitted Shell's policy of importing handguns "on behalf of the Nigerian police force who guard Shell's facilities" (107 Beretta pistols during the 1980s confirmed, others hinted at by way of lawsuits filed by arms dealers due to non-payment).

Achebe – duplicitous character who, although heard to stress the importance of "continuous dialogue" to Owens Wiwa weeks before the sentencing and hangings, avoided contact with anyone synonymous with the international campaign.

Komo – the brutality of Abacha's regime, in many respects, begins here. In April 1994, Komo sent a memo to Okuntimo demanding that those "carrying out business ventures... within Ogoniland are not molested". This was backed up by a policy of strict military intervention. Okuntimo did not disappoint.

Okuntimo – acknowledged even by Anderson as "a fairly brutal person" (either in an effort to disassociate himself with the realities of his lackadaisical and taciturn management policies or in a belated act of culpability). Following the deaths of the four Ogoni tribal leaders (21 May 1994 – Kobani, Badey and the Orage brothers) Okuntimo mounted a vicious campaign of nightly raids which included beatings, torture, rape, monetary extraction and the burning and looting of property. Hardly anywhere was exempt. Sixty towns and villages in Ogoni were punished for their support of MOSOP, whether the affiliation was "real or imagined" or simply a convenient tool of justification for the military. The leaders of MOSOP were detained on 22 May 1994.

Umahi – not enough is known of him, however, simply by replacing Okuntimo in July 1995, four months before the hangings, this individual was complicit – tainted by Abacha's filth.

Odina – arrested Owens Wiwa in December 1993 (held for over a week) implicitly for his role as co-ordinator of the Ogoni Relief and Rehabilitation Committee. Basically a stooge of Governor (Lt.Col.) Komo; part of an arbitrary unit which regularly threatened residents whilst under the influence of alcohol and marijuana.

Mbeki – South Africa, as the other prominent 'African Lion', albeit quarter of a continent away from Nigeria, undoubtedly had responsibilities (itself fresh from years of a different evil, apartheid) and owed a debt of sorts to the persecuted Nigerian dissidents and opposition. Mbeki, who formulated South African policy on the 'Nigerian issue', did not meet any of the Nigerian opposition, however, was involved in 'constructive engagement' on a visit to Abacha's Nigeria in 1995. Although the visit was later seen as the reason behind Abacha's October 1 commutation of death sentences against former Nigerian ruler Abasanjo and other 'coup plotters', the negligence of South Africa's Foreign Affairs Department was quite startling. Indeed, on the day that Mbeki saw Abacha, forty-three criminals were being executed in public by firing squad (not a particularly conducive background to such a state visit). Despite this knowledge – able to be gleaned from newspapers days in advance – Mbeki had been unaware, almost ashamedly so.

Nene – the word 'incompetent' must hang around this individual's neck, if not always, then certainly in the wake of the nine Ogoni deaths. Above him were the Foreign Minister, Alfred Nzo (carrying constitutional responsibility for his department), his deputy, Aziz Pahad, from whom Nene received his instructions as South Africa's High Commissioner in Lagos. The lost opportunity, the tragic unfolding of events appeared to hinge on Nene's interpretation of "maintaining contact" with Nigerian dissidents. For some inexplicable reason Nene had taken this to mean liaising "primarily… on a government level" – quite the opposite. For this not to be monitored is inexcusable. Nzo and Pahad must be compared to Jennings. The ultimate downfall, however, came after the handing down of the death sentences (Tues, 31 Oct, 1995) by the Civil Disturbances Special Tribunal (itself appointed by Nigeria's – read: Abacha's - Provisional Ruling Council). The PRC met on the morning of Wed, 8 November to confirm the death sentences. The news agency, Reuters, reported this at approximately noon that day. However, despite this, despite such information reaching Nene on 8 November – via the following chain: Nigerian opposition groups, South Africa's Lawyers for Human Rights and Johann Marx at the Department of Foreign Affairs – Nene suggested to Marx that they "wait for confirmation in the Nigerian media or work on it in the morning". The morning! An extra two hours per life lost! Thu, 9 November – Nene got his confirmation and then attempted to contact senior Nigerian government officials with the belated message "Don't do this". He failed to make contact. Fri, 10 November (apx. 11am) – Saro-Wiwa and his fellow activists were hanged. Nene made contact. Too late.

Abacha -

'You're onto Abacha, now?' Ragavan asked.

'Yes. Yes, I am,' I replied.

'There's too much. At times there's too much to understand. I've pored through many documents in the two years since. And still, interpretation can be everything. Not on a black and white level as Nene had it, but with shades of grey.'

'But the men you list – they are all tainted in some way?'

'I have no doubts in my mind when it comes to them. But the events – one can never know for sure. I have articulated some of the happenings quite poorly – partly plagiarised sentences in my effort, my scramble to hurriedly know and document. Other things are not in doubt though: Shell's signing of a $4 billion natural gas contract barely a month after the hangings; Okuntimo's promotion to Lieutenant Colonel in December 1994. Rewards for their collusion, their willing of oppression's hand.

'What angers me is that Abacha is still there. Touting a "progressive democracy", fooling some of the world; a world, I suppose, which gladly masks itself behind such 'credible' language should its own business interests continue unharmed. How do we express this though, when everything has been done before at some point in history? One's face cannot invent a new shock or disgust, because humanity has now somehow overreached itself – usurped every available emotion. And so where are we? We are at a place where pogroms, genocide, ethnic cleansing, prison beatings, 'disappearances' and corrupt trials are blinked at.... expected almost. The Civil Disturbances Special Tribunal which charged Saro-Wiwa and his fellows was outside the normal judicial system. It was established by a suspect decree (formulated in 1987) which allows the federal state leniency in trying cases involving civil riots and disturbances – basically any pocket of opposition which seeks to strengthen the country's democracy. There is, in these courts, no right of appeal, no need for actual evidence. Their decisions are entirely at whim – prejudiced by the ruling Nigerian General's desires and wishes.

'I am shifting too far away from my thesis though. Humanity has reached an end point. It needs, requires, a spiritual god – a deliverance. We cannot continue to legitimise life as it is, as South Africa did with the Nigerian regime pre-November 1995. The twenty first century is nearly upon us. There *must* be someone – a god by then. If not old and masterful, then precocious – young and settled.'

Ragavan stared at me. He had a curious wonder in his gaze. I felt uncomfortable too far away from the more solid foundations of his Etc chatter and his Saro-Wiwa storm. I felt an undefinable degree of expectance from him – a 'I have given, now please offer something back. Participate in some way'.

His gaze shifted from me. He became silent, sullen-looking, pensive. I felt the need to say something, although not about gods and spirits. It was now the time – after the lists, as agreed, to discuss Lepanto, to adjudicate with regard to his Ottoman brothers. I thought of how to probe, how to ask – push my discursive line, my non sequitur. And then, the need to approach him from an angle seemed – all of a sudden – to disintegrate. I would be quite direct; the gods and Lepanto after all, amounted to much the same – that is what the voices inside me purported.

'Moses? Jesus? Muhammad? Allah? Who will this god be like? Will he have behind him the Torah, the Bible or the Koran? Which, Ragavan? Do tell me …and what will be his downfall?'

He seemed slightly shocked by my verbal demand, my semi-assault upon his thoughts. The answer he knew, however – knew like a diligent equestrian who had stepped out the course before him.

'The books don't deny the existence of any of these. All four are trumpeted. There is an underlying harmony to the texts which we must begin to concentrate on. Although Lepanto upsets me, it had to be – this last major Muslim / Christian battle. Without it, we would be in a much worse position – at the feet of a sprawling and invidious empire. I suppose my annoyance at the Ottoman naval defeat lies in the numbers. Fifteen thousand slain or captured –

an enormous number then. And half of this, the Christians gladly lost on their side.'

'You're saying that half a Christian equals one Muslim. That Christians hold themselves, because of this, closer to God?'

'I'm saying that people place values on things – stupidly, unnecessarily. That when this god, my god, appears, He should be a god to *all* – a charismatic and discerning 'man' of immense humility, fully able to heal the wounds of history, show mortal man that evil is futile.

'In you, Debrito, I thought I saw some of this. Your presence felt ardent, vehement. I somehow felt the need to weep in celebration at your feet. Yes. Despite my adversity, my fleeing. Nerves. Sheer nerves. Who am I though? Who am I to know such a thing?'

What Ragavan was saying soothed me – made my focused eyes feel sharper, more penetrating. Perhaps… no. Perhaps. Was I to try on some clothes, a robe waiting in the heavens? I had been here before I felt. And yet, my memory of earlier revelations and subtle sentences was clouded – foggy. I had little to coalesce, bind together, comprise and create a thesis from. Innocuous galleys seemed to be sailing toward the centre of my mind, with *me* still scribbling – still patching together reason's intellectual base, its equanimity.

CHAPTER 25

The day before meeting Josie I woke up in a slight sweat. I felt, in myself, a level of prevarication not experienced at any time. Something told me that Ragavan had pinpointed my fate – Level Four perhaps – and yet I could not accept it. There was no mechanism inside of me, no defining staff in my hand which enabled such an eventuality to come about. I was able to view a line through which the bodies of my family, Pendlebury's family, and former work friends were somehow unified, however, the fact of me being 'above them' seemed ridiculous – risible.

My thoughts instead turned to Josie. I ran through my head conversations that we would have, when and at what she would smile, and at what point she would love me. I knew nothing of her, in truth, but our one meeting had offered promise – an unspoken conviction on both sides. I hoped she would be the same – unchanged from the café. I hoped her final year would not absorb too much of her, because such a creature did not belong alone in a library.

In thinking of her, I suppose I was already quite selfish – her movements and preferences, to date, locked in my mind, played forward, rewound, rerun, monitored for vulnerability, benignities, anything that would assist our future togetherness. I would think of a subject – her shoes – and then mention that I had expected elegant footwear and a dress on our first date (even though we were to meet at lunchtime). I simply wanted responses from her that would lead to staged mockery on both our parts, light taps on the arm... and then a kiss.

The play had to come first though; play in lieu of a future playwright's convincing, melancholic productions and everything deemed its opposite (serious and bitter tales of humanity). Lines threw themselves into my mind. Constructed scenes appeared before me – hours and days *ahead* of their release, their physical outpouring. I would mostly prompt the scenes with Josie – unbeknown to her – not knowing for certain her responses, yet having at my disposal three or four follow-ups.

I could not discount entirely the possibility that she might stump me, however I hoped what minimal spontaneity I required would be there – ready to lead, ready to hold firm the mast.

That sentences were even floating around inside me – stacking up and begging to be freed – I took to mean that I had been inspired or annoyed. And Josie could not annoy, which meant her own presence was / would be assimilating that which she had proverbially borne. My words would merely be a reaction to her uniqueness. So in a sense I was a medium through which she understood herself. And vice versa, I supposed. On, into the thick network before us. Without interaction, therefore, our growth was a sham - a poor, modified harvest.

Upon meeting her on the Wednesday – her Egyptian eyes seductive, yet seemingly trustworthy, our chatter continued like a seamless by-product of the second anniversary of Saro-Wiwa's death (two days before). Tonight they would discuss the passing of such a significant date – its ramifications and implicit judgement on the political world given Abacha's untested resoluteness. Now though, before then, I had her company on this quiet campus day – Wednesday afternoons synonymous with strike action every few months rather than lectures and seminars.

We wandered, quite aimlessly. To have plans was to shift the focus too easily away from the nuts and bolts of our kinship. Indeed, we probed each other's history – parents, brothers, sisters, jobs, friends and philosophies. Josie's father was evidently a foreman; a man caught between management and the industrial floor. She had a brother and a sister – both of whom were older than her. Her family was very much steeped in left-wing traditions. They apparently had an innate classlessness about them although, as with James, her siblings had veered off course. Her jobs had been many: assistant manager of a petrol station; charity shop assistant; checkout girl; stable hand; gallery assistant. None had lasted more than two years. Her desire for real happiness had exceeded her stoical bent. Reaching the top, having ambition – as with me – was, if not an anathema, then certainly undesirable due to the elements at the forefront of such endeavour. To be in the middle – somewhere in the middle – was the aim; a hardy place which enabled consideration and hope to be given to the scrappers below, while displaying a working paradigm to those that would play with power – eventually leaving them denuded and wronged.

'*Your* father? And mother...' Josie suddenly asked. 'Are they representative of you? Obvious parts of you?'

I wanted to mention the bruising humility which so often entered my head; those words together indicating my father's mindfulness. I couldn't though. Instead, I mentioned his love of the radio, his forty years of toil in the same industry, how he was only eight years away from retirement now.

'Parts of me? I'm not sure. My mother has a steadfastness. I'd like to think that some of that is in me. My father – he sacrificed things for the family... a more interesting career...'

I found it difficult to continue. There was still an ambivalence in my head concerning Jack Debrito – one which when left alone did not stir. I owed it to Josie to tell her though. I wanted everything straight from day one. Quite how I would articulate the parable, the history, I did not know. My father, a decade ago, refused to say whether he had been certain of the innocence of two men *before* or *after* their pardon and if the latter then I do not have a history. How could I possibly put that across? How could I talk fully ten years after discovering such a gamut of information (while in the company of The Leaf Blower)? An outsider, as Josie still was, would surely rail against the remaining confusion and grey area – seek to simplify and answer that which was not known, rather than question the 'deception' behind it.

'You look worried... intense,' Josie commented. 'Is there something...'

'No...' It was our second 'date'. I couldn't possibly burden her with Debrito family history, religious permutations and the chronicling of my perceived loneliness. But then, I wanted to trust her from the outset. I wanted to see if she was able to withstand the ferocity of the storm. And what emboldened me was the fact that she had unravelled her politics in my presence almost instantly. The personal, therefore by extension, was inherently related and hopefully relatable – a natural follow-up.

'Yes. Yes, there is,' I interjected. And while telling her, while exorcising the leach-like build up inside of me, I thought of how – in a way – this was my wooing, my attempt at making union with her. In the back of my mind was Pendlebury – his whereabouts. Was he still at Lake Vyrnwy? Had he changed over the years? I somehow needed him – his reassuring tone and canter. I needed them all – all the faces that had spoken to me. Everything had to culminate – be together at the final crossing, the final judgement.

CHAPTER 26

My pen was in full flow when he entered somewhat uncustomarily. I was close to completing my final examination paper for year two. Anzia Yezierska, one of my new heroines what with my burgeoning university life, was the focus of my concentration – her work lovingly anatomized and implicitly adored with each stroke of my pen. It was June 1998.

'Abacha! He is dead! Arnold – he is dead!'

Faces looked up at him – this blue-collar intruder shouting loudly, expressing something which didn't quite belong in an American Writing exam.

'Ragavan,' the whispers pieced together. 'It's Ragavan.'

I looked in his direction, immediately nodded and then stared down at the paper before me. A further reverberation of words then sounded: 'The butcherer is dead! There must be change now…'

His sentence tailed off, quite weak and cloying. From his eyes appeared a wetness, a gathering of tears. He tumbled, fell. The adjudicators whose intention it had been to accost with force this intruder, hesitated. What now? What do we do?

The giant frame of Ragavan lay there crying – his initial joy now seemingly mourning for the thousands of Nigerians taken without consideration, without respect and solicitude.

'We *have* to move him. He can't stay here,' came a voice, a realistic call.

They encircled him. Each bent down to lift what they could. He was clearly heavy. Ragavan's weight was very much muscle and sadness, strength and a tempered joy.

'I can't lift him.'

'The same here.'

'Then talk – persuade. We need him out of here.'

'What's his name?'

'Ragavan.'

'OK. Ragavan. I understand what you've come here to say. I appreciate the urgency of it. But, now, we need you to leave. Please.'

Through the damp, inconsolable mist before him, Ragavan gazed. 'You *knew* him? You knew Sani Abacha?'

'I knew of his human rights record – yes.'

'Then tell me – why can I not maintain my joy at his passing? Is there something wrong with me?'

'Let's talk outside. In the hallway.'

'OK, sir,' came Ragavan's humble reply, his unexpected deportment.

The door shut. We were advised there would be an extra ten minutes – five to regain our composure and five for lost time. Somehow we carried on, obeyed the simple edict. Our eyes, apart from those that had either finished or failed anyway, returned to the papers before us. I, personally, re-read the lines I had just written – soaked them into my mind in order to be able to continue, connect with the world in which Abacha had lived in my consciousness. The ending would have to take a different route now. Because of a man's death, my essay had grown partly futile, indulgent even. But, no, I was not to think like that. I was not an anarchist. I did not condone the ripping up of everything that had gone *before*. I was a radical, a changing man, a force beholden only to the remotely-wired signals in my brain.

When it was over, when the screeching chairs had been left or pushed back under their respective tables, I waited in the corridor, the hallway for his appearance. Minutes passed. The adjudicators had gone, boxes under their arms. I had had to indicate to my second year acquaintances that I would follow – see them in the pub, drink to the summer ahead (all three months of it). Eventually, he strode towards me, less confident than I had ever seen him – his head almost bowed, staring down.

'Your teachers – they seem to think I'm normal. The Irish one – he was disappointed by my fall though.'

'He likes fight in a person – reminds me of my grandfather.'

'Is it over now, Arnold? Does Abacha's heart attack mean we're freer?'

'I think we both know it's not. I think we know that the quiet desperation goes on.'

'I was thinking of a new list…'

'Of what?'

'Of everything that doesn't fall under existentialism's banner.'

'That…' I was caught for a moment, spellbound and bewitched. Ragavan had a habit of touching on and then speaking of the neglected, but poignant. '…that would be fine… the right thing to do. Give us hope again.'

'I fear that Wednesday nights will end now. Not because of Abacha, but because they're all graduating… your girl and the others. I don't know how to replace it. It made me comfortable. And without that…'

An emptiness passed through him. He appeared void of mirth. What minor sanguine expressions he had conjured before now seemed at an end – close to expiry.

'Are there not any younger recruits? A new generation below?'

'A few. But they think differently. Technology has them at its bosom.'

'And you're unable to convert them?'

'I'm weaker. Somehow I'm weaker. Age. Experience. In many ways, it is only because I know *you* that I continue.'

'I haven't let you elaborate in the past. For that I'm sorry. You've talked of this discerning 'man', this god. It's odd, because my friend Pendlebury was given a similar mission. To somehow find Him. Sixteen years though. He began in 1982. How will you know it's Him? How will you know He's ready for such a weight?'

'Reluctant messiahs exist – have existed. Often they are better leaders for the very reason that they don't wish to lead. Humbleness has a habit of surprising you – flapping its unseen wings whilst displaying its servility. We have Him in our sights and I would chance that you've always known that. Again, I am not complete enough to know such a thing though. I cannot come out and say it is you.'

'"We"? You talk as if you know Pendlebury, or at least others that are at this point.'

'I know that we're homing in. There will be twelve of us... ready to serve Him. Twelve who have met and perceived His nobility.'

'A 'Last Supper'? You mentioned it. You said "there aren't enough for the table". Before I was beaten, taunted. Is that what I can expect? Will such a knowledge of myself bring me only vehement abuse?'

'Each of us lives with such affliction to a degree. The "being different" arouses other people's discourteousness. But then, a lot of people need educating.'

'You didn't see fit to 'educate' Josie with your beliefs concerning me. Why is that? You've had seven months.'

He seemed to stutter. An air of ashamedness swept over him – something for which he was not responsible. 'You need love – time together, before...'

'Before?' I knew, but I had to prompt him. I had to seek the opposite which would clearly not be forthcoming.

'*I'm* happy being single. I've given my life to books – partook in a Proust-like existence. You, however…'

'Yes?'

'You're not a natural hermit. You're close, but not quite there. That's why we're "homing in"… but still, there's a few years. Time for a normal, domestic life. Josie leaves this summer. She'll get a job. She'll want you to live with her.'

'You're being presumptuous.'

'No. She's made it clear, Arnold. I've known her long enough to know when she's content. And you make her that.'

'And *after* I've lived with her?'

He had already told me. In the manner of his expression. In the awkwardness his face exhibited. She would not be with me beyond my – our – early thirties. She would move aside, allow me to lead, be altruistic.

Ragavan was silent. And so I spoke again: 'I'd be deceiving her. To live with her for just a day, knowing, I…'

I stumbled, spluttered. My life, it seemed, had been decided for me – shorn from my brain. There seemed little point in making any more decisions given the fatalist haranguing of me. Josie was not to be mine – that is what they were saying. I would not retire with her, watch over life together, nor have children with her. My seeing her would dissolve into nothingness. We would eventually stand on separate plinths looking out at the world. And I would shake, knowing that she had been so very right.

CHAPTER 27

'**I**t's a decade – about a decade since I've seen him.'

'And you said his name was...?'

'Pendlebury. Pen-dle-bury.'

'Ahhhh. You mean The Leaf Blower. He's...'

I was there. At Lake Vyrnwy. Amongst the pines. Stood on the road above the dam. Down from the post box. Higher than the thick smoke from the chimney-potted cottage. The noise of the water was rushing, yet reasonably pleasant. The people around me had a distinctly slow gait.

I had been directed, to Pendlebury's abode – his modest living quarters on the edge of the forest. When I arrived, I tingled – stood outside and simply stared. I was afraid to knock. I was unsure what he would look like or whether he would care for my company. We had lived such separate and different lives that, despite his minor encouragement and his wanting me to see the "other side", I now feared that he possessed a certain enmity toward my kind of civilisation.

When the figure stared out from the front room, I jumped. I had turned away momentarily and then – as if conscious of my presence – Pendlebury had suddenly shown himself. His hair was longer, his eyes deep-socketed. The brown rag of a sweater which hung from him in a semi-elegant manner, I was certain was the very same one he had worn during our pretend college days. Other than that, other than these altered artifacts of his youth, Pendlebury was quite simply Pendlebury – the same, magnanimous fellow I had been drawn to even when unnerved by his pariah status.

His figure shifted and he was soon at the door – opening it for me, giving width to his arms in an effort to welcome me. 'My god! Debrito! Is that really you?'

I ignored his question and moved on. 'They've given you a title, I see.'

He looked at me quizzically, more out of non-city slowness than a lack of intelligence. I prompted him. 'The Leaf Blower. They call you The Leaf Blower.'

'Oh. Yes. The locals. They can be naïve. Made merry by the tagging of everything.'

'But you're him. I believe you to be him. Not your uncle.'

'Maybe. We both blow leaves, so…'

His sentence trailed off, at which point I felt it right to indulge in his embrace – a tap of the back, a shake of the hand, an affectionate look from him as if welcoming home a brother.

'It's bigger than that. You were always him. Such a title carries significance.'

He smiled. 'Come in. We'll talk. My trip is in seven days. You've timed it well. I have to be there before my 28th year and wake up there on my 30th, a man. He did it, you see, a century and a half ago.'

'Who?' I asked, not completely uninitiated.

'Why, Thoreau. I've been waiting a while. But tell me of yourself. It's fitting that you should see me off.'

We sat down. I talked briefly about my family, work and the internal philosophy I had slowly constructed. 'Castro's' death had been the real hardship, I echoed. His passing still central to my mother's waking minutes, her morning disposition, even now five years on. Pendlebury seemed to know of the passing. He feigned an ignorance out of politeness though – perhaps because his uncle had told him and he was embarrassed that he had not appeared at the funeral, at the send off. He talked of the hut he was to inhabit. He linked its solitude with 'Castro's' spirit saying that they may chat again, but that there would be no doorbells to remove this time. I felt heartened by his effortless connection, even though I recalled interrogating 'Castro' for his knowing deception in the company of my then new friend.

'"No path, no gate, no front yard – no path to the civilised world!"' Pendlebury suddenly exuded. 'Oh, the "misfortune to have inherited farms, horses, barns, cattle… better born in the open pasture and suckled by a wolf",' he then spoke, in a manner so content that for a moment it was not him.

The hut, *his* hut, was to be deep in forest – what forest this area offered. He would take with him an axe, bring it back sharper as Thoreau had done. He would cut wood, gather his own food, watch the sky, the animals around him. He would eventually live and breathe with the elements – cut out the finery which had plagued him, if only from his vision, not his heart.

'I have to ask: your father – nothing from him in all these years?'

It was his "wolf" quote which had prompted my asking, his almost diaphanous defence which manoeuvred too readily in a sea of justification.

'It's doubtful he's looked. And I've been *here* – quite out of sight anyway. My uncle made clear to me what occurred, so I have no malice inside. He was shocked at my mother's passing and for that I cannot stand in judgement. I cannot hope to ever comprehend.'

Still, after he'd spoken, Pendlebury had a look of sad reminiscence about him – the mien of one born into a different world. His greying hair – the hair which had begun to symbolise his wisdom from his teens – was now virtually camped across every state of his head, save for a thin, Italian-like pocket whose glorious habitation he no doubt smiled at each morning.

'I've practised sleeping outdoors, you know,' he said, attempting to swerve away from my untimely forlornness – make the most of our gratifying reunion.

'Yes? *Where?*'

'South Scotland. Every weekend.'

He then told me, of the dignity he afforded the road dead – animals slain by motor cars, pieces of metal controlled by human occupants. The thin, country roads up there were filled, blood-stained with animal after animal – turtles, hedgehogs, squirrels, birds, feral cats, small mammals of almost every conceivable type. Pendlebury walked the lanes while it was light, with gloves, paper bags, a small shovel, spade and blanket. He also had a kit of veterinary needles in case of suffering and distress.

'The scientists will tell you that most of the needless slaughter takes place when cars drive over 45mph. The lanes are designed for barely thirty and yet we see the legal limit double that. I've had a few close scares myself.

'County councils have odd policies, Arnold. Some will refuse to collect animals smaller than cats. Others have no-go areas: ring roads for example (to interrupt mankind's haste is to obviously pillage us all of a glorious freedom). Animal behaviour is paramount as well. Squirrels see cars as predators and so act exactly as they would with an enemy in the wild. They turn around completely upon sensing danger and then turn a further 180 degrees. Evolution for them shouldn't have to contend with such anonymous brute power.'

Bury them. He would then bury them. Autumn was his nemesis in this respect. Always the fighter of autumn, despite its evocative colours and agreeable climate. More carcasses – too many to count each Saturday and Sunday. But the silent contentment was huge. Despite the wilful recklessness of the metal occupants, Pendlebury had optimism at his side. And one day, there would be none. No twisted flesh or broken, bloodied innocents. He would walk the lanes and simply smile. Not because of scientific advancement – the assisting of lesser mammals than ourselves. But because humanity would come to gaze upon its own hubristic folly. And then flee, into the shadows where its higher thoughts still resided.

'It must tire you…' I lazily prompted, thinking of Pendlebury's refusal to accept a lift after the Forson Watshaw interview – knowing now that he was the *only* Leaf Blower, a chivalrous and valiant man of exception.

'It did. I became very fit though. Walking miles each day. Attending to the undignified, barely recognisable, tyre-battered creatures. The first burials made me cry. I wondered what I was doing, what people would think. But then I had had that. At college. I was able to bypass the chatter – the rude, loose language of lesser beings. Soon I became quite renowned. People would stop. "Has the count gone down, Pendlebury?" they would ask. I would respond. Tell them the average yardage between each of the mourned. Let them know with regard to seasonal factors. Some of them promised to walk more. And I held such comments in good faith.'

Purpose, I thought. How easily its wings are around you, after foolishly treading early on without its hold. George Minty I, Warwick, Ragavan, Josie, and now Pendlebury – acquaintances, friends, lovers, whose goal was to alter something, change the landscape, combine pleasure and work.

'We discuss things well, don't we...' I serenaded, offered ourselves comfort from.

'Yes. We do, Arnold. History – we have a shared history.'

'I need to tell you something then.'

'Please. Go on.'

'I have a girlfriend. Six months it's been.'

'That's... that's good.'

'I met her at university.'

'Then you're close to Level Three. Good. What are you studying?'

'English.'

'The academic connoisseur's choice. You've not let us down. When do you graduate?'

'Next summer.'

'The summer after that my uncle collects me. On my 30th birthday. I'll ask him how you're doing. You don't mind if he tracks you two months before?'

It was an odd request. But 'No,' came my answer. 'Not at all,' I confirmed to him.

Viewing him now in this modest abode, I saw that he was as Thoreau was – a "bachelor of thought and Nature", one whose "days were not days of the week [any more], bearing the stamp of [a] heathen deity... minced into hours and fretted by the ticking of a clock".

'Does she have a name?' Pendlebury then asked, rewinding our chatter, choosing not to ignore my new life with all its intricate folds.

'Josie,' I replied.

'She brings you a new dimension, no doubt. She is unique when it comes to the opposite sex.'

'She makes me feel warm. She...'

We stopped at that. My very effort to think of something apt, something sufficiently flattering was enough. Through the contentment and surety of my expression, my feelings for Josie glowed.

What Pendlebury and I didn't discuss, we implicitly knew. Via the theology which somehow bound us. Via the great works which had fluttered across our minds: Walden; Arrogant Beggar; The Odyssey. The former offered Pendlebury hope and strength in view of his imminent self-imposed exile, his hermitic existence. Its words randomly passed over his lips, particularly thoughts on being alone:

"I find it wholesome to be alone the greater part of the time. To be in company, even with the best, is soon wearisome and dissipating. I love to be alone. I never found the companion that was so companionable as solitude... We meet... about the fireside every night; we live thick and are in each other's way, and stumble over one another, and I think that we thus lose some respect for one another. Certainly less frequently would suffice for all important and hearty communication. Consider the girls in a factory – never alone, hardly in their dreams. It would be better if there were but one inhabitant to a square mile, as where I live."

'There's not going to be a future for myself and Josie, *is there*? That's why I'm here, I think. Some of this solitude seems to have crept over me. Perhaps events will conspire against us?'

Pendlebury looked at me with a distinct sadness in his eyes, a dichotomous understanding. 'It's not for me to say.'

'So I *will* lose her. For what? Everyone else...'

'For mankind.'

'Do you really believe it? Pendlebury? That I'm discerning – ready to take some kind of rightful place?'

'I have to. But there are still a few years left. For you to see what you must see.'

'Isn't it others that have the 'purpose' though? Am I not an imitation, a fake?'

'The table, Arnold. You'll have twelve followers whose lives will be crystallized by *your* lead. Some of whom have a greater knowledge and wisdom now, but when the time comes will excel in the shadow of your resplendence.'

I thought about this. I thought about the signs which were now in front of me at every turn. And all I could say was: 'She holds something back... just for me. She holds something back, Pendlebury – a bit of her personality.'

I would let Josie consume me. I would live out what I could with her, irrespective of the consequences. I needed her to be close. I needed it to be us. And this side issue of becoming a god. Well, I would see. *After* reality. *After* the morsels of life had been

absorbed.

CHAPTER 28

When I left Pendlebury, when I returned, it was for Josie's graduation, her apparent starting of life. After the ceremony – the walks on stage – we met outside, for the chutzpah, the cheer, the mild chatter which she favoured when things became too grand. I directed her parents to where I knew she would be stood – in the shade, away from the crowd, on the edge of the thrum. She looked back, at first with a beautifully-woven gaiety. She seemed content that I was with her loved ones – happy to watch me interact and rove the minds of her mother and father. We then stood around – the four of us. We commented on a few of the, by now, archetypal shouts – bursts of energy which would stay in the mind of the scroll recipient or handshake-laden graduate indefinitely; "Go on, Bob!" being a common interjection, as if observing a striker cutting in from the wing.

'A message from your brother and sister,' Josie's mother then articulated, passing her a folded piece of paper.

She took hold of it cautiously and then slowly read the contents, but not aloud. I leaned over, saw the words for myself ("Go make some money. It's the only way. Otherwise you'll be subsidising the sloths") and then watched her expression.

She seemed to smile through them, for the benefit of her mother mostly. I could see though – a pressure instantly wrapping itself around her, the choices before her reducing, getting thinner already, not quite playing out the imagined career she had had pleated in her brain.

'Food. We should get some food,' Josie commented. 'A drive out of the city.'

'Your favourite pub?'

'Yes. Thanks, Papa.'

We walked to the car park, circumvented the university buffet and wound down the windows for the journey. Josie reached for my hand immediately upon clambering into the back seats. It seemed to be a cry of sorts, an admittance of trepidation – despite her socialist brief, her general air of assuredness. The world now before her was not in any way recognisable. It was, in fact, so disparate to the texts she had read, the seniors she had come to place her trust in, that for a moment she shook. I steadied her hand, her body, without her parents realising. I looked into her face for signs of normality. Her eyes were vacant in a sense, afraid of what was to come. The walls of protection which had allowed her to blossom had been ruthlessly torn down, allowing the Corinthian hordes to peck at her, divest what they could of her purity.

When the car stopped, Josie indicated to her father that we would follow them in. Two minutes, maybe three. There were things she had to say, things she had to confide in me. Her father passed her the keys without question, escorted his wife, Josie's mother, into the public house.

'It's the same, isn't it?' she stressed, or demanded an answer in the affirmative to. 'If anything, it's worse than before. I've cranked it up a level now – agreed to associate with leviathan morons.'

'But what about the theatre group?'

She turned her face away. 'I've enquired. Nothing. They… they're owned anyway, by pricks that would laud Berlusconi…. cultureless megalomaniacs who sweat lies and subterfuge.'

'There must be one – a group that stands apart from the crowd?'

'I'd have to sell tickets for two years though. And even then…'

She began again: 'I'm sorry. I sound self-pitying. We should go in. It's my big day. My parents – I shouldn't worry them.'

'Forget that. Tell me honestly what you want.'

'I want… my own ship, my own business, but I haven't the money. I'm not them – my brother and sister. I don't think my mother sees that though. Also, I want *you*... to be with you. Live with you.'

I was taken aback. Despite Ragavan's foresight. Despite the predilection I had seen in Josie for weeks now. And yet, she had me – I was part of her, I wanted her too. She flagged my conscience and re-directed my individualness like no one before. In her was a pristine loyalty and unfettered devotion I was unaccustomed to. For that, I could but try harder, assist her, stand with her in the crossfire.

'I want the same. And it *is* possible.'

Somehow though, beyond my slight sentences, the constructed reality eluded me. I was not a business man. I did not have an answer which surpassed the hard facts connected with selling one's labour.

'*How*, Arnold? *How*, may I ask?'

I was short. Of all-encompassing solutions. Of smile-prompting lines. And so, I delivered a rash compromise, an unfulfilling and therefore hapless answer: 'We both know the numbers.'

'What!? But that's what I'm afraid of. Us giving up our art... for crass excursions... for chats with Henry and Miles.'

'We could support each other. Do the insufferable work. Buy time for our graceful pursuits. And then sell at a high price our art. Eventually...'

She knew what I was saying, and it – for a moment – gladdened her. What was unbecoming, however, was my own doubt saddled to every part of my expression. I had thought, of course, of other ways, of 'Castro's' cottage – its viability as a starting nest for the two of us. Yet property was rising in value, my parents would eventually use the cottage as a good source of income for their retirement (my father's pension amounting to nothing) and Josie wished to secure our future despite the ugly economics synonymous with such a desire.

The eventual parting hadn't escaped me (if I was to believe my 'disciples'). Nor had the immenseness of my deception in allowing Josie to plan not years, but decades. I simply had to experience her though. I had to defy for a while the prophecies behind my eyes. Quite how it would end, I could not bear to contemplate. We had months, years, and that had to be enough – less torturous than not committing at all.

We went in. Acceded to the normality of a graduation meal. The chatter became lighter. Josie placed the emphasis on her celestial three years – their maturing of her, their richness and wonderful pace. Any suggestion of conflating them with the future was rebuffed – gingerly cast to one side. Because her insurmountable years of education were already whole – not needing of a vile, vocational thread. At least for now. At least for another two to four weeks.

Her father raised his glass, sang the praises of his unique daughter and asked that we – his wife and I – join him in saluting such a wonderful, if anachronistic creature. I pushed my glass against theirs, cried 'Hear, hear!' like a chirpy, yet saturnine politician, and gazed at Josie. She was a daddy's girl, a papa's girl – replete with in-built pride. Her demeanour forced others to reconsider everything they knew about themselves, or thought they knew. Being here – on the same table – as a couple, I felt sanctified, blessed. The day needed lengthening so that I could watch her some more – simply understand the depth of her allure.

~ ~ ~

Weeks after, when she told me she had applied for and indeed received an offer of a position at a city-centre bank, I attempted to gauge her thoughts, her true concerns on such a direction (the very antithesis of that which she had craved).

'It's on the stockbroking side. I know the numbers. You said it. You were right. I should use the part of my brain which gives a definite, tangible outcome or return.'

'It doesn't sound like you. Not the way you said it.'

'Oh, but it is, Arnold. As long as *I* exploit *them*. As long as I stay pre-management. Then I can cope. And we... we can move in together. I'll get a mortgage, *after* the exam, after I qualify –

become a Securities Representative. Twenty plus – that's what they said. It should be enough. We'll be able to start...'

Start. That's what it was about. Not missing the gun. Not limbering up until you were priced into renting. And after that, once *I* graduated, I could take the load. The deal, chalked up in our minds, would bear fruit – keep us sane. We could pretend that the toil was nothing more than temporary. Indeed it was – would be. We were temps. Except, the firms ripe for the picking would not know. We would use *them* – fund our unique existence through their naivety so to obtain the better pay. We would help turn the tables – drop them after twelve months, at a time when they had come to depend on us, rely on our savvy and expertise. Human Resource departments would follow us out of buildings on their hands and knees, pleading that we stay, talking of security – capitalism's 'security' which would feed and clothe us providing we continued to understand the rules of mendacity, the laughter brigade's greater good.

Within days, Josie had glimpsed the world which had embarrassed her mind upon accepting its terms and leveraged gaiety. She had sat in meetings, with pungent corporate habits – the serving of water and biscuits. She had squirmed in her seat, not manifestly but internally whilst in the company of her colleagues and a guest speaker in the company's boardroom. Things – even inadequacies and inefficiencies (which should have pleased her socialist bent) – began to agitate her, yet she learned to cope, 'play the pernicious game'. Seeing the line was important; the line which required your compliance whilst accepting your stash of dissent as part of an on-going peace deal. Authority was odd in that the people above Josie appeared to be automatons – humans treading in a thicker glue than herself. Despite their dashing about and occasional sword-wielding, she had seen them, heard them at their computers talking to their seniors – the empty mammonish language ('escalate', 'mopping up session', 'meet the customer's expectations', 'focus groups we entrust') blighting vernacular's blue sky. And the seniors of the seniors? She didn't think they existed, or if they did then the plane full of people that flew in half-yearly to this, one of the transnational's hubs, was an elaborate guise, a hearty ruse designed to protect an immobile Jabba. But then, looking at the mafia-clad assortment of Wolves – invariably announced beforehand as a pocket of 'very important people' – Jabba hadn't done a very good job. Their stares and bespoke cuff links certainly fitted with the required, self-aggrandizing mode, however, their potbellied skins spoke of excess, a shapeless culture mudded by complacency.

Josie, in the middle of all this, devised certain means of escape, palliative briefs which would see her through. She continued to use her rucksack from university in an effort to persuade herself that this was simply a 'placement' – her real life nucleus synonymous with her lunch time library visits and not the corporate army pounding the pavements (morning concrete and stone full of the previous night's discarded food plus the remnants of erupted, drunken putridness). The company bag, *she had accepted*, however, to display their logo – HSTD – while walking to and from the train station was obscene – a forced sycophancy of sorts. To do anything other than use it for storage at home – away from the public eye – was shoddy, unbecoming. Whilst on the train, she looked around, searched for a depressed sage each morning – someone to offer her hope, someone through whom the false glee of humanity was cast aside. In their world, she imagined, a fuller understanding existed – being blunt was paradoxically part of their armour, their defence. But it was not welcomed where she now resided between 8am and 4.30pm. She had witnessed, first hand, Jabba's deputy speaking about the company's future, spouting "economies of scale, diversified earnings, critical mass, individual excellence and teamwork" and yet when the questions presented themselves before him at the end they were found to be weak, decrepit – lacking penetration or radicalness. The mass in front of him had transmuted into upholstery upon which he now lay - untested, autocratically dominant, victorious in his rhetoric. Individual excellence, he smiled to himself – just as long as it fits *our* mould.

Josie, so far, was in that mould – under its line. Her efforts at conforming, she felt, differed from the vacuous, nodding compliance of the others, however such a hypothesis was not 100%. Perhaps the others were simply good – better manipulators. Perhaps they did 'get it'. Perhaps their turpentine expressions altered upon returning home. But then humanity was not an experiment in acting, Josie attested. To do more than is necessary surely eats away at one's soul – eventually hocks that which you *think* you can return to.

When she walked among the pockets on the dealing floor, on her way to the balcony for a break or to chat with a back-office stooge, she swept her hand against the desks in an effort to pep her confidence – give off a suitable vibe. When dealing, she met her quota (80 deals per day), gathered assets (in the form of unit trusts / mutual funds) so that the company would receive a 0.5% annual 'kick' based on the value and, in time, edited a weekly newsletter of her making full of statistics and analysis. Such behaviour protected her – would act as resistance in the wake of future job cuts. Because they *would* come. The cycle was always there. She would have a stockmarket crash of her own – one to pit against my Monday and Wednesday.

The talk, the products, the client base slowly enveloped Josie over time. And upon passing her exam (one hour of regulation, two hours of market know-how), she was qualified to speak to the market makers, the cockney barrow boys for whom a tit was a tit, and a pert tit, a cheaper offer price or higher bid. The speed of the industry and general conduct within it, while not exactly intriguing her, certainly fascinated her a little. Investors' abilities and foresight in jumping from one asset to another given the geopolitics and economic data at the centre of the securities playing field quite astounded her. Yet she could not conceive investing that way herself – buying Swiss Francs when the terrorist threat was high, selling Yen upon concerns over Japanese deflation, buying bonds in anticipation of lower interest rates, investing in gold or the Australian dollar due to uncertainty in world stock prices, selling equities short or buying an 'index put' due to escalating oil prices and reservations over the world's future energy supplies, buying shares in a small defence company tipped to win a contract with a third world government. Behind each decision was death. But embracing such a fact went against humanity's constructed impulse. Not to 'play' was like giving up an arm and a leg – allowing the Darwinistic swots to take your house, your space, your family, any sense of Creation that you that you had ever derived. So to fight it out, to continue, surely meant that you held them in equal measure – that C & D were still attempting to justify their respective dogmas; that neither had come to the fore in two thousand years. Catharsis. Doom.

CHAPTER 29

Eventually, she altered the newsletter's format. Subtly. Slowly. But consciously. Our moving in together in early '99 and my impending graduation helped lessen the strain, unleash some of her older thoughts, her pre-stockbroking designs.

'When walking behind old people, even middle-aged dawdlers, I'm thinking "Get out of my *fucking* way",' Josie announced one quiet Thursday evening, sat next to me, staring out from our living room at the road. 'The job. It does something to you. Takes over your metabolism, your demeanour. I seem to eat, faster than before. Make judgements more quickly – particularly derogatory ones. It gets inside of you. But to go against it completely … I can't rant about Saro-Wiwa, all my true interests, because no one would listen. You're expected to laugh. Everything's a joke. Even death. There is no sacred ground any more. Language has run dry. It can no longer describe atrocities, acts of barbarism. Because a similar sentence has already defined an earlier, lesser incident. The words – they either need knitting together more forcefully or simply abandoning, perhaps replacing.

'The city. Stocks and shares. Gambling. Financial speculation. It has its eye on world events and yet it, itself, has somehow *become* the event. Catastrophes. Floods. Droughts. Cyclones. Earthquakes. They're incidental. In the world I inhabit they're *fucking* incidental. People don't ask "How many died?" any more. They ask "But has the country's Bourse been affected? Because I'd quite like to trade my way out of this or open up a few new positions". And it will get worse … much worse.

'I've always wondered … when the economic data is released, *who* is in the room, or *who* is privy to the information *before* its release time. Something's coming out at two o'clock, say two fifty … the University of Michigan Sentiment figures. Is the room somehow monitored, tapped, regulated? And if so who's to say that the regulator isn't bent – ready to tip off an anonymous friend? Who "guards the guard"? This is easy money – information. The two are entwined. What is it that we can give to prevent corruption? What is it we can offer though?'

I immediately thought 'hope' and so I said it.

'But from *who*? From *where*?' Business men?! Governments?!'

'Individualism has to be reined in. There should be a compulsory community meeting each week or fortnight. On the wider front, the world needs another Martin Luther … a truly great orator.'

'So that he can be assassinated? Torn apart by vested interests?'

'It's the vested interests that need their wealth trimming, their gluttony and rapacity banishing … purging.'

'But how?' Josie demanded.

I didn't know. Yet. And so I shook my head – signalled our momentary downfall. Josie discussed her strand or strain of socialism, her newsletter and its recent, fundamental shift. She wished to concentrate on the gains, capitalism's humiliation.

'They haven't noticed. The seniors – they haven't said anything. Colleagues have winked at me though, given coded messages, made it clear that they agree with my stance. I'll quote left of centre sources, but attribute the text to the right – the Telegraph, the Evening Standard, the Financial Times. Issues of the day – final salary pensions, GM food, education. They look at the brand, you see – often trust it implicitly. I'm a bloody P.R. woman.

'The usual stuff is still there – the weekly change on the FTSE, commodity prices, rights issues, new issues, the tips section. But when I tip something now, for example an oil or mining company, concerns over pending human rights court cases – perfectly legitimate financial speak – are footnoted. I'm giving the reader almost everything, not just the ashamedly narrow, right-wing cutting.'

'You're doing your bit,' I said. 'So many of you are. Battling the policies of Milton *fucking* Friedman.'

There were rallies later in the year. Josie felt it was the start of something – a people's uprising, an anonymous network of ethical insurgents. She attended her meetings – a post-university cabal, without Ragavan and the people she had known before – and took part in a couple of marches. It was then that I received the call. From the bank. Her senior. Or rather, seniors.

'We've seen her, amongst them. The green-headed crazies and anarchists. And it doesn't look good. It reflects badly on us. We'd rather she therefore stayed away.'

'Who is this?'

'My name isn't important. Just pass on the message. I think we understand each other.'

'Hang on …'

The line went dead. It was happening. They were pressing home their 'ownership' of her. Josie. My partner. My lover. My friend. A new McCarthyism was in the air. And the Romans had scripted, drafted its ideology. I gulped. Turned away for a moment. Stared at the blankest wall in the house in an effort to empty the disarray from my mind. I was speechless. That someone could do this. That we were, in effect, 'fighting' a pathological force which had chosen to disregard its own alarm bells, its albeit fragmented sense of legitimacy. I didn't immediately know whether to tell her, whether to jeopardise her recent, trackless indignation. The voice though. She would ultimately stand in range of its sermons, its corrupt exhortations. And so, I had to. I couldn't have her disadvantaged. I couldn't shield her from that which was intent on seeping through.

She returned later that evening. I watched her walk down the path, rotate her hips like a Latin American senorita. She instantly saw me through the window – blew me a kiss and smiled happily. I raised my hand weakly, tried to reciprocate her beautiful flourish, her too big an effort at contentment.

'Arnold? Arnold, my love. *There* you are.'

She took hold of my arms, attempted to twirl herself round, but fell to one side off balance. 'You're not playing. Play with me ….

please.'

I pulled her to me. Held her tight. Breathed in her hair and scent. 'I will. But there's something I need to tell you. Let me sit you down.'

'But why? *Why*? Play, Arnold. *Play*.'

She had been drinking. A little more than usual. Her concentration was slightly shot, her gaze less flattering now we were inside the house together.

'It's important.' I sounded unintentionally rancorous, aggrieved. I wanted her attention, but my voice was wavering, playing tricks on me almost.

'What? What's important at this time? We should be dancing. And then bed.'

She attempted to stand up again, but I placed my hands on her shoulders. I then said it. Told her. 'They've phoned.'

'Who? Who's phoned? This is silly, Arnold.'

'Your work. Your work have phoned. The bank. And ...'

'Why would they phone – a different shift? Who was it?'

'He didn't say. He *wouldn't* say.'

'What do you mean?'

'The rally. It was on the news. I didn't see you myself, but ...'

She immediately put her head in her hands and then shook. As before. At her graduation. Became afraid. Less emboldened. 'It's started,' she then quietly versed. 'They're as ruinous as Okuntimo. The bastards! *Bastards!* Do I watch over *them?* Monitor their cocktail parties ... their rhetoric?! Maybe I should. Maybe ...'

The seriousness then seemed to hit her more fully. She gasped for air. Her lungs seemed to hyper-inflate. I gripped her sides, knelt before her. 'Slow,' I said. 'Slower.'

'*How?!*' she screamed. 'How can I, Arnold? *Who are they?* Who are they to do this?'

'They're no one. Nothing!'

'But look at us. We're dependent. We ...'

I looked into her eyes, tried to give her something outside of my sentences, my expression. She looked back, but her thoughts had somehow haemorrhaged, burst into microcosms which no longer reflected who she was.

'There's shame attached to it. They don't teach you that, but it's there. Not to manage, deal your quota, be professional, is weak ... it's weak. And I'm good. I'm good with the numbers. I know every product we deal. I'm sure no one else does. Not intimately. Not the alphas and betas, the gearing formulas, the dilution levies. If they don't know I've doctored it, then ... we should be OK. If the newsletter has escaped their attention, then ... You *did* interpret that it was just the rally?'

'*What?* No. I ... What are you doing? Isn't it enough that they've intimidated us?'

'Weeks more. And then *you* ... you'll be in place. Now what did they say?'

'He.'

'He, then. What did he say?'

'Just that they'd seen you. He spoke in a shared sense. But it was him speaking – him only. The bank, each employee as its ambassador. That was the gist. Ownership. He wanted it be known that there are boundaries.'

'So nothing about the newsletter?'

'I don't think so. Not directly.'

'*Any way*, Arnold. Straight. Through a hoop. Round a corner. It's important. *Yes* or *no?*

I stared at her. Refused to verbalise or participate in her one-word language, her 'closing' of me.

She hammered down on my arms, beat me away with her legs. 'Don't you *understand*? I go in Monday not knowing, unless you tell me, prepare me.'

'You shouldn't be at a disadvantage for not knowing. What is it with this world that we *all* must follow the same drummer!'

'You're talking in *riddles!* Your bloody metaphors won't keep us together ... not in a nice neighbourhood. Not on a road with actual trees. Even if I understand you. Even if your 'shouldn't' is well meaning and correct. It's been marginalised, Arnold. 'Shouldn't' has been pushed out. The grammarians have labelled it subjunctive. Doubt is at its heart.'

'Well, I support doubt. Dubiety is better than an extreme confidence. It sails with the small – keeps one thinking.'

'Don't be naïve! If I'm not *ahead* of them, then it falls. The whole thing falls. The newsletter – please. Was there any indication?'

'No.' I was doing as she asked – shedding my callowness, replacing it with a hardened aplomb. Even though I knew it to be a half-truth. Even though I knew the man's intimations to reek of every and any Josie 'transgression'.

'Thank god. I think I can explain the rally – it alone. Anything else though – it would ...'

'*Explain?!* Why the hell should you have to explain yourself, your social life? You're starting to use their language, Josie. You're ...'

'I'm not. I'm just ... I don't want to become Pendlebury. Ostracized. Banished. Made to feel odd, when it's them – *them*. Management is capable of twisting the workforce. Whatever winks and smiles I've had concerning the newsletter, well –

they're nothing. They're rotting as we speak. I've got to manipulate the seniors. Know I'm manipulating them. Even if it's hard. Even if they throw things at me.'

'I'd recognise the voice,' I then said, suddenly with her. 'Put me in a room with them and I'll point him out, isolate him.'

'I'm not sure. What, *who* would it serve?'

'It'll serve *me*. I'll let him know how the land lies, why his polished hyperbole is unacceptable.'

'You sound threatening, Arnold.'

'Not quite. The pacifism will always be in check, but I need to drive close to its borders – evince a careful message to him ... just him. People are inclined to see the wonders when targeted alone – listen and admit to themselves that things are wrong ... if only afterwards, once out of sight.'

She looked at me, unsure. I understood her concerns, but I had to meet this 'Okuntimo', this illegitimate Roman with his unchecked language and white feathered tongue. If Josie objected, if in her considered opinion the sanctioning of my plan was ludicrous, then I would work on her, talk her round, run through my days with Warwick – tell her that numbers were also in the habit of fighting *with me*, flanking me, pitching their integers headlong for a cause, a worthy battle.

CHAPTER 30

'**I** sit with them, Arnold – their puerile faces bowled over by nine hundred channels. They refer to it as "entertainment". Entertainment! Unwittingly hostage to a grand media scheme – a bogus world which bears no resemblance to life. I have to flick through some of the channels, show them the range before leaving. Customer service – that's the emphasis. Customer service. My radio talk, I do less of. They look at me when I do, as if I'm stupid, slow, old. Some of them aren't worth saving anymore. I thought that's what I was doing – I really did. But ... it would take too long. I have to look at *my* life now – the life of your mother and I.'

My father, the radio man. I was sat, in his house, a graduate, a successful student of Yezierska, Emerson and Spinoza.

'Do you believe in conspiracies? That behind the inane front there are people motivated enough to want to quell a person's reach?'

'Sometimes I question things – the path we're on, humanity's blind pride, its manipulative and dangerous pride, so much so that a valid sentence from one family is dismissed by another on the grounds of convenience, not morality. But as for conspiracies, a *world* conspiracy, which is what it would have to be, I tend to think not. If *I* am able to take a certain conscious direction in life, then why not others? I don't credit myself with a superior intelligence, although I *do* despair at some of the sullied minds I have to engage with. To think of conspiracy though – strings behind the scenes – is to be excommunicated in some way, expelled, making life ... quite unliveable.'

'I ask because Josie has had threats from the bank.'

'What kind of threats?'

'Just a phone call, and the Monday after that an anonymous e-mail. They don't approve of her attending rallies. They ...'

'Who have you taken this to?'

'No one, directly. There's a culture in place … a line which is never crossed. The technical people there are quite mummified already. She went to one she trusted a little more, asked him for the sender's name and he promised to come back, but nothing. He avoids her now, looks down, doesn't answer. She phoned Human Resources internally. They said they'd update her file, check the company logs – both electronically and digitally. It's been days though. There's a reticence, a wall which, through its silence, has managed to discourage her. They're professional subjugators. And something somehow worse than violence is their weapon, their claw, their sting.'

'I never imagined them operating this way.'

'Well they do. I intend to meet whoever made the phone call though. They drink every Friday after work. Josie has told me where. They call themselves 'seniors', 'high-ranking players'. I need to stand there, in amongst them – catch the voice which spoke to me on the phone. Follow him into the gents, isolate him …'

'Is that the only way? I don't want you hurt, Arnold. What about the police?'

'Romans. The police are Romans – servants of money. Our life would be picked through – paraded in front of strangers, aliens. *That time* will ultimately come, but for now …'

'You talk like you've moved on – geared yourself up for something, Arnold.'

'You don't know? You have no intimation?'

He studied me carefully. My father tried to see in me what I knew I was to become.

'Perhaps your standards are higher. Perhaps you'll move us on, as a race …'

He was telling me something. He was telling me that forty-three years in the job had finally weakened him, made his ambiguities less sacrosanct. He was letting it be known that his faith in Sacco and Vanzetti had been nothing more than a fabrication, a disappointing yet well-assembled lie. I didn't deliberate over his careful disclosure, nor did I seek explicit confirmation. The shame in his face was enough – enough to set him back, have him turn over his life. In one sense I had lost him as a father, yet the new, blank canvas before us was somehow redemptive – rich and atoning.

-      -   -

They wore ostentatious cuff links and wide ties. The bar they were in had too many mirrors and too many smiles built on nothing but the miasmal surround. I stepped in, at first unsure. There was no mistaking them – a hapless congregation of stockbrokers, laughing ... at elements of poverty walking past, cajoling ... with the reluctant or not barmaid, kitted out to their liking – her breasts tempestuous and sufficiently unravelled.

Josie had wanted me to bring someone – at least look natural in this glass and metal cavern, fit in with the anodyne music and flowing chatter. I had rejected her request, however – sought a surer answer through acting alone rather than stoking their periodic need for a ruck. If I was to be beaten, then let it be me, alone – not a small group of followers who would satisfy them more greatly.

I ordered a drink, a beer, not failing to grab the attention of the cuff-linked cronies. '*Fucking* loners! Shot ... I'd 'ave 'em shot!'

There was wry laughter. Three, initially with their backs to me, turned around – stared blatantly as if I was a foot soldier trespassing at the entrance of their finer barracks.

I responded. I had to in order not to wreck the plan, the timed 'assault'. 'I'd have shot pricks that can't survive on their own!'

I had summarised their investment ethos, their wily, day to day logic. And such a response could not be tampered with nor questioned. Instead, they talked amongst themselves, sometimes in moderation subject-wise, sometimes not. Clusters formed and I began to pick up on the different accents and colloquialisms, the mannerisms of each – some of whom I regarded as 'full braces' stockbrokers and others I viewed as simply basking in the munificent financial warmth.

Before my beer was finished, I had him pinpointed. He wore neither braces nor a sycophantic grin, but rather a dogged, almost fastidious expression. At times he seemed to look my way, keep tabs on me, hark after my reason for being here. And then, eventually, his bladder became too full.

I gave him ten seconds – a count of ten before hopping off my stool and following him. Down the steps. Along the short corridor. And in. Through the in-swinging, male-designated door. He looked up from the long silver trough which acted as a modern-day, communal urinal. I stood at the other end of it, stared at the wall in front of me, yet avoided the customary release.

'It seems odd to me that someone would do it …'

'What?' he replied, seconds later, shaking his appendage.

'Replace the pronoun 'I' with something less personal, less arresting and responsible.'

' *What the fuck* are you talking about?'

I ignored him. 'I mean, to be part of a cabal, but not have any charisma of your own – that must be upsetting.'

He started to run the tap. He then rubbed his hands together underneath the flowing water. 'You'd be better off not doing this,' he said markedly, warningly.

'You talk as if you know who I am.'

'Who are you?'

'I'm Josie's partner.'

'Ahhhh …'

I couldn't tell if his realisation was genuine or if, in some way, he had already seen me – through an album, a subversive catalogue or slide show.

'I tend to keep voices in my head and we've definitely spoken before.'

'I prefer photos,' he responded, removing something from his pocket and placing it on the marble of the sink.

It was of Josie and I; an everyday photo taken within the last month. I took hold of his lapels, pushed him against the wall. '*Who are you* to have this? What kind of outfit are you running?'

He seemed unflustered – used to being manhandled. 'One in which the management must always be aware.'

'There are laws – laws which prevent this.'

'No, Debrito. We do what is in the public's interest.'

'You're a stockbrokers! You talk as if you're a voluntary organisation. This is specious, fraudulent, *illicit!*'

'Josie can come on board – become management. She has the intelligence. We just need to work on her corpulent scruples – lessen them, teach her the way.'

'*What? What?* So that she can become like *yourself* – one of the *unthinking*, the *undead.*'

'You shouldn't talk that way. Not when we and *we only* judge. You're holding her back. What she really needs … is raping, by one of the chaps – perhaps myself. Then she'll become compliant, acq…'

I slapped him with my right hand. Kept a firm grip of him, but slapped him. I told myself I was still at the pacifist border, turning the throttle though close to the line. So close.

'*Don't!*' he replied firmly, however my mind was wrapped up in his use of the word 'rape', his casualness, his degenerative talk.

I continued. Slapped him again and again. Noticed the marks and bruising beginning to appear – unmask him in some way as if they were the colourings of inhumanity, bestialness and depravity.

Eventually, I weakened, seemed to pull back voluntarily, realise my own ruin. He smiled, a sickly blundering grin, an unrestricted mien through the pain and unsettled contours of his face. This was his diet, I realised – testing people, allowing them to initiate conflicts. And then, as underdog, he wrenched in his enemy, played out his dominance, indoctrinated them physically and mentally.

'My turn,' were his words, his ominous parlance. 'I think it is, isn't it …' he said mockingly, boastfully, balefully.

I suddenly choked. The force of his hand, open and U-like with his thumb one side and his fingers the other, pushed against me – my throat and wind pipe. I stumbled back, against the marble laced around the sinks. He lifted his knee into my stomach, kept it there while I instinctively bent forward – compounding my breathing difficulties, adding to my drowning, my fear of suffocation.

'You've never had them intervene, *have you* – the police. Doesn't that tell you something? Doesn't it say everything's in writing already? You're fucking naïve – *fucking* naïve.' The last two words he head-butted me to, like a violent symphony, a nightmarish gathering of symbols and flutes.

I was, by now, slumped. He held me up, however – pressed home his edicts and torment: 'Do you think raping her would even matter? To the world? The courts? Errors slow things down – taint commerce. All contexts are the same. We can't log everything anymore - not desire, anyway. The whole thing has to rumble on. Holistic – that's how you ethical types phrase it. We're a huge organism, interconnected. Except, some of us know where the controls are – some of us bypass the need for redemption.'

I could hear him, yet his wilted lines pressed down on me,

insisted that forgiveness was somehow automatic, freely dispensed, without condition. That rape should be discussed this way was intolerable, party to a contrived madness and horrendous game. His assertion that the world no longer addressed the mistakes of its citizens was surely underpinned by nothing more than ... I failed to say it. I failed to say what I intended, because the ugliness was increasing. This neo-Darwinism I was seemingly witnessing before me was everywhere. On each corner. Plundering each community. Maiming better minds than its own. And ...

I had to speak. The voice within me surpassed the numb, hollow blackness of my being. 'Know that this isn't it. That there are things *your kind* could never conceivably account for. Know that when the day comes, you will be sworn in with the others.'

He laughed. 'A rebellion?! But we have the diversification – we've created enough of it to sap any attempt at unity. Try though – please do.'

I held his gaze – sought his understanding and concession through my incisive stare.

'No. No. No. There is already One,' he responded. 'One that holds sway.'

I thought, of who he could mean: a Roman chief; a demigod; an upper-class master behind it all – in the throes of maintaining this questionable existence. I could not ask him though. I could not purport to be a rival if I did not know or sense fully the lurking shadow.

'That is us done then. Josie – she is beyond your touch.'

'Perhaps,' he semi-acknowledged, conceded in part due to our erudite engagement, our failed attempt at stolidity.

CHAPTER 31

I dreamt over the next few weeks, of my opposite, of an individual whom I believed to be controlling things, steering life with his faceless bluster and unshaven wind. It was a world separate from Josie's – one not at the altar of capitalism, but rather drugged intensely by concerns and wishes. Each evening, unemployed and somehow stripped of my psyche – backward in my aspirations – I sought assurances from Josie that they had not broken her, that they had not in any way carried through their threats. I was poor, impecunious, for allowing her to continue amongst the seniors, bat their words and ideology, but the trees – we needed them, their cover and occupants; our centre of gravity had to be in a neighbourhood of our choosing, not one left filthy without codes and discernment.

Eventually, in the winter of '99, I found myself in sight of work, close to its bosom. What had been magical for a while – religion, the spiritual hold upon me, the belief from others that I had been 'chosen' - seemed to dissipate, loosen. Faith was still in the basement of me, perhaps requiring one final project, mission, person for the table (be they a disciple or Satan-induced warrior), yet its nest was steeped in feathers, extra bedding for rest.

-        -   -

I stood there, next to a barely-above-street level, grey-coloured intercom which immediately sewed a modicum of doubt into my stomach with its crackling and technological stubbornness.

'Arnold Debrito. Debrito,' I said a second time, resonating my name, my character, my history, whilst in ear shot of the bespoke criminals that passed.

I looked around the sizeable street with its neon complexities and damaged gutters. I instantly felt a failing inside myself – the lights blinking at me, welcoming me to their battered and malignant world. In sociologist terms this was a resplendent canvas – one sufficient enough to be pored over for months, even years. Such beggardom had to be surpassed, however, in the desperateness of me wishing to lay down my tools and begin work. What type of work, I was not sure.

An electronic clunk central to the door's mechanism sounded, pulling me from further reverie and allowing me to enter. I tentatively pushed the heavy door, and almost straight away descended a set of stairs. Either side of me, on the walls of the staircase, framed posters were hung:

BOYO KINNOCK WOULD
HAVE STEMMED THE
MULTINATIONALS

LABOUR
BEFRIENDS
LARCENISTS

NOW SHOWING:
BLUE AVARICE

THATCHER
FOR QUEEN

ATOM BOMB
SOFT ON DESTRUCTION
LET'S HARD IT UP
WITH NUCLEAR

The one thing I instantly noticed about the well-assembled words was that, politically, they were hung on the correct side; each scribble accompanied, impressively, by an Orwellian-type drawing. And although over a decade old, the posters struck me as being representative of a somewhat balanced mind; a mind not affected by time and its forgiving qualities, but rather steeped in heavy traditions.

I failed to knock on the door ahead of me, as if encouraged by something to rail against even the slightest of protocol. Instead, I squeezed the handle and entered. The contrast before me was huge: magazines and papers spread out on a mammoth table (The Ecologist, The Economist, Index on Censorship, The Daily Telegraph, The New Internationalist, The Spectator, The Guardian, Time, Resurgence, New Scientist, Socialist Review, Investors Chronicle, Corporate Watch, The Week, Granta, The Times); each opinion displaced by its neighbour; each attitude summoned by the strong-arm council either side of it. Above the table, encased in glass, stood a map of the world – the refusal to hang it seemingly indicative of its owner's style, his less than enamoured view of continent divides.

'This place really needs a clean – the carpet anyway. Would you oblige?'

The voice came from the far end of the room, where the chap responsible for bringing me here today was sat, barely noticeable. Benjamin Chesterton, I suddenly recalled – his name was Chesterton. There was a vacuum, a Hoover near the door, and so I plugged it in and started to push it up and down the room, in the corners – over and over until a patterned cleanliness formed.

'You'd be amazed how many people fail that one test, Arnold. Not a hugely demanding request, but they're above it – not here to play such games.'

'I'm seeking work. Better to be interviewed in a more pristine environment.'

'Aaah, well. I *did* wish to interview you away from here. A walk, perhaps?' He grabbed his overcoat from a quite austere, yet finely crafted hat stand. His singularly rhetorical final sentence bounced in front of me, with my only option being to follow him.

Out on the street once more, I felt like an adolescent lover spared his girlfriend's parents, a commodore banished from the rear admiral's office. I examined him, my interviewer – the chap who contacted *me* without any prompting; the chap who wrote such an articulate letter that I could not ignore it, either through its non-specifics or because of my own semi-petulance. Chesterton, I thought, as I stared unceasingly. His name was every bit him, from the well-worked insouciance, to the manner of dress (efficient and clipped, yet strangely dog-eared and casual). He was somehow less in the 'race' than myself I could not help but feel – more, a selective benefactor handing out gin fizzes and high balls from the sidelines. He was at the same time, however, driven by something raw and non-aristocratic; something that had upset countless uncles and aunties no doubt.

'You don't mind if we chat in here?' he prompted, a few metres on.

The reference was to the Corner House, a multi-faceted social 'dwelling' complete with reception, bar, café and cinema; its title directly gleaned from the fact that it was indeed positioned on the corner of two roads that converged. Indicating to Chesterton that I did not have a problem with such a suggestion in the slightest, we entered.

'I like it in here,' he almost shyly announced, as we walked across the lobby to the foot of the J-shaped staircase which led to the café. 'There aren't many places that a chap feels truly comfortable in, bu…'

'I understand.'

'I think, maybe, it's in the knowledge that everyone around me, us, is a pacifist. I might be generalising, but I *do* get that impression. If the worst came to the worst, the people in here would always *talk* it out.'

We climbed the staircase. I looked around while Chesterton ordered the drinks. His sentiment, whilst a little green, encouraged me. I knew, having been in here before, that the majority of people did indeed offer hope for a better world. At the same time, however, in amongst the French film-goers that it attracted, existed – I was quite certain – Scorsese-type pariahs; brooding, introspective, lugubrious types – only a match light away from anarchy.

Seated now, in the outermost corner of the café, almost on top of the traffic light below, we sipped our drinks respectively. The view, although inherently urban and non-taciturn, was somehow manageable from here. There was a slice of Dos Passos poeticism about it; the rushing, moving bluster able to be contextualised from above.

'I enjoyed reading your dissertation, Arnold.'

'I didn't realise …'

'That's, principally, why you're here today.'

A hush descended. Seconds for me to attempt to pick up the thread. Time for Chesterton to recite the title of my work in a delayed and striking fashion: 'We go forth all to seek America. And in the seeking we create her. In the quality of our search shall be the nature of the America that we create.'

I didn't respond immediately to the goading. I remained locked in thought – almost ethereal or metaphysical in my musing. With his knowledge Chesterton sought to flatter me, yet such a countenance occasionally danced with invidiousness and intrusion. There was nothing to do but stare at the traffic and haste outside, and await the man's next line.

'You're a nihilist, Arnold. Your work smacks of it in every paragraph. I read all the relevant Firsts at five universities before stumbling across yours. Even the introduction is clever. You do as much for Chekhov as you do for yourself. That, to an academic, is honourable ... magnanimous even.'

The words sat on the lobe of my ear, but failed to climb inside close to my mind. I found it difficult to adjust to praise; its brothers, sisters and cousins neglecting me after graduating. Six months of raggedy fighting alongside and against society's most banal. Scrapping for the role of Administrative Mooncalf (as encouraged by the meritocracy of the day). Chesterton's words therefore seemed to echo the cry of a dumb Yank welcoming a party into his hotel; boisterous, insincere, perfidious.

My dissertation. My university days. Why mention them? They were somehow lost in the shake-up of real life, of hard-nosed employers sharing a single interpretation of history, of curiosity being castrated and then thrown onto the altar. Anzia Yezierska. Anton Chekhov. What business were they of anyone, except librarians and lecturers? No one actually cared anymore. No one cared that the Pilgrim Fathers originally set sail from Southampton. Carry on saying it was Plymouth. Please. No one will notice. Continue the sophistry. It'll be OK.

I turned to him incredulously. 'The nihilism skipped a generation. It was my grandfather who taught me to question things.'

Chesterton was unmoved or respectful. I could not tell which. Whatever his disposition, I felt the urge to continue. A listener amongst the hordes of showmen and women! For that, at least, I was thankful.

I told him, about 'Castro'. About his fight, love and drink philosophy, as opposed to food, money and opportunity. About his odd, rustic collection of clothes – sports jackets, woollen jumpers, ties and mustard and beige socks. How we had lived on opposite sides of the golf course. How he had dredged for golf balls for me in the lodge next to their cottage courtesy of an old broomstick and chip pan; the brands found sometimes not quite in keeping with his socialist spirit. How he used to play, drive to opposition courses for competitions, in the process usually parking in the Treasurer's or Secretary's spot. 'He wasn't conscious of it … simply using the available space was his line – had always been his line. It had become such an automatic process … overriding the physical pomp and pageantry,' I said. 'Christ – this was the man responsible for either putting the chip on my shoulder or making me feel elated about the possibilities in life.'

I looked across at Chesterton. Tried to gauge his thoughts. His aristocratic features were somehow involved in a bitter wrangle of their own. Rather than plough on, I chose to fall silent.

'And do you hate him for pulling you from the ship of Cook or Columbus? For stripping you of the day's common uniform?'

'I…' I sensed that Chesterton had plunged into his own personal trove. Quite innocently and perhaps subconsciously, yet very plainly. A metaphor that reeked of a capricious uncle. 'I don't. No. But at the same time, I often wonder what could have been …'

'If you'd been more diplomatic? If you'd towed the line? If you'd followed your father's wisdom instead?'

'You're looking for an absolute, Benjamin … something I can't give you. My father was less dogmatic than my grandfather and so difficult to pin down ideologically. My father is still alive, my grandfather isn't. What I can say to you now is that *I* and *I only* have decided the years … years spent sitting amongst financial chumps because I needed to see – have a concept of who I really was. Figures were the easy way out – yes – what with my 'splendid' maths O-level. I was being geared up for a career as an accountant or financial consultant or something. Contracts were being slid across desks by owl-like individuals. Reports were winging their way back to the special college that I attended, enabling them to hold me up as a shining example. A shining example of *their* teaching methods. Not *my* natural gift with figures or the fact that I had had possibly the finest secondary school maths tutor in all of England. No. *Their* coaching, persistence and general expertise.'

'This was the special college which you attended ... sitting in a lower league than a typical A-level institution?'

'You've done your homework. Yes. Yes, I did ...'

'You have an interesting history, Arnold. We're not that dissimilar.'

'*How?!* How exactly? You're able to listen well enough, but beyond that I can't possibly agree. Aren't you an aristocrat? Your first real salary – was it £52.88 per week? Have you ever offered up a working-class smile in exchange for such a pittance?'

'I can't say I have ...' And at that, Chesterton looked slightly embarrassed.

I wanted to call a halt to my vehemence at this point. I wanted to stop and chat about E.M. Forster – one of the few aristocratic, yet humble novelists to have graced my mind. Instead, something wild and unbound kicked within me; a hangover from the Roman – his lingering threat and attestation that there was One ... One who would quell me. 'Why, exactly, am I here? Is it part of some Oxford-chums machination? Are they going to leap out from behind the cappuccino machine and kick the shit out of me? And the magazines ... why so many? Left wing, right wing. *Where* exactly do you stand, Chesterton?!'

I didn't wish to look at him anymore. The Dos Passos world, instead, pulled me towards it. My left ear remained, in anticipation of a brisk sentence, but the rest of my body was outside. Breathing in acrid air. Allowing the carcinogens to toil over me.

'There is no agenda. I simply saw you as an intelligent chap. I intended to present you with a business proposition of sorts. As for the magazines ... I like to gauge varying opinions.'

'Intelligence is remembering things. I merely have a system ... mnemonics – a poor substitute. I don't even have the excuse of fighting and drinking like my grandfather, of killing the brain cells. I'm virtually abstinent. Repressed. Stiff. *The Minority Man*, in all but appearance.'

'Good.'

'Why good?'

'Because ... because.' At that, he shrugged his shoulders, knowing that an answer would compromise his equivocacy.

The room now seemed to press its dormant guise upon us, its wounded other half. The resultant aura, albeit as ruse-like as effort and interaction, somehow allowed the two of us autonomous grooves in which to 'bathe' or dream. I weighed up Chesterton once more, in the midst of this self-governing trance. He was the purger of something. Quite what exactly, I did not know. His dandyish figure cut an innocuous shadow, yet a torn pocket surely resided. Other traits, affectations, foibles and nuances emanated from him, not least of all the sombre expression which slow danced across his face.

'There's much to tell. Some of it would appear inconsequential were I to tell you now, however. I'd rather we talk about the present before becoming embroiled in the past. That way, we set the stall but reveal the origin of the product later.'

I decided to take heed of Chesterton's prompting. I decided to suspend what lingering fuss still sat in my mind, namely the class chasm which existed. Raking the ground swell mainly for nuggets of disquiet, I began: 'At this moment in time, sat here – not quite knowing whether this is an interview or not – I feel estranged. Twenty-nine-years old, onto my fifth set of skin, yet clutching at belief systems. Science. Literature. Psychology. Religion. History. Sociology. Politics. Philosophy. Economics. I sometimes think that I know less now than when I was sixteen. Or maybe it's just that the information has saturated my brain and everything's become so nebulous and confusing. Perhaps figures were my mainstay. Perhaps an innate gift should be celebrated, not made to go to war with art. I guess I conscripted their exactness in an effort to be free of professionalism ... specifics. But then, I think, justifiably so, as they somehow refused to encompass everything ... all eventualities.'

'Numbers flat refuse to be divided by zero. It breaks the rules. It isn't allowed. Mathematics, economics, commerce, accountancy, or whatever you choose to call it, does not speak from a universal platform therefore. We have, Arnold, a blatant and obstructive device in place. One designed to champion limited ends. Ask me later how to disprove the principal assumptions of your other belief systems, but for now please tell me how you interpret '0'.'

I paused for a moment. The relevance of what we were discussing had long since begun to matter. On thinking about Chesterton's assertion, I instinctively gazed down at the empty cup in front of me. The absence of a liquid, or profound nothingness, hit me immediately. It pressed home an infinitely divisible form when set against the oneness of a simple cup. To show Chesterton that I understood, I unpretentiously lifted the cup, turning it over at eye-level.

'Good. And so the larger truth becomes ...?'

I hesitated, confident in the knowledge that the stage was his. That even if I had known, Chesterton would rather deliver the conclusion like a 17th century medicine man.

'... All numbers are equal. One divided by nothing is infinite. Eight divided by nothing is infinite. And so on. The end of maths! Forgive my plagiarising, but I owe this thesis to the Indian, Bhaskara. The ramifications, thanks to our eastern friends, are many. Western economists would have us think in slightly narrow or incapacious terms though.'

I was beginning to see. The man before me, although quite closed and cryptic, was coming undone – ideologically – with each passing second. I was eager to switch the focus therefore – thus unfleshing the aristocrat further and balancing the knowledge base. 'This wasn't a logic your family approved of, I assume?'

He laughed; a simple, forgiving laugh. 'The present first, Arnold – we agreed. Then the past. But to answer your question loosely: seven sheep will always be seven sheep, despite my best efforts to prove otherwise or dissuade.'

'And so your thoughts now on life? Your direction or karma?'

'That isn't so easy to answer. If I had recently graduated like yourself, then the fire would no doubt be significantly more pregnant. Particularly as, in your instance, English was incredibly alien to you and therefore an exquisite voyage. Soporific. That is the word that comes to mind. I am quite drowsy, not having picked up the educational baton for some years now. Six years in fact, given that I'm twenty-seven. My karma though? My thoughts on life? Disappointment. Concern.'

The words seemed to pack up at this. End abruptly. Chesterton appeared a little worn, a little dispirited. I was beginning to envy him, however. *Him* somehow me. And he saw this the instant I began to think it.

'I'll buy you some time ... expression. I don't know how much, but sufficient to avoid being dependent on the state for a while. Sufficient to redirect you from the appalling indignity of that government hostel, the *Employment Centre*,' he asserted. 'Call it sponsorship if you like. Call it silver-spooned, aristocratic benevolence. Call it my ancestors espousing a reluctant and belated 'sorry'.'

I fell silent for a moment, unable to grasp or indeed believe the magnitude of what Chesterton was saying. Eventually – 'And the business proposition?'

'More of an experiment. 'Business' was the wrong word; a monstrous word and failed locution. All I would require is fifteen hours of input each week. Enjoyable input I should think, based on your existing knowledge or certainly strands of it. The rest of the time is yours. Thinking time. Something which every human being should have.'

I considered Chesterton's pronouncement. Still knowing little about the actual 'venture', I attempted to recall snippets of the "knowledge" he was referring to. At the same time I began to see him as a kind of Engels; myself an over-flattered and perhaps overprized Marx. The comparison left me somewhat worried. What he maybe wasn't aware of – or happily chose to ignore – was that my completed writings and verbal expression *both* depended upon a myriad of vital pauses and checks. I was, in short, still the three O-level Joe who had had to attend night school in order to pass his English O-level at the second attempt. This admittance was in no way meant to be whimsical or self-deprecating, but rather quite candid in its embodiment of my still-limited means. I have a system, I felt like reminding him. Don't apotheosize me or ennoble me when I must revise the answers *before* knowing the questions, when I generally convey two, often contrived sentences, instead of the sought-after native five.

'Beyond this,' I asked him, holding out my arms – '... the political posters, the acute philosophy, the lateral culture, what is there? Inheritance of a thousand acres on your 30th birthday, set against my now powdery degree? A bath of overflowing nepotism waiting to be gotten into?'

'You do me an injustice. I have a degree also,' Chesterton spurted, rather laconically.

'Should I ask what in?'

'No ... because the stall is now fully set. Perhaps another time.' And at that, Chesterton stood up, offered his hand and somehow managed to conclude the day's events in a brisk, yet polite manner: 'I trust that twenty pounds an hour isn't an insult? For that I tap into the workings of quite a rare mind.'

I nearly stopped him. Asked about the specific nature of the job, even the hours of work. But ... something curtailed my instinct. Something skewered the mental scroll that I had only partly unrolled. Even the mention of money failed to unsettle my barter-preferring mind. I simply stared as Chesterton's early insouciance made a rallying attempt at the 'close of play'; his tweed-like garb flapping in the rush and the semi-wind outside.

A distinctive friend, I thought. One to provide me with new perspectives. One to scribble in alongside 'Asian', 'gay' and 'elderly'. One whose origin was incontestably grandiose.

CHAPTER 32

She picked me up in an old Vauxhall; our official, 'shared' car of eighteen months. On glancing at her Egyption-like eyes, dark bob and vibrant features, I still saw the intelligence which enamoured me, which pulled me out of the loneliness and gave me a voice. She then did what she always did: turned on the radio as soon as I was comfortable and mouthed 'This is us.' The random lyrics, at once, stirred:

"... watch the ripples flow
Moving out across the bay
Like a stone I fall into your eyes
Deep into some mystery ..."

Silence after. Just a glazed look. A sad melancholy. A strained appreciation of adulthood. I instantly wanted to protect her. Hold the crumpled willow before me. Push the spent hair away from her eyes. She rubbed the dew before I could do anything though. Attempted to steer the car away from the station, and her mind away from forlornness. My interview didn't matter. The people we passed didn't matter. Not while this ineffable lady was sad. Not while the axis of life had somehow tilted itself against her.

'You can resign tomorrow,' I cautiously enthused. 'Tell the fuckers to keep the globalisation fires burning themselves.'

Her eyes momentarily washed over me; shifting from the road. 'How? Why?'

'Because ... because I'm earning.'

In a sharp, cutting, yet transparent and necessary manner, she managed to shortcut any detail: 'How much?'

I hesitated a little, before the number finally dripped out: 'Fifteen.'

'It's not enough.' She banged the steering wheel with her right hand and raised her voice. 'It's not enough, Arnold! Don't do this.

Don't do it again ...'

The anguish frightened me. I had seen it before, yet not quite at this heady level. She was right of course. It wasn't enough. The lamentable figures plainer to me than anyone. The cusp of our college chatter, our planning, so routinely and savagely blunted. Silence now. There was silence until two miles later upon reaching home.

'I should congratulate you, but ...'

'It's alright,' I assured her. 'I know.' Knew of her mental torture. Of her defiance slowly unravelling in the face of a corporeal assault.

'It gets harder. That's all. I feel my personality diminishing ... abating. It's not what was supposed to happen.'

I lifted the top half of her clematis-like body from off the steering wheel and pulled her towards me. The injustice, whilst there before, seemed ever heightened. The oppression unnervingly close to a state of acquiescence. Examining her young face, I saw that it was somehow blanketed by a popular and crepuscular wisdom; a bacteria which spread its more evil prokaryotes. Everything. Almost everything ... was surreptitiously railing against our original pact. A pact perhaps unrealistic and childlike in its roots and methodology, yet beautiful and auspicious.

'Let's go inside ... Map things out again,' I softly encouraged her. Her - Josie; the woman twelve months ahead of me in graduation terms; the woman, therefore, seventeen months into her vocational 'sentence'.

She nestled herself against me more conducively - moved her right hand up and down my chest, before: 'You said "only one year" though. You promised. It's been longer, Arnold. Much longer.'

Acute optimism's mistake (its transgression); an optimism which had somehow survived against the back drop of both *my* hard, American novels and *her* ferocious and foreboding plays; *my* English curriculum and *her* Theatre Studies tremulousness. We should really have seen it ... the world beyond the classroom ...

the proxy give-ups by Joe Citizen et al in relation to life ... the money coursing through the veins of everybody - all but a handful.

To work one year and take the next off. To continue the 'discovery' like an ethical Columbus. That had been the aim. Me supporting her. Her supporting me. On/Off. On/Off. Something to aim for. Something to contrast the obscene forty-year slog. But only fifteen - fifteen thousand sterling. I had already clocked in six months late and was now found to be inadequate ... incapable of buttressing the desires of my labouring partner.

'I'll find something else. I'll try harder.'

She bypassed my dutiful chatter and cut to it as always: 'No. No. There's something about you. I can tell that the Chesterton interview has made you more content. Did you genuinely like him? Because that's all I need ...'

Chesterton's face immediately transported itself into my mind. Synonymous with it seemed to be the mass slaughter and eradication of words such as 'regular', 'prevailing' and 'wonted'. The man, although probing and personal, had done something. He had marginally altered my tragedy-ridden perception of the corporate agenda. For that, my answer to Josie could only be: 'Most definitely.'

'Then the nature of the job, the salary and any idea of eminence should be irrelevant ...'

'*Should*,' I repeated, half throwing forward my guilt and half worshipping the lady for her smart discernment.

'No should. Just take, take, take.' After which she reached up and kissed me; a kiss which was moist with immense sadness, yet giving and altruistic.

I could not really argue now. I could not really question the lady's - my partner's - motives or rationale, however much it was expected. I merely hoped that she saw it. My countenance humbled. My feelings for her supersonically lapping the heart I imagined to be beating beneath her blouse.

We went inside soon after. Past the small mountain of post. Past the glass dish with used stamps in it. Past the rabble of furniture which wistfully sat in the living room. And on, into the kitchen. She sat at one of the few things which said 'us'; a circular, antique pine table. She then folded her arms in front of her and rested her head upon them (aimlessly staring in the direction of the washing machine, or linen basket). I did not stop to question her. Nor did I physically intervene in an attempt to shift a smile. I simply pulled a recipe leaflet from the drawer and then proceeded to extract the dish's listed, primary ingredients from the fridge.

The whole thing was slow, beautiful, casually precise. It set me thinking that one's 'pincers' should always be covered in the scrub of a vegetable. That modern-day cleanliness had somehow sheltered us from or deprived us of the seedbed of culture. That the service sector was an ill-conceived device put in place by corporate behemoths keen to ensnare our innate ruralness. Thus, our inability to fend for ourselves became immense. Our dependency on the machine got ever greater. (The distance between citizen and soil no longer bridgeable.) We could not bend. The behemoths - they had us permanently upright. We were *serfs*, yet bound not to the land but to the crystallization of a non-Steinbeckian script.

The meal - we ate it slowly, exchanging few words between bites. I looked at her throughout; the continual folding of hair behind her ears; the look of enervation pouring from her like Chesterton before. She was tired. *Everybody* was tired. Of differing things which were so ... similar. Of the shrinking world which no longer boasted the ship as its high-velocity friend. Tied to satellites and moored in by concrete canals, we sat, waiting for an electronic or digital twitch. The world awaiting us. Us awaiting it.

'I don't want it, you know,' Josie abruptly said. 'I want you to have what you crave, but my side ... I can't. I simply can't anymore ...'

Capriciousness. Mercuriality. Schizophrenia. It was one of them, or maybe just the voice of humanity pushed up against a wall. Unable to be consistent. Incapable of a true and full expression whilst its larynx was repeatedly and indirectly gnawed by apathetic politicians. *Who* was out there, I now thought. *Who* actually cared enough to use their dirty money to fight for something so inherently clean? Because, that is what it amounted to: the good, themselves acutely alone on the battlefield, needing the many, needing the money, to ironically *sustain* their cause; Josie's cause.

'We're in a hole. I know that. Let me start this job with Chesterton. That's all I ask. In a few days, weeks ... who knows.'

She looked at me with dew again rising in the corner of her eyes. Any sense of control seemed to have been replaced by an outer rubberiness, a stoical grin laced together with angst. 'Who knows,' she mumbled.

I wanted to repeat my earlier bravado. I desperately wanted to swagger across the eighteen-inch 'canyon' which divided us, which held our sanity. And then whisper 'Resign. I'll take care of you.' But I couldn't. I had no security. My family were working class. A safety net had, unfortunately, not been in the original drawings or plans. In the economic scheme of things, she was 22, I was 15. If I had been 22 then I would have been able to look after her, as she had me ... just. But I was not. I was 15. Fifteen thousand. A charlatan to optimism.

'Let's freshen up. You go in the living room. I'll bring you some wine.'

She slid the chair back, stood with an air of somnolence, and wandered *through* the living room and up the stairs - no doubt to the bathroom. I lingered, watched her legs and feet finally disappear from view; the interlude or respite somewhat necessary. Still seated, I eventually rose myself and began to clear the table - merging the day's pots in the process: glasses and mugs placed at the rear of the kitchen unit; cutlery in the sink; plates, dishes and wares brooding on the right in the knowledge that they were to be 'bathed' last (their smaller sisters and brothers less dirty and therefore less likely to taint the water profusely). It was suggestive, this 'arranging', this marshalling, of one's truer self. A hands up to the accusation of organisational obsessiveness. More crucially, it was a link to second quarter Italy (and America) in the twentieth century. Mussolini. Sacco. Vanzetti. My family. Part of my roots. An all-pervading history which sat in the brain like an incumbent.

'Arnold ... Come up, Arnold,' she uttered; the remnants of the sentence making it down the stairs and into my ear.

I followed the cue - slowly lifted my feet onto each step. The wine, already poured, accompanied me. As I reached the top of the 'climb', I noticed her, sad and folded on the bed in the back room. Like a child almost. Seemingly bitten by a bullying wind. I looked down on her for a moment, paused oh so slightly, yet considered all ... everything. She was losing the fight, I thought. More so than me. She was comatosing on society's ethical vacuum, on the swirling mass of folly which tempered only the brutal.

'The wine. You've got the wine?' she half said, half asked.

'Yes. Right here,' I indicated, thrusting the glasses into her line of vision.

'Good. It's important we have the wine ...' She partially got up and took hold of one of the glasses. '...because wine gives us back our opinions ... our sentiment.' Having spoken, she took a healthy gulp, and then another - finally lying back on the bed.

I removed the glass from her hand, her grip, and then placed it on the desk with my dormantly full one. Depression seemed to clutch the room like a psychotic bear. Dolefulness seemed to walk on through as if attending the funeral of a civil rights chief. I looked at her again: the anguish brimming, rebellion pouring from her in the manner of a fierce sweat. Civilian life, or non-college life, had bound her up. It had taken away her library pass, her ability to assimilate, think and select. Daily inculcations had shorn the dream, the inventiveness. What was left was effectively a shell, a moving apparatus of moribundity.

'Brecht was right you know,' she suddenly pronounced. '"The government has dissolved the people and elected another."' It was the playwright within her talking; a gay abandon which occasionally unhooked itself from the sterile seriousness of urbanity.

'I don't recall you needing the alcohol before,' I cut in, interrupted

- sounded concerned, in perhaps too patriarchal a voice.

'Well before is gone, Mr Sir Arnold!'

It was almost comical. Indeed, had the look on her whilst disclaiming such a thing not been so utterly devoid of hope, then I would have laughed shrilly. As it was, the circles below her eyes seemed ever darker and the tiredness more acute.

'Why didn't you come in anyway?' she asked, referring to her socialist HQ days, me meeting her outside afterwards, never entering.

'Because I would have subdued you. I would have taken the sting out of your reproach. My presence would have compromised your politics.' My answer was different each time she asked, and that was often now – at least three times per month.

She smiled a little; a whimsical kind of slanted lip. 'You had that much of an effect on me?'

'To a degree.'

'And now?'

A sadness seemed to return in her before I could answer. 'Now ... we're confused with modern life. And so, belief is difficult.'

She shut her eyes. Perhaps I had disappointed her. Perhaps she had needed me to restore something in her by professing a few words of sardonic arrogance. The temperature, the false heat, rebelled against it though. The whole autumn manifestation prevented me from looking to the horizon with any level of buoyancy.

I lifted her up. Carried her through into the double room. Her eyelids remained fixed. Her expression taut. Lowering her onto the bed, I watched intently for any give up, any firm sign of attentiveness. Nothing yet. She continued the almost stubborn play, the roving introspection. Shutting the curtains, I managed to block out the orange haze from the street lights. I then clambered under the duvet minus shoes, shirt, trousers and socks. Lying diagonally, I tunnelled under the outstretched legs of my lover - the still, surface presence of her limbs. Just thinking now - simply thinking - I half lost consciousness. It was a delightful state prompted by pure shatteredness and filled with dulcet images; the whole landscape, in fact, was quite celestial and serene; the stone and pastoral hybrid view almost infusing a religious or monasterial tone.

It wasn't uncommon. This 'escape'. This hiding from the world. This mental wanderlust. I do not remember when exactly it started, but if we hadn't conceived it then a diet of television, public houses and sloshed journalism may well have fought perversely for our attention. Now, enshrouded by darkness, we were safe however. As safe as our minds allowed. Stirring in this knowledge perhaps, Josie spread her arms and gave out a minuscule yawn. She then slowly undressed down to her briefs, before joining me under the duvet; her petite-to-average size breasts initially struggling for concealment. Letting my amusement show, I held her. I held her for as long as possible prior to the evening beginning; prior to the contemplation, the reconciliation of thoughts, the talking.

Eventually, and almost on cue, the eight o'clock train sped by; its announcement cheery yet industrial; its reverberations with the track somehow reassuring. We loosened the hold at this point. Began to lie side by side. My hand on her thigh. Hers on mine. Staring up at the ceiling, we imagined it to be the sky, the cosmos - ourselves a mere flicker, yet uninterrupted in our duality by perfunctoriness or trivia.

'Where are you?' I asked.

There was a slight pause, before: 'Away from the bank. Much younger. Hopeful. My eyes still zestful.'

I didn't interrupt, in a similar manner to Chesterton waiting on *my* next word. I didn't interrupt in the hope that time would recede. In the hope that my anachronistic urge would act as a template. But then the ringing came, quite unavoidably. The tuneless follies serenaded and groped. Deference lay in the collective mind lacerated and bludgeoned. Only the exception, the phoenix, was heard...

'... I'm eating toast. Thick, grilled toast with dollops of raspberry jam. My family - about eight of us - are sat around a cloth-laden, rectangular table. A white cloth with simple stripes that fail to dominate ... soft orange, sky blue. They're happy. It's a Sunday of course, but Monday isn't banging at the door. It's different. Things are relaxed, beautifully slack. The faces, the mouths, are moving - almost rudely so, uncivilised, without manners, yet so ... harmonious. I look up at my father. (He's on my right, at the head of the table.) He's jolly. Jolly and simple. Not a hint of boardroom about him. Not a wisp of polish. Just the true look of a labouring man. He leans over me - reaches, as if to make a point to my uncle. I hear the words "work to rule" and for a moment their faces become slightly serious. A second after, the salt cellar is in his hand, and he's shaking it lightly next to his boiled egg. He catches my glance - sees the fascination - and asks if I want to feed him his 'soldiers'. I instantly giggle. My hand over my mouth as always. My mother, opposite, goading me on - her eyes playful and warm. Eventually, I pick up one of the strips of bread. It's a crust, an end, for curling my father's already wavy hair. He looks excited by the choice - his brand of excitement always bordering on a wonderful kind of chumphood. Lifting it - the 'soldier' - to my father's mouth, I find his expression paralysed by happiness and a kind of provincial ... nobility. At this point the food becomes an irrelevance. It's just *seeing* him ... so pleased, so 'full'.'

She smiled, yet looked sadder than ever; her betrothed past never quite making it to the altar; her white dress stained and tarnished by a fresh global apartheid. Re-engaged to the ugly edifice of privatisation, she walked the streets without holding its hand, without chatting or hugging - ashamed of its tasteless garb. People stared. They questioned her animosity, her free will, her general level of frostiness. 'Selfish,' they concluded. 'A loose woman,' they attested (in the manner of a Mid-western cowhand). With a swish of the neck, however, she was past them all. Walking, continuing, with the obligatory shadow in tow, the spectre of an ageless corporation or authority implicitly barracking her. Difficult to shake, she thought. Difficult to *be* truly independent. Too many interconnections. Too many Coca-Cola highways, both cerebral and of tarmac. Where's the past? Where's it all gone? she cried.

'Where's it all gone? The happiness. The nobility. Something concrete instead of specious 'markets' and 'open economies'. Why the apoplectic 'competition' amongst each other? Why not just ... work together?'

'Because there'd be no 'fun',' I interjected. 'Because harmony is dull, staid and traditionally pious. Because whichever country initiated such a utopia would be risking everything. And anyway, there are other, more serious elements.'

She looked at me for a moment, away from the world or cosmos we had recalled and imagined. She looked at me, slightly sickened and disillusioned.

'These words *now* even. They're somehow irrelevant. Nontangible. Because of rhetoric's dominance. Its catching us on the blind side. *All* sentences and paragraphs are now parcelled up using the *same* brown paper and identified using the *same* black marker pen. The one which scribbles 'SUSPICION: THIS SIDE UP'. The whole thing is a war, not just against the government but also the people we pass on the street. We're living an alien existence in the sense that humanity is no longer recognisable. Personally, I'm running from 'the numbers': interest rates; exchange rates; indices; M0s; M3s; LIBORs; GDPs; Public Sector Borrowing Requirements; the Retail Price Index; Earnings per Share; PE Ratios; Net Asset Values; Capital *fucking* employed.'

There was little I could say. And so, I decided to say exactly that. Little. Nothing. The early relationship habit of filling the blanks with rag or doggerel had long since fragmented. I therefore remained hushed. Whipped and beaten by Josie's final shots. Her Marxist sting. At times, it felt as if preclusion hadn't been granted. That *I was* a piece of evil too. That her words had been shorn of even the one thing I held dear: loyalty.

But I needed sleep. The echoes were fermenting. The unrest was...

CHAPTER 33

'**5**760 – that is our year,' Chesterton pronounced upon me entering his new premises, his city-centre dapperness. 'A people hated for nearly one hundred years and then made the prime target in a game of pogrom – party to Aksakov's International Conspiracy Theory. Well, we will laud their traditions, their practices. Behold!' He pulled back a small curtain, behind which was a plaque with the flag of Israel on it and the words: *Jewish Weddings.*

I had wondered about this day, Chesterton's mental state, his apparent generosity and now I knew ... what my fifteen hours would apparently involve, what my "enjoyable input" would be based around. 'I don't understand. They have their shadchans, their marriage-makers already. We wouldn't be allowed to intervene. We're not steeped in their ways – we're not knowledgeable enough. It would be an insult to them.'

'No. No, Arnold. This expression, this enterprise is not for the Jews – it is for Christians and other denominations abound.'

I didn't know what to think. I was aghast, yet somehow beguiled by Chesterton's boldness. I stood, silent, opposite him, beyond his walnut desk which commanded this new entrance foyer.

'The French Revolution – the real start of their decline ... don't you think it odd, quite wondrous that the year was 5550. Not 666, but 555. I know a little. I've come into this not entirely green, but you, *you* are my mainstay. I'm hoping that your dissertation will act as our Torah, our guide; that its beginning with Alexander II will not only veer away the peasant Christians from their DJs and discos, but also unite. Perhaps we'll attract a few Muslims as well – that has to be our higher goal.'

I thought back, to my recently completed thesis, my reference to the Tsar, Alexander II. How his assassination had been a precursor. How the Nihilists had effectively opened the gates to the Cossacks and their cross-carrying, priest-led, pogroms. How

Russia's Pale of Settlement with its fifteen provinces and four million Jews had represented a staggering 50% of the world Jewish population. Without doubt, 1881 had forever altered the Jewish mind. To bear things patiently, to wait for a messianic solution or divine providence was deemed no longer feasible, no longer tolerable. Despite religious thought evolving a "theoretical construct aimed at legitimising passivity", the Jewish collective consciousness had finally revolted, demanded its own land, its own borders, its own national liberty. Pinsker and Herzl (the founder of the World Zionist Organisation) had wished to finally transform their class, their gypsy-like identity into a body of people; a *mentsch.*

'Why the new premises?' I suddenly asked.

'Because ... because we need a look which commands respect ... which attracts people.'

'And did you buy this land or was it colonized?'

'Good. Good. I see, Arnold. You know your history. I bought it of course, as did the early Zionists. Let me show you something now.'

We walked through a side door into a much larger room. Chesterton clapped his hands together loudly. Seemingly from out of the niches and crevices of the room appeared a group of people. Some of them wore skullcaps or kippot. Some of them were simply there to move props and decorations into place. Others appeared solemn, yet sanguine – the inner family including the chatan (bridegroom) and kallah (bride). And then it began: 'Mazal tov,' I heard over and over. 'Mazal tov, my friend – mazal tov.'

I turned to Chesterton. 'Watch and then tell me what you'd like to include and what is perhaps too Talmudic,' he said. 'We have to westernise it a little, but the whole point of the ceremony will be to fascinate, make people laugh and cry. I cannot hope to know myself, so watch – please.' He intensified his stare in the direction of the crew he had hired, whether they were authentic or not. He watched as the chatan put on his prayer shawl.

I looked on, almost blankly. The world seemed to turn without my presence. It was farcical that we should be here watching these hired hands, this unique people, for as I concentrated more that is what they appeared to be – *real Jews.* What must they think? I asked myself. How exactly had Chesterton prepared them for my arrival? It went on though – the 'bedecken' ceremony (the covering of the bride's face with a veil), the saying of a few lines from the bible and then the father taking his daughter into the mock synagogue to stand under the chuppah (bridal canopy). After this, after the kitted-out congregation stood while listening to the Rabbi sing and pray that God bless the chatan and kallah, love was mentioned – their love having to equal their love of God and the Jewish people.

I was already editing them – who I would lose, who I would keep, how they would assist a real-life family, build their expectations and then kick out, partake in the wonderful finale of a Russian dance. This was despite my reservations, my embarrassment at being here. Before then, however, there were more words from the spiritual leader – mention of the Sabbath (a Saturday) and the need to keep a kosher home, blessings over a cup of wine and then the ring.

'... marriage sacred, according to the Law of Moses and Israel ...' I fleetingly heard, followed by the Seven Marriage Blessings, Chesterton indicated. After that a velvet bag was placed on the floor with a glass inside it – the mock bridegroom expected to stamp on it, smash it, as a reminder of the sadness felt at the destruction of the Second Temple (Herod originally beginning construction of it in 19 B.C.). Other potent and symbolic happenings continued: the walk to the bimah (raised platform) to sign the marriage documents; a Rabbi blessing for the plaited loaf (challah); the official welcoming of the new son-in-law into the family plus thank yous to all for taking part in the simcha (joyful celebration); a Hebrew toast to the newlyweds (L'Chaim – 'to life').

'Now we would normally sit down over the meal, cut the cake,' Chesterton imbued me with. 'I didn't think it worth their acting that out though. Watch. Watch now – the glorious meshugoim.'

I had heard the word only three or four times before, but I

remembered its meaning: the crazy people. Suddenly there was music – authentic Hasidic and klezmer music, Russian dancing.

'This is it. This is what we're really selling – this bloody difficult dance. Imagine the peasant Christians used to their romantic slosh and vacuous pop. Imagine them attempting this with its East European bite and speed. They'll be falling over stone drunk. Picture them squatting whilst kicking out their legs, all to the surrounding claps and cheers! What do you think, Debrito? Honestly – what do you think?'

He did something then. Before I could answer, some of his hired hands had pushed me into a chair. I was then lifted – carried around the room like a king on his throne. Thrust into the air alongside the guest kallah. I couldn't help but smile, not just at the woman floating opposite me, but at Chesterton's whole grand scheme.

'King and Queen!' he shouted. 'You are King and Queen!' He lifted his glass from off one of the tables. 'A further toast to the Moses of our time. *Moses!*'

The crowd instantly fell to their feet, moved their arms up and down in unison in front of me. I was being worshipped by strangers, Jews whom I had no apparent affiliation with. And each one of them – including my mock wife – seemed genuine, somehow taken by me.

'Get up. Please. Get up,' I requested. They stood. I was confused and so I left the room. Before closing the door behind me, I heard Chesterton addressing them: 'He flees. Definitely pre-Zion. He has it. He is "God's darling", a red-headed David, not Goliath who we have become, "weighed down by armour".'

I waited for him. Eventually, we stood alone in the foyer. 'What was that? Why the speech?'

'We're acting – every one of us. They're fighting for a job – a role in your enterprise. Not all Jews are rich, as you can see.'

'So I choose them after one rehearsal? Only one? You want me to sack two thirds of the people out there!!?'

'Try and see them as Egyptians and Syrians. Imagine it's '73.'

'They're humans. We're, *all of us*, humans. I'll draft the plan, read a little and decide on a rotation system. Not one of them should be without pay.'

'Good. Good. That's why you're here. To take the reins. To understand the people. I'll tell them we'll be in touch.'

'Tsdokeh. Social justice. Remember it. Please.'

'I will, Arnold. I will.'

I worked long and hard for the rest of the day and into the evening. In my head a Judaic-Christian wedding was being pieced together, complete with prayers, the breaking of glass, cake, music and dancing. Most of it was Jewish, although their Hebraic language I would have to take away. A vernacular used by the 'goyim' would hold sway, although I would attempt to refine it – inject a poeticism. Any reference to God would be just that – there would be no mention of messengers, neither Moses, Jesus, nor Muhammad. I would simply include their communiqués anonymously so to bind everything: the need to welcome strangers as brethren; the final denouement of the Promised Land; almsgiving – charitable donations to the needy. Whether people, couples, would sign up I did not know. Whether the exercise itself was blasphemous in some regard I could not afford to consider. Unity, Chesterton had spoken of, and the more I visualised the paradigm and template before me, the more I seemed to adhere to such blind hope.

One of my first calls the morning after was to Ragavan, the Poster Boy. I imagined him spearheading the advertising – advising me of the various sites. 'Your venture frightens me a little. I see it as hazardous – naïve in its attempted monotheism,' he immediately responded, upon me telling him of the plan, the enterprise.

'Naivety prevents us from seizing up though, doesn't it – forever walking pusillanimously.'

'Not when you're seen as a Christian touting Judaism. You open yourself up to Islamic fundamentalists, conservative Christians, and orthodox Jews. Quite a set of foes.'

'So you're saying don't do it?'

'No. I'm simply warning you of the potential consequences.'

'Would any of these parties commit an act of manipulated reprisal in the belief that they were working for God?'

'Yes. And what is more they would not see it as "manipulated". They are, quite simply, wired to or have the ability to 'hear' His commands.'

'Then they are foolish – deserving of wrath. Because God does not work that way. God is our better thoughts – He channels politeness and consideration into us, He tells us to watch others and not be too introspective. He has never sought destruction. If He did, He would wilt, become fecklessness itself. What they *hear* is the dripping of their ruinous secular tap – an existence which has rusted and so can only be turned properly with a shedding of prejudices and prosaicness.

'Tell me now, Ragavan – will you assist me?'

'Of course.' It was said with slight hesitation.

'Are you sure?'

'Yes. I'll bring some lists. I'll help you.'

We met. Later on. In my new office. The opposite side of the foyer to the hall, the wedding room. Ragavan was still large, reasonably confident, yet he had word: 'Four faces. One behind a grill, one on the crossing, one in a car and another walking a few feet from me just moments ago. I didn't imagine them. Their stares were intense as if trying to tell me something. I have the lists on my person – I removed them from the brief case.'

I got up. Looked out. Through the only window at the front, in the foyer. There was nothing evident and yet I believed him. Ragavan, I trusted implicitly. 'Who knows you're here?'

'Just work. I'm on a job. Meeting a client.'

'They wouldn't send anyone?'

'Not unless they knew of E.t.c. No. They have no reason. I don't like it though. One could easily get paranoid. I've prepared for home – police on my step – but not here ... out here. That is different.'

'Then ... I'll use someone else. I don't want you at risk. Christ! Do they play on our attempt to unify? These pathological brutes - where do they reside, breathe, *sleep?!*'

'No. I won't hear of it. I want this. Look at the lists and *then* turn me away. Please ...'

I pulled them, from an envelope – laid them out on the desk. I didn't have to read them because Ragavan pointed at each line, provided a running commentary, a verbalization of his historical understanding: 'This is bigger than Nigeria and it is one of the few ways in which you can work. I don't take the line that Israel is to blame like many left-wing people of my ilk. Instead, I see that too many characters of significance have faded on the Israeli side – Moshe Dayan, Yitzak Rabin. And on the Palestinian side, the media has failed in bringing to the fore intelligent representatives, speakers of the *real* Qur'an, peaceful speakers. If we look back in Jewish history – most of it unwritten because of a lack of nationhood – we see Jewish exclusion, Jewish land as the Torah (and this only), Jewish suffering on an immense scale (Hitler, the Cossacks, a vengeful Europe). Do you know of a gathering of women – Jewish women – dressed in black who stand silently in a circle each Friday in west Jerusalem with the words 'End the Occupation' written on cardboard hands? Well these nine women, later multiplied into thousands, are what is needed ... despite being labelled "Arafat's whores", "black vermin" and other poorly-imagined defamations. They transcend the words and actions of the somnambulists – those that choose to carp narrow, churlish lines, those that are held by mouse-trap reactionism and popular distortion because they are unable to conjure a life behind their brow. Their excuse of salivating the 'will of God' with a fundamental disregard for others is shameful and a deadening force against humanism. It neither binds human endeavour and spiritualism nor turns the deserts green. I would say, in fact, that this roughshod approach destroys the very Yiddishness that the Jews have cultivated over centuries. It is therefore up to the intellects – both in academia and the Knesset – to set an example to the young generation, being as they are children of soldiers. It is too easy to stoke hurtfulness and politics of fear when leadership in the manner of a sage, a judicious guru is required.

'Look! Look at my other notes. The wish is that in two or three generations the Jewish people will see again – begin a process of cleansing. People talk of the need to lift the Arabs to the same material level as God's supposed children, but this is wrong. Peace will be at its strongest when vehement religion is dispensed with and respect of different cultures is at the fore again. Israel cannot manage the world's thoughts nor should it hold a blanket to its own mouth. Now is the time for *both* sides to begin a resounding dialogue, for a new Zeitgeist to be born. And how – how will I express this in your posters? I will not concentrate on the Occupied Territories representing 22% of Israel. I will not allow the numbing effect and desperation of the region's violence the stage it attempts to construct. Instead, I will push home the juxtaposition of a rich, austere life: dance; music; chatter; friendliness. Class and religion have their positions, their 'loftiness', but such considerations must come *after* decency and deference. Do I have your blessing?'

'Yes,' I replied. 'But I cannot watch over you as I would like. I cannot guarantee your safety. The pathological ones are at each juncture and in every corner. Some of them are motiveless which is …'

'As long as I have my lists, then …'

Neither of us finished our sentences. Neither of us wished to state fully a swab of words whether poisonous or purifying. Ragavan, it was decided, would design and paste the necessary work and I would wait, read and contemplate – prepare to harvest the interest generated, field questions from local officials and appease religious quarters bruised by the enterprise.

Chesterton, over the days and weeks, I saw less of – his dapper appearance occasionally flitting through the office if only to pass me the accounts, agree on what we would charge the Christian faith and discuss ideas. Concerning his family, his aristocratic roots, I learnt very little other than the fact that it was his father's second marriage and that his mother had been ennobled with the blue blood. Of Bhaskara and his lateral economic thoughts, Chesterton still revelled, rejoiced – delighted in the abstract notions of the great Indian.

When the day eventually came, when our first clients agreed to a booking – penned a contract almost in the manner of the 1917 Balfour Declaration (the promise being of a Jewish wedding rather than a national Jewish homeland) – we celebrated, drank a mock wine so to accommodate the Volstead-inspired Ragavan.

'Did I hire the wrong man?' Chesterton announced, acknowledging Ragavan's Jewish portfolio which now adorned much of the north west of England. 'Did I look for a white man when all along he was black?'

'No. No you didn't,' Ragavan replied. 'In Debrito you have honour – an abundance of honour. His silence represents not a dearth of wisdom, but rather a turning mechanism of discernment.'

'I knew as much. A toast! To future enterprises and gods! To Jewish Weddings! To the meshugoim, not discos and DJs and the stiff movements of a crass public!'

We gave a toast – allowed the remainder of the soft liquid to pass our lips. I thought, of something unrelated, of something I had read by W. H. Auden (comparing America's Lower East Side with Russia's ghettos): "Here was poverty still but less absolute, exploitation but the possibility of one day becoming an exploiter, racial discrimination but no pogroms." The subtle diatribe embodied my fears. That such a step from exploited to exploit*er* was the only way forward. That a middle ground did not and could not exist. I looked at them both – Ragavan and Chesterton (the preacher and the aristocrat) – and thought of *where* we would end up, how Level Four would be attained. And then an image of Pendlebury, Pendlebury's uncle – together my wings. I would be with them soon – I knew it. I would somehow be nursed

by them to my 33rd birthday, wherein I would give my all, bring
light upon the earth once more.

-       -   -

I had said that she would have one of her own. And indeed, the
technology crash of March 2000 precipitated Josie's 'fall'. Not
through a slashing of staff or the inevitable revising of the
numbers in the aftermath of such doom (because she was the
bank's pre-management luminary, its star). But through Josie's
bubbling intransigence, her raw rebellion, her fundamental
attachment to an enlightened expression.

'… sell a hundred. Now!'

'No,' she said softly. 'Not until you prove that you are civilised.'

'Civilised!? Civilised? Look at my portfolio, my worth. *Man's
value* is his refinement, his culture.'

'I disagree. Which part of the world you follow is the prime
indicator. And your portfolio – filled as it is with mining and
biotech stocks – concerns me.'

'What do you *mean*, lady. *I* and *I alone* manage this account. I am
not an advisory client.'

'Not in the financial sense, but given this anomalous situation I
feel it my duty to prevent you from selling – usurping blood-
soaked profits.'

'Your name! What is your name? You're costing me … I won't hear
any more of this sanctimonious pap, this … *anarchy!*'

'Josie. And I am not *costing* you. I am slowly healing you.
Diverting your haste.'

Upon the seniors hearing the reports, the catalogue of
complaints, they huddled around Josie, took her phone from her
and demanded answers. She stared at them, one by one –
attempted to make sense of their stance, their reckoning. She
could not speak though. She could no longer converse with the

suited haul before her. They repeated their 'justified questioning', their 'amazement at her complete lapse'. Still nothing though. She looked at them with the expression of a ragged doll, a ravaged enemy weak from the preceding warfare. Nothing – I have nothing left, was what enveloped her mind. She stood, avoided her belongings, and simply walked through the arc of bodies in front of her. No one followed. No one cared to doubt where she resided psychologically.

When I heard this. When I heard that she had imagined herself to be a conductor on the train home, demanding money from innocent fellow passengers, I wept. Delivered to me mumbling and lost, I put her to bed, thought through our life whilst cooling her brow, stroking her arms and neck.

'Lose it. Now we'll lose it. Our sovereignty. Won't we?'

Her reference was to the house. She chokingly uttered loose collections of words throughout the night. On/off. On/off. I was sure she was coming back to me mentally, cerebrally, however I phoned her parents – informed them of her state.

Within an hour they were with us – seated in our semi-rural abode. More questions. Asking. Reasoning. Some of them I could not answer. Some of them I found to be overly pertinent – damning of my dependency on Josie's income.

Chesterton phoned. Ragavan phoned. I spurned their requests – gave a reason for my intended absence other than the one lying before me. This was despite Ragavan's closeness to Josie in the early days, his marshalling of her finer thoughts. I thought her woe to be transient, short-lived and so decided to protect her standing outside the immediate family.

After a while I became uncomfortable. I regretted involving anyone else. Her parents all but kitted me out in a uniform – dondered me with unnecessary chores and errands. When the phone rang a third time, therefore, I assented to Chesterton's wish that I meet some potential clients – strode out of the house uncharitably with the too-easy approval of Josie's parents.

I thought while in the office, of the point we were at. Between articulating the Statue of Liberty's engraving, its 'golden door' pronouncement and the repertoire Jewish Weddings offered, I considered the fact that Josie was moving away from me, that I would ultimately be alone – a single note bound to an invisible scripture. I stuttered, panicked, batted aside the prolonged questioning of the foppish Christians before me.

'Another time. Please – another time.' I shuffled them out, as rude as it was. I then returned to my desk – attempted to phone Josie.

'Hello. Is she there?' I rammed at Josie's mother.

'She's not. No. We've taken her in.'

'What do you mean 'in'?!'

'To the psychiatrist ward. She's still mumbling. We felt it best.'

'You *blind woman*! She should be with me. Don't you understand – they're part of it … they …'

'See. This is what we thought. You're not good for her! We hold you partly responsible. She's in the hands of professionals now – doctors.'

'No! You're not seeing it. *Where is she*? Which hospital?'

'It's a private retreat. No visiting, except family.'

'I *am* family. I'm her partner.'

'No. No you're not. There's no legal attachment. Now *leave us*!'

The line exuded a low-frequency hum. She was gone. She had decamped. I waited. For voices to speak to me. For something which would assist. Nothing. Nothing though. My head fell into my palms. I pushed my hair back, stretched the skin on my scalp. Who could I speak to, burden, I wondered. 'Josie! Josie!' I cried – '*Where are you?!*'

I phoned Ragavan. He answered almost immediately. 'Not in this manner!' I promulgated. 'No – not this.'

He almost whispered back: 'They drugged her … when she left the bank. Stay at the office …'

When he appeared, I instantly catechized him: 'How did you know? How would you know such a thing?'

'Seniors … management – they're all connected. Straight-jacketed into the pseudo-dethroned regalia. The contract I won with you – it's made me privy to more rumours – chatter.'

'What can we do then?'

'Nothing. You knew it would come – perhaps the final catharsis. Just go home before dark each day. Try and equate suffering with an end jolt – rebellion.'

Ragavan's words maddened me. I had, in the midst of this spiritual 'crusade', lost any sense of deism. If there was a God then he was snoozing. And if that God was myself, then I felt much the same as the powerless majority of humanity before me, aside from my new-found truculency, my seething analysis of the system.

'You're asking me to forget, to purge her from my memory? I thought that is what *they* did, not ourselves.'

'An agreeable amnesia, Arnold. You *will* see her again, but now we must build – prepare you. People will not take to you if you have personal or political ties.'

'So we follow Emerson's code? I am to be an individual – at one with myself only …'

'That is how you will shed this human skin. That is how you will fully metamorphose into Him.'

'But who said I wanted this?'

'You have disciples readying themselves. *They* are our gauge – our determiners.'

'*Who?* Who?!'

'I think you know.'

I became silent. Yes. I *did* see their faces, their deference. But my reluctance – how had it drawn them in, how had it shaped a desire on their part to step outside the norm?

Ragavan seemed to read my mind: 'They do not wish to *fear* a god. History has taught us to fear, but *why*, we asked. A god should be gracious and candid but not the inducer of torment.'

'So until then, what do I do? And how will I know?'

'Your questions will stop. You will be omniscient. In the meantime, continue this enterprise – your 'senior bar mitzvahs', 'baptisms', your low culture purges, almsgiving. Now, I must go.'

I looked around, at the small kingdom Chesterton had provided, at the kosher décor, the 'Russification' before me. He had given me complete control. He had entrusted me, redirected me "from the appalling indignity of … the Employment Centre". But his fifteen thousand – it was no longer enough. In Josie's absence, my 'lodgings' would be too grand, too expensive. I looked at the ledger on the shelf close to me in an effort to justify more. The accounts I had failed to study, pore over meticulously, for want of artistic dominance. And now, weeks in, excluding Chesterton's purchase of the building, Jewish Weddings original bank balance of £250,000 stood at £32,458.

I was astounded. I had known the 'peasant Christians' to be an obstreperous set, one not easily drawn or distracted from their turntables and sausage roll buffets, yet my judgement had failed me. I had crashed when Josie had crashed. The liquidity of the enterprise was dire. I would speak to Saul, one of the workers I had befriended (and the best Russian dancer) – discuss lessening the hours of his compatriots or deciding on a few. Chesterton, I would avoid, until the numbers had improved, until my mind was pitted of Josie's touch – armed again in readiness for Chesterton's vein of swashbuckling.

-       -   -

Weeks later he stood in the corner of my office – appraised me like a painter would a landscape. He was direct and serious, yet impish somehow: 'Do you have anything to tell me?'

'It has been different – the enterprise. Not what I'm used to. Stockbroking isn't the front line like this. I've had to adapt.'

'I was aware of that when I hired you – your background, your sea change. But the business – how have you fared?'

'Not well.'

'My quarter of a million – what does it stand at? A few thousand less?'

'Understand that I had to mitigate the human hurt. We committed something to the Jews and I didn't wish to renege on that. They were good. Their choreography worked well.'

'But were you seen as imbuers of culture? That was my plan. I didn't ask that you fund a routine forever with its dust jacket on.'

'At the outset you didn't specify anything. I educated myself with the hours and waited for the business.'

'Business that never came. How many paid-for dances – Jewish weddings?'

'Four.'

'Only four!? Have you been hiding this? Did you choose to please your mind and your staff before the business?'

I paused. I had to answer honestly. 'I think, perhaps, I did.'

'Then you are ... everything I imagined you to be: the possessor of a giant soul; money's executioner; and altruistic. Tell me how much I have lost ...'

'It all, bar three thousand.'

'And when can you lose that?'

'I don't understand.'

'When will you clean me out, Arnold – have me undertake a normal citizen's path?'

'That was your inheritance? All of it?'

'It was. Deposited by my father two years ago.'

'Why then do this?'

'I told you the first day we met: my ancestors espousing an apology.'

'And?'

'And also, I must have *nothing* to be able to follow him.'

'Him?'

'Why, *yourself.*'

'The Last Supper?'

'Indeed. I can only pray for such an occasion.'

'And do you think loss of money spurs me? Do you think it in itself is adequate testimony?'

'I know that you require the two extremes – brothers of humanity. A rich disciple and a poor one – the latter, I believe, you have already met.'

'So you are to be my gold set against tin, great historic injustice set against an open wound on the conscience of all.'

'I am to be a piece of the truth finally coalesced – finally brought together so no one can be in any doubt.'

'And the business?'

'It has to fold, Arnold. That or we give it to Saul – ask him to do something we could never do. Be Jewish. I'm sure he is shrewd – and I talk not in a monetary sense, but one which will help bring about the death of peasant culture (that which drives the evils of the world). Pro bono – I will ask that he do pro bono work in amongst his normal work. The advertising, the significant costs – they must cease.'

'Saul is the right man. Today is my last then?'

'I think we both knew it would come. And I will expect to see you soon – at the table.'

'Yes. You don't mind my seeing out the day though – a last look around?'

'Not at all, Arnold. Breathe in the blueprint that you have created – please. I would reassure you about tomorrow onward, about the 5th June hence, but if I did I would be like a jester to his king.'

I was pensive. I thought about the origin of Benjamin Chesterton – how he had once given me his present with a promise of the past and how that promise had never quite come about; the tangled coil of his history, the experiences which had usurped his orthodox view of the world. I had not asked or demanded too much since our introduction because of something within, however – something which largely fixated my mind on 'the day', the day when I would know anyway, when simply by looking at a person I would comprehend their fears, thoughts and intentions.

We parted. I walked the large hall, alone. The day began to swaddle its sun and embrace dusk. The 'Russification' all around me served to push home a sovereignty which to this day shifted its borders and ravaged peoples and continents. I knelt before the bimah – prayed that my life would not become dust, that my family would encircle me and know that I had had to become different. I knelt through pain, on beyond midnight whilst considering the disciplines and discourses which seduced humanity, which had it shackled and sworn in – never to be radicalised or altered until the pain evolved into wretchedness, the originator's culpability pricked his or her vainglorious rationale.

'Arnold! Arnold Debrito!' I suddenly heard – its cry distinctive and off centre, warped yet magnanimous. *'Where are you?!'*

I turned toward the door. The room was alight, although I could not feel its heat, its combustion. A frame stood over me – a naked frame except for beard, bellicosity and loincloth. It hammered down on an iron block amid sparks and smoke. Hephaistos, I thought. I am in the company of Hephaistos, the Vulcan, the god of fire. I am beneath the earth. I am …

'Debrito! Debrito!' the cry came again; not the voice of the fire god, but something or someone else. 'Come towards me if you're there! They firebombed the building. They …'

'I'm here. *Here!*

The shape moved no closer as if in a different world to me. It stumbled around through the smoke and oxygenless semi-pyre that was now the hall around me. Then it seemed to spot me, for it came in my direction – toward Hephaistos and I, toward the flames which had erupted and encircled us.

'Debrito – indicate that you can see me! Raise your arm!'

I did so. 'The roar of the flames – can you hear the roar?' I replied, drowned out, not quite knowing where I was, in a state of meditation, a post-prayer reverie.

'No! I cannot! I am deaf. Now come towards me slowly … carefully.'

I could feel his pain – whoever this was – but not my own. I could see the orange light mirrored upon his face, the sweat caressing his brow. Myself though – nothing.

'Hephaistos – we can convert him. Allow me to bring him too …'

'What?! What!! Debrito, it is *me* – there is only us … two lives. Just us. Now come towards me … please! Please! I cannot get to y…'

Before I could take a step, it fell, like a marauding pirate - the roof of the mock synagogue, the Jewish temple top, as if wanting me for its furnace, its final ceremony, as the content of its velvet bag of fire.

'No!!!!! Debrito!! No! No!!!!'

Seconds. Then I felt plundered, at variance with the world, still not hot but somehow a charred manifestation, a carbonised effigy. I looked up with one eye from the bowels of this brightness, saw a hell before me, around me – the banging, spluttering madness of arbitrary flames. As I moved through them, they raped me of garments – the fierce entrails of this satanic cauldron had me animal-like and bowed, manacled and tethered. I desperately sought the voice from earlier – called out 'You from before! You from before!' as I now crawled in a barren effort to survive, retain what faculties I had left. I tried to move my left forearm, gain leverage – pull my ailing body forward – but it was somehow fused to the floor, welded by the heat and intensity. 'Not like this! Please! No!!!' I cried. The words I had exuded for Josie echoed in my head – borrowed their posthumous pleas from Sacco and Vanzetti's followers. Please! Don't allow them to be remembered like this – ungodly, knavish, without conviction.

I became unconscious – fell what few inches remained. Black now. Everything was black. And silent. As if my ears were below water's line (its top); myself bathing, nursing my mind, my thoughts, with an unspoiled canvas, the galaxy's refractory swathe of curtains. What of Level Four? I asked. What of the journey? Is there to be no grand or hamlet-like ceremony? Is there to be this darkness only and nothing pivotal after? The stars slowly peeped from out of the blackened cloak. They seemed to ask something of me – politely douse me in a peerless sanctity. There will be no leap across the rapids, but you will get there. One day you will see what has taken us years to amalgamate and forge. When it comes, sit in the most humble chair – deliver to your crowd not a didactic drawl but the remnants of your struggle, the wisdom that has stayed the course.

I blinked – somehow wiped the board before me. But the speckles of light returned – offered their gods and moons, salvaged that which I found unbearable.

Epilogue

'**E**ighty percent third and fourth degree burns. Thermal. We're down to the subcutaneous layers. I'm surprised you made it here. The shock should have taken him. Nurse – a catheter. Keep a watch on his index and output ... Blankets! Dry sheets! This is a very high TBSA.'

'He'll make it?'

'If he's God, then yes. Otherwise ...'

There was a despairing shrug of the shoulders, a stricken mien. The surgeon had not seen a case like this before him in years, if at all – one where the fight had been minimal and therefore the suffering fierce, the mauled structure in his attendance like a grilled piece of fat or hapless semi-corpse.

I watched them from a privileged position above, a celestial pocket which granted me a view of my own reconstruction – the tens of hours which would determine my fate. 'Three days,' I heard them say. 'Then we'll know if the newly-grown blood vessels have knitted in with the allograft or transplanted skin. If the connection is made, if the tissues merge then one can say we're moving forward.'

'The skin – where will that come from, given ...'

'Given the extensive eschar, the nonviable skin which dominates his frame and allows little in the way of self-grafting? From a bank, my friend – a donor establishment which mostly takes the skin of accident victims within twenty-four hours of their demise.'

That was it – I was to be reconditioned as a collection of dead people. My familiar gaze would, for the moment, become a jigsaw, a Bayeux Tapestry carefully 'embroidered' by the crowd of nurses, surgeons and anaesthetists around me – their McIndoe-discernment never waning, placing a value on my pain and offering a cradle to my fear. Physically, to the outside world, I was now a leper, a triangulated wreck. My tendons were in danger of shortening should my joints continue their enervation, their lack of motion, yet my new skin had to rest, not limber up too much. How I felt about this impossible position, my humanity draining away in an aesthetic context, I didn't know. Somehow a higher truth now existed, yet at the expense of what? My physical being? The tangible contours I had quite gotten used to and developed a love of in a pre-narcissistic way?

'We hope to save and indeed rekindle his expression of mood in its infinite variety. That is something we never lose sight of or compromise – one's ability to contort, be true and in harmony with their thoughts.'

It was straight from the guru of plastic surgeons handbook, an Archibald McIndoe biography, and despite its positivism I found myself contending and litigating against its cheery inflection; amidst the fluid replacement and morphine sailing into my body, I was dismayed, terrified, yet amazingly there was no sensation of blame. My thoughts failed to dwell on the 'how' of this outcome, instead fixing their sights on the 'why'. My face was scarred and scorched – devoid of outer skin and acceptability – yet an image of the perpetrator of this did not manifest itself in my thoughts. My immediate preoccupation whilst visualising this medical den – out of body presence inconspicuous to the burn team over my bed – was the non-hospital-like appearance of my surroundings or rather the tepid professionalism of the people, mixed as it was with a strident philosophy. Among the white uniforms and seasoned expressions – I now realised – were ... Pendlebury ... and his uncle. I could hardly utter their names, so emotional was I. They had brought me in to this, their 'Médecins Sans Frontières' outlet, their refuge for pariahs. There was no mistaking the grey mop of hair and unlit pipe respectively. Their concern seemed ever heightened – beyond that which I had thought possible. They asked pertinent questions about my welfare, what my 'recovery schedule' was to entail.

'Some people don't see the rain when it's drizzling. We do. It *is* early though. We need to see how he responds ... Some of the treatment ... well ... let's just say that the illusion of tannic acid won't always be to hand. There will be extreme pain.'

Three days passed. My body experienced saline baths, breakthrough pain, the soothing music of the quarter I was in and an unbearable stinging. Good. Bad. Good. Bad. I developed the ability to speak again though – address my suitors, ask them about the membership once more, its aspirations and presence here.

They initially diverted and deflected my questions – thought them incongruous on an 'occasion such as this'. Talk must be of my health and nothing else – how I had narrowly avoided what they termed 'prophylactic endotracheal intubation'; my airway righting itself within minutes of my arrival.

'Without your voice ... I hate to think of that,' Pendlebury said. 'All the work ... the ...'

'What of your own endeavours?' I asked him. 'How was the forest?'

'I came out only a week ago.'

'And the axe – was it sharper?'

He smiled. 'You're astute. Yes. Yes it was.'

'What did you learn?' I enquired.

'What did I *unlearn* would be more apt. The West – it no longer has me, neither in body or spirit. I see through everything it projects now – *everything.* And the dangerous elements it indirectly formulated which very nearly purged yourself – well, they have been too long in the ascendancy. We have a network of quiet people, Arnold. I will tell you now that the membership has grown – phenomenally so. By the word 'quiet' we don't necessarily denote someone who speaks carefully and reservedly – someone free of turmoil – but rather a mind which avoids the seemingly inane stupor of corporate-speak, the din of charred words which serve only to increase the density of the cloud above us. And that cloud is full of distorted faces, a contrived truth which knows the ridiculousness of its own ethos.'

His use of the word 'charred' set me back. I was suddenly

conscious of my putrid features, my involuntary abandonment of normality. If this was to be the price of transcendence, then I wasn't sure. I would sooner rush back to the fire – seek Hephaistos's revocation, his declaration of anvil, hammer and belligerence; a statement allowing me another way. Suddenly, I turned – spoke firmly in the direction of Pendlebury and his uncle: 'The network doesn't 'see' though, does it. You both attested to the fact that there would be a leap across Three's rapids for me. Well, the rapids were the fire at my face – a turpentine dismantling my skin cells.'

'It's early, Arnold. Perhaps this was ...'

'Meant to be?! A half-destruction? Some kind of crucifixion which would forever perish my lingering humanity at your behest? What if I'm selfish? What if I need this life? Why take *me?* It's been years now and nothing. Years! What if I'm not Him? What if I crave solitude, not leadership – the thing that you yourself have just had. I need a corner, not an audience – a darkness in which heaven's lights will sustain me. Because there is a higher form than me – one whose covering isn't molten. Look at my hands! Treated first and yet I cannot hold things. I am a pathetic collection of woven pelt. My demeanour doesn't speak of spiritualism, but rather a cowardly oscillation. I am *afraid*, gentlemen! My heart asks that God *rescue me*, not suffuse me with Himself. I don't wish to become a template – a claim on what is right. Let the masses choose – indict themselves if necessary. Say I am not responsible for them though. Say that my creed is insubstantial. I would not be here were it not for the 1927 executions. History has me enveloped – gnawed at, however. And that is my downfall – that I do not take its bones and move humanity on, but instead falter and regret, cry at its altar. My communion is with a deep, melancholic lord. I cannot therefore exude a luminous sermon or proffer a band of words which would lift and inspire. My current mode is exemplified through my face – bracken-like and boorish. With my skin has gone my refinement, my restraint. I feel obnoxious, yet hollow – my centre has been taken – pureed out of me. You look at me and accept it. But how can I do the same? How can I accept *this?* My anonymity with the world has been suffocated. I will draw stares for the rest of my life – the pity and disquiet of people I do not know. Tell me I am wrong! Assert the opposite!'

They could not say anything. They were either verbally paralysed or respectful of my forthright claim. Upon them turning away – looking at parts of the room which did not interest them – a silence seemed to take hold like air from an abandoned factory. We were together, yet somehow in three different worlds – harmonised, yet narratorless. Eventually, it was the elder one of us that spoke – through deafness and sagacity, concern and solicitude: 'I don't know sounds – have never known sounds. You know that I have been deaf since birth. For you to have known normality, therefore, is harder ... being as you are now like this. I can trace your thoughts though – I'm aware of a spark worth cultivating. Were I not, I would not have come for you – I would have let the flames finish their meal.'

'You?' I challenged, suddenly seeing his face more clearly in the Jewish hall. 'You carried me here?'

'Only because there was so much of the path that you still had to walk – enrich yourself through.'

'And would you blow the leaves from the path for me?'

'I would. You know I would.'

I shut my singed eyes, drifted off into an abstract easiness. What moroseness I had left soon waned – found itself occupied by a convivial canvas. This place I was in, this refuge, then seemed to unfold itself before me. The people – they were part of a unit actively supporting another world; they were seed bearers of everything overlooked, politicised and manipulated in the name of freedom and democracy. Together they were a powerfully beating heart, of radicalism, of judiciousness, of 'Ya Basta'. And, as with Pendlebury, they – over the days, weeks and months – revered me somehow ... held and retained a look of expectation when dealing with me, sallied a steadfast faith; each action when tending to my skin being an investment in salvation.

I, of course, would be their agent – a redeeming force capable of sapping disorder, devitalising disturbance; the methodology driving this having as its nexus my death, my skeletonization. Why such an outcome no longer embodied a fear in me, why the weeks and months had transmogrified my alarm into a forbearance, I compared to fatherhood. Somehow the cataclysmic change had laid out its wares and lifted before me its most powerful archetype. And my very being had merely cranked up its own tolerance and capability – adjusted to the arduous traffic like a toughened suspension bridge.

Three years. 2001. 2002. And now '03. It passed quickly, in the manner of a vocational degree, only with myself as the hardware, the sodden welt. My parents I hadn't seen since the week of the fire – their faces better than mine, yet sad and outraged at being politely exiled, written to instead, initially with the hand of Pendlebury prompted by my ardent voice. Through letters I was able to construct a finer world, however – one which dipped its head at horror, at the ready intrigue of damage and destruction. My sentences poured out considered thoughts rather than snapshot judgements, worldly observations rather than provincial chaff. Not that the local was prosaic, particularly in its micro reading of things, but I had to universalise that which I felt, saw, tasted and heard.

When the day came – when I stepped out – I was a man of thirty-three. I was to be guided by my senses to a hall, wherein I would meet the disciples; not *my* disciples because I did not own; not my followers either because the tiny Mecca which magnetised us acted merely as a station point, a zenith for our collective rumblings. Yes, I would hold sway over the attendees, but in a manner which suppressed hegemony's boastfulness. I would know power for seconds only – time enough to despise it and reel from its illegitimacy. What control I had would be moderate and purposeful – I would not let its studded tail disregard the elements before it.

And so I entered, the hall, positioned as it was in a barren location, at a symbolically apt starting point – our movement young and to the wider world short on fecundity. I had not been here before – did not know in fact of its existence, until the voices had grown louder, the voices inside the hall which would, each of them, offer a manifesto, a building block. Their echoes and modulations I picked up through a wave somehow coursing itself directly to me. And *their* being drawn here – the disciples … how … why? I had to believe in a poetic providence, in Pendlebury's herding skills at the very least.

Looking at them now – sat around like a theatre group – my gaze became suspended, not of their world, somehow seconds ahead of their awareness, their shrewd cognizance. They were in clusters of three, pockets of commonality: Jack Debrito, Warwick, George Minty I; Ragavan, Saul, Green Suit; Chesterton, Pendlebury, Pendlebury's uncle; Josie, Rose Debrito and, one assumed, the spirit of 'Castro'; each pocket somehow themed, from the old to the young, from the financially polarised to the warriors of the Left. When, eventually, they looked up in unison – saw my changed self – I nearly broke down. There were so many people here that mattered – absolutely, wholeheartedly, without reservation; individuals whose fervour had on many occasions assisted me, ripped my soul from its sheath. Twelve more august individuals I would not meet again or hope to meet, even if that meant facing the caustic tears of my parents and the rehabilitated enigma that was perhaps Josie.

'Look at you. I still know you,' my mother pronounced. 'Not again,' she begged, moving her hands over my newly-knitted skin. 'Don't let us be apart again.'

'You think I'm the same, Mother?'

'My boy's appearance has altered, but you're the same because of your eyes. They are what matters … and everything inside of you.'

'You know why I'm here today though? You know of an inevitability in the air?'

'To a degree, my son. Yes. Your father has pressed such a thing home.'

I took hold of her. Held her close. 'I'll never leave you. You must know that. Haven't you sensed me during these last years?'

'I have, but …'

'Then talk to me as if I were tangible. Don't feel awkward in such an extended world. There *is* more than this outside flux – an inner kingdom befitting our more honest thoughts.'

'I'll try,' she purported, as if dealing with a philosophical contraband, an anomaly of sorts.

My father walked over – added his own strains and notions to the interaction, the generational feyre: 'Something unexpected is going to happen, *isn't it* … something connected to my past.'

'It is.'

'Then we should wait in turn with our manifestos. Allow you to move humanity on …'

I stopped him. Invested more seconds before he sunk back into the crowd. 'Everything I said criticizing you, everything I stirred up – I'm sorry, but …' I nearly didn't say it. I nearly set us back again. Along a confused road. One full of loose stones and snipers. It eventually tunnelled itself out of me though – blinked at the light as it surfaced. 'I'm the son of the man that turned them down quarter of a century ago. I've become too prominent for them, albeit underground – away from their fulcrum, their mainstay.'

'The radio job. You're saying … no … no … they were … it was the frequency of Cold War enemies which interested them. They were safeguarding the country … they …'

'They were spying on their own people as well. And when the Cold War ended, it became more acute; a free people puppeteered by the policies of the few.'

'But … how do you know this? I'm aware of this … 'deliverance', but to your father, Arnold – please tell me. Break down this … theology, this spiritual cavern.'

'There are quarries – quarries of knowledge floating around us. History may have deleted the finer truth, but it doesn't leave our planet. Matter cannot escape. I seem capable of reading this – plucking it from the semi-oblivion.'

'I believe you. So I very nearly myself … Your face though – how can we ever justify that? How have you managed? Ignoring the letters Rose and I received, tell me now ... and please, without a veneer. Tell your father, Arnold. Forgetting Sacco and Vanzetti – forgetting it all ...'

'I'm sorry. I have *this* to do. There isn't much time, before ... I'm in a different capacity now. Present your manifesto like the others, Father, then I'll give my conclusion – the rousing speech which has been stored up.'

Bend to the questioning I could not. Because to fall now through emotion, through tender family promptings, would be to capitulate, prevent my ascendance. For a few more minutes I had to be objective – listen to the 'moorings' of the disciples – before becoming a Luther King, infusing my words with grace and staunchness, shadowing the black god who had pre-dated even my birth.

'Tell Josie I'll come to her after. But now we must begin.'

We wandered through from the casual theatre-circle setup, into a room which boasted a rectangular table and thirteen chairs. In the centre of the wooden mass, there was bread and wine; hand-sculpted flour products uneven in shape, together with a red liquid. What had not been lost on me in the middle of all this was an eagerness on my part to renew acquaintances with Warwick and Green Suit, Ragavan and George Minty I, understand their lives since the fire, since heaven's clerics had uttered my name. I watched each of them as we ambled in – signalled to them that the orthodox proceedings would soon be broken up, tempered by a more personal need, an Emerson-like construct which railed against hypocrisy.

We sat. I took the most humble chair and was adamant that there I would remain, until the mutterings around me guided me to the centre of one of the long sides, the head of the table in all but name plate. Opposite me there was a chasm, a hole between Chesterton and Pendlebury – what was deemed to be 'Castro's spot. I knew, however, that someone else would fill it – a disrupter, the controlling force behind the network of sinewy tramps and corporate management, the One revered by Josie's former colleagues. Here I was though – presiding over a Last

Supper, asking of these followers sober, yet aesthetic analysis, manifestos which would permeate my final declaration, my definitiveness.

Different areas would be addressed. No framework had been laid out, except that of life itself in all its rich infiniteness. Saul stood first. Compared to the others he was like a lesser cousin, yet his patter was strong and fierce, bold and apoplectic: 'The Jews – we – seek to "replace conjectural history with scientific fact" through excavation. We dig and dig near the Mount – for what? For proof that we are the Chosen Ones, for proof that such land was granted to us by God? Is God an excluder? Would He banish other faiths so the purity of His people remained, untainted? I suggest not. I suggest that we are all Arabic, all Asian, all European and all American. As this so called breed or caste, or Israeli construct, we listen to too much news – in lifts, cars, the home, buses, work places, leisure arenas. We are never away from it and so become unhinged by its demands, its killing of time. We are rarely alone – fully and utterly – and therefore do not think in life's stream, its steady patterned flow.'

He continued, rolled out that which was at the centre of his being. And when his words ceased, another stood – took the baton, replaced him, introduced a new theme. Green Suit. George Minty I. Warwick. They spoke respectively of resignation letters, book clinics and small schools – their wonderment in front of the others quite real and polished; Green Suit traversing the norm, insisting once again that good jobs did not exist, that reading one's soul was through the abstract, the piqued blazings of one's melancholic depression, one's expose of office crassness; George Minty I putting forward his steeped idealism, his answer to the world's woes – book clinics on every corner of every village, literary servants to the masses, symptom Baskervilles drooling, able to diagnose through plot and demeanour one's path (and thus piece together one's likely downfall – ward against it – with the assistance of Shakespeare, Homer and Erechtheus); and Warwick, ever the double bluff laughter creator, founder of a small school which harnessed the lower intellects, which positively railed against meritocracy. He claimed, with no irony at all, to have garnered a generation now awaiting my instruction, my utmost calling. He had their minds not trussed up, but supple for the fight – boys and girls (now men and women) whose adult minds were welded to an all-giving force, a bright, salubrious chapter.

My father was next – his enamoured humbleness splayed and latitudinous. 'I listen to seven plays each week. I have given up on television's pixels, its roving around unduly and infiltrating one's score, one's deportment. I wish that my fifty years of life had been different, but at each juncture I heard "just one more decade"… for that I'll have a story – an uncomplicated mortgage. I'll be able to say to people that I was dominant in my trade – a stayer, even if privately mocked. I suppose sufferance has its points – it leans to humour for a release, holds captive an incredulous room of people when you say you gave five decades to one profession. Except … in the final years I was flagging – a daily witness to the nauseous programming directed at humanity. I began to understand that only drama can truly teach – not reality. Because the former has as its captain Miss Poetical Grace. My manifesto thus turns away from a technology which revolutionised my youth and aligns itself with the radio – Radio 4 and its joyous scripts which bring shame upon television's buffoons' cabal. I am sorry for using such harsh words, but when you have sat in the living room of an entire community and watched its merciless scratching, its slovenly etiquette, you begin to draw in your mind alternative worlds – a streamlining of that which doesn't taint.'

They soaked in what my father had said – replayed its simplicity in whispers and subtle chatter. My mother then stood – instantly knew her quota as a multiple of my father's expression, set off down a bespoke corporate path. She talked of James, his reaching the big desk, his changed air, how he had not in fact managed to salvage the innocence that had been with him at the outset. '… something isn't right. His look is glazed. His interest in the wider world has been dissipated. Money has not necessarily consumed him, but it has strangled his selectiveness.'

We listened some more – allowed her to sculpt her manifesto around him, her son, my brother, this congealed example of corporate success. He had a secretary, fellow board members or partners now – his gait had solidified into an upright pre-eminence, blowing away the professional minnows that happened across his path. He wore clothes without thinking of the cost, took four holidays a year, each involving a different ocean. And when inventive trinkets from his trips were passed to our parents as part of his annual visit to them, he convinced himself that their raked smiles were full and unburdened.

'He looks at us now with no depth. And that is my conclusion, I suppose.'

She left the sentence suspended almost, open to differing takes as to James' current level of profundity, his heightened ignorance following his admission to the corporate elite. The consensus seemed to be that blinkers were de rigueur upon one's being seated at the big desk, that seeing 'enough' was preferential to an understanding of the whole – particularly given the squirming awkwardness of minimum pay and deference. James was now party to it – the sandblasting of his underlings' thoughts, the controlling network which acted like a cravat, forever hugging its occupant's neck, keeping him/her warm yet having a minatory hold of their windpipe. Each day brought him more 'gold' and yet the undersurface of his being was becoming tattered, shred-like.

'Exile!' Josie then intervened with. 'I would like to compare my absence with that of the man whose writings so lifted me. It took a porter ironically named Leon to smuggle in the texts and upon receipt of them my world was suddenly meaningful again and incandescent. If 1929 is a year poignant to investors through the Wall Street Crash, then let it also be a year in which fairness was circumvented, in which Stalin exiled Trotsky. I would like to think that the two are connected, that the moneyed droves fled their native market in an act of disgust, but then I know they thought as the world did – that Stalin was an angel, not, as later evidenced, the arms-supplying liquidator of the Spanish Revolution (fearful of his privileged bureaucracy having to slum it should a world revolution take hold).

'1917 though – the Russian Revolution. Not a full-blooded assault on a dominant home government, but a momentary stepping into the vacuum caused by the Great War and national disintegration, "a compulsion of circumstances" rather than an effort at Empire. The poor wanted "bread, salt and candles". After that – would they have liked to have run the country, had a hand in its etchings? Yes and no. Sporadic pockets of resistance existed, however, it was questionable whether the circumstances for self-defence (and thus an instant multiplying of proletarian brotherhood) lay in wait. Certainly the Bolsheviks were driving it, only to be shifted off track by the lack of a tangible enemy, Lenin's stroke in 1923, the German Communist Party's cancelling of its planned insurrection that same year and Stalin's essentially fascist one-country socialism (culminating in the 1934 Hitleresque murder of the Central Committee's favoured son – and Stalin chief rival – S M Kirov).

'I fear now that, in the midst of *our* revolution, two of us will be martyred in the manner of Russia's Sacco and Vanzetti – Zinoviev and Kamenev – that a Moscow Trial is upon us. Don't ask me how I sense this, but a warning burns inside me. My manifesto then, whilst initially exuding optimism, ends with sacrifice. I hope, within it, history's curious twistings and my own 'detention' signal hope, however. What I am trying to say is that just as 1917's 'agitators' and speakers no longer pulled their coats over their heads, no longer concerned themselves with protecting their identity, so should we whatever the consequences – we should allow Trotsky's famous words to graft and comfort us:

I will not ask my accusers to place themselves voluntarily before a firing-squad. No, eternal disgrace in the memory of human generations will be sufficient for them.'

I looked at her and she at me. Everything we had had was now wrapped – not to be undone. Despite our cravings, a dutiful altruism held us. Our paths would slowly begin to divest themselves of likeness yet converge spiritually. My face she seemed not to see – choosing to pierce my recognisable eyes only with her lingering look. When it halted, when – within seconds – our joint transcendence was diffused, I felt empty, otherworldly, inculcated by heaven's reach, its glorious non-indemnity. Yet before I had time to think, muse over Josie's eloquence, her bottled love, Ragavan had stood, filled the space with his exorbitant frame, his seasoned raconteurism.

'What words I have are different to those of my former ally just seated. I used to speak of Abacha, of his henchmen and steers, of whole villages satanically scarred by their oil-filthy paws. I found salvation through the injustices played out in foreign lands rather than through home concerns. Well, that has changed. The masses here disappoint me. I look out immediately beyond my door and see ignorance – a waning of effort. This is to such a degree that changing them through hardened means has become my salvation. *Their* betterment, their amelioration, I see, is so necessary that socialism will no longer do. In fact, socialism excuses them – its semi-radicalness thwarts any designs that better minds might have in saving them. It is with this edict that I propose a network of information wardens – a police of sorts charged with the task of weeding out the inane scourges that choose to roam our streets with philosophy as their foe. Anyone that cannot produce a reasonable sentence should be banished from society until corrected of their deficiency. Anyone daring to exit their abode without something new to say, without fine thought of an acceptable level, should be made to reverse – stand in the doorway of their inadequacies until better read or polished. I hold it that our political ideology has fundamentally sat still – failed to address such a glaring problem which sits alongside the link between education, employment and culture. No longer is it enough to have the tramps as a warning – some will eschew even this forewarning, this dire signal. You may think my words shine with hypocrisy, but I have simply grown uncomfortable with forces outside of the law. I do not wish to dally with randomness and whim. I have therefore drafted what I deem to be my final list – a portrait of this straw dog humanity, the uneven tempos which still pervade one's day, one's existence.'

Across the feast of bread and wine, we stared at Ragavan – slightly dumbfounded and incoherent in the face of his ultra-dogmatic words. We awaited the punch line, the tripping us up, the turning around of his logic with a final sentence. Nothing though. He was being sincere. The quietude which consumed him brought embarrassment to the gathering, concern as to our long-awaited significance.

I spoke. Addressed him before the others. Sought answers in the gaps of his demeanour, his air. 'You once asked that I remind you of your twelve should you fall down. Well, their names are Butalia, Galeano, Shiva, Kumar, Said, Tutu, Berry, Carson, Chomsky, Cahill, Mumford and Schumacher. They are much more than us and would express grave concerns over what you're espousing.'

'What I'm *espousing* isn't that far on from your *own father's* manifesto. We both assert tiredness with regard to the fatuous elements, a level of disdain in relation to the hoi polloi.'

'But my father observes. At no turn did he suggest a ripping up of their freedoms, a fascist edict, however much we agree over the matter of their churlishness.'

He became impatient. His voice boomed with stores of decibels long rested, semi-retired in the aftermath of Saro-Wiwa. 'And that is what is wrong! We pussy-foot, prevaricate, show an assumed respect to these ... these ciphers. They are not deserving of humanity! Their ilk is untrained – liable in its blunderings. Better we save them – show them their errors, not wait another decade with patience as our torch.'

'*Save them?* As Hitler saved the Jews? As Ceausescu warehoused Romania's orphans, prompting their slide into the sewers? What has happened to you, Ragavan? I used to see you as myself, only without a partner and therefore blessed with a greater depth – time to read that which I couldn't, time to digest luminaries thoughts and considerations.'

'But in the end you didn't have to read. It all came to you through the gods. Their wisdom and omniscience fastened itself to your mind.' He turned – looked at each disciple around the table more fully, involved them wholeheartedly. '*Or did it?* The very fact that you still ask questions suggests otherwise. I do not believe you to be God, Debrito. If you were I would be enchanted – taken by your output.'

'I haven't begun though! My way is to *listen* first. That is why you are here. That is why we are all here. In between the question and the answer – that is where I look, Ragavan. My promptings do not aim themselves at what you rightly assert I should know, but rather the mien, the expression of a person behind the voice. By asking the question I understand that person's level of self-deception if indeed it exists. With you it is different. You forego the inner worlds of others. You no longer want to see past the exterior that confronts you – the impure bedevilment which inconveniences your lists, your order, your sense of what should be.'

'Because we cannot analyse why it is these elements exist. Twenty years of wrong would take forty or sixty years to dissect. Time is running short. It cannot afford such meanderings. I don't believe – as you don't – that society is responsible for all the ills. Accountability must be part of the equation – personal ...' He seemed to nearly faint, fall off centre. '... the conscription of one's own benevolence is paramount. All that has gone now though. We have to drive this – punish the hordes ...'

'Come back into the fold. Will you come back into the fold, Ragavan?' My words were few, yet conscious of Ragavan's next fatal line – his admittance concerning his more bellicose approach.

'I can't ...' he whimpered – his manner now exhausted and vulnerable. 'They ... they wanted a name. They said I would be exempt if I gave them a name. I didn't want this, but my lists – they said they'd be protected. I've built them up over so many years. They are my mainstay. Something has altered me though, Arnold. Despite my helping them, I'm not me. Christ! My head – the insides of it tumble around like jelly. I am no longer in possession of *my* history only. Another history seems to have ensnared me – mixed itself with my ... Jesus! *Who am I?* Whence this new land came? Who ...'

He was my Judas – modern-day Iscariot, the retainer of thirty lists or books. The Romans would now come in a matter of seconds, yet I did not think less of Ragavan – his weakness, if anything, was owed in light of his tireless strength, his E.t.c. manoeuvring which fought at the border, the prism of good and bad.

There was a thud on the hall door – an almost psychic reading of the events inside. It was Him, the One, my opposite. I knew through the earth's echoes, the wanderlust of its organisms.

In he came, up towards the table, flanked by a private constabulary – the rotund, bespectacled presence of Webster; my father's nearly-boss and Cold War executive. 'This chair I believe to be mine,' he purported.

'Get out!' my mother immediately cried. 'My father's spirit sits there. Who are you to make sacrilegious his memory?!'

'Ask your son – ask *him* whether I am due here.'

The room looked at me. The answer they were waiting for I could not give, because Webster *was* due – his presence would somewhat ironically save them, his being here would act as my deliverance. 'I am afraid he is right, but do not let that perturb you.'

'You come *now*?!' Pendlebury's uncle then demanded. 'You wait three decades and show yourself at our zenith?'

'Yes ... to hear my sons and you also, my brother.'

'What? What is this?' Pendlebury silently questioned. 'You are the brother of my uncle? You are then ... *no* ... *no*!!! And you choose to wreck our gathering? Uncle – who is this? Please – tell me ...'

'Webster Chesterton. As much as it pains me, I must tell you that this man is your father.'

'Chesterton? *Chesterton*? Father of Benjamin? I have a half brother?!'

'I only realised such a thing today, but yes, the man two chairs from you is your brother.'

'This ... this isn't real. Why then is my surname 'Smith'? Why am I Pendlebury Smith?'

'Because they erased your history upon being fostered. And you couldn't bear to see for yourself through your mother's gravestone that you were in fact a 'Chesterton'. I ... I changed my name to 'Smith' also, so that when you found me there would be less questions. My hope was that religion would supersede one's own small history ... one's lot.'

'So we are all at it – bending histories, stepping in as unauthorised guides. It is not enough that our god, Debrito, should have a false glory surrounding his father in lieu of Sacco and Vanzetti's known reprieve! No! Let every son or nephew be bamboozled – plated with an ephemeral light rather than a solid, infinite truth. Arnold was right. *I am* The Leaf Blower. That title can no longer adorn you, because to interact with nature requires an honest understanding of oneself.'

He looked at Benjamin. 'And *you* – did you know all this? Did it move or disappoint you to know that you were the *second* son?'

'My – our – father talked of his brother in fond sentences.[1] He spoke of his deafness as if nature or religion was to blame. His musings would then turn to anger though – a retribution would cover him, direct his life. It was because of this that I turned to Bhaskara. In this Indian mathematician were factors opposite to those of my father's Government Provisional Unit – qualities seeded in egalitarianism. And so, I decided to trace you – pull away from the upper classes whose ideas were poisoning me. Through Debrito, through his dissertation, I knew – I knew that such expression would place me on a path to you. Not only you, but my uncle.'

'My manifesto has it that your sort, your 'set', are the problem. Not the poor, but the rich – monopolizing as they do the world's policies and resources. I would have assets capped – anyone with one million plus obliged to declare it at a police station as a person caught speeding would declare their licence or a paedophile would declare their threat to society. Tell me, Benjamin, are you for this? Could you manage within limited means?'

'I have already forfeited my inheritance. So – yes. What is *here now* offers much more than a collection of noughts. I find myself suffused with reason again ...'

'Hear yourselves!' Webster roared. 'My sons whom I have come to hear extolling age-old ideas of popular rule and superstition by which the Left are naively nourished. And my brother – apologetic simply because of my presence. Am I not here next to you? Am I not deserving of a welcome? Surely you would not choose one voice, one vote over my fresh policy? Haven't the proletariat had their chance, their play on life? Didn't they disappoint – leave Trotsky out to hang?!'

'Your fresh policy – please tell,' I prompted.

'Ahh ... your god. He speaks. He sounds his broken rifle. But to what end? His are but words, whereas I offer a way out, an iron-cast salvation. Look at us – related through life. Each one of us connected somehow: Warwick – the former manager of my portfolio, now beaten by a false guilt, misguided in his belief that education will alter centuries of human greed; Josie – a client of my former retreat, seduced by Trotsky, happy to blindfold herself when arm-in-arm with Communists; Jack Debrito, who would now be stood behind me were it not for the selfishness of his wife; Saul – a faller at the road to Damascus, my spy, somehow entranced by your god's ways; yes, my spy, *Ragavan* – you who would provide us with a name unnecessarily, you who would value intelligence over loyalty; Green Suit – ahhh, a curious one here – the man that doth not resign from one of my outposts, but chooses instead to wail in a discourse of lethargy and stoicalness; George Minty I – same old lauding of failure, death's charge hand reasoning to all that glory needn't be during one's lifetime; Rose Debrito – your own life empty for so long now, having only been respectful of your father (the insecure hold on your husband symptomatic of disappointment and fear, but not love); my brother – Pendlebury's surrogate father – feigning an anger towards me when aware and understanding of my neglect; my sons – so obviously unnerved, believing that I am a despot of some kind, when in fact I seek to stabilise humanity's course and then buy its individuals' status as mere mortals or citizens. Did the deafness of my brother prompt this line, Benjamin? Was I aggrieved at the injustice of limited senses when others roam making me recoil from their full-sensed stupidity? No and yes. But it was the Cold War which carried me forward – allowed me to build my network. Once behind life's public charade, its curtain, it becomes easy to stay – watch and control. Of course, I missed the changing features of my first son, Pendlebury, but I hope this is understood in the grand scheme. Your god knows of our ways – to have tramps as our eyes (our own people patrolling clandestinely), yet what I don't think he has expressed is our hold on management, our ability to cork the minds of those that rise. We have perfected a system of compliance, a technique which mitigates the threat of anarchists and iconoclasts – those that would disrupt even the smoothest existence.'

'Tell them then. Tell them what this *Holy Grail* consists of,' I stressed. 'And see if they are not repulsed – physically marred.'

'All great causes consist of unusual alliances, Debrito. You must know that with your Zinoviev, Kamenev, Trotsky, Sverdlov, Uritsky, Sokolnikov, Dzerzhinsky, Lenin, Bubnov, Lomov and Kollontai. As General Secretary of the Government Provisional Unit, formerly a wing of parliament but now dominant over even the ministers of this country, I have had to widen our grip, seek ways forward from out of the theological arena, coupled as it is with ignorance and barrow boy loudness. We have engaged with science – brought under our jurisdiction all technological advancements. The thing we clash over I do not celebrate – exaltation does not know me – yet its implementation has been critical. Phase One of our new world has reached fruition. The actuality of that? The tangible coarseness required to counter this perverse thing they call 'free thought'? Yes – we drill through the human cranium. We 'clean' the brain – a nanobot to sit in the head of each man and woman promoted. The very first night they rest as management, in fact, we install our nano device. Because of this, civilisation has flourished. Not only then do we inculcate obedience in the masses through the fear of becoming a tramp, but also through a management ideology of our choosing – a corporate mystification driven by the upper classes.'

A nausea and repugnance enveloped those around me. There was incredulousness – a feeling of paralysis, for without violence, without the harsher tools of confrontation, nothing made the divide, the canyon between spiritualism and science. Words simply fell now – crashed against the perennial sundry which spouted horizontally and diagonally from the walls of the imperceptible abyss, the gap between us and Webster.

'There is no regret?' Pendlebury then asked, moving closer to his father. 'Contrition and lamentation do not visit you in the quieter moments? You do not perceive your actions as being wrong? You do not look back and wonder what fate's other card was?'

'If regret is able to be stripped down then perhaps, but there can be no room for ambivalence. The course we are on does not permit hesitation, nor tolerate procrastination. I must move forward and not make the mistake of Kerensky. The enemy is here, in this room, now and if it will not be converted then ...'

'Including your own son? I stand before you a relative stranger. I am poor and therefore fit your generalised view of the world. I am one of the elements that blocks your 'progression'.'

'It is not you I have come for. It is Debrito.'

'To clean his brain? To enact your prosaic vileness?'

'Circumstances dictate. I am merely piloted by them – their Braille touching my fingertips.'

'That is all you can say?! Each person here represents a lost year of my life - an abominable fracture – and you talk of circumstances. Well, circumstances have it that I should ...'

'Forgive him,' I severed Pendlebury's sentence with.

'Forgive him?! For stripping me of a real childhood? For throwing stones at the world – its unfortunates and insignificants. Why?! Why should I let it go?'

'Because the death of your mother never left him.'

Webster's forehead began to exude globules of sweat. His relatively sedate character became inflamed. A handkerchief was pulled from his pocket to immediately dry the offending aperture in his armour. '*Who?!* Who are you to attest such a thing?! *When?!* When did my history become yours?'

'When you saw winning the Cold War as a distraction rather than your main aim. When you took it upon yourself to play with the minds of humanity including my brother, James, and my esteemed friend, Ragavan.'

'Do you honestly believe them worthy of minds?' Something in him was breaking up – separating itself from his torso. And at that moment, he indicated to his Roman swathes that we were to be fixed in position – made to sense anxiety and fear while he dragooned us with more words. 'Those that would rise the industrial ladder – think themselves gods through the half-covered breasts of a secretary – surely my policy of remedying these ... these ingratiates fits with your own ... When setting out we devised them with society in mind. As long as they didn't touch our land or encroach upon our centuries-earned titles and wealth, then we allowed them scope – it was programmed into them. They were to push the world forward in the aftermath of World War II – restore hope and quash rebellion. And that they did – there has been nothing so threatening since '68 (the miners were a curse to the environment and easily put down). There were Frankensteins amongst our corporate force though – minds which wrestled with the nanobots and somehow picked up signals from a 'circuit board' not of our making. These elements gave little regard for responsibility – they pushed on, continue to push on, without philanthropy. They think of the world as a board game, a gamut awaiting their exploitation and ruthless reconnaissance. What we gave them was not enough. No. They had to shoot not only the pheasant but the satchel from their fellow man.'

'Like yourself? Like the class of people you annexed – the avoidance of dirty jobs, a harbinger to them.'

'No! No!' Webster's thick palms cascaded across his face. His expression descended into a maddening blur. 'We are quite different. We have grace, virtues – aspects to our character which these Phase One cohorts would take two hundred years to marinate themselves with.'

'But ...'

'*And that is why*,' he bellowed, 'we must shift to Phase Two. *Immediately!*'

The ring of blue uniforms and silver buttons intensified – stood, held itself behind us; three or four Romans for each one of us – their faces emotionless and phlegmatic. 'Which? Which one, sir?'

'Saul. It must be Saul. Something quixotic has taken him – rendered him impractical. Perhaps a stronger nano will anaesthetize him where Phase One has failed. Please. Prepare him.'

They lifted him from his chair, pushed him against the wall and relieved him of his upper garments. They then placed a dentist-like protective bib around his neck. Before my words could come out I heard the sound of the drill, its forceful whirring and intimidatory zeal. I witnessed the Romans preparing their human surface with an almost doctrinal, painted 'X'.

'Stop!' I eventually cried. 'Experiment on myself. This man has nothing to give you. He is ordinary. Take a god – see if your science makes tractable and subjugates *my* autonomous mind.'

'Debrito! By saving them, *you* fall down. Don't you see that? I … I wish to beguile them as a dictator – liberate them from responsibility. If the Frankensteins cannot work within my parameters then it is time for them and *all mankind* to lose their citizenship. We, as the state – the upper class echelon – will give them the answers they seek. They will experience the joy of limited inquisitiveness – the safety of our demarcations. For now, in this instance, *I will,* however, accede to your request. Saul is free, as are the others. What, after all, are pious devotees capable of. Count this as a gesture – an indication of the compassion of my peremptory exterior – for they *will* be taken in eventually, either through their own dogged stupidity or through my network, requiring as it does humans to feed the furnace of my new world.'

'Good, let us talk in private then – quarry my future role, understand what it is my nano will inculcate.'

The room lay almost dead through the fear of the disciples and the obedience of the Romans; the former worried that a gesture or word would implicate them, leave them open to Webster's arbitrary furore. Even the faces of his sons – Pendlebury in particular, newly acquainted and loathsomely versed - were sullen, exhibitant of dread and consternation.

Saul was guided back to his chair, overtly sweating, yet relieved. The others watched, waited, as Webster considered his next line – whether to make esoteric our continued discussion, whether to risk his sheen away from hypocrisy's ball.

'Granted,' he finally answered. 'Over there. The room over there.'

We entered and he immediately addressed me: 'What is it that can't be discussed under their glare?'

'Your first wife. I wish to know ... after the haemorrhage – what happened? What support did you get? Seconds on from Pendlebury's birth, did they show understanding?'

His deep-socketed, cavern-like eyes seemed to bathe in a self-generating reservoir. In him now was something else – an isolated facet reluctant to surface. 'Don't,' was his succinct reply, his laconic burst.

'But we're both pulling away from capitalism, albeit in different ways. The professionals on duty that day – were they ...'

'I *created* capitalism – in its pure form. I gave it its heyday. But some of its players – they lost all sense of what it was for. People in their twenties, thirties and forties thinking that life should have heaped upon them a fortune, a spell-binding get-out clause, a day where everything that follows is comfortable because they are finally *themselves* – a selector of opinions, not one obliged (through lack of funds / control) to kowtow. We pit wit against wit, but too many victories lead to hubris and parochialism and too few to resentment and despair. My super-capitalism is the final textbook ideology – it has its benefits over unworkable worlds with no helm ... socialist and utopian ventures – yet I have grown tired of its occupants. Despite my efforts of minimal intervention, some still protect their patch like an irrational tank commander. Some ...'

'*Minimal* intervention, you say?! The exploitation of science for rapacious ends. The attempted colonisation of minds. And you deem this slight – *negligible*?'

'It is kinder than letting them roam. I must treat them like children ... set boundaries ... think for them.'

'And who appointed you in this role? Who passed you the blank tablet?'

'*Who*?! Why, dumbfoundedness – the bewildering realisation

that humans are like litter. But my first attempt at rectifying the detritus that is their grey matter has imploded in part. Maybe 99% I have, whether directly or indirectly. But I now wish for 100% directly – management *and* those below. Production has just finished on our Nanobot '03 – the successor to Nanobot '72, a gesture to my wife on the birth of Chesterton, a promise that I would augment the then seemingly anachronistic upper classes through perforating entrepreneurial minds, enticing their brain waves with a staged neo-corporate agenda. So Phase Two … no more tramp pantomimes.'

'But your first wife … the hospital … you didn't just *become* Ceausescu-like. Was Chesterton in some way an attempt to erase Pendlebury?'

'*I am not* Ceausescu! That my suffering should strip any manifestation of sympathy from me – judge for yourself: When it was over, they placed him in my arms. They seemed to believe that I would accept the trade off – carry my new born whilst in the presence of the sacrifice. My love, *my wife*, everything I had journeyed for! And they passed it off – tried to make rare meat from a bloodied stew. They preferred a half measure rather than a plaintive cry. My emotions were inconvenient to them. *Not one* loosened their professional demeanour – *talked* to me, attempted to understand. And so if God can create such an army of indifferent beings, then count me as an atheist. Let science run the show – better the sophistry that says 'a life for a death'. I have never been so governmental in my thinking before. Chaos has finally acceded to my wishes – agreed to temper its winds and net its butterflies.'

'So my theory is right, that all scientists have been disappointed by the death of a family member and have taken it upon themselves to control that which shouldn't be controlled.'

'And if I didn't exert that control? What would ensue? An irreverent gang of peasants? A corporate cabal believing itself to be invincible? My way is all that is left. The new nanobots will revolutionise the vapid mindset – our prototype tells us that this time there will be no escapees. Everyone will be an adherent to our central knowledge bank.'

'And society will be yours?'

'I am a philanthropist – an altruist. I *give*, so no.'

'*You give*?! Limited inquisitiveness? The alive an undead deportment?'

'"The alive" as you put it have been mudded for eleven millennia. You yourself, even, wish to diminish their individualism. My system is merely one step on from your community ideal. In fact, it offers tranquillity and peacefulness – factors threatened by the anarchy which will always dog your imagined panacea, your perfect world.'

'You offer numbness, not tranquillity. Your henchmen deliver mild threats and menacing glances. In having a clandestine network you admit your fear of more unique and inimitable minds.'

'*I do not* fear anyone! Least of all a specious god unable to save his own face. Debrito – you show contempt in the shadow of my first wife's suffering. You understand nothing but your imagined link with a higher kingdom. Well, if it is true, then let you be our first. Step off the cross with your mind intact – your ideas unblemished.'

I was pulled, from the room, in front of the others in the main hall. They stared, appalled at my stark extraction.

'See your god weaken with no tricks,' cried Webster. 'Where is his flash of light, his omnipotence in the face of my moderate challenge? Isn't this flaccid body an embarrassment – a stain on your faith …'

'No. No,' were the mutters, rising in volume until able to form a sentence: 'We decry the non-pacifist like yourself where everything is judged in an instant.'

'You *decry* the opportunity I provide? You wish, instead, to 'dance' with this feckless specimen?'

'Allow him to speak!' Warwick bellowed. 'We cannot take *any* position without hearing him in full.'

'He has forfeited that right. His seditious gathering has enflamed the goodwill which we – the G.P.U. – have afforded. You, as disciples, I can forgive – your minds not rounded enough nor etched in sufficient clarity to understand. But Debrito – we must wash his brain, exonerate him as soon as his thinking is reasonable again. We wish to pardon everyone – have a society of fair-minded and ...'

'*You yourself* are part of this supper. You may not reach for the bread and wine, but your lips are still coloured with dissidence. I am seventy-four – a decade older than you. Half a century separates myself and Saul. You have in your company three or four generations of people – each one bred on a different world view but harmonised today by the efforts of Debrito. I have seen *every* side of this planet. I have allowed numbers to turn my brain to mulch. I have managed your portfolio, as you well know – helped compound the strength of one of your many tentacles. So we are all damned by deceit, given over to its oily charm, but what *after* the mistakes, the youthful and not-so-youthful miscreantism. That is why we are here – to debate, discuss. And discuss we will. I will *hear* my god. Such finery will not be displaced by a man my junior!'

'Old man! Foolish in thinking that your years count for something! That an automatic deference will find its way into my logic! I should terminate your life now – end the farcical existence which acts as a wood burner to your eccentricity. That you should have one eye on forming an army from today's youth – *indeed*!'

'Stop!!!' I demanded – my mind fried by the bluster, sanctified by something larger than myself. 'We all want a smooth road – that is all there is. To journey forward without being impeded. *And there will be* those moments: a carriageway free of cars; a group of complaisant individuals; the sun, pairing itself with a perfect breeze; a retirement fund able to buy us back our mind. But woven in between is adversarialism – something we must learn to harness and offset.'

Breathing. I was breathing consummately for the first time in my life. A rhythm had entered me, added cadence to my manner. I seemed to arch over the bodies around me, magically loosen the grip of the Romans. It was life frozen – myself its master for a moment; able to hold my eyes on the chocolate-brown blouse adorning Josie's contoured warmth; able to read, in Green Suit, a drive towards vocational oblivion; able to monitor, through the now visual toxins, Ragavan's declining health; and the others – they represented humanity's blend, its insecurity, its fracturedness, its humility and angst. Such qualities, such afraidness, had been trampled in the rush to mammon, mud-packed with a stoical licentiousness. Prioritised now were the superficial wants of a people in disarray – a generation cleverly moulded by Webster et al, made to believe that technology was their saviour, their depth.

'When this happens, when I'm aware of forces out there purposely striving against our fulfilment, against the blossoming of humanity, it cuts me. This is so because *I am everyone*. Each one of you is a part of me. I am *not only* of my mother – *she is* of *me*. George Minty I carries with him my belief that history serves one better *after* their passing. Pendlebury's wondrous depth and celestial bearing have bitten me, leaving no antidote. And his father – yes, we too are from the same egg. *His* determination is mine. *His* guilt is mine to share – work through.'

'I admit that my corporate world is not enough *and you feed* me *this*! I offer a more steadfast world which will allow humanity to peak through its utilitarianism and you roll theology's rubric stones, its random and superstitious code. I deem you a threat to the earth's sanity, Debrito – one that must be counterbalanced. Your disciples may stay. Enough words have been batted now though. And so the time has come ...'

They knew what to do. Each Webster sentence puppeteered the Romans in some way. This seemed to cue their belligerence, for they were more forceful than earlier, unforgiving in the face of crossed swords and new people. Blows rained down, jolting me. I was soon on the floor – my arms like trunks against my stomach, my hands sculpted around my face.

'Leave him! Leave my son!' my mother cried, hysterical and helpless. 'He isn't this man, this god, you think. Mercy! Let him be ...'

I felt no respite, no let up. In fact, the blows hardened, became accurate and pointed in their delivery. My ribs began to ache, a bloodied puss seemed to swim across my face. I looked into the eyes of my tormentors, the perpetrators of this easy massacre. They were black, undistinguished, empty of reason. It was as if they had no insides, no purpose or soul. Their very direction had evidently been crushed and subjugated. Despite the overwhelming sense of radicalness in the room, the Romans were impervious to that which undermined or threatened to challenge Webster's tenets and critiques. To succumb would be to shade things differently – enter a grey unsureness. To veer from their nominated path would require an untangling of something coded, unalphabetised. And as imagination was *no more*, a mere firming of their absurd brutality ensued.

Eventually lifting my stained and battered body from the floor, they had me face Webster, half-conscious and therefore primed for his inculcation. 'There may be a perverted wrath here in this room over your treatment, Debrito, but let me assure you: all is well – necessary. I will gladly enforce the G.P.U.'s will in front of even my children if it means that another strand of anarchism is suppressed.'

I had no words with which to rebuke him. The murmurs and protestations of the disciples I could barely hear – their combined utterances converging into a convoluted mass. He could see my discomfort, yet registered no shame, no compunction. His mind seemed to be paralleled with an ineffable evil – sautéed in an acute McCarthyism, a fascism of sorts.

'You cannot take this man! He is *with me* – his burden is mine. Don't separate us. Please ... don't ...' The words broke through as I was led out to the accompaniment of my captors' muted ominousness. I tried to turn my neck, intimate to Josie that I had never met her like before, but a soporific heaviness had me. I was almost bowed, acquiescent, injurious to everything I had cultivated (and asked others to marvel at). Amongst the boot-laden, gorilla flock, however, I managed to dig out a final set of words for those whom I loved with ease, albeit with my back to them, my mouth aimed at the sky: 'The pamphlet! Find it. It will let you in.'

-            -   -   -

Speech from The Leaf Blower ...

For the last few days He has watched over us. His mind has been washed from the earth, but not His shadow. And now I must tell you, in this dark, cell-like retreat which hosts a golden truth in contrast to the structures above, that we have found it. Not in a safe, a bank, nor a box, but quite aptly amongst the casings, fuses, clipboards and meters which offer a moss-like coating to the interior of His father's car. A place where Webster and his abettors would not have the inventiveness to consider or examine. And that is it – the difference between them and us. Why we must prevail. Why the life of Arnold Debrito will eventually feed itself into *everyone*. Because without it, we die too. Generation after generation. Allow me to read His words:

I am a god. A god who shakes. A god without immediate, effective answers. There is no flash of light in my armour, no instant wooing of humanity in its ignorance and manipulated mindset. Through my fellows in heaven I have learnt sufferance, I have learnt that intervention is not one of our toys. Roots must be changed – not interactions and situations of consequence to them. For without causal amendment, mistakes will be repeated – wrongdoers will merely view the betterment before them and then pillory its outcome, its ill-fitting enhancement. Persuading them, showing them every channel (and link) of their transgression from the outset of its physicalness and mentality must be upmost. Then they will understand that it is the collective which matters. Have your individuality by all means, but do not force its freedom at the expense of the wider good.

Show the bureaucrat how damaging his policies are on the African farmer who is starving and suicidal. Round up all BNP members and take them to Poland – let them speak with survivors of the holocaust and then challenge them *to continue their denial of its existence. Confront society's ills peacefully! Crooks and perpetrators of violence – seat them with the families they have harmed. And see then if their shame is capable of re-wiring them – have them justify their havoc to its sufferants. A mild form of this – deceit of some description – has saddled its wares to me. Each of you has placed chicanery before me at a given juncture in the last two decades. Yet doesn't this in one respect legitimise our membership – this greatness we have forged. Doesn't it make transparent the skewed logic of all nadirs.*

I am asking that we do not let time recede – permit its amnesic cousin recourse through the courts where *and* when *the law of common sense is able to bring parity. I am asking that we end the folly of 'knowing yet having to play by the book'. In being fed Sacco and Vanzetti at an early age, Saro-Wiwa in the unofficial lecture halls of university and Alexander II upon entering the world of commerce, I have been able to weave a history, understand* what *and* who *it is I am. This, albeit, through a prismed deception: my father colonizing Sacco and Vanzetti's pardon; Ragavan failing to mention NYCOP; and Chesterton using Jewish Weddings not to rid the world of peasant culture, but to join the gods, crank up his own spirituality, switch sides. Inadvertently, of course, my journey has been railtracked by you (and the others) – pushed through hilly landscapes (themselves philosophers, informants that not all guilt is loaded with wrong-doing).*

And so here we are, resplendent with your manifestos – the contents of which I knew before you wrote them. Let me highlight Saul's musings and then go beyond them. His disgust is at Israel's continued excavation, its need for 'proof' that its people are the 'chosen ones'. If an artifact is found will they suddenly be imbued with a moral authority? Will God exclude, discriminate, because he has a race of people that are closer to him through their studies, deference and history? I ask that this corner of the world, this people, pull up the sleeves of their Nazi concentration camp survivors – see the tattoos on their arms – and then dare continue *this line. I ask that if science be their card, then let it also hint at Creationism. Across all races we become a Jesus at the age of thirty-three. We have enough in us then to suggest ways forward for our hamlet, our village, our town, our city. This is the hub of what I have learnt whilst in the higher kingdom (both* before *my death when the gods visited me and* after *when they cooled my brow). And how to go about it? How to plough on through the parochialism of politicians and their hubristic masters, the pseudo-dethroned?*
We must go underground. *I have not made this decision easily. Indeed, I have sought input from my fellow gods – those that have*

seen centuries of wars and rebellion, decades of hope and belief become cinder. I once referred to my grandfather and father as A J Cook and J H Thomas, whether respectively or not. Well – it is the former we must exemplify in one sense; his carrying to the surface of a coal-mining pit the body next to his, slain as it was and rubbed out, back to 'its' family. And this, on his first day as a miner (16-years-old) – instantly bequeathed of his childhood. Our duty will be to carry all injustices to the surface – in full glare of humanity's remaining sapience. Through the people that you are and the souls that you have become, you will risk everything for the fate of the earth. The network of 'quiet people' already in existence will strengthen, the 'armies' formed by Pendlebury, his uncle and Warwick will at last have defined roles. Our children will not be the ones with heavy eyelids (despite their clandestine schooling from 6-8am) because inspiration and possibility will drive them on.

Think of every facet of society that needs changing, and through education, 'affordable' mini-rebellions, protests and revolutions, bring a great weight down upon them. And then ... when we represent the majority, or perhaps two thirds (for we do not desire a civil war), let gusto sweep all before it – vacuum the structural pockets which still insist that equality is an ingenuous dream.

It only remains for me to appoint my ministers, to divide up an underground movement which will eventually defy its name ...

Education	Warwick	George Minty I
Employment	Green Suit	Chesterton
Culture	Josie	Jack Debrito
Food & Health	Rose Debrito	Pendlebury's uncle
Housing & Environment-	Saul	Pendlebury

And my patrons? Why, our two Jesuses – Pendlebury and Josie. Allow them to steer you through. And when their time is up, welcome Ragavan – for **he will be there** *to stand with Chesterton.* **He will return** *from the science which grips him.*

----

1 Novel's author, Jeff Weston, celebrated his 34th birthday at this point ... no longer was he 33 (Jesus's crucifixion age).

Printed in Great Britain
by Amazon